UNACCUSTOMED TO WAITING

UNACCUSTOMED TO WAITING

LINDA HUDSON-SMITH

BET Publications, LLC

NEW SPIRIT BOOKS are published by

BET Publications, LLC
c/o BET BOOKS
One BET Plaza
1900 W Place NE
Washington, DC 20018-1211

ISBN: 0-7394-4780-7

Printed in the United States of America

This novel is dedicated to my loving grandson,
Gregory Lee Lewis III.

Dedicated in loving memory of those gone too soon; never to be forgotten:
Kara Gean Cohens
Ralph C. Carter, Jr.
Ethel Mae Stepeny
Joseph Haun
Moses Bailey
Marcus Williams (Uncle Marcus)

Chapter One

Tall, dark, and handsome Reverend Jesse Covington was in deep reflection while seated behind his mahogany desk in the pastor's study at his church, First Tabernacle. He had aged a little, but Jesse still looked good at fifty-two. With his long legs stretched out and his size twelve feet propped up on a straight chair, he thought about all the believable and unbelievable things that had transpired in his life over the past two years, time that had zipped by with the speed of lightning; one had been a year that all hell had broken loose in.

It hadn't been so long ago that he'd been locked up in a prison cell, sentenced to hard time for a crime he hadn't committed: armed robbery, a crime that his son, Malcolm, was thought to have perpetrated. A lot had happened during that awful time in his life, but Jesse felt that he'd become an even better man because of it. His brief incarceration had opened his eyes to so many things that he hadn't been fully aware of. Prison life hadn't ever occupied a fraction of his imagination. Never in his wildest dreams had Jesse ever imagined himself locked behind bars. He hadn't realized how much he'd taken for granted, either, not until his freedom was gone.

It had been the little things that he'd taken gross advantage of.

Jesse hadn't thought of it as a privilege to just walk to the refrigerator and open it up to see what was inside. Eating whenever he felt hungry was a blessing indeed. Taking a shower at anytime of the day or night had been exercised at will before prison. He, or the designee of his choice, had been the only ones to scrutinize his incoming and outgoing mail. His precious right to vote would've been revoked permanently had his sentence not been reversed and his criminal record expunged. Condoms were regarded as contraband in a place where safety and health issues should be a main concern. Watching television programs was often a dramatic occurrence. No one could just go over and change the channel in the viewing room, not without serious challenges. Toothpicks and eating utensils were considered as dangerous weapons.

In making wrong choices in life, the right to choose was given up. Never again would Jesse dare to take for granted the simple things afforded him in life. God had much work left for him to do, and he had jumped into his appointed task with both feet.

Jesse had often visited the prisons early on in his pastoral duties, but once the church had built a viable prison ministry, another pastor had taken over the department. God had worked through Jesse in an incredible way during his incarceration, in a way that many folks still found hard to believe. There were people who found it hard to fathom that the Lord would allow such a circumstance as incarceration to save only one soul. However, Jesse believed wholeheartedly that God had sent him to minister to the soul of one Richard James Du Boise, who had later been murdered by another inmate over the use of the telephone.

It was never Jesus' intent to lose a single one of his flock. Jesse was in no doubt that the Lord had sent him to save and then deliver unto Him one of the sheep that had strayed far from the Master's fold. Richard James Du Boise had been led back, back into the loving arms of the Father who art in heaven. It was Jesse's prayer that he and R.J. would one day meet in the sky.

A loud knock on the door instantly interrupted Reverend Jesse's faraway thoughts. He quickly removed his feet from the other chair and tucked them under the one he was seated in. "Come on in," he shouted to the visitor.

The door cracked open, and Faye Browning poked her head inside. "Brother Samuel Carter needs to see you. Says it's kind of an emergency. Do you have a moment to spare?"

Jesse smiled broadly at his administrative assistant. "Of course. Send Brother Samuel right on in. Thanks, Sister Faye. By the way, the intercom is working now. You no longer have to do as much legwork as before. You can let your fingers do the walking over the dial-pad."

Twenty-five years young and very attractive, Faye smiled at him. "Thanks for the update, Reverend Jesse, but I don't mind the extra steps. I like popping in on you. Sometimes I do it just to make sure you're really back here with us. We all missed your loving smile and kind ways. Two years have gone by, but your absence is something your congregation will never forget. I can't tell you enough how thrilled we all are at having you back home where you belong."

Jesse smiled warmly. "Thank you, Sister Faye. I'm still thrilled to be back."

Jesse's assistant departed, but came back within seconds. Samuel Carter was right on her heels. Once Sister Faye ushered the visitor into the room, she turned around and left in haste.

Jesse stood up and extended his hand to Samuel, a young, God-loving man of thirty-five. "How are you, Brother Samuel? Please have a seat. It's good to see you."

After shaking Jesse's hand, Samuel took a seat. "To answer your question, I was fine up until about a half-hour or so ago. It's Yvonne, Reverend Jesse. She's gotten herself into a heap of trouble with the law. I need your help."

Jesse frowned, finding Samuel's statement hard to believe. "Your wife, Yvonne, in trouble with the law! What kind of trouble?"

Samuel looked thoroughly embarrassed. "Shoplifting up at the

Beverly Center. She was picked up a couple of hours ago. I need to bail her out, but I'm low on funds. The bail's been set at twenty thousand. I have to come up with ten percent of that amount, two thousand dollars. Do you think I can get a helping hand from the church?"

Jesse raised both eyebrows. "Shoplifting, Yvonne! What are they saying she stole?"

"A variety of things, mostly items that can fit into a large purse and shopping bags."

Jesse looked puzzled, frowning heavily. "Brother, you don't seem the least bit outraged or shocked by these allegations. Am I right?"

Samuel nodded. "This isn't the first time. She has a serious problem. Kleptomania is defined as a compulsion to steal without any relation to need or monetary value of the object."

All Jesse could do was shake his head. Only thirty years old, sweet, shy Yvonne plagued with that kind of disorder stunned him. There hadn't ever been a thing in any of the Carters' demeanor to suggest what he'd just heard. Samuel made good money, so there was no need for her to steal. Samuel did mention needing funds. Were they in serious financial straits? According to her disorder, though, that wasn't a reason for stealing. Jesse had every intention of standing behind the Carters and their young family, two boys and a girl, all under the age of ten.

Jesse got up from his seat only to drop down on his knees. "Brother Carter, we need to pray on this. God has all the answers, but we have to give it to Him before He can supply them to us. God will provide your needs through the provisions He provides for the church. Your situation would normally have to be met with board approval, but this is an emergency, which gives me full authority to move forward without calling a board meeting."

Jesse's voice was strong and clear. His words were powerful, soul stirring, filled with humility and thanksgiving. Brother Carter's numerous amens were softly spoken, as tears fell from his walnut-brown eyes. Samuel loved his wife, but her problem had already begun to destroy their marriage, not to mention their children's lives. God hadn't heard or answered Samuel's supplications, because he'd always been too embarrassed by them to bring his burdens to Him in prayer. It wasn't that God didn't know about Samuel and Yvonne's situation, but God was always patient in waiting on His children. In turn, He loved to have His flock to wait on Him to act before taking matters into their own hands.

The great-smelling meal that Marlene Covington, Jesse's wife, had placed on the table out in front of him had his mouth watering. It had been a long, disturbing day for him. Having his wife's companionship and sparkling conversation while eating one of her delicious home-cooked meals was a great way to begin a relaxing evening. Taking to the leather recliner/massager and reading the daily newspaper were next on his list of things to do. For right now, his undivided attention belonged to Marlene.

Jesse smiled lovingly at his wife as she sat down to the right of him. She looked good enough to be on the dinner menu. Marlene had recently lost over forty pounds, and she had joined a health spa just to firm up. Some of the weight loss was contributed to stress, but her desire and strong will had kicked in to help her trim away more of the unwanted pounds. It didn't take long for her full figure to start slipping away. Jesse had always loved her for who she was, not for what she looked like. This fantastic woman had long ago caught his attention, and she still held it.

"Wildflower, you look as delicious as the food smells. I'll first pass the blessing, and then I want to hear all about your day." He reached down and took her hand.

As she closed her dark brown eyes, no longer saddled with puffy bags and dark circles, Marlene smiled adoringly at her husband. Her smooth, mahogany brown skin glowed with health. While she was well aware that Jesse loved her no matter what, thin or obese, crazy or sane, Marlene was thrilled by all the extra special attention he constantly showered on her. They'd always had a healthy physical appetite for each other, but as of late, her man had become a little more amorous than normal. She couldn't deny the fact that his being locked up for a long time still played a part in his hot pursuit of her. However, she was sure that he found her more physically attractive at a size fourteen as opposed to her old size twenty.

As always, his deep voice soothed her. His humble prayer of thanksgiving lifted her spirits even higher. Marlene was ecstatic to have things back the way they used to be. With no more bars and locked gates to separate them, she was as happy as a lark.

Jesse kissed each of her fingertips before letting go of her hand. He then took a few bites of the creamy mashed potatoes and mixed vegetables. Closing his eyes momentarily, he moaned with sheer pleasure. After breaking off a chunk of tender, well-seasoned meat loaf, he put it into his mouth and chewed it slowly, savoring the delicious taste of the tangy tomato sauce. A tall pitcher of ice water and another glass container filled with a mixture of ginger ale and cranberry juice was there to satisfy his thirst. Marlene always tended to his every need and desire.

He took a long swallow of the cranberry concoction and followed it with a sip of water. "What have you been doing all day, Mar, besides cooking this fantastic meal?"

Before speaking, Marlene chewed the food she had in her mouth. She then put her fork down. "I ran a few errands before going to the spa. Did a little grocery shopping for Sister Wiley and us. Dropped in on the children at the church nursery school for a hot minute or two. Later on in the afternoon, I went to the beauty shop only to find out I was a day early. My appointment is for tomorrow." She laughed heartily. "My memory must be slipping. Lately, I've been having my share of 'senior moments'."

Jesse laughed along with her. "You and me both. I got somewhat of an excuse, but you're not yet fifty. Don't tell me you're going to have to start writing yourself little notes like I do."

"Lord, how I wish not. I've already got enough Post-it notes stuck here and there and everywhere. As for the age factor, I'm getting pretty close to fifty. I fondly remember the day when my brain could just about hold my entire schedule for a month. Now I have to look at the calendar at least three to four times a day." They both had a good laugh over that. "How was your day, Reverend Jesse? With all the good that you do, I know it was busy but fulfilling."

Jesse got a disturbing look in his eyes. "Brother Carter came by the office to see me today. Wildflower, you'll never guess what I spent my afternoon doing. I still can't believe it."

Marlene was curious. "It doesn't sound as if you enjoyed it, whatever it was."

He shook his head. "Not in the least bit. Samuel and I had to bail Yvonne out of jail."

Again? Without thinking, Marlene gasped, silently praying for Yvonne. "What?"

"Shoplifting, of all things. It seems that she's a kleptomaniac of some sort."

Marlene's eyes instantly filled with tears. "Oh, no, I thought she was in recovery."

Jesse raised an eyebrow. "You knew about her problem?"

"It's been going on for years. But this must be the first incident in a very long time, at least the only one that I've been made aware of. I'd actually forgotten about it until now."

"That long! Why didn't you ever tell me about this?"

"You were always so busy with other things, Jesse. Besides that, she was too embarrassed about it. She didn't want you to know, but it's too late for that now. I'm surprised Samuel even came to you with it, since he's so embarrassed by it. He knows how she feels about too many people knowing. But I guess the cat's out of the bag now."

Jessed sighed hard. "You can say that again. I didn't stay until she was released. I just went there with Samuel as a support system. He also told me she'd be embarrassed, but I don't know why. Maybe I'd be able to understand her reluctance before I got locked up, but she should surely know by now that I'd never stand in judgment of her. At any rate, she doesn't know I know, so we should keep it that way for now. However, she does need ministering to."

With her appetite lost, Marlene folded her hands and placed them on the table. "I'll counsel her, as I've done before. I'm sure she'll come to me when she's feeling a little better. She has in the past. This is a terrible thing for her to deal with, not to mention the pain the entire family might have to one day go through. Sarah, David, and Joshua are now old enough to understand what's going on, but I'm sure Samuel and Yvonne won't share the bad news with them. That's a hard thing to share with your kids, especially when it's about their mother."

Jesse stroked his chin thoughtfully. "After I left the county jail, I began to think a few things through. The circumstances with the Carters have me wondering if there is a large number of men supporting women behind bars. A lot of women are in prison, so I'm sure there's a man somewhere in the picture standing behind them. What do you think, Mar?"

While giving a minute's thought to Jesse's questions, Marlene shrugged. "I don't know. I'd certainly like to think so. I guess it's easy enough to find out. Perhaps I can visit a women's prison and do a little hands-on research. Possibly I can get permission to do some observing during the visiting hours. The first step is to get an appointment with the warden. Would you like me to do that, Jesse?"

Jesse nodded his approval. "That would be just great, Wildflower. I'm really curious to know if men are as supportive of women in prison as they are of them. Please try to get as much info as you can. It looks like the Lord may have another serious mission for us."

"I will, Jesse. I'll dig up as much as I can. If you're not too tired, why don't you come down to the church and sit in on the Ladies In Waiting support group? Perhaps you can say a few encouraging words to the women. Rosalinda and Keisha are supposed to be there, but I'm not so sure about Alexis. She hasn't called me back yet. She pops in and out of our lives at will, just as she does at the meetings. Alexis reminds me of a hyped-up jack-in-the box."

Laughing at Marlene's comments, Jesse's eyes widened with excitement as he snapped his fingers. "Support group! I'm glad you mentioned that. I'd love to come and sit in after two years of wondering what really goes on in those sessions. But the idea of starting one for men suddenly came to mind. We should do this, especially if we find out there's a need for such. What do you think of the idea of starting a support group for men supporting women behind bars, just like the one you and your friends are running for the ladies in waiting?"

Marlene couldn't help smiling her approval, wondering why she hadn't already thought of it herself. "I think it's a great idea. If you really want to do this, like I've already said, I'll do all I can to help you. The research has to come first. There's a women's prison up near Norco that I can check on. I'll try to make an appointment with the warden for early next week. Right now I'm going to get up from here and call Keisha to make sure she's still attending the meeting this evening. So many things can happen to change your plans when you have little ones."

Seated in the center of the bed, her legs curled up beneath her, Keisha was rereading for the tenth time the letter she'd received from Zachary Martin, the father of her two children, Zanari and little Zach, his daddy's namesake. Zach was still in prison.

The thought of Zach being released in a month's time had her insides trembling. It wasn't his release that bothered her as much as what he'd asked of her. Zach wanted to come live with her, and she wasn't at all sure she wanted that to occur. They had never lived together, though he had spent many nights with her and the children.

Zach had always lived with his doting mama, Lucian Martin. Lucian was crazy about her son and would defend his wrongs as easy as a right.

According to Zach's letter, Lucian had told him that he couldn't come back to her house to live. That had come as quite a shock to Keisha. Lucian loved her son, Zach, like crazy. She had a new man, and she didn't want her adult son under her roof and in her face at every waking moment. In order for Zach to get parole, he had to have a permanent address. A halfway house was an option for him, but he hated the idea of living in one. He saw it as only one step from being locked down in prison, because there were almost as many rules for him to abide by.

As far as Keisha was concerned, Zach still had a lot to prove to her. Before their future could ever be decided, she wanted to see him with a stable job, paying child support on a regular basis, as well as turning his life completely around. If he were to come home and start hanging out with the same crew, it wouldn't be long before he'd once again find himself on the inside with no windows to look out of. Neither did she want any criminal activity around her kids. They were two years older and she didn't want Zach to be doing the same criminal things by the time the children were old enough to understand what their daddy was all about.

If Keisha hadn't figured anything else out about her relationship with one Zachary Martin, she was adamant about wanting a better life for her and the kids. It was what they deserved, and she was determined to see that they had all the reasonable goodness this life had to offer. Allowing Zach to walk into her apartment without any means to support at least his own habits would only have disastrous effects. Zach needed to stand on his own two feet and not start his freedom by looking for and accepting handouts. Her budget was so tight, it already squeaked.

The phone rang and Keisha only stared at it, fearing that it was Zach on the line, calling collect, wanting an immediate answer about the living arrangements. Still somewhat of a coward where he was concerned, she had planned to give him her decision by answering his letter with a letter. She could better explain it in writing; a letter wasn't something he could argue with. But if he got her on the phone, an argument would ensue, because she knew he wasn't going to accept her total rejection of his idea. He was a master artist in the arts of persuasion and manipulation.

Keisha continued to stare at the phone until the answering service picked up. Upon hearing Marlene's sweet voice, she snatched up the receiver. "Hey, Mizz Marlene, I'm here. Are you all ready for this evening? I'm looking forward to seeing you."

Marlene chuckled. "That's just what I was calling you about. I can't wait to see you as well. Have you spoken to Rosalinda? If so, is she coming to the meeting?"

"I haven't talked to her today, but I'll contact her as soon as I get off the line. What's Malcolm up to lately? You haven't mentioned him in a while. Is he doing okay?"

Marlene closed her eyes for a brief moment of silent prayer. Every time someone mentioned her gorgeous twenty-three-year-old son's name, she had to stop and give thanks to the Lord for keeping him in check. "Girl, if he was doing any better, I'd be scared. As you know, he's been on the same job for close to two years now. He really loves working in the sports program with the kids down at the Los Angeles County Department of Parks and Recreation. He was recently promoted up to special assistant to one of the program directors. You know he has his own apartment, but he just bought a brand new car, financed it himself through the county credit union. So, I'd say that the young brother is doing okay for himself. Praise God!"

Keisha laughed softly. "Okay, Mr. Malcolm Covington! I ain't mad at you, brother! Sounds like he really does have it going on. If I wasn't so in love with Zach, I might make a play for your son. How would you like to have me as a daughter-in-law?"

Marlene groaned. "I like you just fine as a surrogate daughter. If you and Malcolm ever got together, you two young folks would drive me insane, not to mention what you'd do to each other's sanity. We'll all be insane in no time at all. It's not like you two don't dis each other every time you meet up." Marlene laughed heartily. "I have to run, sweetie. See you in a few."

Keisha disconnected the line and then immediately dialed Rosalinda's number. Keisha listened to it ring several times as she mentally prepared herself to leave a message. Rosalinda picked up just as the machine came on. "Hey, girlfriend, are you getting yourself together for this evening? I just got off the phone with Marlene." There were several seconds of pregnant silence. "Rosalinda, are you there?"

"I am, but I can't talk right now. Can I call you back?"

"Yeah, sure, but you don't sound like yourself. Your voice is so strained, and it sounds stressful. Is there something wrong? Are you stressing about your mom's death?"

"Everything is fine. I'll call you back." Rosalinda hung up the phone before Keisha could get in another word.

Rosalinda's odd behavior had Keisha a little frightened, but she didn't have a clue as to why. Keisha thought back on the strange sound of her best friend's voice. Something was definitely up, but what? Keisha thought about the incident for a few minutes before deciding she might be making too much of it. Rosalinda had said she was fine. At any rate, she was going to stop by her friend's apartment on her way out. She only lived in the next building. They hadn't planned to ride together because Rosalinda had personal plans for after the meeting, but that wasn't going to stop Keisha from checking her out beforehand.

Rosalinda twisted her hands in anguish. Had she known Ricardo Munoz would be on the other side of her door, she certainly wouldn't have opened it. Cursing herself inwardly for not looking out the peephole first, Rosalinda found it hard to make eye contact with her ex-boyfriend, who had just been released from prison. The words to the old Gloria Gaynor song "I Will Survive" were rolling around inside her head, making her crazy, yet she was proud that she'd survived Ric. How long would she survive with him back on the street was the fifty million dollar question. Changing the stupid locks had been necessary when she'd decided it was over with them; finding out who was on the other side of a closed door before opening it would've prevented the serious predicament she now found herself in.

Ric got to his feet and started pacing the floor. "I don't understand what has happened to you, Rosie. You were never this cold. I thought you'd be happy to see me. I know what you said in your letter, but I never did believe you were through with me." He hit the spot over his heart with a closed fist. "We're inside of here with each other, man. Been here twenty minutes and you have barely spoken a word. What's up, Rosie? *El gato* got your tongue?"

Rosalinda flinched as he came toward her. When he reached down and lifted her head with his two fingers under her chin, she shrank back, expecting him to squeeze her face hard or slap it silly. Then a familiar pain ripped through her scalp. Ric's hand held her by the hair so tight it felt as if the blood supply to her scalp had been totally cut off.

She blinked back the tears. "Please, Ric, you're hurting me!"

"Whatcha think you be doing to me? You think it feels good to have the woman you love cut you off without even looking back? I ain't locked up no longer, and I finally got your undivided attention." He pulled her up from the chair by her hair and brought her in close to him. "How's it feel to be back in my arms, Rosie? Feels pretty good, huh? You love it, don't you?"

Rosalinda had always hated it when he called her Rosie, but it now sounded far more vulgar to her ears. He only called her by that name when he was highly perturbed with her. The sour smell of alcohol on his breath nearly made her gag, and it also caused her fear to escalate. She was in no doubt as to what he was capable of. If she didn't give him what he wanted, she knew Ric well enough to know that he'd simply take it, by brutal force if necessary.

A hard knock caused both Rosalinda and Ric to look toward the door.

His grip tightened on her hair. "You better not utter a word. If you so much as whimper, I'll rip your scalp right off."

"Please don't do this," she rasped painfully. "If that's Keisha on the other side of the door, she's not going to leave until she talks to me. She knows I'm in here, and she'll call 911 if she thinks I'm ill or in some kind of danger. Do you want to go right back to jail, Ric? Haven't you had enough of that place already?"

He appeared to be thinking over what she'd said, but Rosalinda wasn't at all optimistic. Ricardo hadn't cared jack about being locked up thus far. He'd always had his own rules and was determined to live by them come hell or high water. His answer came as his fist met her eye.

"Rosalinda," Keisha shouted through the door, "I know you haven't left the house because your car is still in the parking stall. What's wrong with you? Are you okay?"

Keisha knew exactly what was wrong with her best friend. The second she'd spotted Ric's posse hanging out in front of the building, she'd slipped back inside of hers and approached Rosalinda's place by the back entrance. She had been fully aware that Ric's boys could also be stationed there. She had already called 911 on her cell, though she hadn't given an apartment number, thinking the sirens would be enough to scare everyone away. If Ric were rearrested because of this incident, he more than likely would instruct his boys to come after both her and Rosalinda. Now she felt that she needed to make some noise to cause a distraction for whatever was going on inside Rosalinda's apartment, since the police weren't fully informed.

"Oh, God," she screamed, "I've already called 911. Help is on the way. I know you must be sick, Rosa. The police will come with the paramedics. It'll be okay. Hang in there."

Keisha hoped that what she'd said would send Ricardo packing. When the front door suddenly flew open, Keisha stepped back, ready for battle. Seeing Rosalinda standing there, looking as if she had been terrorized out of her wits made Keisha sick. Her friend's right eye looked swollen, which was indication that Ric may have physically abused her. Keisha prayed that the physical aspects hadn't gone any further than that. Rosalinda was fully dressed, though terribly disheveled. Still, it was a good sign that she possibly hadn't been sexually assaulted.

As he stepped out into the hallway, the deadly look in Ric's eyes had Keisha's heart racing. Though she feared him something awful, she was determined to stand her ground. Showing that she was the least bit intimidated by him could get her killed. Ric and his posse weren't to be taken lightly. They were all crazy; he was their leader, the craziest of the bunch.

Ric glared back and forth between Keisha and Rosalinda. "This ain't over! You both better watch your back. Rosie, you will see me again. If this witch of a friend of yours hadn't shown up, you would've eventually given in to the demands of your sweet body. You want me just as much as I want you. You haven't forgotten what it was like for you and me, the way it will be again, real soon." Ric kissed his two fingers and pushed them outward toward Rosalinda. He then took off running, shouting and spewing out every vulgar word he had in his vocabulary, taking the downward stairwell like he was in a race with the devil.

Crying out from the sheer fear of it all, Keisha rushed into the apartment, slammed the door shut and immediately put the locks in place. With both women trembling like leaves, Keisha and Rosalinda went straight into each other's arms. Something she'd been doing a lot of over the past two years, Keisha began to pray hard, thanking God for keeping them safe from serious harm. Tears streaked their faces as they held on to each other for dear life. Keisha said a silent thank you to Marlene Covington for teaching her how to pray. It came naturally now.

A few minutes later, somewhat calmer, Keisha led Rosalinda over to the camelback, overstuffed sofa, where they both sat down. Wiping away her own tears, Keisha turned and wiped Rosalinda's. "First off, are you okay? I can see that he hurt you since your eye is already turning colors. How in the world did he get in here? I know you didn't just invite him into your place. I had no idea he was out of prison. Zach has never mentioned Ric's release to me."

Rosalinda shook her head in dismay. "I'm not hurt too badly, but I don't know what would've happened next had you not shown up. He was getting pretty physical with me. I feel so stupid. Keisha, I didn't even stop to think about who might be there before I opened that door. That is so unlike me. I tried to slam it shut in his face, but he's quick. He was inside before I could blink an eye." Rosalinda's voice trembled with fear. Her body shook as she thought of all the years of abuse she'd taken from her crazy ex-boyfriend. "You're not the only one who didn't know he was out on the streets. But I can't imagine Michael not knowing, since he was once Ric's defense attorney." Rosalinda sighed in distress. "This is so unreal."

Keisha jerked her head about. "As hard as the fine Michael Hernandez, attorney at law, has been trying to win your heart, I'm also surprised that he didn't know. Anyhow, we should call Michael and get him over here right away so he can help us figure this out. I'm going to also call Marlene and have her come. She can probably get someone to cover the meeting for her. A lot of the women are regulars, and they should know how to conduct things."

Keisha looked down at her watch. "I'll have to reach Marlene on her cell. She likes to get to the church early."

Rosalinda stilled Keisha's hand, keeping her from dialing the phone. "I don't think we should involve Marlene or Michael. It can only mean trouble for them. They have enough going on in their own lives. They don't need to take on my burdens, too."

Keisha sucked her teeth hard and rolled her eyes. "Neither of them will feel that way, and you know it. If we don't tell them, we're going to get blessed out by both of them. If something happens to you, I'll feel responsible, especially if I didn't do everything I could to help out. Calling Marlene and Michael is the right thing for me to do, so chill."

Marlene looked terribly troubled after getting off the phone with Keisha. Glad that Jesse had come to the meeting with her, she summoned him from up in the church balcony to come down to where she was seated. Jesse had planned to observe the support group meeting from the upper tier. He had also agreed to say a few words to the members once the session was over.

Jesse noticed the stressful look on his wife's face as soon as he reached her. "What's up, Mar? You don't look too happy. In fact, you look downright terrified."

She got to her feet. "There's been some trouble over at Rosalinda's apartment." She relayed to Jesse what Keisha had told her. "Would it be possible for you to run the meeting for me? They want me over there right away." The door swinging open caused her to look toward the back of the sanctuary. "It's early, but they're starting to file in. Can you handle it?"

Jesse shrugged. "I don't know how they'll receive a male facilitator, but I'll give it my best shot. However, I feel like I should be going to Rosalinda's with you. You may be walking into more trouble than you realize. I've seen firsthand what kind of a bad boy Ricardo can be. He was always into some kind of trouble on the inside. If the boy is just out of prison, which I'm totally surprised at, it doesn't seem as if he's learned too much. I don't want you or the other women hurt. This mission could be a dangerous one, Wildflower. I want to go with you."

Marlene waved off his concern. "Michael Hernandez is also on his way there, so we will have a male presence. Keisha duped Ricardo into believing the police were on the way. She did call 911, but she didn't give them the apartment number. However, her cell number and address would've automatically come up on the emergency screen, and they will eventually track her down. I told her to call them back and explain herself in order to keep out of big trouble. She promised to do so. With Ricardo threatening Rosalinda, the police should be informed."

"Good advice, Mar. I have your back as far as the meeting is concerned. Be careful."

Jesse had stood in front of hundreds and hundreds of people as a servant for the Lord, but there was something a little different about standing in front of this formidable-looking group of women. He'd been in the building during the meetings on several occasions over the past two years, but he'd never sat in on one. Being a male, he wasn't sure if they might view him as the enemy or see him as a friend. He prayed for the latter.

According to Marlene, many of these women had been hurt badly by men on lockdown. On the other side of the coin, there were just as many who had good, strong relationships with incarcerated loved ones. As an ex-con himself, though proved an innocent one, he wasn't too sure if he'd be received with open arms.

Jesse quickly decided that it was too late for analyzing the situation. Marlene was already out the door. He would just have to go for broke. A prayer asking for divine guidance from God was right on the tip of his tongue.

Smiling broadly, he looked out over the crowd. "Welcome, ladies! For you that don't already know, I'm Reverend Jesse Covington, the pastor of First Tabernacle, the man responsible for making my wife, Marlene, a Lady in Waiting. It's nice to see you all."

Several gasps echoed throughout the room, followed by a healthy round of applause.

Jesse recognized a few of the women who had not so long ago joined his church as a result of Marlene's spiritual guidance. However, he wouldn't think of pointing them out.

"Thank you. Thank you," he said, his humility apparent. "Due to an unavoidable situation, Marlene has been called away and has asked me to stand in for her. Rosalinda and Keisha won't be with us this evening either. I must warn you. I've never facilitated a support group. But, if no one minds, should I fail as a facilitator, we'll just have an old-fashioned prayer meeting. Would that be okay with you nice ladies?"

The enthusiastic applause was deafening. With his audience completely won over, Jesse sighed with relief. His silent voice of heartfelt thanks to the Creator followed.

In the next instant, Jesse knew exactly what Bible text he would share with the women before the conclusion of the evening. Luke, chapter 23, spoke to Jesus' false imprisonment, which eventually led up to His crucifixion. Just as Jesus was falsely imprisoned and later sentenced to die, even when neither Herod nor Pilate could find any wrongdoing in Him, Jesse knew firsthand that many of these women's men were probably experiencing the same plight. The numbers of falsely convicted inmates were great, greater than most people knew.

Luke, chapter 23, also spoke of the group of women who waited, standing and beholding far off from the prison in support of Jesus. They then followed after Jesus, weeping and wailing, as He, bound in chains, carried on His back the burden of the cross that He would eventually die upon.

Jesus turning unto the weeping women had said this: "Daughters of Jerusalem, weep not for me, but weep for yourselves and your children." (Luke 23:28)

As he thought of the thief that was crucified alongside Jesus, he fondly embraced the memory of Richard James Du Boise, the self-proclaimed thief; the man that he often wished was still alive.

There was no doubt in Jesse's mind that he and R.J. would've become great friends, brothers of the soul, kindred spirits. The one thing that Jesse was overjoyed about was that R.J. had received the gift of eternal life—not only because he had come to believe in God, but because he had also wholeheartedly accepted Jesus as his Lord and Savior.

Chapter Two

Inside of Rosalinda's warm, cozy, moderately furnished apartment everything and everyone had calmed down considerably. The police had come and gone and an official report had been filed. Keisha had been given a stern warning about the proper use of 911. Quick to apologize for giving misleading information, Keisha was extremely glad that she had recalled 911, as advised by Marlene. Seeing herself behind bars wasn't a bit appealing.

Rosalinda was instructed by the Los Angeles police officers to seek an immediate restraining order against Ricardo Munoz, who was in violation of his parole. Before anything could happen in this instance, Ric's parole officer would have to be contacted in order to have his conditional release violated. Ricardo would eventually be rearrested and returned to prison.

However, Ricardo had to be caught up with before anything could happen.

That daunting revelation had everyone worried, especially knowing exactly what he was capable of. He was a leader in a tough street gang, one that he'd still controlled from on the inside. Ricardo and the bad reputations of his posse were known all over the streets of L.A.

Rosalinda knew that Ricardo wasn't through with her yet; he didn't make idle threats.

The small group of friends sat quietly in Rosalinda's living room, enjoying the coffee Marlene had brewed. Tall and dashingly handsome Michael Hernandez had brought along a box of freshly baked churros and donuts. He had already purchased the baked goods from his favorite Mexican donut shop, when he'd received on his cell phone the emergency call from Keisha. He had made plans with Rosalinda for them to spend a quiet evening in his home, after her meeting, so the pastries were for them to enjoy.

Michael Hernandez deeply felt Rosalinda's turmoil. During the time he'd held the ice to her eye, all he'd wanted to do was hold her in his arms and comfort her. It had been a tender moment, but the circumstances had been wrong, not to mention the timing. The swollen and discolored condition of her eye had him wanting to annihilate Ricardo Munoz. As Michael thought of excruciatingly painful ways to make Ric pay for all the suffering he'd caused the woman he himself cared so much about, his anger continued to escalate.

Wearing a brooding look in his coal black eyes, Michael was still a little upset that Rosalinda hadn't wanted Keisha to notify him about Ricardo coming to her place. Michael had developed a serious penchant for Rosalinda while serving as Ricardo's legal counsel. Eventually plagued by the certain conflict of interest, Michael had removed himself as Ric's lawyer only a short time after revealing to the stunning, dark-haired Rosalinda his romantic interest in her. Michael's unusual, highly insensitive test of Rosalinda's character still bothered him to no end.

In his quest to find out if she was even worth his time and energy, he had made her a terribly offensive offer: *sleep with me and I'll reduce Ricardo's legal fees.* He had spent the better part of two years trying to make up for his callousness toward Rosalinda, the woman he loved to spend all of his spare time with. While their relationship had not taken the serious romantic turn he still desired, he was extremely grateful for every moment they spent together.

Rosalinda had become his social butterfly. He was always inviting her to the social functions that he had to attend. Rosalinda had once revealed to Michael that she'd never had a man treat her like he did. He made her feel so special, yet she still kept him at a safe distance from her heart. He couldn't help thinking of the speech she'd once made to him regarding personal relationships. It had been such a bold statement coming from the shy, young woman who'd let a man walk all over her. She had presented him with a challenge he had been more than willing to take her up on. Getting Ricardo out of her life had been his first challenge; keeping him out was an even bigger one.

If it's only my flesh you're pursuing, I want you to know that the next time I lie down naked in bed with a man, I'll be the missus.

The memory of that impertinent speech never failed to make Michael smile.

The sudden knock on the door had Michael leaping to his feet. Upon seeing the alarming look on the women's faces, he gave them a reassuring smile. "It'll be okay. I'll handle the door. Just be very still. . . ."

"Wait a minute, Michael." Rosalinda looked terrified. "That might not be such a good idea. You could be putting your life in danger and your career in jeopardy if Ricardo is on the other side of that door. If he sees you in here, he's going to wonder about you and me. If he thinks something is going on between us, he will probably make even more trouble for me than he's already threatened. Ric is also known for carrying a weapon."

Michael walked over to the sofa and knelt down in front of her. Taking her hand in his, he squeezed it tenderly. "I will first look through the security window. If it is Ricardo, I simply won't open the door. Then we'll call the police. Okay?"

Marlene and Keisha were held spellbound by the sweet, gentle tone that Michael had spoken to Rosalinda in. Each of the women had grown extremely fond of him. He was around them a lot, and they found him to be a genuinely caring man. They'd stopped questioning his true feelings for Rosalinda right around the time of Jesse's homecoming celebration. It was some time later that he'd earned a permanent place in their hearts. When Rosalinda's mother's health had taken a turn for the worse, he had been there every step of the way for both women.

Paulina Morales' death had come unexpectedly, because she'd been doing very well during the previous year and a half. It had once appeared that her serious health issues had become manageable, but she had eventually succumbed to kidney failure, which had come as a result of systemic lupus. Before her death, Paulina had come to have high hopes in a future for Rosalinda and Michael. She thought he would be a perfect husband for her lovely daughter.

By the time Michael finally reached the door, the insistent knocks had practically turned to hard pounding. Upon looking out of the tiny viewing window, he gave a huge sigh of relief. Then his mouth suddenly broke into a huge smile. "It's Reverend Jesse. You all can relax now."

Michael released the locks and opened the door wide to Jesse. The two men exchanged brotherly hugs before taking a seat alongside the women. Prayer ensued next, led by Jesse.

After voicing a hearty amen, Marlene reached for Jesse's hand. "How'd it go?"

Jesse squeezed her fingers reassuringly. "We'll talk about it in a couple of minutes, Mar. First, I need to find out how everyone here is doing, especially our dear Rosalinda." Jesse only then caught a glimpse of Rosalinda's swollen eye as he looked over at her. He winced within, shaking his head from side to side. "I'm sorry, Rosalinda. I can see for myself how you're doing physically. I wish I could've done something to prevent what has happened to you. How are you doing emotionally?"

Rosalinda smiled weakly. "I'm an emotional mess, but thanks to all of you, I'll recover soon enough. No one is to blame for what happened here. I was extremely careless by opening the door without knowing who was there. I'll be fine in due time. For sure, once Ric is caught and taken off the streets. We're all anxious to hear about the meeting. How *did* it go, Rev Jesse?"

Sensing that Rosalinda desperately wanted to change the subject, Jesse dared to grin with smug satisfaction. "I had all those beautiful spirits eating right out of my hand. You three ladies were certainly missed, but I was the *man*, the man of the hour!"

Everyone laughed as Jesse pounded his chest in a boasting way.

Marlene closed her right eye. Out of her left eye, she eyed Jesse with skepticism. "Is that so? The man of the hour, huh? So you think you got it like that? That's okay, just as long as you remember exactly whose man you are twenty-four-seven, three-hundred and sixty-five!"

Laughing, Jesse slipped his arm around Marlene's shoulder. "Woman, I know I'm all yours. After all this time, you should know that, too. Feeling a little jealous?" Jesse joked.

Marlene and Jesse never failed to keep others in awe of them. It wasn't something they tried to do or even wanted to do; they were just an awesome couple. Their deep love constantly shined bright, and they exulted in the joy of it and in the reverence they held for each other.

Just being around Marlene and Jesse was exhilarating for the others in the room. The older couple had taught their much younger friends the true meaning of fellowship, which was exactly what they indulged themselves in for the next couple of hours, despite the growing lateness. All enjoyed the pastries and fresh coffee as Jesse told them a few stories regarding his early days in the ministry and how he'd tried to run away from his divine calling.

While all of her guests had departed, leaving the two of them alone in the apartment, Michael looked intently at Rosalinda. Anxiety burned in his dark eyes as he tried to find the right words to say to her. Her living alone had always made him nervous, but it was more so now that Ric was out of jail. She wasn't a bit safe in her current residence, which had already been proven by the unexpected violence visited upon her person by her ex-boyfriend.

Just as it had been with the passing away of her mother, which had occurred only several months ago, Michael once again felt the need to convince Rosalinda to move into his guesthouse, an offer he'd first made to her two years prior. She had flatly turned him down each time.

Though Rosalinda now worked part-time in his law office, he often pressed her to change her status to full-time. She was smart and extremely efficient, and his other employees loved working with her, loved her bubbly personality and great sense of humor. Her present job was taking her nowhere. The part-time telemarketing job hadn't offered much financial gain, either.

Rosalinda looked as anxious as Michael felt. "Michael, I know you're still upset because I didn't want Keisha to contact you, but could you please put it aside? I have enough to cope with without having you mad at me, too. I can see the agitation in your eyes."

His expression softened. "I'm not mad at you, Rosalinda. Disappointed that you didn't want me to know about it? Yes, a little, but I'll get over it. It's certainly not an altering-of-feelings kind of situation. I don't feel any differently toward you."

Rosalinda looked relieved. "Thank you for that. I feel much better now."

His eyes grew somber. "Now you can make me feel better by packing a bag and agreeing to stay in my guesthouse tonight. In fact, a permanent move would not be out of order in this instance. You can put your things in storage. Or, I'll have my furnishings stored, and you can move yours in so that you'll feel right at home. I promise to respect your right to privacy."

Rosalinda smiled softly. "Seems to me that we've already had this conversation a few dozen times or so." She laughed, looking around at her modest furnishings. "Sometimes, when you're making a new start, you have to strip everything down. There are very few things in this apartment that I'd want to keep. Any and all reminders of Ric will have to go. That's a must."

Michael looked bewildered. "Is that a yes?"

Rosalinda smiled broadly. "I really do like being alive, Michael. Until he's caught and put back behind bars, Ricardo is definitely a threat to my existence. Even then, the threat will still exist through his homeboys. For now, your gated community is the safest haven I know of. I'd like to take you up on your offer until I can find another safe place. Should I go pack?"

Grinning like a Cheshire cat, Michael leaped to his feet. "I'll help you."

Michael brought Rosalinda into his warm embrace and hugged her fiercely, which gave her much needed solace. Smiling, hand-in-hand, the couple proceeded down the hallway toward her bedroom. Rosalinda had decided to only pack enough clothing for the night and next day, but she couldn't wait to permanently move out of the apartment that held more bad memories than good ones. Although her eye had been blackened, her future suddenly looked bright and sunny.

Keisha couldn't believe that someone could be knocking at her door this late. Then she thought of Ricardo. He and his homeboys knew where she lived. Would he dare to come there, knowing the police had been called on him earlier? Her legs shook as she made her way to the door, relieved that the kids were with Zach's mother. Perhaps she shouldn't say anything. If no one knew she was inside, they'd probably just go away. *Or break in. . . .*

"Keisha, I know you're in there. I can practically hear you breathing. Open this darn door before I kick it down."

Keisha definitely knew that voice, but what she didn't know was why Malcolm Covington was standing on the other side of her apartment door. The thought that something bad might've happened to Marlene or Jesse had her jerking the locks off without thinking about her near complete state of undress. A gray tank style T-shirt and matching boxer shorts were all she'd worn to bed.

Nearly running her over, Malcolm moved inside before Keisha could blink an eyelash. She couldn't help noticing how good he looked. His pants were pulled up and not hanging off his behind. They actually fit his waist, unlike the baggy stuff she'd often seen him in. In her opinion, he was looking rather *GQ*. Handsome as could be, the young brother still had the most beautiful ebony-colored bedroom eyes she'd ever seen. With his pretty brown face all clean-shaven, his tall, lean physique dressed to impress, Marlene and Jesse's son was quite a looker.

Keisha put her hands on her hips. "Why are you here?"

He smirked. "Not for what you think, though I know you want me to want you. If he stood you up, I can give you what you need. I'd say you were expecting someone to do a drive-by? You know, that late night booty-call."

"In your dreams!"

"By the way you're dressed, I think it was in your dreams. Got kinda hot for you, huh?"

Realizing what she had on, or didn't have on, Keisha's hands immediately went up to her face. Trying to ignore Malcolm's howling laughter, she streaked from the room and flashed down the hall. Keisha's hands shook as she threw on the pair of jeans and sweatshirt she'd had on earlier; a robe would not conceal enough of her body from Malcolm's probing eyes. The boy's imagination was already overly stimulated. And he was attracted to her, she knew.

By the time Keisha returned to the living room, Malcolm had made himself comfortable on the sofa. "Do I need to repeat my earlier question, as to why you are here, Malcolm C.?"

Malcolm patted the sofa cushion beside the one he was seated on. Keisha ignored his gesture as she dropped down in the chair facing the couch. "Okay, I'm feeling you, Keisha Reed. To answer your question, I came here to check on you."

Keisha raised an eyebrow. "For what?"

"My parents told me what happened to Rosalinda."

Keisha rolled her eyes. "In that case, shouldn't you have gone to her house instead?"

Malcolm chuckled. "They told me Michael was looking after Rosalinda. Since you have darn near stolen my parents away from me, I thought I should start acting like a big brother."

"If anything, you'd be a little brother. I am older than you, remember?"

"Whatever! You are only slightly older than me, but you haven't reached the maturity level that I have, which is several years older than how you always act."

Keisha sucked her teeth. "Get real! Now that you've checked on me, why are you still here? The door swings both ways. Besides, you've already worn out your welcome."

Malcolm got to his feet. "I know you got a Coke up in here. I'm thirsty."

"How many 7-Elevens did you pass by on your way here?"

"You're going to deny a brother a Coke after he drove out here this late at night to check on you? Keisha, you better get up and get me something to drink. Didn't anyone ever introduce you to the word 'hospitality'?"

Keisha couldn't help laughing. "I can see that you're not going to leave here until you have me ready to throw you out on your tight butt. You sure love to harass me. Let me get this Coke for you so you can get your tired, trifling behind out of my apartment."

"That's not exactly the spirit I'm looking for, but I guess it'll have to do." Malcolm followed Keisha into the kitchen. Without being offered a seat, he plopped down at the table.

Keisha slammed the ice-cold can of soda down in front of him. "This is a to-go order. If you're not trying to hear me, Malcolm, you need to start! It's late and I'm sleepy."

Malcolm shook his head. "Girl, you know you ain't ready for me

29

to shake spot. Grab a cold one and join me. We can sit here and do some catching up. You can start by telling me why you're still dealing with that joker behind bars. I'm real curious to hear your sorry excuses for continuing to run up to that prison every week, especially after he played you the way he did. How many women did he have tramping up in there to see him? I heard it was four or five."

Keisha suddenly felt tired, too fatigued to fight any longer with Malcolm. Besides, she thought it might be nice to have someone to open up to about Zach. Perhaps she could bounce things off of Malcolm in regards to Zach wanting to come live with her. Malcolm was a man, so he surely knew how a man might react to having his ideas rejected. Wearier than she'd ever been in her life, Keisha grabbed herself a Coke from the refrigerator and plopped down in the chair opposite Malcolm's. "For your information, it was only two, Tammy and Celeste."

"You mean the only two that you caught up there with him. Why are you in such denial?"

Eyeing him intently, Keisha ran her thumb across her lower lip. "Why do you care?"

"Good question, but I don't have an answer to that yet. Let me rephrase my question. How can you still be loyal to a man who's been constantly cheating on you from behind bars, of all places? That's some deep doo-doo, Keisha. You have to admit it."

Keisha looked exasperated. "Malcolm Covington, the pot should never call the skillet black. You were cheating on your woman, Sheila, too. How you gonna come down on Zach for the same darn thing? You're no better than he is in that regard."

Malcolm shrugged. "That was a long time ago. I was dead wrong. But Sheila didn't have my babies to take care of. Perhaps that's why it was easier for her to move on."

"There were no kids involved, but she was sure taking care of you. You couldn't even wipe your behind without her; she was the only one supplying the toilet paper. Now that's what you call deep doo-doo, as you so dramatically put it."

Malcolm raised an eyebrow; unable to believe they were having a real conversation, though spicy. It was a first for them. When he'd been living with Sheila, taking all that she had to offer, giving very little in return, he hadn't thought about things like that. On the other hand, he hadn't given much thought to anything back then. He'd been all for one, himself. Malcolm had stopped looking back a long time ago, because it had brought him nothing but pain. He hadn't been a nice guy two years ago, marching to Satan's tune. All that had changed, drastically. He was now moving forward in his life, continuing to take it in a very positive direction.

"I've changed, Keisha, for the better. Has Zach?"

Keisha formed praying hands and pressed the sides of them into her lips. For several seconds she pondered Malcolm's very pointed question. "I don't know." She shook her head. "I'd like to think so, but I'm just not sure. He's about to get out of prison. Wants to come live with me. Surprisingly enough, he can't go back to his mother's house. Wants me to still be there for him. He has the option of a halfway house, but he doesn't want to live in one. Says he wants to be with me, right here where his kids are."

Malcolm sighed hard, showing his impatience with the subject matter. "All I've heard you say is what Zach wants. You've used 'want' several times. Zach wants this and Zach wants that, but what does Keisha Reed want? Furthermore, what does Keisha desire for little Zach and Zanari?" Malcolm held up his hand. "Don't answer that yet. Hear me out first, okay?"

Keisha nodded, wondering where he was going next.

Malcolm fell into a moment of silence. "Listen up." He rubbed his hand across his forehead. "Think about where you were two years ago and where you are now. You were a single mom on welfare, struggling all by yourself to make ends meet. You also took a computer class in hopes of bettering yourself. You constantly pushed yourself. How am I doing so far?"

Keisha grinned. "If you weren't listening to your mother about

31

anything else, you sure were busy listening to her talking about my business. But what are you getting at?"

"That's 'cause I was trying to figure you out. These are the facts for right now, girl. You completed your computer course and quickly landed a data entry job with a major health network. You have moved up in your department three times in less than two years."

Keisha blew out a stream of shaky breath. "Will you just get to the dang point? Don't you think I know all that already?"

"Patience, woman! Your department head is now training you to become a supervisor and you're also going to school two nights a week to eventually earn a degree. You have health benefits and you actually know where your next meal is coming from. You were even able to take a trip to Atlanta to pick up Zach and Zanari. Your kids are in day care, compliments of you and only you. Are you going to be able to maintain all that if Zach comes here to live? If he's just going to be another mouth for you to feed, is that what you really want out of this deal? Is that all you think you deserve out of life after working so hard to change your circumstances?"

Keisha had to admit that Malcolm had summed up everything quite nicely. Just like his parents would've done, he hadn't pulled any punches. "You *are* acting just like a brother! Do you really look at me like you would if you had a sister?"

Malcolm's dark gaze settled on her pretty face. "That's 'cause you won't let me look at you any other way. I don't mind being a big brother to you, but I'd also like to be your friend."

"Correction, *little* brother!"

"Whatever, girl! Think we could stop the verbal jabbing and become friends?"

Wondering if friendship was all he had in mind, Keisha eyed him with deep curiosity. It would be nice to have him as a friend. He had certainly changed his life, and she thought him now to be a positive influence. But if he wanted more than friendship, he was knocking on the wrong door; she was in love with Zach. If she weren't involved, she'd surely give him a chance.

Keisha extended her hand for him to shake. "I think that can happen, but you need to understand that I don't want you all up in my personal business. If I need your advice, I'll ask for it. Is that okay, Coolio?"

Smiling broadly, he shook her hand and quickly released it. "Yeah, but I wish you didn't have to put any restrictions on me and our relationship. I'm only looking out for your best interest. You got it going on now and I'd hate to see you start backpedaling. You deserve the best, but you have to believe that in order for it to happen. No one can believe it for you."

"Are you saying that Zach isn't what's best for me?"

"Wow! How did you ever come to that conclusion? Duh!"

"Okay now! We've gone and found some common ground; step lightly."

Malcolm laughed at her warning. "I hear you. I'll turn off the sarcasm button." He got to his feet. "I'd better go. It has gotten late."

"It was late when you got here. But could you stay another minute or two? I want to run a couple of things by you. The kind of stuff that only a man might be able to answer."

Malcolm dropped back down in his seat. "Let me hear what's on your mind, girl."

Keisha suddenly looked apprehensive, as if she wasn't sure she should be baring her soul to a man. Malcolm wasn't just any man. He was Marlene's son, and she had to tread lightly. Rosalinda and Marlene could offer her sound advice, whether she took it or not would be up to her. But it wouldn't be the same as a man's point of view, which would be more helpful.

"Okay, here goes. I'm feeling really scared about Zach coming to live. . . ."

"You should be scared, scared straight by now," Malcolm interjected.

Keisha sucked her teeth. "Can you please let me finish what I'm about to say?"

He threw up both his hands. "Okay, okay. No more interruptions."

Keisha didn't feel like she wanted to go on, but she needed to. Another opportunity to solicit a man's view on her troubling issues wasn't just going to fall into her lap like this one had. She could always talk to Reverend Jesse or Michael, but that would be too embarrassing for her.

"As I was saying, I'm scared of him coming here because I don't know if he's changed. I don't think he can know that himself until he gets out and faces life on the outside. If he goes back to his old lifestyle, he'll be putting our kids and me in jeopardy. My other problem is that if he comes here without being able to take care of himself, my financial burdens are going to get even heavier. But what I want to know from you is this. How would you take it if you were in prison and I wrote and said that you couldn't come live with me, that I didn't think it was such a good idea? Then I tell you how my finances were already stretched to the limit."

"That's easy enough to answer. But since I think differently now, I'm going to tell you exactly how the old Malcolm would've reacted. I'd be pissed. I'd think that you deserted me when I needed you most. Then I'd question you to death to see if you had found someone else. If you said you didn't have anyone else, I'd call you a liar and accuse you of wanting to get rid of me to be with another man. I'd threaten you with what would happen to you if you had any other man around my kids. I'd make you feel guilty and I wouldn't stop hounding you until I got my way and had you back under my complete control. Sound like something that could happen?"

Sighing hard, Keisha held the cool Coke can to her forehead. She closed her eyes for a brief respite. "More than I want to admit to. Thanks for your honest input. I appreciate it."

"Don't sweat it. It takes a manipulator to recognize one. So what you going to do?"

Keisha shrugged. "I honestly don't know, but I don't have much time to make a decision. Zach needs a permanent address before he can get paroled. I have to let him know something pretty quick so he can make other arrangements if I decide not to let him come here."

"If? Girl, you haven't heard a word I said." Malcolm stood. "I'm out."

Keisha looked injured. "I know you're frustrated with me, but does that mean you no longer want to be my play brother and my friend, Malcolm?"

Keisha's question caught Malcolm by surprise. He hadn't thought she cared about his friendship one way or the other, not before now. It seemed that circumstances were changing for them. He liked that. "I'll be your friend no matter what your decision is. I just hope you make the right one. What about taking in a movie or dinner next weekend? As friends, mind you."

Seated at one of the larger booths at the Red Lobster restaurant, Marlene smiled brightly as she received big hugs from both Keisha and Rosalinda. She got up and let the two women scoot toward the center of the booth so she could be on the end, since Alexis had yet to arrive. Queen Alexis always opted for the end; her royal court usually obliged. Everyone knew that she didn't like to be cramped up in the middle, so they always accommodated her.

While looking over her young friends to see how they were faring, Marlene was happy to find both of them looking relaxed and well rested. Rosalinda's eye was still badly bruised and discolored, but it wasn't nearly as swollen. Only a couple of weeks had passed since the incident with Ricardo, who hadn't yet been caught, so Marlene expected Rosalinda's nut-brown coloring to return shortly. Marlene had attended a Christian women's retreat the previous weekend, which had put her out of daily contact with the others.

Marlene looked down at her watch. "Well, dears, since we're a little early, why don't we catch up. What's been happening with you two beauties?"

35

Rosalinda blushed. "Michael is still happening for me. I'm glad he finally convinced me to move into his guesthouse for safety reasons. Until Ricardo is caught, I don't want to be in that apartment alone. It recently dawned on me that Ricardo probably thought he could've gotten into the apartment without me opening the door. Since he used to live there, he still had a set of keys, but they were to the old locks. If he'd been able to get in, I can imagine him just sitting inside waiting for me to get home. I'm glad Michael's in my life. We've become such good friends."

Keisha rolled her eyes at Rosalinda. "When are you going to get off that 'just friends' kick? You two are so into each other, it's sickening."

Rosalinda shook her head, her long, black hair swaying with the movement. "Friends, Keisha, that's all. Michael and I have not slept together, and it's not in my future plans."

Keisha laughed. "I can believe that. Sleep rarely occurs when two people of the opposite sex come together. That's such a tired term."

Marlene playfully swatted Keisha's hand. "If Rosalinda says they're just friends, that's all there is to it. Why would she need to lie about the nature of their relationship, especially to her close friends?"

"Oh, so you're going to double-team me, Mizz Marlene?" Keisha charged. "It's like that, huh?" All three women dissolved into laughter.

"Speaking of relationships, how are you and Zach doing?" Marlene asked Keisha.

"Zachary Martin," Keisha said, her eyebrows lifting. "He may be getting out fairly soon. He comes up for parole next month. Since he's been on his best behavior lately, he will probably get approved for release."

"That'll really be nice for him, but what about for you? Are you prepared to have him released back into your life on a full-time basis?" Marlene inquired.

Keisha scratched her head, avoiding eye contact with Marlene.

"This is crazy. Malcolm asked me the same questions a couple of weeks ago. . . ."

Marlene looked stunned. "Malcolm! When did Malcolm call you?"

"He didn't call. He came over to my place the same night Rosalinda was attacked by Ric. He said that you and Reverend Jesse told him what had happened at the apartment."

Marlene didn't know how to take this bit of news. Malcolm certainly hadn't mentioned anything to her about him being at Keisha's apartment. Marlene couldn't help wondering why he'd gone there, but she had made up her mind not to ask; she wasn't sure she wanted to know.

"I can see that Malcolm's visit to my place has come as a surprise to you, Marlene. He just came over to check on me to see if I was okay, since Michael had Rosalinda's back. Malcolm accused me of stealing his parents away, so he thought he should slip into a brotherly role. We've agreed to become friends, nothing more."

Marlene sighed with relief, inwardly. "I'm surprised only because he hasn't said anything about it. You'd better watch out for Malcolm. His interest in you goes deeper than any sister-brother relationship. He's always grilling me about you." Marlene briefly thought back to the question Keisha had asked about how she'd feel having her as a daughter-in-law. That wasn't going to happen. Marlene was confident that Keisha was still crazy in love with Zach. Malcolm wasn't ready for marriage, and he certainly had no clue on how to take care of small children.

"Back to my earlier question, Keisha. Are you ready to have Zach back at your place?"

"I don't know, but he has to have somewhere to go. He can't go to Lucian's. She got a new man living up in there. The kids need their daddy in their lives, but only if he's changed. Zach always talks a good game from behind bars. But once he gets out, he goes right back to the very things that got him locked down in the first place. I'm really torn about the matter. A halfway house is the ideal solution, but he doesn't want that. I really don't want us to live together.

I may not be able to keep the boundaries in place if that happens. The last two years have been a new day for me practically every single day. I'm not sure I want that to change."

Rosalinda looked troubled. "For your sake, I hope that Zach changes. Your circumstances are different from mine, as you've pointed out a hundred times, but I pray that I never fall back into that kind of dead-end emotional trap. Ric will never change. I'm sure of that."

"Don't be too sure. God has the power to change all men," Marlene said. "He can do a mighty work in someone when He takes a mind to. Ric's soul is salvageable but he has to want it saved. You don't have to be with him to pray for him, Rosalinda. It's so obvious that he needs it. Prayer is the only thing that can save him now."

"Do you think Zach has changed enough for you to be able to deal with him, Keisha?" Rosalinda inquired.

Marlene's ears perked up. She wanted to hear the response as much as Rosalinda did.

Keisha looked uncomfortable, but the troubled expression only lasted a fleeting moment. Her smile was a confident one. "Of course he's changed, somewhat. For better or worse?" She shrugged. "Your guess is as good as mine. They all say certain things when they're locked up. He's been saying all the right things lately. He always asks me how I'm doing, and he genuinely seems to care about what's happening in our everyday life. Before, when he called, it was all about him and how much money he could get from me. The kids and me were never a priority."

"That's certainly a positive change," Marlene remarked, genuinely glad to hear that.

"Yeah, I know. He seems more sensitive to my needs. Will that carry on once he's on the outside? Will he do all that he can to take care of his family? We'll have to wait to see." Keisha shrugged as she turned her shoulder into Marlene's playfully. "How's Reverend Jesse?"

The mention of Jesse's name always made Marlene smile. "He's real good." Marlene glanced at her watch again. "Alexis is late again, ladies. Should we go ahead and order lunch?"

Keisha scowled hard. "With her track record, she may not show, period. I don't know why we keep putting up with her. She only sees us when it's convenient for her, and it always has to be on her terms. She's as flaky as she's always been."

Alexis Du Boise suddenly appeared and flung herself into the booth next to Rosalinda. She looked as if the world was her oyster and she was the precious black pearl found within its shell. Her figure was still stunning. The low-cut red blouse and designer jeans she wore made an exciting statement. Her Ralph Lauren double-breasted, gold-crested navy blue blazer fit her to a tee. Alexis, with her beautiful face and pixie haircut, could easily pass as Halle Berry's double.

"Oh, ye of little faith! As usual, Keisha always says a mouthful. But I have to wonder what you two might've had to say about me if I hadn't shown up when I did," Alexis remarked.

"That you're totally unpredictable and unreliable," Rosalinda joked, hugging Alexis and then kissing her on the cheek.

Marlene blew Alexis a kiss from across the table. "You look darn good, girlfriend. Glad you could make it, even if you are over thirty minutes late. Maybe you think that us poor paupers don't have a life and that we won't mind spending our time waiting on you." Marlene's tone wasn't malicious, but her remarks were right on the money. "However, glad you're here."

"I'm really sorry. My lateness couldn't be helped this time." Alexis's eyes zeroed in on Keisha. "You don't look too happy to see me. I know you're not embarrassed by your little cutting remarks, 'cause you still love to tell me exactly what you think of me, all the time. I've never known you to miss an opportunity yet."

Keisha grinned, her eyes glowing with warmth for Alexis. Keisha had come to love Alexis despite her inconsiderate ways. "I don't know why I bother. It never does any good."

Her eyes gleaming with fondness, Alexis smiled at Keisha. "Yes, it does," Alexis countered. "I just use what I learn from you on everyone but you. If you think your comments are getting me in line, you might stop checking my shapely behind every chance you get."

All the ladies laughed as Alexis pulled a variety of faces at Keisha. Imitating Marlene's loving gesture, Alexis blew Keisha several kisses.

"Girl, you shouldn't have told Keisha that. Now she'll be bossier than ever at trying to check us all," Rosalinda said, laughing.

Keisha blew on her fingertips and polished them on her sweater in a gesture of arrogance. "I'm good at checking folks, but only when they need to be checked."

"Too bad you haven't checked yourself when it comes down to Zach, your babies' daddy," Alexis shot back. "He could definitely use some serious checking."

Marlene and Rosalinda stifled their laughter; Keisha would see it as betrayal.

Feigning injury, Keisha rolled her eyes. "I know you're not trying to go there, Alexis. Let's order lunch before you storm out of here mad at me for what I'd dare to say in retaliation. That is, if I hadn't learned from Marlene that I don't have to say everything I'm thinking."

"That's great to hear, Keisha. But you two ladies are running true to form. Getting together with you all is like sitting here watching an episode of *Girlfriends*. Those sisters don't cut each other any slack, either," Marlene teased. "But I have to admit that watching you two go at it is better than any *Girlfriends* show I've seen."

"What else do you watch on television, Mizz Marlene?" Keisha challenged. "For a preacher's wife, you're sure into a lot of worldly things."

"In the words of Harold Melvin in the blue notes, 'If you don't know me by now, you never will.' Because I know about the world, and constantly checking out the world doesn't mean I'm *of* the world. Big difference, my dear Keisha. When you're wearing the full armor of God, you can walk in and observe any world. That only makes you a visitor, not a resident. Now, young ladies, when you use the tools you learn from the world to lead others that are out in the world to victory, a journey into the world can be rewarding. Are you hearing me?"

Keisha turned toward Marlene and raised her hand for a high five. "You're still putting it down. I love the lessons you teach. So effortlessly."

"And I love that each of you continues to teach me. I'm very blessed by your friendship," Marlene confessed. "We were born into sin and we will die in sin. Like I've said a thousand times before: justification is instantaneous, sanctification is a work of a lifetime."

"Now that we're through with the sermonette, can we please order lunch?" Alexis asked.

Rosalinda gave a hearty harrumph. "Alexis, you're all late and stuff, while we've been waiting on you to get here before we could order. Now you have the nerve to get testy." Rosalinda giggled. "But since I'm starving, I'm with you on your suggestion. Let's order!"

Marlene summoned the waiter to the table even though no one had taken so much as a glance at the menu. The ladies ordered their drinks first, which would give them time to decide on the entrees. After everyone made a selection, they engaged in conversation, filling each other in on the recent happenings in their lives.

Keisha went deeper into her fears about Zach wanting to come live with her. She told everyone that she was worried about the effects it might have on her kids, especially with him being there full time. The kids' welfare was her main concern.

Marlene first shared Jesse's idea for a male support group, and then she proudly spoke of Malcolm's numerous successes.

Alexis talked about her upcoming trip to San Francisco, hinting that it could be considered a romantic liaison. When pressed on it by Keisha, Alexis backed away from the subject. It was too soon to reveal her uncertain secrets, especially when the plans weren't yet confirmed.

The conversation eventually got around to Rosalinda's troubling situation with Ricardo and then moved on to her decision to move into Michael's guesthouse.

Alexis was the only one of the four who wasn't privy to all the information discussed. The other three ladies spent more time together than they did with Alexis, so they shared stories all the time. Alexis was still very much a part of the group, but only when she wanted to be bothered with the others. Most of their invitations to her were turned down with one flimsy excuse after another.

Today's meeting for lunch had been Alexis's idea.

Chapter Three

J esse was reading the Bible when summoned by his assistant via the intercom. He marked his place with a cross-shaped bookmark and then pressed the talk button. "Good morning, Faye. What can I do you for?" he joked.

Faye laughed at his flippant comment. "Eric Eldridge, the gentleman that Mr. Hernandez referred to you, is here already. His appointment isn't for another half hour. Shall I have him get some coffee until you're ready for him?"

"Have him get a cup of coffee and come on in. I can see him now."

"Are you sure, Reverend Jesse? He realizes he's early."

"There's no reason to keep him waiting. I'm caught up for the moment. I was into the scriptures preparing for my next sermon. Please send Mr. Eldridge in, Faye."

Only a couple of minutes had passed when Eric Eldridge was ushered into Jesse's private office. Well over average in height with an athletic build, Eric was a very attractive man with keen features and large sable eyes. His almond-brown skin was clean-shaven, and his dark brown hair was cut short and neatly trimmed. His overall appearance was very pleasant to the eye.

Jesse got to his feet and came from behind his desk. After introducing himself to the young man, he shook Eric's hand and offered him a seat. Instead of returning to his seat behind the desk, Jesse opted for one of the high-back leather chairs, his way of putting his guest at ease.

Jesse smiled endearingly. "Mr. Hernandez didn't go into a lot of detail when he asked me to see you." Jesse chuckled. "He thought it best that I hear everything straight from the horse's mouth, so to speak. So now that we have all the formalities out of the way, Mr. Eldridge, what is it that I can help you with?"

While having a hard time getting his voice to work, Eric looked nervous. He wasn't used to sitting down talking with a man of God, especially inside of a church. Jesse's very presence was somewhat intimidating to Eric, but only because of Jesse's spiritual connection with the Man upstairs and his own lack thereof. Eric revered God, but in a very fearful way, since he believed that the heavenly Father was quick to dole out severe punishments for those who sinned against Him. Eric considered himself an unsalvageable sinner; therefore, he kept God at bay.

Eric shifted his body to a more comfortable position. "Reverend Covington, I need some sort of counseling. You see, I have an ex-girlfriend behind bars. Cicely Kirkland's a drug addict and a small-time dope pusher. I don't know what to do about her anymore."

Since it was something that happened all too frequently in America's communities, especially among his own people, the drug use or the selling of illegal substances didn't surprise Jesse. The young man's honesty about it was refreshing. Jesse stroked his chin, a habit of his thought process. Eric looked clean-cut, and he seemed to carry himself with dignity, Jesse mused.

"Since you referred to Cicely as your ex, I'd like to know if she earned that status before or after she was arrested? That is, if it's not too personal of a question."

"We had been apart a couple of months when the bust occurred. We were together two years before she started in with the drugs. I

44

put her out of my house because I found dope stashed here and there throughout my place. We'd already been there and done that a few times prior to the last incident. I've seen her through rehab more times than anyone should come to expect." Eric moved his hand across his throat in a slicing gesture. "I've had it with her."

The corner of Jesse's mouth turned down in a sad frown. "Sorry for your frustration. So what else is going on with you now? What's on your mind?"

"Cicely is pregnant. She's twenty-seven now and hasn't gotten any wiser."

Jesse wasn't surprised by that remark either. In fact, there wasn't too much that surprised him in the climate of the world today. The two had obviously lived together, which had made the circumstance ripe for what had eventually occurred. Jesse didn't want to make snap judgments, but he figured that a condom probably wasn't used because of the cohabitation, which didn't necessarily make it a monogamous relationship. "Will she be released before the child is due?"

Eric blinked hard. "That's the problem. My child will be born behind bars if I don't find a way to stop it. Just the thought of that kills me inside."

Jesse looked troubled. "You're not talking about her ending the pregnancy, are you?"

Eric shook his head in the negative. "No way. She doesn't even know that I'm aware of her condition. Her best girlfriend, Destiny Powell, told me. But here's the real kicker." Eric shook his head from side to side. "Because I put her out, she's planning on putting our kid into foster care until she's released. That's two years or more from now, mind you, if she gets paroled. This is hardly her first offense. Cicely has been waltzing with disaster and the devil."

"How is it that Michael Hernandez is representing you? He's a criminal defense attorney. He didn't say, but I did wonder why you'd seek him out."

"I've known Michael for quite awhile. Since he doesn't do family law, he referred me to a friend of his that does. I guess you assumed I was in some kind of legal trouble?"

Jesse laughed, shaking his head. "I've learned not to assume anything these days. However, it does seem that you have legal problems, just not of the criminal variety."

Eric found it hard to smile. His situation was far too sad. His heart was broken, the kind of break that never mended. "I still love Cicely, desperately. But I had to make a clean break from her for both our sakes. Had I stayed with her, she would've eventually brought me to my knees." He couldn't forget their wonderful times together. But the only times he wanted back with Cicely were all those days and nights before the drug use had gotten serious. He'd met flight attendant Cicely Kirkland on an airplane. Instant attraction. Seated next to each other on an East Coast to West Coast flight when she wasn't on duty, they had talked and talked until there wasn't too much they hadn't learned about each other by the time the flight was terminated. The countless things they had in common had them wanting to see each other beyond baggage claim.

Needing more time to fully assess Eric's situation, Jesse saw the need to break into Eric's thoughts. He didn't want to rush this session, but the clock was ticking away and he still had a pretty full schedule ahead of him. "What kind of work are you into, Mr. Eldridge?"

Eric closed his eyes for a brief moment. He then took a deep breath. "Everything should become crystal clear for you once you have the answer to your question. I'm a cop, a ten-year veteran with the LAPD."

Jesse showed no visible signs of being stunned. "Did you ever use drugs with Cicely?"

"I admit to once smoking a joint or two from time to time, but not with Cicely. But I've never used any hard drugs, sir, and I don't smoke cigarettes, drink alcohol, or gamble."

"Does that mean you lied on your application about drug use

when you applied for a job with the police force? It seems to me that you were already a cop when you met Cicely."

"I *was* on the force when we met. My days of smoking marijuana had long been over by the time I applied for the police academy. Yes, I lied on my application, specifically where it asked if I'd ever used marijuana. If I had been honest, I wouldn't be on the force today. I'm a darn good cop, one that's dedicated to protecting and serving. I didn't want such a youthful indiscretion to hold me back. I had every intention of being a good man, a good cop."

Jesse smiled gently. "I see what you mean. I guess that's enough personal information. I don't think I should know anymore about your drug use as it applies to your job application. Though you lied to land a good job, your honesty with me is admirable. I respect you for that. What's your game plan and what can I do, if anything, to help you out with your situation?"

"I've hired Michael's friend Orin Mayberry to help me win custody of my child once he or she is born. Michael says Orin is a great attorney and a real good brother. I'm not only seeking child custody, Orin is going to fight hard for my child to be born in a regular hospital." Eric suddenly looked chagrined. "I can't confess to being a Christian, Reverend Covington. Religion wasn't taught in our home, and I've never had a desire to pursue it as an adult. It's not that I don't believe there's a higher being, I just can't ignore the troubling conditions of the world. Things are really bad out there on those streets, Rev." *God's punishment is too severe.*

"I read you. *Why*, if there's a God somewhere? Is that your burning question?"

"No disrespect intended, Reverend Covington, but I have asked myself that question a couple of hundred times or more. There's a lot of suffering going on in the world. Why indeed?"

Jesse's mood turned somber. "You and a trillion others have asked that question, including me. We often direct that question to everyone but the only one who can answer it: God. If you ask Him the question, you will eventually come to know the answer. But if you're not here to seek spiritual guidance, I need you to spell it out for me."

"Oh, sir, but I am here for exactly that. I'm thirty years old and I'm just starting to figure out that I can't do this alone anymore. Trouble keeps finding me no matter how hard I try to dodge it. I can't find any more hiding places. I do need spiritual guidance, lots of it. With what I'm about to take on, I need every thick layer of armor that I can get, religious and otherwise. You see, I'm in no doubt that Cicely will probably throw up my past drug use to the courts. In getting to know her, I was stupid enough to mention that I'd once used marijuana on occasion. How's that for honesty? She's terribly angry with me for throwing her out. I may lose my only child right along with my job. Without the gig, I can't take care of the baby."

Seeing the sincerity in the young man's eyes, Jesse leaned forward in his chair. "Count me in, Mr. Eldridge. While you're trying to win custody of your unborn child, I'll be busy trying to win custody of your soul for Christ. Fair enough?"

Eric grinned broadly. "Fair enough, though I have to warn you, you have your work cut out. It may take you a while to complete this work in progress. For the most part, I'm unaccustomed to waiting, but I'm beginning to believe that patience is a virtue. I've never been a patient man, nor am I an extremely impatient one. But I'm ready to settle in for this one, for however long it takes. I don't think there's any other way."

Unaccustomed to waiting: Jesse instantly thought of Saul. "Since we have that settled, let's shake on forming a spiritual relationship. We can take it as fast or as slow as you want."

Eric pumped Jesse's hand. "My friends simply call me Eric."

"I'd be honored if you'd call me Reverend Jesse, just like all my other friends do."

"Thank you, Reverend Jesse. I'm looking forward to all that I believe you can teach me. Although I haven't mentioned it, I closely followed your trial two years ago. I couldn't imagine a minister committing armed robbery, though stranger things have happened, so I had to stick with it to see the outcome. I'm glad you turned out to be the hero; that had me wanting to meet you, to come and visit your church. But it has taken me a long time to finally work up the courage to try and make your acquaintance. When Hernandez mentioned your name to me as someone who might be able to guide me through this nightmare, I couldn't believe it. It was in that instant that I'd been given a sign to meet you. I see it as fate."

Alexis always had a noticeable glow about her, but she looked even brighter and fresher. Dressed conservatively in a basic black, crepe, Kasper pants suit, a superb fit, she looked chic and classy. Her face was flawlessly made up, and the expensive perfume she wore was a definite male-magnet. The dashing man seated next to her inside the quaint Hollywood Café was every bit as attractive as she was. He was also well dressed, conservatively and expensively.

Alexis had known Mathis West for a couple of months, yet she had only casually hinted about him to her friends. She wasn't sure that enough time had passed since she'd laid R.J. to rest. Her and Mathis's not-so-frequent outings had only consisted of lunch, dinner, and visits to a couple of art museums thus far, but she still wasn't sure that she was ready to take the relationship to the next level. A little weekend rendezvous in the Ritz Carlton or some other luxury hotel would certainly make things much more interesting, but she wasn't too sure of him.

Mathis, whom Alexis had met at a posh party, was an extremely successful architect who owned his own engineering firm. At forty-five, never married, Mathis was no R.J. With all her late husband's flaws and numerous shortcomings, there'd never be another R.J., not for her.

Forever, until death do us part, was what she'd come to expect from her only marriage. Alexis had never loved another, never thought she'd be in a position to give her heart away a second time, thought it was impossible. She might have to consider a lengthy tryst at some point, but for now her heart was buried with R.J. Widowhood, as an outcome for her, hadn't entered her thoughts, ever. R.J., not quite middle-aged, had been cut down in the prime of his life.

Mathis covered her hand with his, disliking how preoccupied she seemed. "I've missed you, Alexis. What have you been doing with yourself all week?"

His hazel eyes fixed on her so intently made her blush like a silly teenager. He looks so darn scrumptious, Alexis mused, her eyes eagerly drinking in his smooth, cocoa complexion and mixed gray hair, considered by some folks as "good hair." "A little bit of everything. Redecorating the house has been a real challenge, a bewildering one. It takes up quite a bit of my time, since the place is so large. So many choices in interior design boggles the mind. Since I've been unable to make my own selections, I've finally hired a design firm, what I should've done in the first place. I've only been gearing up for this project for nearly two years."

He nodded. "It seems that you're having no regrets about your decision not to sell."

Alexis took a sip of her iced tea. "I have a twinge of regret now and then, especially when I'm feeling overwhelmed by the total makeover. But there are too many memories that I don't want to part with. Believe it or not, I find comfort in all the rooms R.J. and I spent time in together. While I've already moved out of the master suite we once shared, and into the smaller master bedroom in the other wing, I still have a tendency to go into our old room and sit for long periods of time. I find peace there. The room was left just like it was before R.J. passed away."

"I can see how things might still be difficult for you, Alexis."

Despite his comforting comments, Mathis did not want to hear about her deceased husband. If he had his way, he'd extract every single memory Alexis had ever had of R.J. He'd do away with quite a few of his own nightmarish memories if it were at all possible. It wasn't.

Mathis picked up one of the menus and handed it to her. "What do you have a taste for?"

Alexis took the menu, only to lay it back down on the table. "A salad will do for me. A lemonade instead of another iced tea might be more refreshing; I stay so thirsty lately."

He frowned. "Your eating habits concern me. You eat next to nothing. I'd like to see you order more than just a measly salad, Alexis. You could be ruining your health."

Alexis hated it when Mathis said things like that. It reminded her of R.J. and how he used to question her every choice. It was a way of gaining control of someone's every thought and movement. She often wondered if she had "indecisive" written across her forehead. While she was uncertain about a lot of things, she'd eventually make up her own mind. Since it was her mind, the choices on how to make it up were also hers. The new Alexis would maintain control of herself. No one would ever run her life again. Mathis would just have to accept her "as is."

Alexis looked Mathis right in the eyes. "The choice I made for my meal is the right one for me. I'm the one who has to eat it." Her tone had been soft and deadly sweet; her message was concise. Though he hadn't voiced a word, she both saw and felt his reaction to the challenge in her statement. It was easy to see that he didn't like it. His body language was evidence enough.

Tough luck! Alexis thought. She loved how easily she had exercised control.

Mathis eyed her curiously, intently. When she didn't avert her eyes from him, or so much as blink one of them, he turned his attention back to the menu. An awkward silence immediately settled between them. It looked to Alexis as if he was sulking, but she didn't let it bother her.

As the silence continued on, even after the waiter left, Alexis once again began to second-guess her relationship with Mathis West. It was beginning to dawn on her that she didn't like many of his petty ways. Being handsome, intelligent, witty, rich, and charming was no longer enough for her. She was more interested these days in integrity, morality, and niceties. Alexis was well aware of a man's knack for being charming and solicitous when trying to wend his way into a woman's heart. Though Mathis had been accommodating to the slow pace she'd set for their relationship, that he was starting to grow impatient with her had become apparent.

Alexis thought about the fact that she'd never been to his home, nor had he visited hers, though he was very impressed with her Bel Air address. Visiting with each other wasn't the kind of ingredient that should be excluded in any relationship recipe. A person's habits and environments could reveal a lot about an individual. But she wasn't ready to have him in her personal space nor did she have a desire to be in his. That was the only explanation she had for keeping him at a distance, but she had an odd feeling that there was something more to it.

"How about a movie, Alexis? I've been dying to see one of the new war movies."

Alexis wrinkled her nose, wishing he'd been thoughtful enough to ask her what movie she'd like to see before voicing his desire. It would've been the gentlemanly thing to do.

After taking a sip of lemonade, Alexis set her glass back down. "That's not the kind of movie I'm interested in. I have my own war to deal with. I'm sick of senseless battles."

A look of disdain came again in Mathis's eyes. Alexis laughed inwardly. It felt good to finally make decisions for herself. Saying what she thought without worrying about how someone might feel about it felt pretty darn good. Always keeping quiet on the issues had really hurt her and had kept her aggravated from within, making her a prime candidate for ulcers.

Exercising her own independence felt so good that her joy leaped up and down within.

* * *

Rosalinda loved the homey feel of Michael's plush guesthouse. The color scheme of oyster white, soft hues of beiges, rust browns, and splashes of autumn gold were warm and welcoming. Living there was like residing in a mini-cottage; it had the same kind of cozy feel. She was thrilled that she'd gotten the chance to burn real wood in the fireplace. Spring was already in bloom, but Southern California was still experiencing a cold and rainy climate. The weather felt like it did in the dead of winter, especially during the early evenings and nights. Rosalinda smiled as she stared at the colorful flames roaring inside the fireplace.

While thinking of her lovely mom, Paulina, Rosalinda regretted not taking Michael up on his offer sooner, wishing she had done so when Paulina was still alive. Paulina would've loved it here. The lush greenery and colorful flowerbeds surrounding the grounds and the magnificent view of the pool may have provided a source of healing for her. Instead, Paulina had passed away in an impersonal atmosphere, a small hospital room. Although Rosalinda had turned the room into a cheerful spot for Paulina's eyes to behold, home, it wasn't. The fact that Paulina hadn't died in a nursing home or a rehab center brought Rosalinda the most comfort.

Michael took Rosalinda's hand in his. That she'd actually invited him over when he'd called the guesthouse surprised him. He'd been there nearly two hours already; that was promising. Most of their evenings out together were spent among people, at the movies, or some other social function. A good bit of their time together was also spent in the company of her friends, Marlene and Jesse, Keisha, and on occasion, Alexis was present, too. Jesse and the other women had also come to mean a lot to him. He enjoyed spending time with all of them.

Rosalinda looked down at their entwined hands. It felt so good, seemed so right, which kept her from pulling her hand away.

Although Rosalinda knew how deep Michael's feelings ran for her, since he'd told her enough times, she'd never revealed to him how she really felt about him. Despite their rocky, near scandalous start, they'd grown extremely close as friends. Michael was her hero in more ways than one. He just didn't know that he'd become the swarthy Spanish hero of all the romance novels she loved to read and the hero who starred in all her good dreams.

Taking him up on his full-time job offer had to be reconsidered by her, she conceded. He'd offered her way more money than both of her jobs combined. The extra money could help her continue on with her education. Rosalinda had already decided that she'd like to take a few psychology courses. To have a wonderful job, counseling women just like her, would be an awesome challenge and a rewarding experience.

Michael squeezed her hand. "How do you do it, day in and day out? When you're not working, how do you spend so much time by yourself? Aren't you ever lonely, Rosalinda?"

She smiled gently. "Always. Loneliness is a choice, Michael. Learning that I have choices is still so new to me. I haven't gotten completely used to thinking for myself yet. I like the right to exercise my choices, but it's still a challenge for me in determining the good ones from the bad. In spending time alone with myself, I get to discover who I really am, Michael."

"Really! How's that?"

"It's simple; my life was always controlled by others. When I spoke, my voice wasn't heard. The reason for that was because I was often mimicking what I was told to say and to do, and what to think, how to feel, and how to act. My voice wasn't heard because it wasn't mine doing the talking. Now, I get to make all the choices for me. Mommy's gone now. She was the only person who ever had the right to control me. But when I became an adult, that kind of control should've stopped. It did, but only with my mother."

Rosalinda leveled her eyes on the floor.

Michael scratched his head. "You look like you need to say more. Go ahead and talk. I'm already intrigued by what you have to say."

Rosalinda was glad that Michael had prompted her to continue speaking. She needed to talk, needed to share her deepest feelings and fears with someone she could trust. She trusted Michael and Reverend Jesse, the only other men she'd ever trusted in her life.

Rosalinda's father, Mario Morales, had died when she was young, but he wasn't someone that deserved anyone's trust. Although she'd been young, she wasn't so young that she didn't remember the terrible physical and verbal abuses he'd rained down on her mother. The images of such were not eradicable. Her maternal grandfather, Raphael Rodriguez, hadn't been a kind man either. But he died before Rosalinda was old enough to have any tangible memories of him. Raphael hadn't treated Paulina's mother, Maria, any better than Mario had treated Paulina. It appeared that Raphael had loved Paulina and Maria from the pictures Rosalinda was shown of them. Paulina had labeled the pictures as blatant lies. When Raphael fell into poor health, Maria cared for him until he passed away, but she was happy that she'd won her freedom.

Rosalinda's gaze fixed itself onto Michael's handsome face. "When my mother's role changed in my life, and simply became a guiding force rather than a demanding, insistent one, I let others pick up where she left off."

"Men?" Michael inquired.

Ashamed, she lowered her lashes. "Yes, men, but Ric was my only sexual partner. There was a guy before Ric, another bad boy, a criminal misfit. Yes, I imagined myself in love with him, too. But I wasn't. Just as I wasn't ever in love with Ric."

Unable to believe his ears, Michael raised an eyebrow, his heart racing. "When did you discover that you weren't in love with Ricardo?"

Rosalinda swallowed the painful lump in her throat. "The very moment I realized I didn't love myself." She licked her lips, tasting on them the bitterness of her acid tears mixed with the deep anger she felt about Ric and his ill treatment of her. Still, she felt sorry for the man who'd never learned to love, a man who might never be free long enough to find true happiness.

Ricardo Munoz was nothing more than an empty human shell, devoid of all emotions.

Pain and suffering had matured Rosalinda. Her mother's death had sped up the maturation even more. She had often felt alone in the world, but now she had God and lots of new friends, true-blue ones. Marlene Covington had especially made a big difference in her life.

Two years ago Rosalinda was an immature girl, despite her legal age. Rosalinda had once been a silly girl who'd thought she should trade sexual favors to pay for her boyfriend's legal appeal, a process he'd had no chance of winning. Her decision to lay down in bed with Michael couldn't have been based on love for Ricardo, since she first had to love herself before she could love another. Though she'd had a pretty good start, Rosalinda had to admit to herself that she still had a long way to go to achieve total unconditional love for self. No matter how far it was to the end of the road, her strength of heart and her endless determination were up to the challenge.

"You have grown so much over the past two years, Rosalinda. I'm proud of you."

"Thanks, Michael. I have made many new friends: Marlene, Reverend Jesse, Keisha, and Alexis, just to name a few. One of those friends is also you, of course. Would you like to know something about a new friend, one that I haven't ever mentioned to you?"

Rosalinda never failed to amaze Michael when they conversed. He always found himself in eager anticipation of what she might say or bring up. The mention of this new friend had caused more than just a spark of fire to light in her eyes; a bonfire was more like it. That alone made him curious to hear more. "I'd love to learn about this new friend of yours."

"Okay, we'll start with her name, which is Rosalinda Morales."

Rosalinda grinned at Michael's surprised reaction. "Rosalinda had to become as naked as the day she was born in order to completely tap into her psyche. They were such awesome revelations when she actually freed her spirit and then later learned that it was a pure one. She also discovered what had tainted her spirit. It was the kind of people she foolishly allowed to rule her world."

"Wow! Sounds like a great beginning for a new friendship with yourself."

"Yeah, I know. I've gotten all inside of Rosalinda's head. I'm getting to know her, but still not as well as I want to. She's a nice lady. I like curling up with her and sharing a good book and even the scriptures that Marlene gives me to study. My new friend and me have great conversations, honest-to-goodness ones. The types that strip the soul bare and leave nothing there for us to hide behind. I can't wait to get to know her even more. One day I hope to know her inside and out. Once you really get to know her, I think you'll like her too, Michael."

Rosalinda had come such a long way, he mused. Michael always felt horrible when he thought back on the derogatory offer he'd once made to her. *Flesh for fees!* Testing her morals or not, his actions had been downright obscene, even to the point of setting up a sleazy motel rendezvous, where he was to orchestrate the seduction of the beautiful Rosalinda Morales.

Michael would never know if he could've stopped himself had she not run out on him that fateful night, hating herself for the reason she'd come there. Some men had a tendency to take what was offered them, without giving the possible consequences any thought whatsoever. He'd like to believe that he would've called a halt to things before they'd gotten out of control. Because she'd done it first, he'd never know for sure.

Rosalinda had forgiven him, but he had yet to forgive himself.

Rosalinda looked at him with concern. "Michael, you're looking a little pale. Is everything okay with you?"

His dark eyes probed her lovely face. Rosalinda had turned out to be everything he'd thought she was from the very beginning. His heart was breaking at the thought of what might never be between them. Testing her in that way may've killed any chance at love and happiness and for them to become a real couple. He loved being her friend, but he wanted so much more. "Just thinking back in time. Unpleasant thoughts. The truth of the matter is that I've never forgiven myself for setting you up like I did. I won't say I'm sorry again, Rosalinda. The words seem so empty, not nearly enough to right a wrong. I've already said it a thousand times."

Rosalinda touched his face with her fingertips. He was a beautiful man, with a genuinely giving heart. His actions had been offensive, but he'd already more than made up for that awful episode of mindless thinking by showing her how thoughtful and kind he really was. Michael had no way of knowing how much of a changed woman she'd become because of what he'd done to expose her. The silver linings behind a lot of her misery had been discovered.

She took his hand. "Marlene once told me that the worst mistake people make in trying to right a wrong is to not forgive themselves for the wrongdoing. I've been making the same mistake all of my adult life. The way Marlene explained it to me seemed so simple. She told me that Jesus had already paid the price for my sins and that God would forgive me for any sin if I confessed it to Him with my mouth and then asked for His forgiveness. Most important, though, she taught me how important it is for me to forgive myself."

He shook his head. "I did a terrible thing to you, Rosalinda. My intentions were good, but the way I went about it was so wrong. That night haunts me more than you'll ever know. I don't believe that forgiving myself can be as easy for me as you've put it, Rosalinda."

"I didn't say it was going to be easy. It was the way Marlene explained it that seemed so simple. Perhaps I should've said that it was only simplified once I began to practice what she told me. The hell we're living down here on earth is not God's doing. We've created our own hell, and we throw ourselves into the burning fires at least two to three times a day. I'm learning to forgive myself; still have a long way to go in surrendering all. But I forgave you a long time ago. Please forgive yourself, Michael. Only then will you have complete vindication from the hell you're putting yourself through over something that you can never go back and change."

Michael looked astounded. He desperately wanted to kiss her. She had a way of freeing his soul and making his spirit soar. He quickly leaned forward to pull her into his arms, only to back away. Once again, his timing was off. Rosalinda needed more time. He was sure of it.

Rosalinda smiled at his reluctance. Deciding to take matters into her own hands, she kissed him gently on the mouth, as only a friend would do. Then she kissed him passionately.

As Alexis and Mathis exited the restaurant, a man much taller than herself ran right into her. Her smart retort died on her lips as she looked up into one of the most beautiful pair of gray eyes she'd ever seen, familiar eyes. These eyes she had connected with before, numerous times.

Concerned for Alexis, Jarreau Thornton studied her closely, making she sure she was okay. He then looked at her even harder. Seemingly totally bewildered by Alexis, he appeared to take a second to catch his breath. "No, it can't be. But it has to be. Your beautiful face is unforgettable. Alexis Gautier, I can hardly believe my eyes. It has been a long, long time, lady. This is too unbelievable to be real."

Alexis's face glowed as she smiled broadly at her handsome high school friend, forgetting all about Mathis West who stood dutifully on her other side. Alexis had dropped Jarreau like a bad habit after R.J. had come on the scene. While they hadn't been involved in a romantic relationship, they had been the best of friends. Jarreau had been crazy about Alexis.

Alexis stood on her tiptoes and gave Jarreau a long, warm hug.

She then stepped back from him. "You can go ahead and believe it, Jarreau Thornton. I'm as real as real can be! It has been a long time. What are you doing in L.A.?" The small group moved off to the side.

Jarreau showed all of his healthy white teeth as he smiled back at Alexis. "I've been living here for several years now. No more family left in New Orleans." Jarreau suddenly became aware of the man at Alexis's side. "Sorry, didn't mean to be rude. I was so caught up in seeing my old friend, I'm afraid I'm just now noticing you." Jarreau extended his hand to Mathis. "Jarreau Thornton. Alexis and I grew up together in New Orleans. We go way back."

Mathis shook Thornton's hand, but his reluctance to do so was not lost on Alexis. She saw his slight yet noticeable hesitation before he'd extended his hand; just another of Mathis's characteristics that didn't please her. His juvenile behavior had Alexis seething within.

Alexis turned to address Mathis. "Jarreau and I grew up together, graduated from kindergarten and later on from the same high school graduating class. As he said, we go back a long way." Alexis dug around in her purse and came up with a business card. Though she had no legitimate business to speak of, the card made it easier for her to pass her personal information on to those persons she wanted to keep in contact with.

Alexis handed Jarreau the white seashell-shaped card embossed with fancy gold lettering. "I'm sorry I can't stay and chat longer with you, Jarreau, but I have to be going. However, I'd love to hear from you, would love for us to stay in touch."

Jarreau grinned, wondering how R.J. would feel about Alexis's old friend calling his house. As he thought of how possessive R.J. had been of Alexis, he couldn't help wondering what role Mathis West played in Alexis's life. He couldn't imagine her having an affair if she was still married to R.J. Perhaps she had divorced R.J. That thought made his heart sing. "When would be a good time to call you, Alexis?"

"Whenever you'd like. I'd love for us to catch up. Later this evening would be fine if you don't have any other plans."

Mathis looked stunned, unable to understand why Alexis would ask Thornton to call her knowing she had a date with him. Mathis looked on in dismay, thinking of the things he'd have to say to her later, in private. Alexis had gone too far this time. She was ruining his plans.

"I don't have a thing planned for later, Alexis. Wish I had run into you before you'd eaten. I'm going to let you go now, but you will hear from me later. Nice meeting you, Mathis."

Mathis grumbled something indiscernible under his breath as Alexis opened her arms to receive Jarreau's warm hug and slight peck on her cheek.

Mathis was beside himself with anger by the time they reached their cars, which were parked side by side, but he remained in control. The trip to San Francisco was still on the table, but not yet decided on. "Have you figured out what movie you'd like to see, Alexis?"

Alexis rubbed her right temple with her fingertips. "I'm sorry, but I suddenly have a headache. I think I'll go on home and rest. Let's talk later in the week. Thanks for dinner."

Mathis reigned in his temper. Alexis had insulted him terribly. He didn't know what to do about it. This wasn't the ending he'd expected for their evening. Mathis was smart enough to know it wasn't his choice. Alexis had been calling the shots from day one. He hadn't come close to figuring her out yet, but he would; it was imperative to his agenda. Alexis was conquerable, just like every other woman he'd ever dated or had an affair with. Yet he had no choice but to let her think she was in charge. Once his mission was over, she would find out who was in charge.

Her lying in bed talking on the phone with her high school friend wasn't a visually tasteful scene for Mathis. Her sudden headache seemed to have everything to do with the unexpected appearance of Jarreau Thornton. That she'd cut a date short with him to have a

61

phone conversation with another man was downright galling. He hadn't expected any feelings for her to come into play. She was very beautiful, but he couldn't lose sight of his real interest in her.

"Good night, Mathis. Talk to you soon."

Alexis was in her car, backing out of the space before he could come up with a suitable response. This insufferable defeat was one that he'd have no choice but to take as personal, but Alexis didn't stand a chance in hell of getting away from him. She hadn't seen the last of him.

Chapter Four

Observing the interaction with the female inmates and their visitors during the prison visiting hours, Marlene Covington, quiet as a church mouse, sat on the back wall. One of the African American counselors, Starla Connors, sat beside her, explaining some of the details on how things worked at the California Women's Correctional Facility, often referred to as CWCF.

Marlene was surprised to see that very few of the visitors in the room were men. Could it be too early? Visiting hours weren't over until 7:30 P.M. It was also a weekday. She then thought of visiting at various times in order to arrive at a fair assessment. The room probably overflowed with visitors on the weekends, when people were off work. Folks did have jobs.

Marlene made eye contact with Starla. "I noticed that there aren't a lot of men visiting today. Is that the norm, or is it because it's a weekday?"

Starla looked around the visiting room with interest. "This is the norm. The majority of the men that come to visit the women are fathers, brothers, male cousins, or others who are related by blood. And then there are the really good friends. Female visitors come more often."

"Really! What about husbands and boyfriends?"

Starla shrugged. "They come, but not in record numbers. In fact, the men that these women are in romantic relationships with are very rarely supportive of them. It's very different when the shoe is placed on the other foot. Women are very loyal to their men who've gotten themselves into trouble, as you already know. Sorry to disillusion you, but the show of support from men to women is as different as night and day. Another amazing fact is this: a lot of these women are in prison behind some man and the mess he's actually responsible for."

That revelation caused Marlene's interest to further increase. "Explain, please."

Starla laughed with cynicism. "Just think of it. Women get caught up in all sorts of crazy scams run by men. There's the prostitute who's managed and grossly damaged by the pimp, emotionally and physically. Let's not leave out crimes of passion, especially when a woman loses it altogether after finding out that her man is cheating on her. The woman who kills to keep from being killed behind domestic violence is also in the mixed bag of serious felonies women have committed because of a man. Oh, I left out an important one, though there's plenty more. Taking the fall for running that little package across town as a favor for their man without knowing they're running illegal drugs happens way too frequently. Have I made my point?"

Shuddering, Marlene shook her head in dismay. "Vividly so. It doesn't look like Reverend Jesse may have a chance of getting his support group off the ground. If the support's not there, attendance won't occur. He's going to be disappointed in my report."

"Maybe not. This is just one of many women's correction facilities in this state. The church pews may not be filled like they are with your women's group, but there are probably numerous men who may see it as beneficial to be involved in a structured support group. I have a couple of referrals that I can make to the group. I'd go ahead and do the advertising and set things up the same way you got the LIW group going. Your husband just might be pleasantly surprised. I think he should go for it. He has my support, and I have a lot of contacts."

"Reverend Jesse will be thrilled to death if he can just help save one soul or guide one person in the right direction. I'll give him my report and let him decide what he wants to do. I'll keep you informed as things progress or digress. Thanks so much for this very informative session. You've been a big help. I've been enlightened once again. Please keep us in prayer."

"Sure thing, Marlene. Please feel free to visit us anytime. Come on. I'll walk you out."

Sister Annie Wylie was thrilled to see Marlene. Though she was almost eighty-four, Sister Wylie hadn't lost a single bounce in her step. She was as active as ever. Along with her daughters, Sara Leigh Walters and Carrie Louise Madison, and her only son, Reginald Wylie, Marlene was involved in planning a surprise birthday party for Sister Wylie at a first-class hotel. They had discussed waiting until her eighty-fifth birthday, but too often things had a way of changing without notice. People could be in the greatest shape healthwise one day; the next one could find them in ill health. It was decided by all concerned that the celebration should go forth on her eighty-fourth birthday rather than waiting on the next one.

Marlene had dragged all the grocery bags into the house. Immediately, she began emptying them, putting the food away. Because of her visit to the prison, in the interest of time, Marlene had decided to get a list from Sister Wylie via the phone instead of taking her shopping.

"Would you like a cup of tea, Sister Wylie? I can turn on the teapot."

"That would be nice, Sister Covington. Thank you. Were the lines in the grocery store as long today as they usually are?"

Marlene turned on the kettle she'd just filled with bottled water. Sister Wylie didn't trust tap water even though she had a filter on it. "It wasn't that bad. I got through with everything in pretty good time. Even picking up your medication at the pharmacy was a breeze. It was probably the time of day, right after the lunch hour was over. A lot of people pick up things from the grocer during their lunch breaks. Maybe we should think of changing our scheduled time."

Sister Wylie nodded her head in approval. "You would think that no one would be in the stores early on Monday morning, since most people shop on the weekend, but that's not the case. I have no problem going after the lunch hour on Mondays if you don't mind."

"Not at all. What kind of tea do you have a taste for, Sister Wylie?"

"The mint flavored comes to mind. I'm sure you didn't forget to pick up my chocolate chip, white chocolate, and macadamia nut cookie orders from the bakery. You know how much I love Sister Taylor's baked goods. As good as I can bake, I've been patronizing her store for years. Sister Thelma Taylor sure taught her daughter how to get around in the kitchen."

Chuckling, Marlene picked up the large pink bakery box for Sister Wylie to see. "It's right here. It just couldn't be seen from behind all the grocery bags. I know you were just fooling around with me on that question. You know I wouldn't dare to show up without this pink box."

Marlene went about her duties, making sure all the items needing refrigeration were put up first. She often had a good inward chuckle over why Sister Wylie kept so much food on hand. Her handsome beau, Brother Paris Shelton loved to eat. More than that, he loved to cook for Sister Wylie, good old southern cooking. According to Sister Wylie, he paid for most of the groceries.

Brother Shelton was a good man, had already been widowed for thirteen years.

Once Marlene placed half a dozen cookies on a paper plate, she set them on the kitchen table in front of Sister Wylie. After pouring two cups of hot tea, she carried them back to the table with her. Realizing she'd forgotten the spoons, she quickly grabbed them from a kitchen drawer and then took the seat opposite her dear friend.

In amicable silence, the two women sipped on the tea, enjoying all the fringe benefits their friendship afforded them. Marlene and Sister Wylie adored each other and had helped each other through some pretty tough times. The older woman reminded Marlene a lot of her own mother, Zelma, who was one of the kindest, gentlest women anyone could ever meet. Zelma and Marlene's father, Benjamin, had been gone so long. If it weren't for the pictures she had of them, Marlene feared she wouldn't be able to bring their faces to mind. But their angelic-like spirits were ever present in her life. For that, Marlene was grateful.

Sister Wylie eyed the cookie plate. "I guess I can't entice you into having one of those deadly sweets. I know how much you're enjoying that new Coke-bottle figure. Would you like something else? In anticipation of your visit, I made some sugarless Jello for you this morning. I know you can have that. If you picked up the Cool Whip on my grocery list, you're in business."

The love Marlene felt at this moment for Sister Wylie shone brightly in her eyes. "See, that's what I love so much about you. You always find a way to please others. Thank you for the sweet-but-sugar-free offer, one that I wouldn't think of passing up." Marlene got up from the table to fix her a dessert bowl. Heartfelt love and warmth for Sister Wylie permeated her being.

"I love pleasing others, but sometimes I forget to please myself. It would please me greatly to go ahead and marry Paris and forget about my hard-earned pension. We keep talking about moving in together, but we never seem to get around to it. Our love for God and His laws make the decision a hard one for us. We practically spend every waking moment together, but I want him around twenty-four seven. I want us to share the same bed every night for the rest of our lives." Sister Wylie cracked up. "Now, I've finally said it! My way of thinking may be bad, but it sure does me a wealth of good. Paris is one fine man."

With her delicious-looking dessert in hand, Marlene came back to the table with a wicked grin on her face. "I'm not going to ask you if you're trying to say that you and Brother Shelton don't spend the night together on occasion. That would be too much information."

"Not to mention none of your darn business!" Sister Wylie's eyes twinkled with devilish brightness. The two women had a good laugh at that.

"You are right about that. At any rate, I think you should just forget about the money and concentrate on the man. He's told you enough times that he can take care of you. Don't you believe him when he says that?"

"It's not that, Sister Covington. I worked hard for the money that's due me up until the day I die. I worked slave jobs before I finally landed that job at the gas company. I washed and cleaned for white folks until my hands got bleached out from all the Clorox and other abrasive cleaning agents that I had to work with. When you can go from doo-doo to sugar, you feel that you've made it, that you've somehow beaten the odds. Then Social Security messes you up."

"I understand. Please don't cry." Marlene wiped Annie's tears with a paper napkin.

"Though I'd still have my retirement, to now give up my Social Security income would be like washing away all my accomplishments. That would be hard for me to do. As for the man, I concentrate on him all the time. Paris has become my soul mate. But I just can't forget that the money Social Security sparingly dishes out every month is mine. Why should we have to struggle during our golden years? Not only that, Sister, we stand a good chance of going platinum, God willing. Paris and I probably have another good twenty years or so left in us. Our hearts are stronger than a lot of those much younger folks."

Marlene covered Sister Wylie's hand with hers. "It seems to me that this is just another one of those times you might have to step out on faith. If you truly love him, don't let money be the issue that comes between you two. You may gain the money, but what is living with him going to cost you? Will the price you end up paying be the loss of your salvation? That's a question only you can answer. I'm sure you've already asked God what you should do."

"Only a thousand times."

"Now all you have to do is wait for His response. Maybe he's already given you His answer and you're just not trying to hear it. Ask again. This time listen for His whispers on the wind or even in the silence of your bedroom in the quiet hours of darkness. With all your heart and soul, no matter where you are or what you're doing, listen for His gentle voice. I promise you this: If you'll just be still, you already know that He is God; you'll eventually hear Him. Maybe you should stop concentrating on Paris and the money for now. Focus your thoughts only on what God's will may be for you. He's brought you through the storms of life many times. He'll bring you through this one, too."

"Thank you, Sister Covington. You are always a godsend, always right on time, right when I need you the most."

"The same as it is with God. Always right on time," Marlene voiced with conviction.

Keisha smiled at hearing Malcolm's voice on the line. He had called her but hadn't come by the apartment since he'd asked her about seeing a movie and going to dinner with him. Since he hadn't brought up his suggestion of a date, she hoped he was calling to do so and to set up an exact time for them to hang out. Keisha was lonelier than she'd ever been in her life. With school, work, and taking care of the kids, she needed to indulge in some sort of fun thing.

Malcolm first asked how she was and then he asked about the kids. That pleased her. She felt good about anyone who showed genuine interest in her children. Malcolm had shown and voiced his sincere concerns for little Zach and Zanari every time he'd gotten on her back about continuing to hang in there with Zach.

If Keisha thought Marlene might approve of him and her starting a more personal relationship, she might be more open to having Malcolm in her life. Although he'd never expressed wanting her as a girlfriend, the attraction undoubtedly existed.

However, Keisha's love for Zach and their history together would probably interfere in any new relationship that she might get emotionally involved in. That's just the way it was.

"What's on your mind, Mr. C?"

"Remember when I asked about you and me going to a movie or something?"

Keisha suddenly felt nervous. "Yeah, what's up?"

"I'd like to get you out of the house but thought we should do something that included the kids, especially since we're just building a friendship. Would that be okay?"

Keisha was speechless. His words spun around in her head, making her feel dizzy. Malcolm, the kids, and her! What was up with that? She had to wonder.

"Keisha, are you still there? Caught you off guard, huh?"

"I'd dare to say so." She sighed. "I don't know, Malcolm. Zach would not like it. He can be a real butt to deal with."

"There you go, true to form, worrying about what Zach thinks. Zach is locked up. Even if he wanted to, he can't take his kids anywhere right now. Why should they be deprived because he's un-available to them?"

"Don't start with me. I don't want to go there with you, Malcolm."

"You never do, 'cause you can't deal with the facts. All Zach is right now is a deadbeat dad. You know it, too. One day you're going to wake up and smell his stench in your nostrils."

"Okay, let me warn you. You've said enough already. I'll think about your suggestion."

"You don't have much time for that," Malcolm shot back. "The bus leaves first thing in the morning for Sea World in San Diego. It's Saturday, you're off, so don't try and use that."

"Sea World? San Diego? Are you joking?"

"The County Recreation Department is sponsoring the trip. The bus has a few seats left, and I thought about you and the kids. If you want to go, I need to know within the next hour."

She and the kids had never been to any of the large entertain-ment parks in California, or anywhere else fun for that matter. Entertainment prices were off the chart for three people. The thought of her kids at Sea World filled her with eager joy. The re-ality of it scared her to death.

"We're going! Fill me in on the details."

Chuckling inwardly, Malcolm thoroughly enjoyed laying out the plans for their first outing. It was not his desire to become a father figure to Keisha's children; he just wanted them to experi-ence some of the finer, fun things that life had to offer. They de-served a well-rounded life, like the kind his parents had provided for him. Working with kids had given him a totally fresh perspec-tive on how to help out the youth of today's society, especially those at risk.

Keisha's kids and their future were definitely at risk.

* * *

In a room lighted only by candles, Marlene and Jesse, dressed in pajamas and cozy robes, sat on the sofa watching the colorful flames of the firestorm, listening to the gentle crackling and popping of the pinewood burning in the fireplace. The pine scent was heavenly, tranquil. Half-finished cups of coffee and an empty dessert plate rested on the coffee table in front of the couch.

Jesse put his arm around Marlene and guided her head close to his chest. "That we have managed to stay in love all these years astounds me, Mar." He kissed her forehead. "I guess we really like each other."

She smiled. "Yeah, but it's a little more than us just liking each other. Don't you think?"

"I would have to say so. I'm happy that our love has survived so many fiery trials. I never thought you'd get over the loss of baby Mason, yet you did. You really suffered a lot through that painful ordeal. Look at you now, though. You're as strong and beautiful as can be."

"Thank you for the compliment. What you've said is true enough, but you weren't easy to console during Mother Covington's final departure at her going-home celebration. You adored her and she was crazy about her Jesse. I'll never forget the day you sprinkled her ashes out to sea. Your pain was unmanageable. Though you were against cremation, you loved her enough to put your feelings aside and honor her last request. I thought I couldn't love you anymore than I did on that sorrowful day. I was wrong. My love increases for you daily."

He kissed her behind the ear. "I feel the same. My love for you also continues to grow. Though we've had a host of tribulations, we came through together in triumph. I don't ever want to fly a mission without you, Wildflower. You'll always be my wingman."

Marlene giggled, wrinkling her nose. Jesse knew every button she had, knew how to push the right one every time. "Wingwoman sounds a little more feminine. There's nothing manly about this old girl, Reverend Jesse."

"Woman, you don't have to tell me that! I'm familiar with all your feminine charms."

"Speaking of feminine charms, I'm getting the impression that some charm is happening between Malcolm and Keisha. I just don't know who's trying to charm who."

"How did you come to that end?"

Marlene told Jesse how Malcolm had gone to Keisha's the night Rosalinda was attacked by Ricardo. She also conveyed to him that Keisha had once asked her jokingly how'd she like to have her as a daughter-in-law.

"Daughter-in-law! She came up with that after one visit from Malcolm?"

"That question was before his visit. I was certainly surprised when she told me Malcolm had come to her place. There's not much my son doesn't let me in on. That is, since we've mended our mother-and-son relationship. He sure didn't mention that visit to me."

"Maybe he didn't tell you because he wasn't sure how you'd react. I'm curious. How would you react if those two fell for each other?"

Marlene sucked in a deep breath, looking thoughtful. She glided her fingernail over her lower lip before letting it come to rest at the corner of her mouth. "If I'm to be honest here, I have thought about it, a lot. My initial reaction wasn't a positive one. I couldn't imagine Malcolm getting involved with a ready-made family. I want him to have a fairy-tale wedding and a fairy princess for a wife. But isn't that what every mother wants for her son?"

"I would think so. Including Martha, Keisha's mother. But the reality is never as simple as that. Mistakes are often made, life-altering ones. Keisha is only one of countless young women who find themselves in trouble before they're old enough to know how to make the right choices in life. Teen pregnancy is an epidemic in this country, the same as incarceration of black males. As Malcolm's father, I'd be happy for any choice in a wife that he made, as long as he was happy. My son's happiness is extremely important to me. You said your initial reaction wasn't positive. Does that mean you changed your mind?"

"What it means is that I was being judgmental again. Then I thought about all that Keisha has been through and all that she has done to turn her situation around. I'm very proud of that girl. She's come so far and still traveling forward. How can I say I love her like a daughter and not think she's good enough to be my daughter-in-law is the question I had to ask myself."

Jesse stroked his chin. "Did you come up with an answer?"

"It was a tough one to answer, but I finally managed to peel away all the layers and get real. That I can love her like a daughter and not want her as a daughter-in-law is the truth of the matter. Some people would see me as a hypocrite, instead of just being true to myself. After much soul-searching, I do believe I can truly be happy with it if Malcolm chose to get involved with Keisha. However, that doesn't mean I wouldn't be concerned. The children have a father in this world, one that might not want another man around his off-spring. Knowing of Zach as we do, he won't take lightly to Keisha and his kids being with our son. That's what really scares me."

"That's one of those things that we can't control, so we have to turn it over to God. Keep both the big and little kids in prayer. We don't know for sure that Malcolm and Keisha are even interested in each other on a personal level. It's not something you have to entertain right now."

"You're right, Jesse. Thanks. Would you like more dessert before we go to bed?"

Jesse grinned. "Sure would, but what I have in mind doesn't come in a bowl or on a plate. I'm feeling a little frisky right now. I have a deep burning for you under my skin. Why don't we turn our evening's end into an intimate rendezvous and move into the bedroom, Mar?"

Flushed all over, her eyelashes fluttering uncontrollably, Marlene picked up a magazine from the coffee table and fanned herself with it. Of all times to have hot flashes, this wasn't it. "Why not stay right here, where we already have the fire going and the candlelight? Malcolm hasn't had a key in quite some time, so that's certainly not a concern for us."

She reached up and kissed him gently on the mouth. "We haven't made this old couch sing a hallelujah chorus in a long time. If you're ready to relieve that sweetly tortuous burning and familiar yearning, I'm willing to help you stoke the fires and eventually put them out. However, dousing the flames will come much later." Marlene's giggles filled the air.

Taking her in his arms, Jesse allowed his lips to respond to her intimate challenge.

As Alexis dressed for bed, her thoughts turned to Jarreau Thornton. Finer than the finest, Jarreau had been very well thought of by her family. As far as her father was concerned, he would've made him a grand son-in-law. He had trusted Jarreau way more than he did R.J., the man who eventually married his daughter and ended up calling him Mr. Gautier, never Dad.

Alexis turned to face the door when she heard the light knock. Marietta Grainger, her housekeeper, a native of the West Indies, was the only other person on the premises. "Come on in, Marietta," Alexis shouted through the closed door.

Marietta entered her employer's bedroom. Already dressed for bed, she looked relaxed in a cotton floral print gown and matching robe. Her smile, bright and loving, never failed to warm Alexis's oftentimes cold heart. "Missy, can I do anything for you before retiring for the night?"

Alexis tossed Marietta a glowing smile in return. "What about loaning me one of those sensitive ears of yours? I feel like I could talk up a storm. I suddenly seem to have a lot to say, but only if you're not ready to go to sleep yet. I know you've had another long day."

"I normally lie awake for an hour or so once I get into bed, especially if I lie down before I'm sleepy. I was going to watch a television program or two, but I'd much rather have a nice conversation with you. Should I sit down over there?" Marietta pointed at the brand new, comfortable-looking, overstuffed lounge chair situated near Alexis's canopied king-size bed.

The bedroom suite Alexis had moved into was fit for southern royalty. White plantation shutters graced all the windows, except for the large picture one, which elegant gold satin draperies hung from. A gold satin comforter set decorated with delicate white hand-sewn roses covered the huge bed. Gold and white accents complimented the elegant décor. While Alexis slept every night in the lap of luxury, she had begun to learn how to fully appreciate her numerous blessings. Alexis had become more sensitive to those less fortunate than herself.

"I have a better idea. Let's go into the kitchen. I'm in dire need of a sugar injection. Any more of the cinnamon rolls left from the ones that you baked for breakfast?"

"More than a full dozen. None of the outside workers were around for me to hand them out to. By the time the decorators arrived, I was on my way out the door. You brewed it up the last time we had a chat, so I'll go and get the coffee started. That is, if you want a cup or two."

"That'll be so nice. I'll be right along, Marietta. Thanks for always being so thoughtful and accommodating. You're so good to me."

"Think nothing of it, Missy. You are just as good to me."

As Marietta cleared the doorway, Alexis put on the silk robe that matched her deep raspberry and soft pink gown. She then ran a soft bristled brush through her short hair, fluffing it slightly with her fingertips. Her smooth-as-satin skin was now stripped of its light layer of foundation, but her face was nonetheless beautiful without it. She still looked radiant.

Alexis stared longingly at the bedside phone as she passed by the nightstand. She noted the time on the clock radio, hoping Jarreau would call tonight, since he hadn't done so a couple of evenings back, when she'd run into him at the restaurant. She wasn't sure why it bothered her to no end. Maybe an emergency or something had come up. Alexis was sorry that she hadn't gotten his number. But if he were married, he wouldn't have given it to her.

Normally a man of his word, she couldn't help wondering what kept Jarreau from keeping it this time. His actions were downright puzzling to her, since he sounded so sincere about calling. He still looked darn good. Though she hadn't paid much attention to him after she'd met R.J., they'd done a lot of things together before R.J. had swept her off her feet. She had loved Jarreau more like a brother. Alexis hadn't ever considered their social outings as dates.

The situation was indeed ironic; she had never paid Jarreau any personal attention, though he had constantly vied for it; in an under-cover sort of way. A lot of males had begun to take special notice of Alexis during her sophomore year in high school. She'd never been an ugly duckling, but the last stages of her transformation into a beautiful swan had suddenly swung into full bloom. Male heads had started to turn every which way just to get a glimpse of her.

That Jarreau hadn't asked about R.J. hadn't come as a surprise to Alexis. He'd always thought of R.J. as the archenemy, a major con-tender for her affection. Jarreau had tried every trick in the book to keep her from R.J., but nothing had worked. Still, he hadn't given up on their friendship becoming more until the day Alexis had ac-tually walked down the aisle to wed R.J.

Alexis's wedding had finally spelled out the end of any chance for them as a couple.

Alexis had to admit that she didn't know what kind of man Jarreau had become. He could've turned out to be the worst kind. But she somehow doubted that. Though only a teenager at the time, he'd been extremely considerate and respectful of her. He was actually one of the nicest boys at school. That's probably the reason why she'd swooned at R.J.'s feet.

The bad boy in R.J. had instantly turned her on back then. R.J. had lived as a bad boy, had died as one, though redeemed, thanks to God and Reverend Jesse. God rest his weary soul, she mused, praying silently for her husband's peace.

If Jarreau was married or not was now the million dollar question in her mind. The curious cat had suddenly come back to life to claim one of its remaining lives. Alexis sighed. "Oh, well, what's a girl to do when a man doesn't keep his word? Jarreau's loss, not mine."

Alexis left the room, wiping a single tear from the corner of her eye. Despite her attempts to move on with her life and get back into the game of living, she still missed her husband like crazy, didn't think she'd ever stop.

"Sweet potato pie!" Alexis screeched, taking a seat at the kitchen table. "When did you bake this?"

Marietta beamed. "Not long after you left this morning. I made three. I thought you'd prefer the pie to the cinnamon rolls."

"You guessed right! The pie looks divine." She practically devoured the entire slice in one bite. Alexis then closed her eyes to savor the delightful culinary experience.

Marietta cracked up at how Alexis had attacked the generous slice of pie with gusto. "I can certainly see that." Marietta took a sip of her coffee and set the cup down. "Missy, my ears are perked up and ready to hear what's on your mind. What do you want to talk about first?"

Alexis looked up, tears suddenly brimming in her doe-brown eyes. "How to move on without R.J. in my life. I need to know if I can, if it's even possible for me to do so. I feel so empty inside. I want so badly to be filled again with the pleasures and goodness of love. I want my cup to overflow with it. My heart feels so broken, irreparably damaged."

Marietta wiped Alexis's tears away. "Don't go making yourself sick, Missy. Try to pull it together now. It's going to be okay. You'll see. That kind of healing takes a lot of time."

Alexis flailed her hands about in desperation. "I can't continue night after night to make love in my dreams to a corpse. I can't keep on daydreaming about the way it used to be. It wasn't always good for us, but neither was it so bad that I couldn't stomach him. Our physical relationship was awesome in every way. When I awaken, only to find I've been dreaming about us, I'm shattered. Then the uncontrollable sobbing follows. Marietta, do you think I can find that kind of love twice in one lifetime? I desperately need to know."

"I wish I had the answers for you, Missy, but I don't. God does, but you have to ask Him to send them to you. You've been so thrilled that R.J. found his salvation before his death, but I've been watching you ducking and dodging God since I've known you; more so since R.J.'s death. It may be time for you to seek out your own salvation, Missy. You have Marlene and Reverend Jesse at your disposal. None of us are immortal. Death will eventually visit us all."

Fresh tears spilled from Alexis's eyes. "I will, starting right now. Will you get down on your knees and pray with me, Marietta? I have got to find peace in my life."

Marietta reached for her employer's hand. "I will pray with you, Missy, but you are the one that should lead out. God needs to hear from you. He hears from me quite often."

While R.J. would always be the love of Alexis's life, she had to know if there was room left in her heart for someone else to share in. Spending the rest of her life alone wasn't the least bit appealing. Alexis needed to adore and be adored. Life without the warmth of human contact would eventually kill her. Mathis West had intrigued her in the beginning, but something about him was unsettling. There were numerous small imperfections in his character that she'd already discovered, but she feared the possibility of him being too flawed for her to reconcile with. The imperfections that she had yet to discover in him concerned her. Sure that they existed, the larger ones were what terrified her most. Who was Mathis West really? Should she even try to find out?

Alexis had to make darn sure that she didn't repeat her past mistakes. As good as R.J. was to her, he had been controlling and possessive. He had purposely kept her away from her family, not to mention all the dark secrets he'd held within, secrets that had destroyed him and could've left her with the same ending. She didn't like to think of the negative aspects of her late husband, but if she was to keep history from repeating itself, she'd better not forget a single one of them. This time she had to fully know what and to whom she was opening herself up to.

Alexis then vowed to first seek and explore the love of God.

The sun had barely peaked over the horizon, but Reverend Jesse and Michael Hernandez had already started their day. Seated in a booth inside the Serving Spoon, a soulful restaurant in Inglewood, both men were having the first cup of coffee.

Rosalinda Morales and Ricardo Munoz were the main topics of conversation. Neither man could believe that Ricardo was still roaming the streets. Until he was caught and put back behind bars neither Rosalinda nor her friends would have any peace. Even then, concern would remain, mainly because of Ricardo's ability to control his homeboys from within the correctional facility.

"How is she doing with all this, Michael? She seemed so fragile the last time we all got together. Marlene is terribly concerned for her safety."

Michael had a somber look about him. No one was more worried about Rosalinda than he was. Now that she resided on his property, her safety had become even more important to him; he now considered it as his job to protect her and keep her safe.

Unbeknownst to her, Michael had his LAPD friends and county sheriff buddies on high alert. Whenever Ricardo was so much as spotted on the streets of L.A. and surrounding communities, Michael had asked the officers to contact him personally. Michael had also convinced Rosalinda to report her whereabouts to him at all times. It would be difficult to ensure her safety without knowing her every move.

Michael lightly tapped his nails on the table. "She says she's fine, but the false bravado is apparent to me. Rosalinda is not the kind of woman to cower in fear, but she has every reason to be extremely fearful. She doesn't like reporting her every move to me, but she understands why she has to. She knows Ricardo better than anyone else, knows exactly what kind of violence he's capable of. It still amazes me that a woman like her ever got involved with a man like him."

Jesse laid his fork down on his plate. "Good people get involved with bad people all the time. However, I want you to take a minute to consider Ricardo and what may've caused him to turn out the way he did. As humans, we are always quick to judge. Ricardo could've had some pretty terrible things happen to him in his lifetime. As an abuser, he could've been abused."

Michael took a couple of moments to digest Jesse's comments. Thinking of the abuse children often suffered at the hands of adults aroused his empathy. Young boys were just as susceptible to abuse as girls, including sexual abuse. As boys grew into men, their painful ordeals weren't something they'd easily allow themselves to talk about with anyone. When boys weren't taken seriously as children, many of them never spoke of their pain as adults.

"Though Rosalinda has talked very little about Ricardo's background, as his former lawyer, I know a lot of his history. He's the only one of his siblings who ran in a gang. His loving family has completely cut him off because of their deep disappointment in him. However, I don't know of any issues of abuse from his family."

Jesse stroked his chin. "Abuse doesn't have to come from inside one's home. The big city streets like those found in L.A. are often mean and dangerous. As a gang member, Ricardo was more than likely jumped into the gang with a horrendous amount of violence. That's how it's done. Some kids think they want to belong to a gang because it will make them tough. A lot of times the kids who are picked on and bullied at school join gangs for protection. I don't think a lot of them are fully aware of what gang life is really like until after they join one. Then it's often too late. They can't get out without the risk of being killed. Just another catch-22 for America's youth."

"Then you have the ones who are abused at home and looking for a real family to belong to, one that will love them," Michael added. "They don't understand that the gangs only love them as long as they do what they're told. The minute they rebel, the abuse will once again become their reality. I was once a runaway, but only for a very short time. I was only thirteen when I ran away and began to learn the codes of the streets of L.A. Those tough experiences came during a period of total confusion in my life, but they also helped me. It didn't take me long to carry my tail back home and accept the game plan my parents had laid out for me. The Hernandezes wanted a lawyer in the family. As the only child left at home, the youngest of three, I was the chosen one. My older brother and sister were already in medical school at the time."

Jesse nodded. "I see, a life of privilege. A lot of people growing up in the same situation as you did don't always take advantage of the privileges afforded them. I'm glad to see that you did. You've done very well for yourself, Michael. Are your parents still living?"

"Both of them are alive and well. Now living down in San Clemente, they left Los Angeles many years ago. I see them several times a month."

Jesse smiled wryly. "Have they met the fair lady Rosalinda yet?"

Michael grinned. "Not yet, but I'm hoping for that to happen real soon. Her background won't bother them. My mother is from a poor, uneducated family. My father changed the course of her life. He saw a beautiful woman that he wanted desperately, the same as it was with me when I first met Rosalinda. My parents will see the same wonderful things in Rosalinda as I do."

Jesse swallowed the last of his coffee. "It seems that we've talked about everything but what you asked me here for. You said you needed some advice, Michael. On what?"

Michael rubbed his forehead with his thumb and fingers, bringing them together to meet in the middle. "I'm concerned with the street mentality I've been thinking of resorting to. I want Ricardo hurt really bad, but I have no intentions of getting my hands dirty. I know a few guys who will take him out for me, with or without payment, but I don't want him dead. The problem is this. I know it's wrong. I'm an officer of the law and I shouldn't even be thinking this way. What's worse is that I can't stand the thought of what he might do to Rosalinda if he somehow manages to get to her. I'm consumed with finding a way to stop that from happening."

Jesse folded his hands and placed them on the table. "You shouldn't be thinking that way, but you are. You're also a flesh-and-blood man, one that's in love. A man's first instinct is to protect self and then those that he loves. However, that kind of behavior can land you in jail right alongside Ricardo, with a felony conviction. What good would you be to Rosalinda then?"

"The answer to that question is what keeps me from putting my desires into action. She expects more from me than that. I'm sure of it. Rosalinda is extremely grateful to me. But that poses sort of a problem for me."

Jesse looked puzzled. "Why's that?"

"She's grateful and I'm in love. I'm afraid that she might begin confusing her gratitude for love. It's her love that I want, not her gratefulness."

"I understand the concept, but why are you saying that? Did something happen to make you believe in what you're saying?"

Michael couldn't help smiling. "She kissed me on the mouth the other night. The first one was friendly. I definitely felt the passion behind the second one."

Jesse cracked up. "I don't see your problem, man. The woman kissed you. Twice! You should be jumping for joy, not sitting here whining and complaining about her being confused. I'm sure Rosalinda knows the difference in what she's feeling and what she's not. It seems to me that you're the one who's confused, Michael. Is that a possibility?"

Michael suddenly looked awestruck. "I sure hope so."

"I hope so, too, Michael. Is our business finished?"

"One more thing. Orin and I have been talking a lot about the support group you're interested in starting. We're both going to do referrals for you. As a family lawyer, Orin has more situations involving men that could use some spiritual direction. In fact, he's planning on sending another of his clients to you. This guy's girl-friend is also locked up. From what I was told, he was all but forced to take custody of their child when his own mother passed away. He's terribly angry about his new role in life. Apparently his mother had taken the child into her home when the mother got locked up. Her death put the responsibility for the child squarely in his lap, something he hadn't had much to do with before. He hasn't been a very responsible father."

"This one sounds like we won't be having a laugh a minute. Any referrals you and your colleagues can send my way. In fact, I'm having an impromptu meeting next week with a couple of guys I've been counseling. Send to the meeting as many referrals as you want. It will be appreciated, Michael."

Jesse got to his feet. "It also looks like your personal dilemma is resolved." He quickly sat back down. "Michael, I hope you heard what I said about ending up behind bars. If you do something to Ricardo, or have it done by someone else, you'll be guilty of committing a crime. I don't have to tell a man in your profession what that means. You have to be stronger than your strongest desires in this instance. Try kissing Rosalinda more and leave the thoughts of violence and mayhem completely alone. Do you hear me?"

Michael extended his hand to Jesse. "Loud and clear, my friend. I hadn't been praying too much a short time ago, even though I attend church services regularly. It seems that I can't pray enough since Rosalinda came into my life. I guess I needed to get back to the basics."

"Continue to pray, Michael. It works."

Chapter Five

M arlene and her best friend, Myrna Jacobson, were seated at Marlene's dining room table preparing to work on some of the plans for Sister Wylie's surprise birthday party. Their major issues of two years back had been long since resolved between them. The two women were now back to acting like loving sisters toward each other, the same way as before the serious misunderstanding that had nearly torn them apart. Godmothers to their only sons, Malcolm and Todd, the two young men had come between them when each woman thought the other's son was guilty of the crime that Jesse had been imprisoned for.

Todd Jacobson and Malcolm had remained the best of friends throughout the horrific ordeal. It turned out that neither son was guilty, but that both had played a part in what had occurred to Jesse. Malcolm had stolen the church van and had lent it to Todd, who had lent it to Latrell Johnson, his girlfriend's brother. The van was involved in the armed robbery the same night. It was later learned that Latrell Johnson had committed the crime.

"What's Sister Wylie's favorite color, Marlene?"

"She has two. Lavender and blue. Those are the colors I'll order for the cake."

"Are we doing the room decorations in the same color, Marlene?"

"It wouldn't be her party if we didn't pander to her likes. The crepe paper to make the decorations is in the spare bedroom. Flowers in the same color will be ordered for the centerpieces, but we should add some white baby's breath to break up the lavender and blue. In fact, we should use a little white throughout all the decorations. We still have a while to go before we need to order the cake and the flowers."

"If that's the case, then why am I here so early in the morning?"

Grinning, Marlene reached under the table and picked up one of many lightweight boxes. "To help write out the invitations. I picked these up from the printer yesterday." Marlene opened the box and took out one invitation. "Aren't they beautiful? White card stock with lavender and blue script writing in bold print. Sister Wylie is going to be thrilled to death. The little raised pink rosebuds are a perfect complement. I can't wait to see the expression on her sweet face."

Myrna groaned, looking down at her fingers. "Writer's cramp is not something I relish getting, but I guess somebody has to do this. Since her kids all have full-time jobs, looks like we're the ones. Being housewives has it drawbacks." Both women dissolved into laughter.

"We could use the computer to do the address labels, Myrna, but I don't think that's personal enough. Labels seem impersonal to me, though they don't look bad at all. However, we can be grateful for self-stick stamps. No licking any nasty glue for us today."

"What you guys doing in the dining room so early? I thought I'd find you in the kitchen," Malcolm remarked, leaning his lean frame against the doorjamb.

Marlene looked startled. "How'd you get in here, boy?"

Malcolm laughed at the fearful expression on his mother's face. "Either you or Dad left the garage door up. I just came through the side door. So you don't get shook up again, Todd is with me. He stopped to use the bathroom."

Marlene looked relieved. The thought of Malcolm still having a key had caused her to instantly think of her and Jesse's previous late-night rendezvous. That's not something she would've wanted Malcolm to walk in on. They had gotten pretty loose that night. Jesse had been feeling his oats and someone else's too. Marlene couldn't help smiling as the delicious memories filled her head.

Marlene's dreamy-eyed look turned to a sheepish one. "Jesse and I are the guilty parties. I went out into the garage early this morning to see him off. Both of us must've thought the other one was going to put it back down after he backed out. It appears that neither of us did so. Thank you, Jesus, for covering us with the blood of the Lamb."

Todd popped into the room, rushing over to kiss both his mother and godmother. "Hey, ladies, what you up to so early?"

Todd was lousy at keeping secrets, which had Marlene and Myrna exchanging apprehensive looks. He had spoiled the last surprise party, the one thrown for his mother.

"Just doing the Lord's work," Myrna responded. "What are you and Malcolm doing over here this time of morning? Shouldn't both of you be on your way to work?"

"I took the day off," Todd remarked, taking a seat at the table.

Myrna looked concerned. "For what? You don't need to start missing work without good cause, Todd. That's a good way to get yourself fired."

"Mom, it would've been nice if you'd given me time to respond before scolding me. It's not like I've been irresponsible over the past two years. There's an opening at Malcolm's job and he recommended me for the position. I'm going with him on the field trip to Sea World to see how things go with the kids. The bus leaves from the local county park. I didn't just call in sick either. I took a vacation day. Malcolm is off today, too." Todd worked at one of the Wal-Mart Super Centers, where he served as an assistant store manager.

Myrna reached over and hugged her son. "I'm sorry for jumping to all the wrong conclusions. I didn't mean to imply that you weren't being responsible, but I guess that's exactly what I've done. Please forgive me, baby."

"For sure, Mom. It's all good, but you need to stop worrying about me. I'm still doing the right thing. Both Malcolm and me have serious goals to accomplish. We've even talked about me moving in with him. We're also thinking of starting our own music production company. You know we're the best rapping duo around." Todd and Malcolm exchanged high-fives.

Marlene still smelled something funny despite Todd's explanation. It was very rare for them to come to her house this early in the morning. "With all that said, I'm curious as to what really brings you here this morning. My house is not in the same direction you're headed."

It was Malcolm's turn to look sheepish. He balled his fists tight and brought them down in front of him. "Mom, I was just hoping you might have some pancakes on the griddle. This is Saturday, you know. I've been dreaming about those little tasty hotcakes all night."

The pancakes weren't the only things that had been on Malcolm's mind when he'd decided to come and see his mother. Malcolm hadn't mentioned that Keisha and her kids were going to Sea World with him. For that matter, he hadn't told her about being at Keisha's apartment. He wasn't sure if he should tell her these things before the trip or afterward. He knew for a fact that she loved Keisha, but would she still feel the same way about her if they got involved in a romantic liaison? He really wanted to talk to Marlene about Keisha. His mother's opinion was important to him, but he'd gotten cold feet. If his Aunt Myrna hadn't been there, he probably would've opened up dialogue with Marlene.

While he didn't mind sharing his situation with his godmother, Malcolm didn't think his mother would want him to discuss it in front of anyone until after they'd discussed it in private. Out of respect for Marlene, he made the decision to wait for a more favorable opportunity. The fact that he'd met Keisha through his mother made it even more important to him to have Marlene weigh in on the issues.

Marlene pulled a face. "If that's true, why didn't you call to make sure that I'd have a little something for you?" Marlene joked with ease. "You know I don't mind cooking for my baby. But since you didn't give me any advance warning, you're going to have to stop off at a Denny's or an IHOP somewhere along the way."

Malcolm's jaw dropped. "I can't believe you didn't cook pancakes for Dad this morning. You've only done it every weekend as far back as I can remember."

Marlene shook her head in the negative. "He had a breakfast meeting with Michael Hernandez. Dad left the house before the rooster could belt out the first cock-a-doodle-do."

Malcolm looked dejected as he glanced at his watch. "I guess I'll have to settle for less than the very best in buttermilk pancakes in Southern California," he flattered his mother knowingly. "Let's hit the road, Todd. Looks like we can't get no play here. And we still have close to two hours to kill before the bus leaves."

Both Marlene and Myrna jumped to their feet at the same time. "I'll fix them," they both sang out simultaneously. The two women cracked up at their willingness to please their sons.

"We can do it together by dividing the duties," Marlene assured Myrna. "My kitchen can hold two women at the same time, but only if we leave our egos out here in the dining room. Just don't get in my way," she said jokingly, taking her best friend into her warm embrace.

Malcolm was careful to hide the smugness he felt inside as he looked at Todd and winked in a covert manner. Though Marlene kept Malcolm in check these days, he knew that there were some things she still couldn't deny him.

Unassuming and even-tempered, Todd looked on, grinning from ear to ear. He was thrilled that the Jacobsons and the Covingtons were just one big happy family again.

* * *

The phone bell jerked Alexis out of her bad dream. Alexis looked at the clock and moaned, reaching for the receiver. As she listened to Jarreau's deep voice sincerely apologizing for not calling sooner, her moaning ceased instantly. A smug smile tugged at the corner of her full lips. Knowing that she still had it going on caused her laughter to break within. Jarreau couldn't seem to apologize enough. She'd once again have him eating out of her hand in no time at all. That is, if he wasn't married. Alexis mentally reminded herself that she had changed. The old Alexis would've had him begging for forgiveness. Fortunately, for all concerned, a lot of Alexis's old ways had died with R.J. Finding favor with God was more important than anything.

"I hope I'm forgiven, Alexis."

Alexis giggled. "Of course. Don't give it another thought. It has been a long time, Jarreau. Tell me all about yourself and what you've been doing."

"It has been that. First things first! How's R.J. and are you still married to him?"

Alexis had difficulty swallowing the sudden lump in her throat. His direct questions had knocked her a little off kilter. "I'm a widow, Jarreau. R.J. died two years ago."

Jarreau wished he could've bitten his tongue off. He had no idea that R.J. had passed away or the circumstances surrounding his death. How he'd died wasn't something he'd dared to ask. Alexis would tell him about it if she ever saw fit to do so. "I'm sorry, Alexis. I didn't know. Are you doing okay?"

"I'm doing much better than I had been. I wasn't sure if you knew or not, but I had wondered." Alexis went on to tell Jarreau about her situation, holding many things back.

"That must've been incredibly painful for you. That had to be a really tough situation for R.J. to be in and a horrible one for you to find yourself saddled with. I hope he's at peace."

"He is. I'm sure of that. So let's get back to you. What's going on in your life?"

"Why don't we talk about that over lunch this afternoon?"

Alexis bit down on her lower lip. "I planned to go to the cemetery today to put flowers on R.J.'s crypt. I always go there before noon."

"Why don't I meet you there?"

His request stunned Alexis. "Why would you want to do that?"

"Why wouldn't I? It's not like I didn't know R.J. And I'm sure you could use some support from one of your oldest and dearest friends."

"Yeah, you're right, Jarreau, but I'm still surprised. You've always viewed R.J. as an archenemy. You two guys had a serious rivalry going on back in the day."

"That was a long time ago. R.J. was a couple of years older than us, but you and I were not yet twenty-one. Mad male egos flared up in that situation. You were the prize and both male beasts wanted to win the town beauty. I'll always believe that the best man lost, but that's all in the past now. Where is R.J. buried, Lex?"

Tears sprang to Alexis's eyes as sweet memories of yesteryears leapt into her mind. Jarreau was the only person who had ever called her "Lex". The warm affection he still felt for her could be heard in his voice. "Forest Lawn, Beverly Hills." Alexis went on to give him the directions to exactly where she'd meet him on the cemetery property.

"Is one o'clock okay with you, Alexis?"

"Perfect timing." Alexis once again bit down on her lower lip, feeling nervous about the personal question she wanted to ask. She drew in a shaky breath. "Did you and Nina ever marry, Jarreau?"

"If you don't mind, we'll talk about that over lunch, too. It's kind of a long story."

Alexis wanted the answer right now, in the worst way. "I'm curious, but not so curious that I can't wait until I see you," she lied. "One o'clock."

"I'll be there waiting. Until then, be safe."

Malcolm helped Keisha get the kids settled into the blue and yellow metal strollers they'd rented, while Todd and his girlfriend, Arlissa Johnson, patiently waited for them. Keisha couldn't help noticing how Malcolm handled her kids with gentle hands. Zanari was looking up at him as though she were looking into the face of a hero. Keisha didn't like the look of adoration in her daughter's eyes; Zach would like it even less. She'd have to be careful not to compromise the hearts of her children. Malcolm was just a friend.

Zach was Daddy.

Keisha had been surprised when Malcolm had shown up with his friends, though they were friendly enough toward her. While she had expected it to be just the four of them, she was rather relieved to have the extra company in the park. That way, Malcolm wouldn't get the wrong impression about her acceptance of his invitation. Even though she'd considered it as one in the beginning, she no longer saw this outing as a date. This trip was strictly for the pleasure of her kids. She'd been trying to convince herself of that all morning.

No matter how hard she tried, Keisha couldn't deny Malcolm's attractiveness or how much she enjoyed talking with him. He made her laugh, something she hadn't done a lot of since Zach went to prison the last time. She couldn't even come to terms with how fast her heart palpitated when Malcolm was around. Getting a grip on her emotions was a must.

"We're all set," Malcolm said to the others. He took control of one stroller while Keisha steered the other. "What do you want to see first, Little Zach?"

Little Zach grinned, showing all of his pretty white teeth. "Shamu!" he said, giggling.

Malcolm eyed Keisha. "I thought you said they'd never been here. How does he know about Shamu, girl?"

Keisha stopped and put her hand on her hip. "We do have a television, Malcolm Covington. Ever heard of commercials? Besides that, I've been talking to them about Sea World and Shamu since you first called and invited us. We do live on this planet, you know. Just because we've never been to any of these places doesn't mean we don't know about them."

"My bad, Keisha. I thought you were trying to pull one over on me."

"That's more your style than it is mine," Keisha countered sarcastically.

"Time out," Todd intervened. "I thought we came here to show the kids a good time."

Malcolm felt silly for purposely baiting Keisha, something he promised himself not to do anymore. "I'm sorry, Keisha Reed. Let's start over." He extended his hand to her.

Though Keisha had the urge to ignore Malcolm's good-will gesture, she took his hand and called a truce. "I accept your apology. Now let's go catch up with the rest of the group."

"I'm not an assigned chaperone on this tour, but Todd wants to see how it is to interact with the children since he's applying for a job where I work. They're all right over there," Malcolm said, pointing out the large group of shouting kids. "Let's go."

Eager to have a fun day in the park, Todd and Arlissa moved toward the children. Arlissa Johnson was medium in height and possessed a nice, solidly built shape. She wore her dark brown hair at shoulder length and she had pretty golden brown eyes and a sweet smile.

Keisha slowed her pace and turned to face Malcolm. "Since you're not on duty, can we talk a minute? I have something to ask you."

"Sure. What's up?"

"Your mother, does she know that the kids and me are with you today?"

He scratched his head. "Not really."

Keisha rolled her eyes. "Would that be a yes or a no?"

"No, I didn't tell her. I ate breakfast at her house earlier, but my Aunt Myrna was there. I was going to talk to her about it. Thought I should do it in private. She doesn't even know I've been to your apartment."

"Why not?"

"It just hasn't come up."

Keisha sucked her teeth. "You are sure enough a mama's boy! I thought you had matured. What, you afraid to tell her?"

Malcolm frowned. "Stop tripping, Keisha! I already told you what happened. I can't make you believe me and I don't see what the big deal is. Contrary to what you might think, my mother is not privileged to my every move. You can call me a mama's boy, or whatever else you like, but that doesn't make it true. When I get ready to tell her about today and being in your apartment before, I will. The right opportunity just hasn't presented itself."

"Save your breath on the visit to my apartment. She already knows. I told her."

Malcolm actually looked relieved. Marlene already knowing about the visit had taken some of the pressure off of him. He didn't think for a second that his mother would forbid him to see Keisha, but he wasn't sure that she'd encourage it either. Since he'd begun acting responsibly, Marlene was treating him like a man now, unlike before when he was immature and irresponsible. Jesse's false conviction had had a lot to do with the change in him. More so than that, his mother's willingness to love him from a distance had opened his eyes wide. Kicking him out of her house was one of the best things she'd ever done for him. He had been forced into acting his age as opposed to his number twelve-and-a-half shoe size.

"I see that you still have a big mouth, girl. Oh, well, what's done is done." He came to a dead stop and put his hands on Keisha's shoulders. "Do you want the kids to have a good time or do you just want to continue arguing with me, knowing you can't win? It's entirely up to you."

Keisha looked slightly ashamed. "I want us all to have a good time."

"Thank you!" Malcolm shouted happily. "Let's catch up with the others."

Standing in front of the marble steps leading up to the mausoleum that housed R.J.'s crypt, Alexis looked like a beauty queen to Jarreau. His thoughts immediately carried him back to the junior and senior proms. Alexis, princess of all his nights, had been on his arm for both events, yet Alexis had still refused to call him her date. She had looked beautiful on those occasions, too. She was a real stunner then, just as she was now. Alexis appeared to have hardly aged at all. The woman still had a way of making his heart stop, yet he'd never so much as shared an intimate kiss with her. He didn't know whether to be happy about his heart's reaction to her or be fearful of it. He'd already had his heart severely broken by her once.

Knowing that Alexis Du Boise was widowed was one thing. Wondering if her heart would ever be eligible had kept him deep in thought all morning long. The one thing he could never kid himself about was how much Alexis truly loved R.J. Although R.J. was now deceased, Jarreau had the strangest feeling that any man who got involved with Alexis would find himself constantly competing with R.J. for her love, something he had no intention of ever doing.

In celebration of the sunny day that had finally visited L.A., Alexis wore a large white straw hat with a bright yellow band. The lightweight knit shell accenting the white linen trousers suit was in the same sunshine color. Her clothes were grossly expensive and her entire demeanor reeked with wealth and prominence. No matter what she wore, she looked rich and classy.

A huge grin spread across his face. "Hello, Mrs. Du Boise. You're certainly looking very lovely today. But then again, you always do."

Jarreau had smooth, clean-shaven, mocha skin, long eyelashes, and his gray eyes had unusual depth to them. His satiny hair, mixed with silver and black, was cut and trimmed neatly, as was his silvery-threaded mustache. He appeared to be a dignified man of character.

In response to the nervous butterflies attacking her stomach with a vengeance, Alexis's eyelids fluttered wildly. If Jarreau didn't know better, he might think she was flirting with him. But Alexis hadn't given him the least bit of play back in the day, so why would she act any different toward him today? He could always hope and pray for a miracle.

"Mr. Jarreau Thornton, you're not looking so bad yourself. You are still gorgeous!"

Alexis was once again reminded of R.J. when she saw how neat and clean-cut Jarreau looked in his attire. Like R.J. had been, Jarreau was also a slave to fashion. The man definitely knew how to dress with class and style. She'd never forget what he'd looked like in a tuxedo.

The khaki-colored slacks and chocolate-brown polo shirt looked magnificent on his tall, lithe frame. The color-coordinated sports coat was a perfect fit. Jarreau was every bit as good-looking as R.J. had been, but in a more rugged, athletic-type way. R.J. had often been referred to as a pretty boy, one who wouldn't think of getting his weekly manicured fingernails dirty.

Jarreau briefly touched her hand. "Ready to go inside?"

Smiling sweetly, Alexis boldly took hold of Jarreau's arm. "I've already taken care of R.J. What I'm ready for is lunch. How about you?" Alexis felt strongly that R.J. would resent her bringing any man to his final resting place. He may've been dead for over two years, but she was ever mindful of her late husband's numerous idiosyncrasies. Alexis had catered to R.J.'s every whim for so long, she was having a hard time adjusting to her newfound independence.

"Where would you like to have lunch, Alexis?"

"There's a beautiful park right over the hill. I brought along a picnic lunch. It's so beautiful out today, too lovely a day to be indoors." Alexis liked the fact that, unlike Mathis, Jarreau had asked her preference, rather than choosing a place without consulting her. It wasn't that she didn't like a man who made special plans for their enjoyment, but she just didn't want her life to be overtaken yet again. The picnic lunch had allowed her to choose for a change.

Jarreau took a step back, laughing. "I've never eaten lunch amidst dead folks before, but I think I like the idea of lunch in the park. The grounds are beautiful." As it dawned on him that his remark had been unkind, he suddenly looked disturbed. "I didn't mean to be disrespectful to your husband's memory with my comment, Alexis. I wasn't thinking. I'm sorry."

Alexis waved his apology off. "I've never eaten with the dead either. But it'll probably be more interesting than some of the living folks I've had lunch or dinner with. My car is right over there," she said, pointing out her dark blue Jaguar convertible. "You can follow me to the area."

Alexis was glad that she no longer owned the Rolls Royce. She had sold it to one of R.J.'s colleagues. The expensive car had always been intimidating to some people, especially members of the opposite sex. The Jaguar had kept a lot of folks at bay, as well, but it didn't set her too far apart from everyday people in the same way as the Rolls had done. The Jaguar and a silver Mercedes Benz 500S were now the only cars she owned. Though very expensive automobiles, they were a lot less daunting. There was a time when she and R.J. had owned seven cars at once. Two of the seven had been sports utility vehicles.

* * *

Alexis chose a large tree under which to spread the blanket out. In a matter of minutes, she and Jarreau had begun to enjoy the sandwich and salad lunch Marietta had prepared. She had also made a plastic pitcher of iced lemonade to satisfy their thirst.

Alexis wiped her mouth on a paper napkin. "Curiosity about you and your life has nearly gotten the best of me, Jarreau. I guess it's time for telling all. The first question I'll ask is the same one I asked this morning. Did you and Nina Sutton ever marry?"

He looked at her with a straight-poker face. "I never married. I'm not into women."

Nearly choking on her own saliva, Alexis coughed and sputtered as she tried to clear her throat. Jarreau's comment had her stunned. *Not into women?* her brain echoed. How could that be? *No, don't tell me*, she thought. *He can't be!*

Jarreau found it hard to keep a straight face since the look on Alexis's had him wanting to howl. He wished he could capture her image on film. It was obvious to him that she'd forgotten what a jokester he'd been in the past. She had been an easy one to shock senseless. It looked as if nothing had changed. He thought Alexis still looked adorable when thoroughly embarrassed.

Seeing the look on his face, Alexis narrowed her eyes at him. "Should I be feeling really stupid right now? You've gotten one over on me again, haven't you?"

He threw his head back and laughed. "I'm afraid so, Lex. You were always vulnerable to my serious expressions and straight-faced confessions. Although I've matured considerably over the years, I couldn't resist finding out if I could still dupe you with one of my not-so-true assertions. I won't ask for forgiveness 'cause I don't deserve it."

"How gracious of you!" Seeing no point in feeling stupid and allowing a joke to ruin their day, Alexis had to laugh, too. After all these years, he had found a way to dupe her once again. The new Alexis would not shrink away in embarrassment this time. Jarreau would definitely get his, when he least expected it.

"Still want the answer to your question, Lex, or have I totally ruined the moment?"

"I'm dying to have it answered."

"Nina and I never married. We lived together for several years. But when I became a born-again Christian, I no longer wanted to live my life that way. I asked her to marry me, but she wasn't ready to change our living arrangements to something permanent. She ended things."

"I'm sorry, Jarreau, sorry that you were hurt."

He shook his head. "It's nothing to be sorry about. We had our problems before that came about. I've never been a man who likes to run from woman to woman so I did everything I could to make it work. It didn't. That's life. I learned a long time ago how to turn sour lemons into refreshing lemonade, just like this drink we've been sipping on. Life is much sweeter these days. I'm very happy with how I've chosen to live my life, Alexis. I'm totally blessed."

Alexis was glad that she hadn't nearly choked to death again, but his statement about being a born-again Christian had shaken her up a bit. His religious conviction shouldn't have surprised her but it had. Much like her family, his family had also been regular churchgoers. Singing in the church choir had also been a parental requirement for Jarreau. He'd been able to recite the books of the Bible backward and forward. His ability to quote countless scriptures had been nothing less than miraculous. Reading the Bible, unashamedly, had been a favorite pastime of his. That he loved the Lord shouldn't have been so surprising.

"Jarreau, you haven't changed all that much from the days of our youth. A lot of our friends and me were sure that you'd one day become a preacher. Are you a minister?"

He laughed, shaking his head from side to side. "Not even close to one. I am deeply involved in service to my church, though. What about you, Alexis? Have you been baptized again? I know we all got baptized as kids, before we understood what it really meant. It seemed like it was the in thing to do back then. If your friends went up front to join church during the invitation, there were many of us who thought we should do it, too. I know that's what happened to me the first time."

"Will my answer affect our friendship if it's not what you want to hear?"

Frowning, he shrugged. "Why should it?" That's a strange question for you to ask."

"It's not so strange considering how judgmental some people are. Anyway, I haven't been baptized since we were kids, and I don't belong to a church or even a Bible study group. Are you disappointed in my response?"

He laughed at the somber look on her face. "Lighten up, Lex. You're way too serious about this. Of course I'm not disappointed. I'm not even going to ask you why you haven't gotten baptized again or why you haven't found a church home. At least, not this time around. Think there'll be another opportunity for me to ask those questions?"

"Only if you promise not to try and save me from entering the gates of hell."

"I can't promise you that. With that in mind, has my answer affected our friendship?"

Alexis ran her fingers through her hair as she thought about his question, one that had unexpectedly turned the tables on her. Since they were only friends, she couldn't see what harm it would do for them to see each other every now and then. His great company could only do her good. He still knew how to make her laugh and she certainly needed more of that in her life.

For sure, she wasn't going to get romantically involved with a religious fanatic, if that's what Jarreau turned out to be. The term born-again Christian frightened her in a way that she couldn't begin to explain. If Jarreau was looking for the right woman to share his religious convictions with, she was definitely not the one.

Alexis hadn't returned to structured religion in all this time, though she did believe in God. She hadn't forgotten her recent vow to seek God and His love, but she first had to find Him again and establish a trusting relationship with Him before she could think about what Jarreau might need from a woman.

Alexis was aware that she had to discover how to meet her own needs first.

Her scattered thoughts instantly turned to Marlene, the woman she'd never measure up to when it came to pureness of heart and spirituality. Selfishness and spirituality were worlds apart. Alexis had yet to find out how to make the transition from her old world into a brand-new one.

"I don't see any reason why we can't get together again, Jarreau."

"I'm thrilled, Lex. Now that we have that settled, what about us having dinner together tomorrow evening?"

Alexis smiled warmly. "My place or yours?"

Marlene was doing her best to remain calm and to make Malcolm feel at ease. The topic of their conversation was Keisha. Marlene was surprised to learn that her son had taken Keisha and her kids to Sea World with him. The fact that he hadn't mentioned it at the time had hurt her, yet she somewhat understood why he may've chosen not to share it with her earlier.

"What are you really saying, Malcolm?"

"No more than what I just said. I took Keisha and her kids to Sea World."

"Is there a reason you didn't tell me this morning when you were here?"

He shrugged. "Aunt Myrna was here. I thought we should talk about it in private."

"Yet you brought Todd along with you. That isn't what I'd call privacy."

"Mom, you know that Todd would've been happy sitting at the kitchen table eating breakfast or watching television while we had a private conversation in another room. He's been like that forever.

On the other hand, Aunt Myrna might've been offended. She already thinks that she should know every little thing that goes on in our lives."

Marlene stifled a chuckle. His statement was true enough. Myrna meant well, but she always did have a need to know every small detail of what was happening in the lives of her friends. "So, you're seeing Keisha. What do you want me to say, son?"

"Say what you feel."

Marlene raised an eyebrow. "I'm not the one that needs to feel something. What you're feeling about the matter is what's important here."

Malcolm shook his head. "Mom, why are you making this so difficult for me?"

"Malcolm, I honestly don't know what you're expecting from me. I'm not a mind reader, boy. Maybe you need to tell me exactly what it is you're after."

"Your approval."

Marlene took a deep breath to calm down her heart rate. Malcolm seeking her approval had her choked up. Trembling with emotion, Marlene got up from the sofa and sat on the arm of the chair where her son was seated. Looking into his eyes, she took his face between her hands.

Marlene kissed his forehead and released him. "You've had my approval much longer than you've had to live without it. We encountered some seriously bumpy roads over the past few years, but we've had far more good ones. I'm proud of you, proud of how you've managed to turn your life around. Your choice in a woman will never make me disapprove of you. I've never disapproved of you, only of the wrong things you were once doing. I may not like something you might do, but it won't ever take away my love. My love is your birthright."

Malcolm was misty-eyed. "Thanks, Mom. So are you saying that you don't think it's wrong for me to see Keisha?"

"Seeing Keisha socially isn't wrong in my eyesight or in your dad's. But I do want you to stop and take a minute to think about her man, Zach. He could cause you both trouble. He *is* due to get out pretty soon." Malcolm hugged his mother before she returned to her seat on the sofa.

"I have thought about him and his relationship with Keisha. But let's understand something here. Keisha and I are not romantically involved. We're just getting to know each other. I like her and she likes me, though she pretends not to. I can't predict an outcome for us."

"But surely you already know if you're leaning toward and hoping for a certain outcome, Malcolm. I can't imagine you going into this totally blind. Right?"

"Wrong. I just don't know, Mom. But I do know that I'm trying to do things differently when it comes to women. I want to do the friend thing first. If I try to do it the old way, I'm going to fail at it. Sex before feelings are even developed is not happening for me right now. I want something different, something very much like what you and Dad have had all these years."

Marlene looked embarrassed. "Whoa, wait a minute here! You can save the sex subject for your Daddy. He can better advise you in that area now that you're a full-grown man."

Malcolm cracked up. "Okay, I see your point. I guess it was easier for you to have those kinds of talks with me when I was younger."

Marlene had to laugh, too. "Yeah, but back then, you were the one trying not to hear me." Her expression turned serious. "I'm glad that you want a wholesome relationship like Jesse and I have, son, but you also need to know that it's hard work and you have to work at it every single day to maintain it. We've had some extremely tough times in our marriage, have been through the fire and the raging storms together, but our love for God, self, and each other got us through it all. Our ship has made it safely through life's choppy waters. We're coasting now, sailing on calm waters. We're happier than we've ever been in our lives and we're still in love. But the dark clouds and rainstorms could come again, without warning. So we have to be prepared."

"Boy, do I know how much you two are into each other! You can barely keep your hands off one another. I may not say this often enough, but I love you and Daddy so much, I love what you stand for. I love seeing the look of love in your eyes and feeling in spades the love you have for each other. I hope I can teach my kids the same valuable lessons you've taught me."

"We love you, too." Marlene cleared her throat to ease the emotion welling inside her. "Speaking of kids, Malcolm, I hope you'll be very careful with Keisha's darling babies. Zach and Zanari will be greatly impacted if you park yourself in their lives only to back away from them later. This isn't my business, but since you asked my opinion, I'm going to weigh in."

"I asked because I want to hear what you have to say, Mom. Don't start biting your tongue now. You never have before."

"Okay, here it is. Perhaps you should try doing things with Keisha that don't include the kids, for now. Like you've already said, you can't predict the outcome. Those innocent babies *will* get attached to you if you're around them on a regular basis. Make no mistake about it. They are young and impressionable and their own daddy is away right now. Until you know for sure where you and Keisha are headed, please don't add to their grief by blowing in and out of their lives on a whim. That's all I ask of you in this instance. Is that too much to ask?"

"I hear what you're saying. I feel it, too. I plan to give this situation a lot of thought before I jump in any deeper. Thanks, Mom, for the great advice. That's why I come to you. Sorry I didn't discuss this with you sooner. I know you already know about me being at Keisha's apartment the night Rosalinda got hurt. Keisha told me you knew."

Marlene grinned. "You wouldn't have heard a thing from me on the matter if you hadn't brought it up. I admit to being a little shocked when I first heard Keisha mention it. But that's only natural for a mother who's used to her son telling her everything. I understand that you're now a man. Just be careful. Being responsible in every aspect of life is what best defines the word 'man.' It is just another word if one doesn't take on all the serious responsibilities that come with manhood. Anyone can call himself a man, but without understanding what it truly means to be one and acting upon it, the word carries no weight whatsoever."

"Thanks, Mom, for more good advice. Love you."

"Love you, too, baby. Before you go, I have a confession to make. I've been very apprehensive about the possibility of you and Keisha getting romantically involved. It really bothered me for a short time. It was only after I did a lot of soul-searching that I realized I'd be okay with the relationship. I want you to know that you have my blessing and your Dad's."

Malcolm smiled broadly. "That means the world to me, Mom. I'll talk things over with Dad as soon as our schedules can accommodate it. While I intend to proceed with caution, I won't forget any of the advice you've given me."

"Son, whatever you decide for your life, please don't forget to go with God. Without Him, you will surely lose your way."

Chapter Six

Jesse was somewhat uncomfortable with Easton Chapelle, the young, medium-built, Caucasian man seated across from his desk in the pastor's study. Easton's steel-gray eyes were seething with something akin to hatred and his ash-blond hair was disheveled from constantly pushing his fingers maniacally through it. To say that he was resentful about his current situation would be an understatement. He had even expressed downright anger with his late mother for dying and leaving him the responsibility of raising his three-year-old son, Kyle, his own flesh and blood. Michael had told Jesse what he could expect, but Jesse hadn't imagined the session to be quite this intense. So much hate and anger coming from a man so young concerned Jesse.

Diana Harper, the child's mother, had so far received the full brunt of Easton's raging anger. Diana was locked up in prison for numerous crimes, including running money scams on men of wealth and power. The use and sell of illegal drugs, prostitution, and fraud were the worst of them. She was currently serving a five-year sentence, a repeat offender.

Easton was terribly upset about the prospect of having to raise

Kyle alone. Their son would be eight years old before Diana ever saw the light of day again.

"Now that you've told me your story, how can I help ease your situation, Mr. Chapelle?"

Easton glared at Jesse as though he were an enemy about to attack him. "I don't know that you can. I'm not so sure anyone can solve this mess. To be frank, had I been told you were an African American, I would never have come here."

Jesse thought that that was odd since the nearby communities surrounding the church—Inglewood, Fox Hills, Culver City, and upper-middle-class Ladera Heights—where Jesse resided were densely populated with African Americans from a variety of socio-economic backgrounds. The heavily populated African American communities of Crenshaw, Baldwin Hills, and View Park were also close by. In Jesse's opinion, that he might be a black man should've at least crossed Easton's mind. Michael Hernandez and Orin Mayberry were also men of color.

"Since I don't know how I should respond to that remark, I won't. But the facts are these: you are here and you have already told me your story. If my skin color bothered you so much, you didn't have to take the seat you're sitting in. No one put a gun to your head to make you stay or to talk about your issues. You're operating on free will. Am I getting through to you?"

Easton tossed Jesse a defiant look as he got to his feet. "I don't need to hear this crap from you. I'm out of here. I don't even like black people, especially you men. There's nothing no black man can do for me, anyway. You all can't even help yourselves. You got major problems within your own race. How do you think you're going to help someone out when you people can't even identify your own issues? If you could identify them, you wouldn't know what to do about them, 'cause you can't shake free of the slave mentality. It's easier to blame someone else for what ails you. On whose authority do you get off trying to counsel a white man?"

Wearing a silly grin on his face, Jesse rocked back in his chair, his eyes fixed directly on Easton. "God's authority, Mr. Chapelle. His instructions are all the power I need. You should try talking to Him some time. There's no doubt in my mind that He can solve your problems. In fact, He's the only one that can solve them. Just ask Him and then wait for the answer."

"Yeah, sure! I hear you. But I'm not accustomed to waiting on anyone, and I don't intend to start now. I guess you're going to try and convince me that God's a black man, too. Save your breath, old man. I'm not trying to hear you."

Jesse couldn't stop himself from laughing inwardly. This young man was making a downright fool of himself; Jesse knew there was nothing he could say to get Easton to stifle his ignorance. But he sure was going to try and make him stop and think about what he was saying. His racial views could get him hurt, or worse, killed, if he expressed them in the wrong forum.

The fact that Easton was still there and still talking, despite his unkind opinions of blacks, let Jesse know that the young man was crying out for help and that he didn't care where it came from, as long as he got it. Jesse saw that there was a very real chance to get through to Easton, and he wasn't going to pass up an opportunity to win yet another soul for Christ.

"I'm not going to try to convince you of anything, not in the state of mind you're in right now. However, when you have a little time, pick up the Bible and read the entire book of Revelations. You'll see that the descriptions given there are very fascinating indeed. Pay close attention to chapter 1:14-15."

Jesse picked up a flyer from his desk before he got to his feet. He then moved steadily toward Easton. When he came face-to-face with the young man, he handed him the flyer, surprised when he took it. "Please read it. I hope you'll consider joining us for this very worthwhile evening. You have a lot to say, and I think you should be heard. I won't pressure you, but I hope to see you at the first meeting. You just might get some of the answers you're looking for." Jesse extended his hand to Easton, which was totally ignored by the younger man.

"I wouldn't count on it if I were you." Without uttering another word, Easton turned on his heels and left the office.

Jesse blinked back his tears as he knelt down in front of the chair Easton had occupied, where he prayed fervently for the young man who was so full of anger and hate.

Up off his knees now, Jesse rushed to his desk and sat down. He then took out his notebook and began writing. "Unaccustomed to waiting," he wrote down on the paper. This was the second time he'd heard that phrase in a short period of time. The young police officer was the first person he'd heard it from. Unwilling to wait indicated a state of impatience to Jesse.

Saul once again came to Jesse's mind. His next thought was of Sarah.

Keisha was all smiles when she opened the door and saw Tammy Arnold standing there. Keisha had met Tammy, who was just one of the many women Zach had scammed and used for his personal gain, when both of them had shown up at the same time to visit Zach at the prison. That was when Keisha learned that Zach had been putting singles ads in the newspapers. Tammy had answered his ad. After several letters had passed between them, Tammy had begun to visit him. Zach had never bothered to mention to Tammy that he had a girlfriend and two kids.

Keisha had to do a double take. Tammy was much thinner than she'd been the last time Keisha had seen her, only a couple of months back. Tammy also looked all bright-eyed and bushy-tailed. Keisha noticed that her dark brown hair was now cut in a shorter style and highlighted with shades of bold copper; she liked the new look. Her lovely face was even prettier now that it was thinner—and she still had that warm, friendly smile. Tammy's style of dress was somewhat provocative, but Keisha saw that she appeared very confident in her new look.

The two young women warmly embraced before Keisha led Tammy into the living room where they sat down on the sofa. It was rare for Keisha to have a weekend free, but since she hadn't been running out to the prison as frequently in the last few months, she had more time for herself. Lucian and her new boyfriend, Thomas Gleason, had taken the kids for the weekend.

Keisha was now glad that she had changed her mind about visiting Zach today. Their last few phone conversations had been quite volatile, so it was probably for the best. During the course of the last call, Zach had hurt her deeply by calling her all kinds of names. The vulgarity had come when he hadn't been able to accept Keisha's decision to not let him come live with her. Zach had thrown everything in the book at her, all that Malcolm had told her Zach would.

As Keisha and Tammy took a few minutes to catch up on things, Keisha complimented Tammy on her weight loss, the new style of clothing, and the dramatic changes in her hair, telling her that she really looked great. Tammy thanked Keisha and then politely inquired of what was happening with her college courses and her job. Keisha was proud to reveal all.

"Would you like something to drink, Tammy?"

Tammy smiled sweetly. "Thanks, but I'm fine. Just had a Diet Coke on the way over here. Too much caffeine makes me crazy." Tammy suddenly realized how quiet it was. "Hey, where are the kids? It just dawned on me that they haven't come out of their rooms."

"They're with Zach's mom. I know you stay as busy as I do, Tammy, so what brings you over here today, besides the fact that we haven't seen each other in a couple of months?"

"Yeah, I know. I've just been thinking about you. Have you heard from Zach?"

A red flag went up for Keisha. "Zach! Why are you asking about him? Are you still in contact with him?"

Tammy entwined her fingers, looking nervous. "I got a letter from him a few days ago, followed up by a phone call." Tammy gulped hard. "Keisha, he's asking if he can come live with me until he gets on his feet. He's really desperate to get a permanent address in order to get paroled. Why isn't he coming here to stay with you and the kids?"

Keisha blew out an uneven stream of breath. That Zach had had the nerve to try and push himself back into Tammy's life surprised her, but it also let her know the depth of his desperation. "Tammy, he can't come here until he proves himself. I don't want to take care of a grown man, and I can't afford to feed another mouth, not on a regular basis."

"But, Keisha, he's the children's father. That seemed so important to you at one time."

"It still is. But I've changed, and I don't want to go back to where I was with Zach. He totally disrespected me in so many ways. I let him walk all over me in the past. If given half a chance, he'll do it again. In fact, he already has, after I told him he couldn't stay here. The fact that he's contacted you tells me that he hasn't changed. That took a lot of nerve on his part."

"Keisha, he needs a place to stay if he's going to get paroled. How can he prove himself to you from behind bars? He told me that he only needs a temporary situation."

"Yeah, that's what he says until he gets all settled in. If I let him through that front door for one measly night, he's going to park his butt up in here until he's ready to move it. That's the way it'll be. Trust me. Zach has a long way to go before he gets it, if he ever does."

"He only asked me for a month."

Keisha sharply raised an eyebrow. "Are you telling me that you're actually considering Zach's request to come live with you?"

Tammy nodded in the affirmative. "The brother needs a little help, Keisha. I wouldn't have to consider it if you'd just give him another chance."

Keisha was extremely disturbed, but she fought hard not to show it. Another bailout was the last thing Zach needed. One month would lead to two months and so on and so on. Was it her place to try and get Tammy to see that Zach needed to stand on his own two feet? He'd have no choice but to do the halfway house if everyone stayed out of it and let him do his own thing. He would never become a man if everyone kept acting like his momma. "Tammy, you do what's best for you. I advise against him coming to your place, but that's not my decision to make."

"Will I lose your friendship if I let him come live with me, Keisha?"

Keisha wrung her hands together. "Where's Zach going to sleep, Tammy?"

Tammy looked as if she was highly offended. "In the guest room! Where else?"

"Just asking. You two were once talking about a baby. I see no reason why we can't stay friends. But if Zach starts acting up, and you can't find a way to get rid of him, please don't bring the drama to me. I want nothing to do with it; don't want to know anything about anything that might go down in your house after he comes there to live. Is that understood, Tammy?"

Unable to believe her ears, Tammy appeared shocked. "Have you fallen out of love with Zach? If so, I can't believe it! Zach won't be able to believe it either."

Keisha shook her head. "No, but I have fallen in love with someone else. Myself. Since I'm still learning how to put God first, Zach will soon be running a distant fifth in my life."

"Sounds a little cold-blooded to me, Keisha."

"I can see why you'd think that. What was cold-blooded was my neglecting my children and their needs to see that Zach's wants were met. As far as I'm concerned, Zach's books can remain empty from now until hell freezes over, but my babies' bellies will always be full. Zach has to face reality sooner or later. I've done a complete one-eighty. When it comes down to the welfare of my kids and me, I'll be as hard-nosed as I need to be. My kids and I come first."

"You have made some serious changes. I'm proud of you." Tammy covered Keisha's hand with hers. "Keisha, you know I have a soft heart, although some people see me as a fool. Many folks take my kindness for weakness. I know now that I'm not a fool, nor am I weak. It took me a while to figure it all out, but I'm just a large person with a big heart. If I can do something to help change the course of someone's life, I just have to do it. I don't worry about the outcome until it happens. My grandmother was the same way. She taught me that you have to give it away to keep it. I'm going to help Zach. If he doesn't come correct with me, that will be on him not me. I just think he needs another chance to get it right. I really believe that he wants to change and do the right thing by his family."

"I hope so. If not, I hope it doesn't come at your expense, Tammy. You are a good person and you have to live your life the way you see best. That's why I have to continue to live my life for me. Zach may very well have a place in my life again. I don't know. But should that occur, he has to be the one to fit in with my lifestyle. He will be the one who has to adapt. I wish you the best of luck in trying to reform him. Because I failed at it doesn't mean that you will."

"Thanks for the encouraging remarks, Keisha. I only want to be of help."

"You're welcome, Tammy."

Tammy began telling Keisha about all the things happening in her life. Her beauty salon was so successful that she'd opened up another one on the other side of Inglewood. She had rented out the booths to stylists who already had a heavy clientele list. Though she had hired an experienced stylist to manage the second shop, she still ran back and forth between the two salons on a regular basis. She also made extra money by selling to her clients the finest in beauty products. Tammy believed in staying on top of her own business affairs. She told Keisha that nothing went on in her shops that she didn't know about. Before opening her second salon, Tammy had gone back to school to brush up on accounting in order to stay on top of her books.

Keisha filled Tammy in on her latest job promotion and the new college courses she was taking. Keisha liked Tammy as much as she had in the beginning, if not more. But she was concerned. For Tammy to even consider Zach coming to live with her told Keisha that vulnerability might still rule Tammy's heart. It was true that she was a great person with a big heart, but Keisha was still frightened. Low self-esteem was always easy to identify. No one knew that better than she did. Low self-esteem was what had allowed Zach to manipulate her while making her believe she couldn't do any better than him for a man. Well, she could do better, and from here on out she would entertain only what was best for her and the children.

Could Zach still manipulate Tammy into doing his bidding despite how badly he'd treated her? How many times had she herself gone back to him under the same circumstances? There were too many times for her to have kept records of. All it proved was that Zach had made fools out of numerous females. Well, there was one fool that he'd just have to cut off his list, Keisha cited inwardly. Keisha Reed would no longer be a fool for one Zachary Martin.

Keisha couldn't hold against Tammy anything that she was about to do to help Zach achieve his parole, but she wasn't going to allow Tammy to hold her responsible if Zach messed her over again. However, if Zach actually accepted the help he'd asked Tammy to give him, Keisha would know exactly where he was coming from and that nothing about him had changed.

His asking Tammy for help had been bad enough, but accepting it would be the worst thing he could do under the circumstances. Zach's real test of character was coming very soon.

Marlene sat quietly in her kitchen listening intently to what Yvonne Carter had to say. With tears streaming down her honey-brown face, Yvonne's hands shook each time she put the coffee cup to her mouth. Marlene saw the fear in the younger woman's hazel eyes as she talked about her husband, Samuel, threatening her with filing for a divorce. He'd told his wife that he could no longer take the arrests and the embarrassment that came with her kleptomania. Samuel had also asked her to relinquish custody of the children to him without a court battle. He didn't want them raised in a home where they were subject to Yvonne's out-of-control disease. Samuel didn't ever want his children to actually see their mother getting arrested. That would change who they were forever, not to mention the hurt they'd no doubt experience.

Yvonne had pleaded no contest in the criminal offense, which had helped her to garner two years of probation. She was also ordered to seek counseling once a week for twelve weeks. Once that was completed, the judge would call a probation hearing to check on her progress.

Yvonne brushed her tears away. "I don't want to lose my family, Sister Covington. I love them dearly. I've been with Samuel all my adult life. If he leaves me, I don't know what I'll do. I've never been anything but a housewife. How will I live without him there to take care of things? I don't have any money saved, and I don't have any special skills to speak of."

Marlene felt awful for Yvonne and it showed in her painful expression. "No matter what happens between you and Samuel, Yvonne, you can't forget that God will take care of you. The reasons you cited as to why you couldn't make it without your husband are the very things I counsel young women on all the time. A housewife and a mother are the most respectable jobs a woman can have. However, there are times when those important jobs don't seem to quite measure up to other professions, especially when faced with the sort of dilemma you're now finding yourself in. As for your skills, I beg to differ. You have a lot to offer."

Yvonne stared at Marlene in disbelief. "Like what?"

"I can easily recollect how you filled in for the church secretary when she was out on disability for two months. Computer literacy is a significant skill. It also takes a special person to handle all those phone lines at the church. You did both of those jobs with ease. I shouldn't have to remind you of how well you work out in the nursery when called upon as a temporary fill-in."

Marlene paused a moment, pondering how to express her thoughts to Yvonne without offending her. She was considering that perhaps Yvonne needed something more in her life than what she currently had. With the kids now old enough to be in school all day, Yvonne just might have too much time on her hands. Boredom could bring about a lot of unsavory thoughts and actions, which could all come down to an idle mind being the devil's workshop.

Despite the fact that kleptomania was considered a medical disease, Yvonne's problem with shoplifting could be a direct result of sheer monotony. Although Yvonne had had the same problems with stealing when her children were just babies, she could've suffered with boredom then, too, and possibly even depression. All babies did for the first several months of their lives was eat, sleep, and soil their diapers, though motherhood was still a tough job to reckon with.

"Have you ever thought of going back to school or possibly working part time?"

Yvonne looked at Marlene like she'd spoken in a foreign language. "School, job! I'm too old to go back to school. As far as a job is concerned, who would hire me?"

"You're never too old to go back to school, Yvonne, but you have to want to do it. I'm sure Reverend Jesse can find something for you to do at the church part-time. If no opportunities exist there, I can help you find a job somewhere else if you decide that's what you should do."

"I don't know. It sounds like that would give Samuel more of a reason to divorce me."

Marlene looked puzzled. "How so?"

"If he thinks I can take care of myself financially, he won't feel obligated to stay with me. Having an income would just give him another excuse to walk out on me."

Marlene shook her head in dismay. "Oh, Yvonne, that is some terribly misguided thinking. You never want a man to feel obligated to you. If he's going to stay in the home, it should be because he loves you and wants to make the marriage work. Never do you want a man to stay with you because he feels duty-bound. Deep resentment will well up inside both of you if that were to happen. If Samuel is considering divorcing you, getting a job will show him that you're asserting independence and that you're willing to do whatever it takes to take care of yourself. That can only gain you his respect."

"You and Sister Jacobson are housewives, too. Neither of you work outside the home."

While thinking of all the duties she had inside and outside of the home, as well as the numerous church social events she headed up, Marlene had to laugh at that. Myrna had only been a housewife for about three years. "I only worked for the federal government for over two decades, Yvonne. Myrna retired from her profession, but she keeps her nursing license current."

Yvonne put her hand to her mouth. "Oh, I darn near forgot about your government career. Did you work long enough to get a pension?"

Marlene nodded. "I'm fully vested in the retirement plan, just need to meet my age requirement. I may not have a steady, paying job now, but I do work outside of the home. I also make a tidy little sum on the patchwork quilts and the various other arts and crafts I create and sell. Volunteering here and there and everywhere is almost like having a real job. Different hospitals and other agencies depend on me for the number of hours I commit to them each month. I also help Jesse run numerous errands to help meet our senior church members' needs."

Marlene leaned forward in her seat. "I've been tiptoeing around what I need to say here, but I'm going to go ahead and spell it out for you. I don't think you have enough to keep you busy, Yvonne. I believe you may be bored stiff. That might be part of your serious problem."

Marlene continued to listen to Yvonne as she gave one tired excuse after another as to why she shouldn't or couldn't get a job. Even Marlene's suggestion of volunteer work didn't go over very well with her. It seemed that Yvonne's main objective was to stay dependent on Samuel versus learning to depend on herself. For Yvonne to compare her situation with that of the other two women hadn't made sense to Marlene. There was no comparison. She and Myrna were two of the busiest women in their circle of friends and acquaintances. Marlene and Myrna were constantly active. Yvonne wasn't. Until Yvonne decided to change her circumstances, Marlene knew there wasn't anything she could do to help her out.

"Why do you think it's important for a woman to be independent? Isn't that what causes a lot of marriages to fail?"

"Because of the very situation you're in right now. I vowed a long time ago to never totally depend on anyone but God, never to solely depend on someone else for my livelihood. I have to keep my business skills honed. If I had to go back to work tomorrow, part- or full-time, I'm prepared. My investments and skills are what kept me out of the poorhouse when Jesse was incarcerated. It's true that the church members assisted by raising funds for his defense and appeal process, but I would've found a way to take care of it alone, had it come down to that."

Yvonne eyed Marlene with curiosity. "You didn't answer the part about the marriages breaking down."

"That may very well be the case in some marriages. There are just some men who can't handle women who are independent and can make it without them. There are also some very controlling women, those who like the men to be dependent on them. However, there are both men and women who can put all that foolishness aside and work together in achieving their goals. If they want their marriage to survive, it won't matter who makes what. The key is doing it together, creating a balance."

Yvonne looked puzzled. "How do you create a balance?"

Marlene rubbed her hands together as she thought of how to answer the question in the simplest way. "Let me give you a few examples, Yvonne. Jesse's strengths are my weaknesses and his weaknesses are my strengths. Jesse could care less about finances and interest rates and all, but that is one of my major strengths. He loves to work in the garden and plant vegetables and flowers and watch them grow. That's something I could care less about."

"What about cooking, Sister Covington?"

"He likes to cook way more than I do, but we share that particular duty. Jesse also takes care of the heavier household chores like washing windows, scrubbing floors, and cleaning the bathrooms. I do the lighter chores, like dusting, running the vacuum, and washing the clothes. We normally do the dishes together. Then there are all the other things we have in common: all kinds of sports, travel to exotic places, sharing romantic evenings together, only to name a few. Our marriage is well balanced. We also allow each other to have our own space when it's needed. Giving a person his or her space is something we all should be very mindful of."

Tears pooled in Yvonne's eyes. "Sounds like a great recipe for maintaining a strong marriage." Yvonne looked down at the palms of her hands, as if she could find the answers within the numerous lines. Her hands appeared to be much older than she was in age. Born of years of housework, Yvonne's hands were dry and cracked. She felt as old and as cracked as her hands looked. The sadness in her watery eyes was darn near tangible.

"Samuel never encouraged me to work. He likes being the head of the household, just like his father and grandfather did. After hearing what you've said, I think he likes me being dependent on him for everything; it might make him feel manlier. I just don't know, Sister Covington. I have always tried to please him, but it appears that I've failed him somehow."

Marlene sucked her teeth quietly, careful not to show her displeasure. The last thing Marlene wanted to do was alienate Yvonne and make her think she was judging her. This young woman was emotionally fragile, and Marlene had to somehow help her to shore up her self-esteem. Yvonne was too young to give up on herself and her children. She could make it without Samuel if it came down to that, but she had to be there for herself in order to keep from losing her mind to the stresses that came with the possibility of starting her life all over again.

Without Samuel to lean on, Marlene had to convince Yvonne that she could make it if she had to. However, Marlene had high hopes that this union wouldn't end in divorce. She would do all that was humanly possible to keep that from occurring. Counseling Yvonne was a great way to start. Marlene made a mental note to have Jesse talk to Samuel about getting counseling.

"Who you've failed is yourself, young lady. It's easy for us to take someone else's inventory instead of taking our own. We're too busy trying to figure out what are the problems of others when we should be looking inside ourselves for the answers to our own issues. We can only fix ourselves. Have you even talked to Samuel about any of this stuff?"

"I guess I've assumed everything I just shared. I've never discussed any of it with him."

"You should try doing that right away. Then you have to figure out exactly what's missing from your life. It's never too late to realize your dreams, but you first have to know what they are. Do you have any dreams for yourself, Yvonne? What are your aspirations?"

Yvonne laughed softly, which softened her facial expression. Twinkles of light appeared to be back in her eyes for now. "I've always wanted to be a beautician. I love fooling around with hair. It drives my Sarah wild to have me mess in her head, but she always likes the final outcome. I'd also like to learn to play the piano. I do get bored being at home all by myself while the kids are at school and Samuel's at work. Do you really think I can fulfill my dreams?"

"Wholeheartedly. But the belief has to come from you. If you believe it, that's all there is to it. I can help you if you want me to. I can have my little friend, Keisha Reed, talk to her friend who's a successful beautician. Maybe she can help steer you in the right direction. We'll also check out all the local cosmetology schools. And Sister Wylie will be glad to teach you to play the piano. To have you as a music student would tickle her pink. She's the one who taught me to play. Are my plans for trying to get you started on the right path okay with you?"

Yvonne grinned. "I think I'd like to check everything out. Maybe doing something creative might help me to cope with all my numerous stresses. Thanks, Sister Covington."

"You're welcome. Glad to be of assistance. God will guide us the rest of the way."

Eric Eldridge looked at Cicely Kirkland as though he couldn't understand why someone so beautiful and vibrant had practically destroyed her life. He once loved the texture and the glossy sheen of her wavy almond-brown hair, but now it was drab and dry with numerous split ends. He missed the sparkle that used to be in her sable-brown eyes.

Cicely had had everything going for her at one time. Then some jerk, a so-called female friend, had introduced her to cocaine. It hadn't taken Cicely long to lose herself in white-powdered dreams. Now she was just a rail-thin shell, only a fraction of her old self.

He locked his gaze on to hers. "Why didn't you tell me you were pregnant, Cicely?"

To hide her surprise at his comment, Cicely allowed her eyes to toss him a dagger-sharp glance. It didn't take her a moment of thought to figure out how he'd found out. She would deal with her best friend later. Destiny Powell would get an earful. Her anger with Eric was written all over her face. Her body language was telling him that she was uncomfortable with him being there, even somewhat embarrassed by it. Eric had seen her behind bars before, but never in the horrid condition she was in now. He hated seeing her looking so pathetic and terribly unhappy.

She tore off a piece of her fingernail with her teeth. "Who says I'm pregnant, anyway?"

It wouldn't surprise him one bit if Cicely had been able to score some coke while in jail. She, in fact, looked high to him. She was very resourceful when it came to keeping up her habit. When she could no longer afford the white powder that sent her into orbit, she had immediately switched to the crack pipe. She was well aware that she looked skinny, haggardly, and totally burned-out. That's because she was tired and worn out all the time from lack of sleep. Cicely had been sleeping fitfully from the first moment she'd spent the night as a guest of the state.

Though she played tough and hard, and had been in and out of the system a time or two, Cicely was scared stiff of her own shadow. She knew by heart the role she had to play to survive. The difference in Cicely's old lifestyle and her new one was as different as night and day.

"Don't be coy, Cicely. This is not a fool you're talking to."

"Really? You could've fooled me."

"Sarcasm is always your way out of a tight spot, isn't it? Could you please answer my question?" He gripped the edge of the table so hard that his knuckles turned colors.

"You seem to already have the answer."

He blew out a ragged breath. If he were a different sort of man, it would be so easy for him to shake her like a rag doll, shake her until she came back to reality. "I guess I shouldn't have expected this visit to be any different from the ones on previous lockdowns. If you don't want me to come here, why is my name still on the visiting list?"

"Just in case."

He narrowed his eyes in anger. "Of what?"

"I need something. Like you've said numerous times, I only come running to you when I need something."

He lowered his head to the table for a brief moment. It was all he could do to keep from crying his heart out. He'd never felt more frustrated with her than he did right now. If only he could walk away from her and never look back. He thought he had accomplished that; then he'd learned from Destiny that Cicely carried his child.

Many of his personal friends had asked him how could he be sure that it was his baby. His response had come swift and with certainty. Cicely was a drug addict, not a tramp. He couldn't even entertain the thought of her being a wayward woman. Just the thought of her with another man would bring about such excruciating pain for him. Still, Eric Eldridge wasn't a complete fool. He wasn't foolish enough not to have a DNA test performed once the child was born. Paternity would be proved one way or the other. For now he was content in holding on to the belief that Cicely Kirkland carried his child, his only offspring.

As painful as it was for him, Eric made eye contact with her again. "Are we that far apart emotionally, Cicely? Having a child together should bring about some sort of change for you. I know it has changed me, has changed the way I feel about our situation."

Her eyes grew bright with surprise. "How?"

"It has changed my way of thinking. I now want to try and help you get straight again."

Her glare was cold and hard. "Because I'm pregnant?"

"In part, yes. But, Cicely, I've never stopped caring about you. I just couldn't deal with the destructive behavior any longer. In my profession, I couldn't stand by and allow you to sell drugs from my home or use them there. You know you were dead wrong in doing that."

The coldness melted in her eyes. Shame replaced the icy glare. "That's over and done with. I'm paying the price for it. You helped see to that." The wintry look returned to her eyes.

"As I said before, time and time again, I'm not taking the fall for your crimes, Cicely."

"Yeah, I know. I've heard it all before, just like you've stated. I'm sorry I disappointed you so badly."

"You should be sorry for disappointing yourself. You've done far more damage to yourself than you've ever done to me. I have my freedom, Cicely. What about you?"

"That was cruel."

"Factual is what it is. Believe it or not, I want you to be free, too, in more ways than one. I also want you to be drug free."

"Well, I am that. Contrary to what people think, there are no drugs in this facility. Usually when people start a sentence with 'believe it or not' they're normally lying. Are you?"

"I'm not lying to you." He didn't believe that she wasn't lying to him about getting drugs in the facility, though. His experience as a police officer led him to believe she was high on something. "I'm trying to tell you how I feel about this situation. I don't want you to place our child in foster care after he or she is born. That wouldn't be fair to any of us."

"What isn't fair is my being locked up like this. I need help, not jail. I'm not a criminal, Eric. I'm an addict."

"Recreational drug use is one thing, though still a crime. When you start selling illegal substances to maintain your habit, you committed a serious criminal offense, a major felony. The child, Cicely, what are we going to do about the child?"

She rolled her eyes in dramatic fashion. "All of a sudden it's 'we.' All I heard from you before is 'I. I could lose my job. I want you out of my house. I can't take this anymore.' Glad to learn that you've added a new word to your vocabulary. I guess that's a good thing."

Her sarcasm had always bit hard into his resolve. She had become so nasty, even nastier on drugs. The use of drugs always changed who she was. Cicely was a perfect stranger when under the influence of alcohol and illegal substances. Out of all the talks they'd had over her habit, he still didn't know why she'd started using in the first place. If she would just open up to him about it, he thought they could conquer it. Whatever got her started on drugs was the key to her eventually getting clean and sober. Keeping silent on the matter was slowly killing her.

He got to his feet. "I'm going to go now. Your mood is getting funkier by the minute. Please think about what I've said. I'd like to take custody of our child without having to fight you for the right to do so."

"All neat and tidy, right, Eric?"

"That's how I like it. It's easier that way. I'll wait to hear from you."

"Keep an oxygen mask handy. You just might have one hell of a wait if you're planning on holding your breath."

"Perhaps. I'm patient enough to wait on your decision. You don't have too many options in front of you."

His smugness was really getting to her. She thought him to be arrogant beyond understanding, yet she couldn't help wondering how they'd gotten to where they were. They'd been so happy in the beginning. The more Cicely thought about the past two years she'd spent with him, the more she seethed inwardly. There would come a day when she'd have enough courage to tell Eric that he was responsible for all her problems. Until that day came, she wasn't about to let him have any peace, or have the last word. He had injured her deeply, and she needed to hit back with a vengeance. Arming herself with just the right weapon, Cicely wanted nothing more than to bring him down to his knees.

"What makes you so sure that the baby I'm carrying is yours, Officer Eric Eldridge?"

Chapter Seven

Lying flat on her back in bed, looking up at the ceiling, Keisha nibbled on the tips of her fingernails. Darkness had fallen and she was grateful that the kids had gone to bed tonight without incident. Little Zach and Zanari were good at fighting sleep and hated to have her announce bedtime. They often begged for a few more minutes of television or they'd begin asking for something to eat or drink and anything else they could think of to delay the inevitable.

Keisha closed her eyes for a brief moment. As she refocused her gaze on the ceiling, her smile beamed radiantly. "Hello, Father, it's me, your eternal daughter, your fairly new friend, Keisha. I've mostly prayed with my head and within my heart, but I'm gonna pray out loud today. Mizz Marlene told me that it's okay to converse with you like I was talking to a friend. I've never tried it like that before now, wasn't sure if it was respectful, so I hope it's okay."

While fingering the pillowcase, Keisha thought about what she'd say next. Prayer was only two years new for her. Lately it had become a constant force in her life. When she forgot to pray, she could always tell; those days usually turned out to be crummy ones.

"I know I should make more time for us to communicate, but I stay so busy. That's a weak excuse, I know, but it's the truth. I

127

should never be too busy for you 'cause you're never that way with me. You always seem to have time to hear me out. Thanks for that."

Keisha remembered Marlene telling her that God's ears were always open to His children and that He never tired of hearing them calling His name. She was happy for that, since she'd been calling His name a lot lately. "Father, I need some sort of sign about Zach. Am I wrong for not letting him stay here? I already know how you feel about unmarried people living together. But is it wrong for me to let him stay here if he sleeps in the room with the kids, especially if he's really trying to change? Marlene told me that you have the power to change the worst into the very best. I know that for sure. Look how much you've changed me."

Keisha fought her tears. Just the thought of how far she'd come often made her emotions erupt. Before knowing God, she'd been totally lost. No God, no peace. Know God, know peace; just something else that Marlene had taught her. Marlene was good for her and the kids. That had been proven time and time again. Keisha didn't want to imagine where she might be without her.

Keisha smiled as a powerful image of Malcolm's handsome face popped into her head. Their friendship was still growing by leaps and bounds. Malcolm never failed to come to her aid when she called on him. Just like Marlene, he was a true-blue friend. She frowned slightly when she thought about them becoming more than friends. Was the potential for such really there?

She looked upward again. "Then there's the little issue of Malcolm and me, Father. Am I sending him mixed signals? Where do you see our relationship going? Is it insane for us to get romantically involved? I have asked you numerous questions, and I have so many more, but I think I should wait until you answer these before I throw anything else at you. Father, thanks for listening to me again. I'm going to try to be still while I wait for your answers."

Before Keisha could voice a hearty amen, a knock on the door interrupted her private prayer time. It was kind of late for visitors and she wasn't expecting anyone, she mused, looking over at the clock to see the exact time. Noticing that it was just a little before nine, she shrugged. Before going into the hallway, she slipped on a pair of jeans. While remembering the night she'd opened the door to Malcolm, barely dressed, she cracked up. The thought of it being Malcolm on the other side of the door sobered her quickly, causing her pulse to accelerate.

A peek through the security window revealed a nervous-looking Rosalinda. Wondering why Rosalinda hadn't used their special code for knocking when visiting each other, Keisha removed the locks and opened the door. A couple of warm hugs and animated greetings passed between the two friends before Keisha ushered Rosalinda into the living room.

Keisha plopped down on the sofa. "What are you doing out by yourself, Rosalinda, especially so late?" Keisha reached over and gently touched Rosalinda's hand, glad to see her.

Rosalinda sat down in the chair. "I'm not by myself. Michael brought me here. He'll be back to get me. While we were on our way to have a late dinner, he got an emergency call from one of his clients. Instead of me going down to the jail with him, I asked if he'd mind dropping me off here until he was through. The police precinct is located in this area. I should've called you first, but I didn't think about it until I was at the door."

"You looked kind of nervous when I looked out the security window. Are you okay?"

"Not knowing where Ricardo is keeps me on edge. He's bound to pop up sooner or later. Michael did walk me to the door. He didn't leave until you opened up. He said to tell you hello."

"Tell Michael I said hey! I can't believe they haven't caught that boy. They're probably not putting a lot of effort into finding him. They know it's just a matter of time before he slips up and ends up in custody again. Ric is no different from all the other repeat offenders. He can't stay out of trouble, and it looks as if he doesn't even want to try anymore."

Rosalinda scowled. "Let's change the subject, okay? He's on my mind enough as it is. I stay so worried because of him. But listen to this. I had to run an errand for Michael today in Beverly Hills. I later stopped off at the post office there. You'll never guess who I ran into."

"Alexis? She's the only person that we know of who might hang out in that area."

Rosalinda laughed. "I guess you're right about that. The girl was looking hot, and she has a date tonight. Someone she knows from her hometown. He's coming to dinner at her place."

Keisha howled. "That means Marietta's putting in overtime. I'm sure Alexis is getting her to cook the meal. Alexis still can't boil water, and she thinks she's too cute to try. Despite her trifling ways, I've learned to love her. Speaking of water, what about something cold to drink?"

Rosalinda got to her feet. "I'll go into the kitchen with you. I'm starving. You have anything to snack on? No telling when Michael will get back. Both of us were very hungry."

"I know we can rustle up something good. I just did my weekly grocery shopping."

While walking around in the kitchen, Keisha smiled inwardly, covertly studying Rosalinda, whose expressions carried all the tell-tale signs of being in love. Her dark eyes were soft and moist, wide with intrigue and wonder. Her nut-brown complexion was rosy with a blushing innocence, a dew-kissed appearance. The soft smile she wore on her full lips showed that she was somewhat content. Other than Ricardo being on the loose, wreaking periods of havoc in her life, Rosalinda looked as if everything else was right with her world.

Keisha set down two cold sodas on the table, along with a chip and dip bowl of Lays potato chips. A creamy onion dip accompanied the salty snack. She then went back to the counter and retrieved a small platter of cheese, crackers, and Vienna sausages.

Keisha finally pulled out a chair from the table and sat down. "So, Rosalinda, have you given Michael any yet?"

Rosalinda nearly choked on the small amount of drink in her mouth. "There you go again, trying to be all up in my personal business!" Rosalinda smiled softly. "You know something, Keisha? It's not like that with us."

"Just how is it between you two, my beautiful friend?"

"It's something very special. I admit that there's a strong physical attraction between us, but we're hoping to build something together that will last long past the bedroom antics. What's been happening in our relationship is so sweet and tender."

Keisha felt like crying happy tears. She was ecstatic for Rosalinda. "I'm thrilled for you. I want to hear more. The dreamy look in your lovely, dark eyes is exquisite."

Rosalinda's eyes glazed over as she thought back on the numerous days and evenings she'd spent in Michael's loving presence. A considerate and honorable man was he. Though he still talked of feeling guilty over the unsavory proposal he'd made to her, Rosalinda had put the unfortunate incident completely out of her mind. Michael was so much more than what that proposal had been indicative of. He never failed to make her smile. Constantly, he told her how special she was to him and how much she deserved to have everything her heart desired.

Blushing all over, Rosalinda looked up at Keisha. "There's not a lot more to tell. We're really getting to know each other without all the pressure of sex and other intimate acts. We've shared a few passionate kisses, but we've ventured no further than that. He's such a romantic. Loves to buy me roses and enjoys doing everything by candlelight, even watching television. He likes to read poetry to me, loves to weave all sorts of romantic sagas for us to enjoy. I have never had these kinds of wonderful experiences, ever. It's often overwhelming. I feel like royalty."

Keisha looked spellbound. "You are royalty! Oh, I can't help wondering what it would feel like to have a man treat me like his queen."

Rosalinda giggled. "It's unexplainable. The feeling is indescribable. I wish Mommy could see the transformation in me. I find my-self smiling all the time, day and night. I giggle and act silly quite often at work. Sometimes I feel out of control with happiness. My coworkers surely think I'm crazy. Michael doesn't hide his feelings for me at work, though I wish he did."

"So what if he wants everyone to know? You are both crazy. Crazy in love." Keisha reached for her best friend's hand again. "Do you love him, Rosalinda?"

Rosalinda placed her free hand over her heart. "I honestly can't think of another name for what I feel. I believe I do love Michael. But my feelings for him only came after I learned to love me. I hope you'll one day find what I've found. I hope that Alexis will also find love again."

Keisha sighed hard. "How nice would that be for all of us? Then there's Zach! Ugh."

Looking scrumptiously debonair in his impeccably creased, dark dress slacks, a form-fitting body shirt, and a camel-colored double-breasted blazer, Jarreau pulled out Alexis's chair. Before seating himself directly across from her, he waited for her to get comfort-able. His nostrils were filled with the delicious scents of the food spread out before them. Jarreau wasn't sure if Alexis prepared the meal herself. Though he doubted it, since she'd instantly become R.J's pampered brat. But he was surely going to enjoy it. The Cajun-style foods had his mouth watering.

Alexis looked quite delectable, too; another dish he wouldn't mind sampling. Dressed in simple white elegance, consisting of a sheer halter-top and crepe pants flaring slightly at the hemline, Alexis was always the epitome of class. It was obvious by her golden glow that she'd been in the sun. A slender diamond choker graced her neck, and she also wore large diamond studs in her ears. A horse would choke on the diamond rocks she wore on both her hands and the diamond bangle bracelet adorning her right wrist. Her perfume was sensuous, seductive.

"Should I go ahead and pass the blessing, Alexis?"

Alexis nodded. "By all means."

Jarreau had no problem in voicing his thanks to the Father above. His prayer was simple and humbling. His reverence for God came through clearly. Alexis stared at him in awe.

Alexis looked surprised when Jarreau reached across the table and picked up her plate. Using his fork as a pointer, he pointed to each food dish to see what she wanted. Before placing the selection on her plate, he waited for her nod of approval. Once her plate was filled, he passed it back to her. That he had fixed her plate utterly fascinated her, but that he'd consulted her on each dish made his gesture even more special. Jarreau had chalked up a few points for himself.

Alexis looked on as Jarreau then filled his own plate with small portions of all the dishes. Alexis thought a man his size would have an appetite requiring heaping helpings of everything. His moderate food portions were another surprise for her. But his physique *was* lean and solid.

She smiled broadly as he poured ice-cold lemonade into each of their glasses. "Thank you, Jarreau. That was so sweet of you. I like being waited on."

He smiled wryly. "I remember. All too well. My pleasure, Lex." He winked at her as he took his first bite, taking a moment to savor it. "Are you the chef? This jambalaya is divine."

Alexis grinned, wishing she had cooked the whole meal. "I can only take credit for helping out with this one. I'm not much of a cook. My housekeeper, Marietta Grainger, is the master chef around here. She knows how to put out a grand feast. You'll get to meet her."

"That's obvious from this huge spread on your dining room table. I'll look forward to meeting Marietta and complimenting her. Why don't you like to cook, Alexis?"

Alexis shrugged. "It's not that I don't like to cook; I've just never had to, at least not after I got married. R.J. insisted on hiring someone to take care of all our chores, domestic and otherwise. He made enough money, so he thought we should have a staff of people at our beck and call. As dirt poor as my family was, having people around to do anything and everything we needed was foreign to me, yet I adapted quite easily. R.J. thought we should have it all."

Alexis couldn't help thinking of how much it had been her desire to take care of her husband in the same way her mother had taken care of her father. Her high hopes of becoming a loving housewife and eventually a doting mother had come to an end rather quickly, only months after they'd married. All of her meager-but-exciting plans for building a life with her husband had been squashed beneath R.J.'s grandiose ideas for living a lavish lifestyle. Alexis's simple needs had gotten lost in his grand desires. Had R.J. lived, Alexis was sure they could've turned things around, as long as they had allowed God to come in as the head of the household.

Jarreau smiled smugly. "That sounds just like the R.J. I came to know." He looked at Alexis with a sober expression. "What really happened to R.J. in that prison? That is, if you don't mind talking about it. You touched on it the other day, but I sense there's a lot more."

"It's definitely not dinner conversation. Mind if we discuss it later, perhaps over coffee?"

Jarreau nodded, mindful of her feelings. "Fine with me. This is a huge place you have here. I guess it can get pretty lonely in a place this size, especially with you practically living here all alone. Your home dwarfs mine in every way. I'm sure your housekeeper has time off every week, which leaves you to your own devices. What do you do to keep busy, Alexis?"

Alexis looked pensive. "I hate to admit this, but I don't do much around here, Jarreau, other than eat and sleep. Scoping out the nearby malls is my favorite pastime, but I'm really learning how to cut back on my frivolous spending. Less shopping equates more downtime on Alexis's hands. Do I get bored? To tears. This hasn't been an easy two years for me."

Jarreau smiled sympathetically. "I can only imagine. Perhaps this year will be better."

"When you spend all your time living your life the way someone else designed it, you can become totally lost once that person is no longer there to direct your path. The death of a lifelong partner is difficult. I'm now trying to build a life around my needs, my likes, and my wants. It's not easy. I have a lot of fears about how to proceed. That slows me down. I also worry about being selfish in trying to live my life just for me. I often wish I could find something worthwhile to do to fill the void in my spirit. I just don't know what that something might be."

"You can come work with me on major fundraising campaigns. I think you might be good at it. You probably have a host of influential friends to reach out to. I am founder and president of BIC, Blacks In Crisis, a foundation that benefits blacks with serious medical issues. Lupus doesn't get nearly enough exposure in the African American communities. Sickle-cell anemia can never be overexposed. Bringing about AIDS awareness and finding effective treatment plans and a cure is a high priority for our agency. These diseases are all incurable. Statistics show that all of these maladies affect our people more than any other ethnic group."

Deeply interested in what Jarreau had to say, Alexis folded her hands and put them on the table. "I wonder why that is? Why are most of the diseases that mainly affect blacks incurable? It seems like a conspiracy to me. The diseases that affect mostly whites seem to get most of the attention in our so-called land of equal opportunity and treatment."

"Thought provoking, huh?"

"Darn right it is! R.J. gave money to a host of charities, but I don't think he ever gave one single dime to benefit medical dilemmas that affect our people. If R.J. had lived, I believe that he would've changed his thinking in that area. He just wasn't informed."

Jarreau looked skeptical. "What makes you think he'd do that, Alexis?"

Smiling softly, Alexis lowered her lashes. "He had gotten saved before he died."

Jarreau's eyebrows shot up at a sharp angle. "R.J. got saved?"

Alexis chuckled. "Yeah, but why do you find that so hard to believe?"

"You already know the answer to that one. If you don't, you should. R.J. was one of the biggest devils out there in the world. He was never one to cloak his evil in sheep's clothing. I don't like speaking ill of the dead, but R.J. was a straight-up con man. You know that better than anyone, Alexis. You have only lived your entire adult life with him. How could you not know?"

Alexis's tearing eyes brewed with unleashed anger. "Maybe you should leave, Jarreau. I never thought you were the kind of person to insult a man in his own home."

Jarreau was clearly stunned by her anger, yet his expression was one of empathy. "The truth hurts like hell, doesn't it, Alexis?" He got to his feet. "Sorry I offended you. I'll go now."

She reached for Jarreau's hand. "No, don't go. Please stay. I'm being silly. I know exactly what R.J. was. I loved him regardless. No one knew him. He had a lot of goodness in him." Biting on her nails, she waited for Jarreau to sit back down. "Don't you think God has forgiven him? It seems to me that He actually put one of His saints through a lot to save R.J."

Jarreau looked perplexed as he thought about Alexis's statement. "What does all of that about one of His saints mean?"

Alexis went on to tell Jarreau how she believed that Jesse Covington had been imprisoned to save her husband from hell. Jarreau listened with keen interest as Alexis told him that she thought God released Jesse from prison just in time to preside over R.J.'s funeral.

"That's an incredible story, Alexis."

"Do you believe it could happen that way?"

"You obviously do. You sounded very passionate about your belief. To answer your question, most definitely. I believe it could happen just like that. God works in mysterious ways. He gets the job done anyway He can and uses anyone He so desires. I also believe R.J. was saved and that God has forgiven him. I'm sorry for being disrespectful to R.J.'s memory. Very sorry."

Out of the blue, Alexis began to cry. Her hard sobs caused her body to tremble. Jarreau instantly went down on bended knee in front of her, where he took her into his arms. The softness of her flesh overwhelmed him. His breath caught at how beautiful she looked, even in distress. A frown did little to mar Alexis's flawless beauty. His hand found his way up to her hair, where he ran his fingers through her short tresses. Her hair was as soft as a cloud, silky, too.

His hand moved downward, where he used his thumb pad to wipe away her tears. "You cry a lot, don't you, Alexis?" He caught the next teardrop with his lips.

"Enough tears to drown in," she sobbed brokenly.

"I bet you'd like to have the sunshine hurry up and come out in your heart again."

She nodded. "Desperately so."

"It will happen, then. In the meantime, you can borrow some of the sunshine from mine. Is that okay with you?"

Fresh tears plopped from her eyes. "A bright ray or two might be just what I need. Did you mean what you said about me coming to work for you on a fundraising committee?"

"Of course. Are you willing?"

"I'm willing to try anything about now. I think it might keep me from being so lonely."

"Only if you like the job. I think you should at least take a stab at it. It can be rewarding."

"I think you might be right. I'd love to find out." Smiling, she dried the last of her tears.

Alexis looked startled at the sound of the musical doorbell chimes. Visitors couldn't gain access to the house without using the front gate intercom. Deliveries were made at the back entrances. Marietta was out for the evening, so she'd have to get the door. Remembering she hadn't closed the inner gates made her realize it was her own negligence that had allowed someone to approach the house. She had no clue as to whom she'd find on the other side.

"Excuse me, Jarreau. I'll be right back, though I can't imagine who could be calling on me at this hour. I don't have anyone who visits me without letting me know."

"Maybe I should go to the door with you."

She gave his suggestion a second of thought. "I'll be okay. Make yourself comfortable."

Alexis panicked at seeing Mathis West standing before her. That he'd never been given the address to her home, nor had she ever invited him there, gave her a weird feeling. Of course he knew that she lived in Bel Air, because she'd told him that much. Had that been enough information for him to go on? How he had managed to get a hold of her exact address had her gravely concerned. The Internet instantly came to mind. The possible reasons for him putting himself through so much trouble to seek her out made her concern deepen.

Reluctant to hand her the roses that he had behind his back, Mathis shuffled his feet nervously. "Did I come at a bad time?"

Alexis couldn't believe his nerve. Her fingers itched to slap his arrogant face. "There is never a good time to visit me without calling first, Mathis. Phoning a person first is a sign of respect. It's not like we've ever been to each other's homes before."

Agitated with her rude remarks, Mathis narrowed his eyes. "You haven't returned my phone calls, numerous ones. I thought something might be wrong."

"Now that you know everything is okay, I'm going to have to put an end to this little visitation. I'm entertaining guests." Alexis had barely finished her sentence when Jarreau appeared in front of her, causing the moment to intensify.

Jarreau looked from Alexis to Mathis. "Is everything okay, Alexis?"

"All is well. Mathis was just leaving. I don't know why he thought it was okay to come here unannounced, but he did." She turned to face Mathis. "I need you to know that I don't like having my private space invaded. At this very moment you're an unwelcome intruder. I can't imagine what made you think this unexpected visit would be okay with me. It's not."

The murderous look on Mathis's face was not lost on either Alexis or Jarreau. Guests indeed, Mathis mused, sure that the only guest Alexis had was standing there with her. By the sexy way she was dressed, Mathis believed that this was a date for them rather than a casual evening between old friends. His anger with her only deepened. He was at a complete disadvantage with her having a guest there, but she hadn't heard or seen the last of him yet. Alexis had everything that he wanted and needed, and he wouldn't give up on her until he got it.

Alexis suddenly had an attack of conscience, realizing she had been far too rude to Mathis. She had also been downright unfair. Alexis knew that she really should've returned his phone calls. He needed to know that she had no intentions of seeing him again. Alexis found him too controlling and opinionated. She'd had enough of that from R.J. to last her a lifetime. Her lifestyle change required her to call all the shots for herself, but she didn't have to be cruel.

Alexis stepped forward. "Mathis, would you like to come in? We've finished dinner, but there's plenty of food left. Or you could just come in and join us for dessert and coffee."

Mathis was knocked off balance by her offer, but he wasn't about to take her up on it. Three was a crowd in any country and in any language. "Thank you, Alexis, but we can meet another time, one that's more convenient for you. Good evening."

Without handing her the roses, Mathis walked out into the cool night air.

Once settled on the couch in the family room, where freshly brewed coffee and strawberry cheesecake were within easy reach, Alexis began to explain to Jarreau her relationship with Mathis. A few minutes into the conversation, Alexis wasn't able to draw any conclusions from Jarreau's expressionless face. She liked the fact that he was a good listener, but she also wished that he'd moan or nod to give her some indication of what he felt about what she was sharing with him.

"You really didn't have to explain all that to me, Alexis. What you do in your private life should never have to be explained to anyone. You're an adult, lady."

She chuckled with sarcasm. "Now you tell me. I'm sure that you were a little more than curious about our relationship."

He nodded in the affirmative. "Yeah, I was. He doesn't seem your type. Not worldly enough. No polish and very little personality."

"Oh, he's worldly all right. The man has been around the block a few times and has experienced living on the international scene for a while. He's just too controlling for my taste. I don't want another R.J., not that there could ever be another one. He was one of a kind."

"I second that. R.J. never would've tolerated you talking to him the way you talked to Mathis. I wonder how Mathis might've reacted to your rudeness had I not been here. The dark look on his face made me believe you had gone too far with him. I haven't forgotten how you always took the opportunity to speak your mind, but I don't recall the nastiness being there in your tone. You sounded so angry and bitter. It wasn't pleasant for me to see that kind of evil come out in you. Why are you so bitter? Maybe this is a perfect time for you to tell me how R.J. died. That might somehow explain what I witnessed."

Alexis braced herself for the pain she was about to endure. It nearly killed her every time she thought about how R.J. died. Once she told Jarreau the story, she vowed to never repeat it again. Mathis hadn't been told the details of R.J.'s death either; she'd never felt comfortable enough with him to share her pain. All Mathis knew was that she was widowed. It was different with Jarreau. Not only had she known him practically all her life, she had explicit trust in him despite the years they'd lost touch.

For the next thirty minutes Alexis poured out her poisoned secrets and painful grief to a very attentive and sympathetic Jarreau.

Glad the story was over, Jarreau gave her a warm hug, though he desired to lose himself in her, if only for a moment. Things between them were so familiar, yet so much was unknown. "Since we now have all that out of the way, what about us getting back to our evening, Alexis?"

"Great idea!"

Looking dead serious, Jarreau lifted up Alexis's chin with his two fingers. "What is it that you need from me, Alexis? Don't be shy. You never have to be that way with me."

"Friendship."

"You already have that. When and if you need more from me, please don't hesitate to let me know."

"What do you need from me, Jarreau?"

"I don't need much, Alexis. I'm easy to please, easy to get along with. I don't demand from others what I myself am not willing to give in return. I've never stopped caring for you in all these years. Yours is a memory that's eradicable. But I'm a changed man, Lex, not the teenager you once knew. You were brutal with Mathis. I don't know if he deserved it or not, but you singed the brother's eyebrows with that fiery tongue of yours. Getting right to the point, I won't put up with what I took from you back in the day. You catching my drift?"

She smiled sweetly, loving the new Jarreau. The take-charge kind of man turned her on. Laughing inwardly, she gave a silent growl. Had he been a bad boy back in the day, they probably would've had a real relationship and might've eventually gotten married. "I like clarity. If I'm hearing you correctly, I think you're telling me not to tamper with your heart or your dignity. I won't. I promise. I've changed, too. Thanks for putting the cards on the table."

He grinned. "What about another glass of wine, Ms. Lex?"

"Sure. I think we can find a couple of things to toast to."

His eyes gently caressed her face. "For starters, us." He kissed her tenderly on the mouth.

Starving for affection and the warmth of human contact, Alexis deepened the kiss, wanting it to never end. Pulling slightly back from him, she looked into his eyes. "Real nice."

Seated in his car, parked on the same block as Alexis's home, but only a few houses down, a brooding Mathis West checked his watch for the hundredth time. He then looked at the digital clock on the dash of his fancy black Lexus, hoping his watch had gone haywire. Much to his disgust, both timepieces were running neck-in-neck. Midnight was slipping up on him like an enemy prowling around in the darkened shadows of combat; Jarreau Thornton had yet to leave Alexis's place.

Mathis tried to give little thought to what might be going on inside Alexis's house, but the image of her in Jarreau's arms constantly menaced the inside of his head. Without warning, his heart ached with the familiar twinge of jealousy. He willed himself to remain calm, knowing he had to keep on checking his emotions at the door whenever he was with Alexis. She was a knockout, killer beauty, sensuous as any woman he'd ever known, but he had to keep her outside of his heart. This was all about business. He had a job to do. Getting emotionally involved with her could mess up all his plans. In fact, it was out of the question, period.

Mathis West falling deeply in love with Alexis Gautier-Du Boise was strictly taboo.

Chapter Eight

Keisha went stiffly into Zach's embrace, totally immune to his false charm. He looked good and well rested, but he appeared too thin to her. His hair was cut neat, and she could see that he'd recently shaved. The kind of clothes he wore was a shocker. It seemed to her that both he and Malcolm had transformed into normal beings by wearing tasteful clothes that actually fit. His face was void of the acne he suffered with, which surprised her. His skin looked very clear.

Out of prison for over two weeks now, this was the first time Zach had contacted her, period. She had learned from Tammy that he was out and staying at her place. He hadn't even bothered to call about the kids until this very morning. His aloof behavior made her wonder what was really going on between him and Tammy. That she didn't feel even the slightest twinge of jealously also surprised her. She and the kids hadn't been up to the prison in over a month; her job and college courses kept her schedule tight. Time had become a precious commodity to her.

There'd never been this sort of awkwardness between them, yet it didn't seem weird to her as Keisha mentally groped for an opening line. Being at a loss for words was a rare occasion for her. She always had something to say, even if it was sarcastic.

"Have a seat, Zach. I'll go back and get the kids. They're in the bedroom watching a Disney movie, one they've already seen a hundred times." Dumb opening line, she thought.

Eyeing her curiously, Zach took a seat in the chair. "Can we talk first?"

Keisha couldn't believe he wanted to talk to her before seeing the kids he claimed to love so much. She was away from them a better part of the day, but she could barely wait to hold them in her arms when her work and school schedules were finally over. Zach and Zanari filled her up in every way, though it hadn't always been that way. Now that she was no longer wrapped up in Zach, she saw her children in a totally different light, had come to view them as the beautiful angels they truly were. Zach and Zanari were her precious gifts from God.

Looking skeptical, Keisha sat down on the sofa. "As long as it's not about you moving in here with us. It's not going to happen."

Zach appeared highly perturbed as he narrowed his eyes at Keisha, wondering what had happened to the woman who'd always been there for him. The coldness in her embrace had stunned him. It was as if she'd been hugging a perfect stranger instead of the father of her kids. Zack knew that he had a lot to atone for; he just didn't know how to go about making amends to all the people he'd hurt, including his mother. Lucian hadn't been all that happy to see him either. Her new man had far removed her both emotionally and physically from her only child. All Lucian could talk about was her new life and how ecstatic she was to have Mr. Wonderful.

"You know that's exactly what I want to talk about. What's wrong with you? You've been acting crazy for over two years, baby girl, and you're only getting worse. Are you smoking crack or what?"

"That fits more into your lifestyle, Mr. Man. Maybe I have been acting weird, but you've been acting crazy a lot longer than I have.

You've been out of prison two weeks and not so much as a phone call has come from you to check up on your kids until this morning."

"How do you know when I got out? It's not like you've been accepting my phone calls either. I can't even remember the last time you came to visit me."

"Tammy."

His shock at her response couldn't be denied. He didn't need to be a genius to figure out that he was cold-busted. He couldn't believe Tammy had given him up. She had promised not to. Couldn't anybody be trusted? Just in case Keisha was fishing without any bait, since the sister was darn good at that, he thought it best to play coy, though aware that things could backfire on him. Sisters knew how to get blood out of a turnip if they put their mind to it. He couldn't remember all the times Keisha made him believe she knew something when she didn't know a thing. That is, until he'd already confessed under duress. "Tammy! What are you talking about?"

Looking like a dark thundercloud, Keisha threw up her hands in disgust. "The last thing you want to do is come up in here and try to play me again, Zachary Martin. I know that Tammy let you come to her house to live. I also know that she went downtown to pick up your trifling behind from the Greyhound terminal when you got released. Though she's as big a fool as I've been over you, Tammy's cool with me. But you, you're still the devious, doggish person you've always been and will always be."

He quickly decided not to mount a counterattack. It could have disastrous affects, as if things weren't already bad enough. "Are you letting me take Zanari and Zach over to my mom's place for the day, Keisha?"

"How you gonna get them there?"

"I have Mom's car."

"With no license?"

Zach rolled his eyes to the back of his head. "Here we go!

Keisha, stop tripping. I've driven them around before without a license. You wasn't saying nothing then."

"That was before. This is now. You aren't even trying to get it, are you? In case you haven't noticed, baby girl has really changed, has turned herself completely around," she mocked him. "This is no dress rehearsal, Zach. This is life. It's for real. I'm for real. If you want to take them, I'll follow you over there and come back for them later. If you get busted driving without a license, my kids can end up at children's protective services and your mom's car will get towed to the impound yard. You could end up in violation of your parole for breaking the law yet again. So much for a new start."

"*Our* kids, Keisha!"

"Don't remind me."

"What *is* your trip? You haven't even given me a chance to prove myself. Why's that?"

"You proved yourself to me when you contacted Tammy and asked her to let you stay over there with her. Then you come here and try to play me off stupid about it, like you didn't know what I was referring to when I mentioned it. Add in driving without a license to the long list of *Stupidities R Zach*, and I don't need any more proof to know you haven't changed one bit."

"You wouldn't let me come here, Keisha!"

"Dang right! You should've gone to the halfway house, got yourself a job, and then started doing all the things you promised. You're still such a big, fat liar."

Keisha instantly recognized that brooding look in his eyes, the one that normally preceded a slap across her face. "Don't even try it, Zach, not if you don't want the county coroner to haul out the body bag with your name on it. No fighting and arguing in front of the kids either. Those days are over, buster. I finally got your footprints off my back."

"What are you going on and on about? Your gums been flapping ever since I got here."

"I think you already know, so I'll leave it at that. I'll go get the kids."

Zach stared hard after Keisha as she left the room, hating that his cover had been completely blown. Tammy had broken her promise to him. It looked to him like these two sisters had set him up once again. Tammy had a royal cursing out coming. It didn't take him too long to rethink that strategy. Cursing her would more than likely end up with him out on the streets. Tammy was all he had for right now. It would be foolish of him to bite off the hand feeding him. Until he could win Keisha back, he decided it was best for him to cool down.

Keisha was glad that the kids had fallen asleep and hadn't heard any of what she and Zach had said to each other, but it troubled her to see how shy they were acting around him, especially little Zach. Zanari had even backed away from him when he'd tried to pick her up. That surprised even Zach, hurting him as well. His little princess was acting like she didn't even know him. It *had* been a long time since she'd last seen him. Could she have forgotten her daddy? Little Zach had come straight to him, but the silly giggles that always came with seeing his father were absent. Zach realized he missed the sound of his son's childish laughter.

Zach suddenly looked defeated, gazing at his children as if he were really seeing them for the first time ever. He found himself looking at his kids in a way he'd never looked at them before today. These weren't just his kids, nor were they toys, something to play with to pass the time away on the weekends inside the prison; they were flesh and blood, little people with real feelings and beating hearts. It suddenly dawned on him that his precious babies needed a real daddy, not just a weekend father. Just as Keisha had been a lady in waiting, Zach and Zanari were children in waiting. If he couldn't change his ways for them, then what was living his life really all about? What would be his sole purpose for living if it were not to live his life for them, to have a better one than he'd had? A mountain of questions with so few answers was the only conclusion he could come to at the moment. Realizing he was simply not equipped with the right tools when it came down to parenting was a rude awakening. He'd been merely playing daddy.

Keisha instantly felt sorry for Zach. She could clearly see how much he'd been hurt by all the negative reactions he'd received thus far. He had definitely recognized the difference in her attitude toward him, but it was the children's detachment that affected him most. She figured that he'd eventually get around to blaming her for their less-than-positive responses to him. Accusing her of turning them against him would surely come to pass. Unfortunately, he'd accomplished that feat all on his own. Absence didn't always make the heart grow fonder.

It was in the presence of being that kept the heart alive.

Looking downtrodden, Zach turned toward the door. "I'll be outside waiting for you."

"Go in your bedroom for a minute, guys. Mommy will be right there." Keisha smiled at her children as they ran out of the room, looking happy to finally escape the tension.

Keisha took on her warrior stance. "Oh, no, you won't be waiting in the car, Mr. Man," she hissed, careful to keep her voice down. "You're going to help me get *our* kids situated in their car seats. I've done this by myself for too long as it is. Before taking them downstairs, you can get their backpacks and carry them out, too. If you're going to be coming around here, you'll have to take on your half of the responsibility. Charity's over, even if it does begin at home."

Zach started to protest, but thought better of it, realizing it was the very least he could do.

The silence was near deafening as Easton Chapelle walked into the church vestibule. Seeing all these black men in one room immediately freaked him out. He thought of turning around and walking out, but all eyes were on him. Every head in the place had turned before he'd managed to clear the entryway. Everyone looked just as stunned by his presence as he was of being there. The only white man amongst a room full of men of color was a scary thing.

Easton instantly felt threatened. Black men were dangerous. He feared them, was afraid of their brutal strength and criminal minds; he strongly envied the hype behind their capabilities in the area of sexual prowess. He was no match for a black man from the streets. He was a white country boy, thrust into the big city, with a passionate dislike for all men of color. In his opinion, they were all thugs, even the ones who wore suits and held respectable positions in society.

Easton Chapelle was a proud bigot, but a closet one. He rarely voiced his convictions to others outside his circle of like-minded friends. With Jesse as a man of the cloth, Easton hadn't feared any retaliation from the devout minister the day he'd spouted his racial views to him.

Although his attorney was a man of color, Easton hadn't been told that when he was first referred to Michael Hernandez, who in turn had referred him to Orin Mayberry. He'd stuck with Mayberry since the price was right, only learning that fact after he'd checked out the fees of a white attorney. Easton was also a cheapskate; one who'd never paid steady child support.

His steps were labored as he forced himself forward at a snail's pace. If Maybelle Jasper, the counselor at child welfare services, and his attorney, hadn't strongly suggested that he make Reverend Covington's first MIW support meeting held for men waiting on women to get out of prison, Easton definitely wouldn't have come here. In his mind, the day he'd walked out of Jesse's office was the last time he'd ever lay eyes on the slick-tongued, black preacher man. Easton believed that the only difference between Reverend Covington and the jackleg preachers who wore fancy clothes, shoes, and flashy jewelry was that he wasn't on television trying to dupe the world into believing he was down for God and not for the money and fame.

Easton decided he would stay at this meeting, but this would be his first and last time to attend. Hanging out with the brothers wasn't his brand of liquor. He was only accustomed to the fine stock located on the top shelf. Cheap whiskey was known to rot away a man's guts.

Reverend Jesse had been no less stunned to see Easton entering his sanctuary. Once he'd recovered from the shock, he had immediately given thanks to the Almighty. He didn't know what in the world compelled Easton to show up, but it didn't matter. He was right here in the one place Jesse could minister to him. Jesse felt sure that Easton wouldn't get up and walk out on him as he had before. Nor would he be eager to readily spout his racial views. There were too many onlookers for that. However, it was possible that he might never show up again.

Easton wasn't that brave in the presence of those he probably deemed as his enemies.

Easton had right away come off as a coward in Jesse's point of view. It was often the cowards that were the easiest to turn into the strongest of fighting men. Once Jesse equipped them with the right protective covering, the full armor of God, they were always the first ones to take up positions on the front lines, especially when it was time to charge into battle for the Lord.

Reverend Jesse opened the meeting with a warm welcome, followed by a humble prayer. Though the number in attendance was nowhere near the large attendance that Marlene and the LIW group were used to, Jesse felt optimistic. The first three pews to the left were nearly filled, and a handful of men had taken up seats on the right side of the sanctuary. The majority of the attendees were black men, but he was encouraged that several Hispanic males had also shown up. That he didn't speak Spanish that well concerned him, but he hoped the men could understand English. If the attendance of Hispanics grew large in number, Jesse would see to it that the group had a translator. Rosalinda and a couple of other ladies acted as translators for the LIW group.

As Jesse looked over the small group once more, his eyes eventually zeroed in on Easton. He had to laugh inwardly, wondering what sinister thoughts were going through Easton's mind. Finding himself amidst so many men of color, all of whom he disliked with a passion, probably had him in deep shock. Easton looked scared to death. If someone let out a loud boo about now, Jesse was sure the young man would hightail it out of there in fear for his life.

"Okay, fellows, we're going to get this meeting going. In a few minutes I'd like to open up the floor to those of you who have a desire to speak. Before I do that, I'd like to tell you a little about myself and my mission for this group."

Jesse went on to briefly talk about his short stint behind bars and how he'd come into his vision regarding the male support group, patterning it after the highly successful women's group. He told the guys how his wife and her friends had started the group and how it had caught on all over the country. He also mentioned how the group had touched and changed the lives of many.

"I love the title "Ladies in Waiting"; it's so appropriate. But when I applied it to our group, tossing around inside my head the title "Men in Waiting," it just didn't say as much, nor is it nearly as profound as the other. After thinking it over, I came up with a unique name, one that describes quite a few of us men. I heard this saying from a couple of young men that came to see me, and I found myself writing it down. Unaccustomed to Waiting, UTW for short, is the most appropriate name for this group. As men, rarely are we willing to wait on anything. We're always in a hurry to go nowhere. Patience is not our strong suit, nor do we see it as a virtue. So, from now on, this group will be known by the name Unaccustomed to Waiting, or UTW, whichever you prefer. I plan to do a lot of tie-ins to show why this is the name for our group. You will one day come to understand its full meaning. It will prove to be a perfect fit for us."

Jesse then ended his small speech on a short, but powerful, prayer.

Jesse wiped his sweaty brow with a white handkerchief and then he took a long swallow of the ice-cold water that had been placed on the podium for him. "Now that we have that out of the way, we can get started, fellows. Who'd like to begin the session?"

Jesse looked slightly dismayed when he saw no hands go up. "Come on now, there has to be a couple of volunteers in the room. We're here to talk, not clam up. We're all here because we have some sort of need that we want to get met. That's the purpose of the group." Jesse's eyes went to Eric Eldridge, but only stayed there long enough to give the young man something to think about. Jesse didn't want to pressure Eric, but he could sure use his help. Jesse knew it would do him absolutely no good to look in Easton's direction; he already looked ready to bolt.

Eric reluctantly got to his feet. He quickly gave his first name, but he knew that he had to keep his official status as a police officer confidential. That's the last thing he should make the others aware of. He already had enough problems as it was. Cops, white and black, were often considered the number one enemy, especially out on the streets. While all of the citizens didn't see them as the adversary, there was definitely no love for them by quite a large number of folks.

Eric scratched his head. "I'm here because my girlfriend is in jail on drug charges. I was referred to Reverend Jesse for counseling a short time back. He's already helped me to see some of the issues more clearly. He will help you, too, if you let him. Like he's helped me, I tried to help my girlfriend on so many occasions, but she wasn't willing to help herself. Not only did she use drugs, she started selling them. Bad combination."

"How long has she been in jail?" a Hispanic guy asked.

Jesse looked pleased to have someone else get involved. Intent on hearing Eric's response, he stroked his chin thoughtfully.

"Four months," Eric responded. He had wondered if the Hispanic guys could speak English and now his question had been answered for him, at least about one of them. A definite heavy accent was present, but he had spoken clearly enough to be understood.

"When's she getting out?" another guy inquired.

Eric shrugged. "You probably know how it works. She could get out early, right on time, or end up doing more time than her original sentence. It's a gamble any way you look at it. I wished more people realized that. Once you enter the system, the powers that be literally become your master. To answer your question more specifically, two years if she's granted probation."

"If she's your ex-girlfriend, why do you even care?" the same Hispanic guy questioned Eric. "You should be able to just walk away."

Eric looked terribly hurt. "She's carrying my baby." Though Cicely hinted that the baby might not be his, Eric had a gut feeling that it was. Cicely was no tramp. Drugs turned people into all sorts of things, had them doing things that they wouldn't normally do, unsavory things. But he had to hold steadfast to the idea that the drug use hadn't caused Cicely to sleep with a bunch of other men. He had to admit to himself that it was a real possibility, but he wasn't going to entertain it until he was actually faced with it, something he hoped would never happen.

A hush came over the room but all eyes stayed intently on the speaker. It appeared to Jesse that everyone was hoping Eric would give up more information. Curiosity was in the eyes of many. Jesse knew how difficult and painful it was for Eric to tackle this subject in a public forum, but he also knew it would eventually do him a world of good. Matters causing grave concern were best dealt with by getting them out in the open as opposed to stuffing them deep inside, where they had a chance to fester and cause all sorts of emotional fiascos.

Eric paused a moment and looked around the sanctuary. He'd never been to any sort of support group meeting before, but he'd been in a room full of men on countless occasions. The booking room at the county jail had instantly come to mind. It was often a zoo up in that place.

This crowd of men was somewhat different, yet he was sure

there were more than a few criminals among them. Some of the shady characters had a certain look about them, the kind of look that Eric was all too familiar with in his line of work. But it was the smooth criminals that were the hardest to detect. They had a way about them like no other; could practically smooth talk themselves out of anything and everything. There were probably a few like that in the room.

Eric knew firsthand that men had women do a lot of silly and crazy things for them, those of the criminal variety. Women were arrested all the time for something they'd do behind some male joker. It was normally someone that could care less about them, a lover who wouldn't think twice about setting them up. He'd also seen women take seriously hard falls for their men. Just to keep their men out of jail, they'd implicate themselves and end up doing the men's time. It was crazy, but so unbelievably true. The type of crimes they'd commit for a man pretty much ran the gamut.

Eric cleared his throat. "I only learned of her condition a few weeks ago. I've hired an attorney in order to seek custody of our baby once it's born. I'm also hoping to keep the baby from being born behind bars. That's an awful stigma to attach to a child, one that they'll have to live with for the rest of their lives. Don't want that to happen to any kid of mine."

"Are you still in love with your ex?" Jesse had asked the question already knowing the answer. Eric had admitted as much to him, but Jesse thought that it would help if he never allowed himself to deny his true feelings for Cicely. True love had a way of conquering all things. He hoped that Eric would one day come to see that for himself.

Eric couldn't help smiling. He didn't know why Jesse had asked the same question of him again, but he figured that Jesse had a good reason for doing so. "I'd have to say so. She was such a beautiful spirit before drugs ravaged her inner and outer beauty. She simply chose drugs over love, and I still don't know why. Thanks for letting me share." Eric took his seat.

Easton couldn't believe what he'd just heard. This guy actually wanted custody of his kid, and here he'd been all but forced to take custody of his son. Curious as to how this brother planned to take care of a child by himself, Easton raised his hand.

Surprised but pleased that Easton wanted to participate, Jesse summoned him to rise, at the same time praying that he wouldn't say something offensive. The last thing Jesse wanted was to see the young man suffer through a possible beat down for popping off at the mouth.

Easton shuffled his feet nervously, clearing his throat repeatedly. There was no doubt that he was out of his element. The others were just as intent on what Easton had to say simply because he looked so out of place. The arrogant aura about him stuck out like a sore thumb.

"I'm assuming you have a full-time job. If I'm correct, how are you going to raise a child by yourself?" Easton inquired of Eric.

"The same way I was raised, with lots of love and care. My job allows leave for parents when their children are born, or when someone adopts. I plan to stay at home with my kid as long as I possibly can, and still get paid while on leave. When it's time for me to report back to duty, I'll have someone come into my home and care for him or her."

An older gentleman on the front pew chuckled. "So you're gonna have a live-in nanny, huh? I dare to bet that she'll be young and pretty."

"That's not what we're here for," Jesse scolded. "No heckling allowed. Everyone needs to read the rules before the next meeting. If you didn't get a set, see me after we adjourn."

Eying the older gentleman with understanding, Eric laughed. "It's cool, Rev Jesse. I'm not offended. Back to your question, sir, age and looks won't be a prerequisite. Responsibility and reliability are what I'm mostly interested in. A live-in person works for me because I pull a lot of different shifts. That way, my daughter or son can remain in his or her own environment, without being shuttled from pillar to post."

The older gentleman smiled as he got to his feet. "By the way, my name is Marc. Sorry for hassling you, brother. Nothing malicious intended. Just trying to lighten things up a bit. My youngest daughter is in prison. She's also in jail behind some no-good man."

"Sorry to hear that," Eric remarked.

"Stealing expensive electronic equipment from her job for him to hustle on the streets. She never saw a dime of the money he made off her stupidity, nor did the kids. Said he didn't make enough to pay child support. A pair of shoes or a new outfit every now and then was his definition of taking care of his kids. I'm taking care of all three of my grandkids, alone. My wife is deceased. Sounds like you have a good plan in mind, brother. Good luck in raising your child." With nothing else to say, Marc reseated himself.

"Thanks. None of my plans can be executed if the judge doesn't grant me custody when the time comes. Out of her anger at me, my ex is hell-bent on sending our child into the foster care system until she's released. I'm going to fight that with every ounce of breath in me."

Easton found himself admiring Eric despite his feelings about men of color. He thought Eric seemed very sincere in his quest to get custody of his kid. Easton began to feel a little ashamed of himself, a feeling that was totally foreign to him. For the first time ever, he really began to seriously think about his child, who'd been nothing more than an inconvenience to him thus far. His anger hadn't let him see that his child wasn't responsible for his mother's death.

If anyone was to blame for the burdens of his mother, he needed to look at himself and then begin shouldering the responsibility. His fragile mother cared for her grandchild because there were no alternatives. With no one to relieve her, even when she was ill, she had taken care of the child without any help from the parents. Both parents were too caught up in themselves and their desires to even try and understand the needs of the child. Both parents were self-ish.

Still, no matter his thoughts, Easton was going to search every avenue on how to relieve himself of the responsibility for his child. Without any thought to the child being his own flesh and blood, Easton was even considering giving up his parental rights in order to be totally free.

"Why are you at this meeting?" Eric asked Easton.

Surprised by the question, Easton looked puzzled as he scratched his head. "Just out of curiosity. Nothing more than that." Jesse was the only one in the room that knew he was lying, but Easton didn't care about that either. The smirk on Jesse's face didn't faze him a bit.

"You don't have a female friend or relative behind bars?" Eric asked in a probing manner, raising an eyebrow.

Easton slapped his hand down on his thigh. "Like yours, she's an ex."

"That still doesn't explain why you're here," one of the other men challenged.

Easton's eyes clouded with indignation. "That's my business."

"Yeah, it is," Eric said, "but you didn't seem to mind getting all up in mine a few minutes ago. I at least gave you the courtesy of answering your questions."

"Maybe that's the difference between you and me, besides the obvious," Easton tossed back with undeniable sarcasm. "Night and day."

Looking uncomfortable at the scathing reference made regarding differences, Jesse shot Easton a warning glance, sure that his remarks had to do with skin colors. "Watch your mouth," Jesse muttered lowly under his breath. "This is not the time or the place for you to share your views on differences." Jesse threw up another silent supplication.

Eric shrugged Easton's remarks off. "Man, I'm not here for you.

I'm here for my kid and myself. I'm not going to let you or anybody else get under my skin."

Jesse stood up when Easton glared hard at Eric. Keeping the peace was a must, and Jesse was fondly known around his congregation as the peacekeeper.

A medium-built Hispanic man had put up his hand and had stood at the same time Jesse had. "I'm Pedro. I'd like to share something if you don't mind. I need help. That's why I'm here."

Everyone clapped, verbally encouraging Pedro to speak. Jesse sighed a breath of relief, happy that he hadn't had to intervene. Eric keeping his cool was what had kept the situation with Easton from escalating.

"My sister is in jail. Prostitution," Pedro confided to the group. "Her own boyfriend is the one who turned her out onto the streets. Made a real tramp out of her. We don't play that. Family is family. But one of my brothers here, Enrique," he pointed to the guy seated next to him, "got locked up when he took her boyfriend down hard. Beat him real good, much worse than he'd been beating on our sister. We recently had to stop and ask ourselves if it was worth it for each of us to end up in jail for her when she refused to stay away from him. We all have wives, children, and jobs. We're still worried about our little sister, but we don't know what else to do. We can't afford to be locked up every time we turn around. Does anyone have any suggestions on how we can keep her away from him when she gets out?"

Jesse stepped up to the podium. "I'll take this one on first. Please have a seat, Pedro. This might take a minute or two." Jesse stroked his chin. "My wife and I often talk to our acquaintances, friends, and family members about choices when they come to us with problems regarding loved ones. Being with this abusive guy was your sister's choice, not your choice for her. Bad choices come with dire consequences. It was those choices that landed her behind bars. Your sister is an adult, which means you won't be able to keep her away from the guy if she starts back up with him. You have no legal ground to stand on. But I have this suggestion for you. Get someone to counsel her while she's still on the inside. Sounds like she needs help."

"Do you have anyone you can refer us to?" Enrique queried.

"My wife is a wonderful spiritual advisor, and I'm sure she'd be happy to counsel your sister. I'll talk to her about it tonight. You can leave me a contact number or call me at the church office on Monday. You also might want to think about what's in your sister's background that might've made her turn to prostitution. Low self-esteem is usually at the core of making bad decisions in life. Instead of taking the guy's inventory, you might want to help her take her own. Something bad may've happened to her to make her think herself unworthy of better treatment. I don't know. But you can't blame yourself for her misguided decisions. I know a kid that came from one of the best families around, but he still made some very bad choices in his life. I know him extremely well. He's my son. I'd also like to share with you that he turned himself completely around before it was too late. He's now working with our youth. Once a follower himself, he's now doing a fine job as a leader." Jesse beamed with pride.

Reverend Jesse walked away from the podium, only to turn around and go back. "One more thing, Pedro and Enrique. Two wrongs never make a right. It is against the law to physically attack someone regardless of what he's done. Leave the punishment phase up to the law and up to God. God will take care of things in His own way."

Everyone turned around when one of the sanctuary doors swung open. The meeting was just about over, so there were many puzzled glances directed at the latecomer, who appeared to be in another zip code as he took a seat on the back row.

"Welcome, young man. Come on down front and have a seat," Jesse boomed into the microphone. "We're just about ready to adjourn, but if you'd like to talk we can hold the meeting open a while longer." One more male added to the group pleased Jesse. It saddened him that the attendance was so low considering the number of women behind bars. Since this was the very first meeting, he had high hopes of the attendance picking up in the near future.

"Thanks for the offer. I'll be fine right here. I don't have anything to say."

"Mind if I ask your reason for being here?" Jesse inquired.

"I'm Frank. Only here as an observer. If that's a problem, I can leave."

"No, no, that won't be necessary. We're glad to have you."

Jesse had a gut feeling that the young man had very good reasons for being there, but that none of them had to do with observing. He wasn't going to run away a single person. People didn't just stray into these kinds of sessions; this meeting had been heavily publicized through newspaper advertisements and numerous other mediums. Something compelling normally caused folks to attend a support group meeting. Jesse would wait to see if Frank would come again, but something he couldn't explain told him that he'd definitely return.

Jesse picked up the microphone and tapped on it. "Is there anyone else who has a desire to speak before we adjourn?" He waited several seconds, but no hands were raised.

"Since no one has anything else to say, I'm going to end this meeting. But I'd like to do a little ministering to your soul before we go our separate ways. I'm going to tell you a little bit about a man named Saul, a biblical character. Saul was like many of us; he was a man who was unaccustomed to waiting. . . ."

Chapter Nine

Jesse carried the double-sized, wicker bed tray into the bedroom and positioned it on the king-size bed so that it would be between him and Marlene once he got settled in. The tray held two plates of steaming-hot, home-fried potatoes and onions, turkey sausage, scrambled eggs with cheese, and freshly squeezed orange juice. The coffee and morning newspaper had been brought in earlier. Careful not to tip over the tray, Jesse got back in bed and made himself comfortable.

Marlene leaned over and kissed him gently on the mouth. "You are too special. Thanks for fixing this wonderful breakfast. I just hope I can do it justice. I should've been the one taking care of you this morning. You were out so late last night."

"You told me you weren't feeling well, Wildflower, so I'm supposed to take care of you. Let me pass the blessing, then we can chat away to our hearts' content."

Jesse led them in a short prayer of thanksgiving, asking the Lord that the food might nourish and sustain their bodies. Once the prayer was over, the couple dug into the morning meal with gusto. Marlene started out with a good appetite, but after she'd eaten less than half of her food, her stomach began to hurt. Not wanting

Jesse's efforts to be wasted, she took smaller bites in hopes of eating enough to keep her husband from worrying about her health. She was sure it was nothing more than a stomach virus, but she hadn't ruled out the possibility of something more serious. There were times when the pain in her abdomen was quite incredible.

Jesse had gulped down most of his breakfast. He was a man who enjoyed his food to the utmost. He loved his own cooking almost as well as he did his wife's. But there was something about Marlene's cooking that kept him happy and satisfied. He often teased her about putting her finger in it to make it so delicious. On the other hand, Marlene thought he was the better cook. Malcolm loved both of his parents' cooking. He saw it as having the best of both worlds.

"How are the plans coming for Sister Wylie's upcoming surprise birthday celebration?"

"Myrna and I are doing our best to do it up right. Sister Wylie's girls are of no help whatsoever. They merely want to be supervisors and seem to have no interest in getting their hands dirtied. We still have a lot of time to pull things off, but it would sure help if they'd give us a little more assistance than they have thus far. I realize they both work, but the week does come equipped with weekends. We're not even interested in soliciting help from Reginald."

Jesse chuckled. "I hear you. Reginald Wylie is too unpredictable for you to count on, but he's Sister Wylie's heart despite the things she says about her only son. But the Marlene I know is probably happier with things the way they are. You know how you like to have it done your way. If you're honest with yourself, the girls would probably just be in the way."

Marlene cracked up. "You know me too darn well. I'm having a hard time as it is with Myrna, since we both like to have it our way. So far we've managed to work together harmoniously. Rosalinda showed us a very creative way of doing crepe paper roses a couple of evenings back. Since Myrna and I were having such a hard time learning to make them, Rosalinda offered to do them herself. By the way, she and Michael are coming over for dinner this evening. I also invited Alexis and told her she was welcome to bring her new male friend, the one none of us has met and are just dying to. Though she accepted, we'll just have to wait and see if she shows up. Keisha is coming by, too, so I invited Malcolm. He seemed genuinely pleased by the gesture. Oh, I forgot to mention that the Jacobsons are coming over, too."

Jesse looked at Marlene with concern. He knew his wife hadn't been feeling well off and on over the past couple of weeks, and it appeared to him that she wasn't getting any better. "That's quite a crew. Are you sure you're going to feel up to cooking dinner? You're looking a little fragile right now. I can see that you're struggling with your meal, though you've been doing your best to try and hide the fact from me. And how'd you forget about Zach in all this?"

Marlene grinned devilishly. "Are you saying I should've invited him and Tammy over?"

Jesse laughed heartily. "Not at all. That doesn't sound like a very good idea."

Marlene put her fork down and laid her head back against the pillow. "I didn't forget Zach. I asked Keisha did she want me to invite him. She wasn't too keen on the idea. In fact, she was totally against it. But when I told her Malcolm would probably be coming by, she didn't have a problem with him. Zach will be keeping the kids overnight at his mother's place."

"Sounds like you have all your bases covered. If you don't feel like cooking, I can do it for you. I'd love to whip up a batch of my famous teriyaki chicken wings. Okay?"

"Neither of us is cooking. I ordered the food from Bertha Sharpe, your favorite cook, before I started feeling ill. I called her right after I invited everyone over. I know it was short notice, only two days, but Bertha said it was no problem at all. Her soul food is some of the best in this area. I hope my stomach will be strong enough to handle some of the spicier foods. You know how she likes to spice up her collard greens." Just thinking about Sister

Sharpe's delicious cooking caused Marlene to moan with pleasure. "The guest list is bigger than I anticipated."

Jesse laughed, making a few moaning sounds of his own. "I know what you mean, girl. But I can hardly wait to taste those greens myself. What else did you order, Wildflower?"

Marlene reached over and removed her food list from the nightstand drawer, quickly looking it over to refresh her memory. "Besides the collards and mustard, I ordered short ribs of beef, salmon croquettes, hot wings, macaroni and cheese, and candied yams. I plan to fix a huge tossed salad. Sister Sharpe is also baking up a few sweet potato pies and two apple-cinnamon cobblers. I didn't do the lemon pound cake this time, but I was sure tempted. Since cake is one of my major weaknesses, I didn't want to blow my diet completely. Doing too good for that."

"You've done very well for yourself, but I don't want to see you lose another pound. Too much weight loss can't be good for you, sweetheart. That might be why you're having problems with your stomach and feeling so poorly lately. We have to do everything in moderation. I'm going to love you no matter your weight. It's the inner package that I love so much. The skin you're in is a bonus for me either way." He leaned over and kissed her on the mouth, savoring her sweetness. "It doesn't get much better than this, Mar. You and me is how it'll always be."

Marlene couldn't help blushing. Jesse still turned her on. He always knew how to make her feel like a million, even when she wasn't feeling her best. "Thank you, sweetheart. I'm so grateful for your unconditional love. And I promise not to overdo it on the weight loss. You're probably right about it affecting my health. I'll be more careful. I want to be around so you can continue to spoil me rotten and vice versa. With that said, we'd better get out of this bed and get our day started. Sick or not, I have numerous chores to attend to before our guests arrive."

Jesse moved the bed tray and then pulled Marlene into his arms, sprinkling her face and neck with butter-soft kisses. "No work for you today. I want you to just lie here and look pretty and dainty for me. I'll take care of all your chores for you. You're going to need your energy for entertaining tonight. That's a lively bunch you invited over here for dinner. I got your back."

Marlene gave him a lingering kiss. "I know you do, Jesse, as always. I love you."

Although Alexis had just finished eating lunch with Mathis West at a posh Beverly Hills eatery, her mind was on handsome Jarreau Thornton, whom she hadn't heard from in over a week. She had called to invite him to Marlene's for dinner, but she'd had to leave a message and she hadn't heard back from him yet. She hoped he would call back and leave her a message before it got too late. She wasn't sure she'd make the dinner engagement if he couldn't go with her. His odd behavior had her puzzled. He seemed to run hot and cold with her. One minute he was flirting and coming on to her in a delicious way; in the next instant he seemed so aloof.

Alexis was quite familiar with the concept of running hot and cold, since she still had a tendency to do that with her girlfriends. She had to wonder if it was some sort of internal defense mechanism used to protect oneself from others. Whatever it was, she and Jarreau were both guilty of practicing it. Noticing the same peculiarity in him let her see firsthand how undesirable a trait it could be in anyone. Her friends had often complained to her about her drastic personality temperature changes, but she never really understood what she was being accused of. Now that Jarreau was using the same keep-you-at-a-distance tactics on her, she knew exactly what they'd been talking about. It wasn't a pleasant experience by any stretch of the imagination.

Perhaps Jarreau was as scared of getting into a relationship with her as she had been of forming the ones she now had with Marlene, Keisha, and Rosalinda. While she had no clear indication as to where their relationship was going, she had a pretty good idea of where she wanted it to go. Jarreau seemed like a good man, and she needed some goodness in her life.

Seated in a booth with Mathis across from her was the last place Alexis wanted to be, but she had promised to make things up to him for her rude behavior. Alexis felt guilty over the way she'd treated him. In trying to draw nearer to God, consideration of others was something Alexis deemed as a necessary change. She was also doing her best to make sure she kept her word once she'd given it, unlike before, when the feelings of others just didn't matter to her.

The seven-dozen roses, a dozen a day for the past week, had also been instrumental in earning Mathis more time in her company. Though she wished that the flowers had come from Jarreau, she was nonetheless flattered by the kind gesture extended to her by the other man.

If Jarreau wasn't truly interested in her in the romantic sense, she thought Mathis might be okay for her to have an occasional date with. An outing with him would surely beat sitting at home being lonely. While she'd been taken with Mathis in the very beginning, the control issues he exhibited were a big problem for her. No one would ever control her again.

Alexis had also considered the fact that Mathis could change. If she laid her cards out on the table regarding how she wanted to be treated, he wouldn't have a choice. Although he had shown some sensitivity toward her lately, she didn't think that alone was enough to build a relationship on. However, until something better came along, she just might allow Mathis to help keep the loneliness away. That is, if Jarreau wanted them to erect only a friendship. Mathis was intelligent, witty, and a great conversationalist. Still, he was no prince charming. *Why do I seem to have a tendency to settle for less than the best, knowing I deserve so much more?*

Mathis reached across the table and covered Alexis's hand with his, leaving it in place for only a brief moment. Alexis was still a bit touchy, and he wanted to be careful with her since he wasn't fully back in her good graces. "Are you okay, Alexis? It's unsettling to see you so quiet."

"Is that because I talk non-stop?" she teased, eager to lighten her own dark mood.

He grinned. "Not at all. Hearing you talk is a turn on for me. I don't hear your voice often enough. I hope that will change one day."

"Ugh," Alexis moaned lowly, cringing inwardly. She thought his tired line to be lame and tasteless. She instantly checked herself, vowing to have at least a halfway decent time with him. She could do much, much worse. "So how's business at your firm?"

"Brisk. Business is booming despite the sluggish economy. Making money has always been my top priority in life. Lots and lots of money."

Alexis stretched her eyes wide, scrutinizing him closely, making sure that it wasn't actually R.J. sitting across from her. Mathis had sounded just like R.J. How many times had she heard her late husband say that very same thing? Another man with an obsession for money was daunting. Of course, she loved the finer things that money afforded her, but she was finally learning that there was more to life than seeking riches and material wealth. Her new mission was to find those things God provided for His children and then try them on for size.

The walk in the park with Jarreau came to mind. An expense-free outing amidst God's creations had been one of the most pleasant experiences she'd had as of late. Recalling how she'd loved to be close to nature in her youth made her smile. The memory took her back to a time when she loved to dig around in the soil and plant things so she could watch them grow. In that instant she decided to try her hand at gardening again. That should prove to be a refreshing challenge. Her first project would be to plant a rose bush or two in memory of R.J. Just the thought of taking on something new and wonderful excited her to no end.

Alexis looked up just in time to see the heavy scowl on Mathis's face. She could see that she had once again offended him. Her cell phone rang just as she was about to apologize for zoning out on him. "Excuse me, Mathis. I'll be right with you."

"I can hardly wait, since you've been absent for some time now," was his sarcastic reply.

Alexis didn't hear him; she was already listening to the caller's voice. "I really want to come, Marlene, but I haven't been able to get a hold of my friend."

"Alexis, you don't have to have someone with you. I just thought it would be nice to have you bring your new friend along. Please come anyway. You can leave our address and phone number on Jarreau's answering service if you like. That way, he can call or come on over if he doesn't get your message until later. Sound like a workable plan?"

"Very much so. I'll be there. See you tonight. Kiss, kiss, Marlene."

"Kiss, kiss back to you, Alexis. Later."

"Plans for later on?" Mathis asked as soon as Alexis put her cell phone away.

"Dinner with friends. We try to get together a couple of times a month."

"It sounded to me like you don't have a date. Mind if I tag along with you?"

Alexis hid her surprise and dismay at his question. Him tagging along with her to Marlene's was out of the question. "Perhaps another time, Mathis. This is kind of a girl thing."

He raised an eyebrow. "A girl thing, huh? I guess I got the wrong impression."

"Yes, I guess you did. And let's go ahead and change the subject."

"Are you going to have dessert, Alexis? There are many delicious choices."

"No thank you, Mathis. But I'd like to have a cup of coffee before I take off. The restaurant employees are probably wondering when we're going to vacate the premises since we've been through eating for over thirty minutes."

"At these prices, we can stay as long as we want. Don't let that run you off."

"I won't, but I do have to run from here very shortly. I have a salon appointment at two. I usually go first thing in the mornings, but when you called me for an early lunch, I decided to change the time. I was lucky that my beautician had a late afternoon cancellation."

"If you hadn't said it was a girl thing, I was thinking you were getting dolled up for another man. That would break my heart. You wouldn't resort to playing me, now would you?"

Alexis didn't like the tone he'd used, though she could tell he'd tried to keep it light. He'd hardly meant his statement as a joke. "Mathis, no disrespect intended, but there'd have to be an exclusive relationship established between two people before one could get played or get their heart broken. As for my getting all dolled up, I get my hair done every week, standing appointment." She looked down at her watch. "Forget the coffee. I don't have time now." She got to her feet and began gathering her things.

"Wait a minute, Alexis. Please don't leave. It seems that I've stepped out of bounds with you again. I don't know why I can't keep it together when I'm around you. I think I'm trying too hard in showing my personal interest in you. Try not to hold this latest gaffe against me."

"I don't, but I still have to run." Feeling slightly indignant with Mathis, Alexis removed fifty dollars in cash from her purse and placed it on the table. "To show you there's no hard feelings, my treat. Talk to you later." Without giving him a chance to respond, she hurried from the restaurant, hoping he wouldn't come after her. He needed to learn to keep his dignity.

Seated on the sofa in her living room, Keisha looked exasperated and exhausted. For the past twenty minutes or so she had been listening to Zach go on and on about how she was no longer there for him and how much he needed her to be. It seemed to her that he had covered every spot in her living room during his pacing. She'd already heard more than enough, but she thought it best to let him get all his issues out in the open with her. Then she could set him straight once and for all; she thought she'd already done that at least a couple of dozen times.

"You didn't have any problems with me spending the night here before. You're asking me to baby-sit for you, yet you don't want me to stay and do it here."

Keisha rolled her eyes at him. "Baby-sit for me? Is that how you see it? If that's the case, I guess I've been babysitting for you for over two years. Seems to me you have a lot of catching up to do in that area. When we talked about you watching the kids, you said you'd do it at your mother's house. My place never came up in the conversation."

"I don't know why you keep acting like we're perfect strangers. I used to practically live here with you. We have kids together. That means we know everything there is to know about each other. You just keep on tripping with me. Why is that?"

Keisha blew out a ragged breath. "How many times do I have to tell you that this is a new day, that things aren't the way they used to be? I guess I'll have to keep repeating myself until you finally get it. You are not spending tonight or any other night in this apartment."

"I don't know why I can't sleep on the couch if you don't want me in your bed."

Keisha glared at Zach. "No! Go back to Tammy's. You have a bed over there."

He seethed with anger, but tried hard not to show it. "Jealous, huh?"

Keisha laughed with derision. "If you knew how unaffected I was by you, you'd know how stupid you sound. Tammy's a great catch. Maybe you should try casting your rod in her direction again. She still just might be stupid enough to take the bait."

Keisha immediately regretted the scathing remark she'd made

about Tammy. She believed that Zach was only at Tammy's because Tammy really wanted to help him. She silently prayed for forgiveness. Tammy hadn't deserved her nasty remark. It had been so unfair to her.

Zach looked stunned by Keisha's comments. "Wait a minute here, Keisha. Are you saying that you're never going to be with me? You made me believe that if I got out and got it together, we could try to make it again. Was that a lie? You were lying, weren't you?"

Keisha's frustration was growing by the minute. Looking like she wanted to scream, she pushed her hand through her hair, making a mess of it. Zach looked so vulnerable, hurt, too. It was now that she realized he had feelings, too, that she had hurt him deeply. Keisha felt torn. She had to admit that Zach still had a strong hold on her, but she couldn't come apart at the seams because of it. Things had changed drastically, and he needed to get used to the way things were now. If she needed to resort back to being a fool for him in order for them to make it, she had to get him to understand that it wasn't happening. All bets were off for that.

"Talk to me, Keisha, damn it! What are you really saying to me? You've been sending me all sorts of mixed signals, baby girl. I liked it better when you spelled it out, when you gave it to me straight up." He scratched his head. "Is it over between us? It is, isn't it?"

Tears sprang to her eyes. "I honestly don't know, Zach. I'm confused on so many of our issues. But I do know that I can't go on being involved with you if it means losing myself in our relationship. Zach, I've finally found me and I don't want to lose me yet again. I know what makes me happy now. I can never go back to the way it was with us. Please understand that."

Zach stopped his pacing and took a long look at her, studying her hard. "I finally see what's going on here. You got another man, don't you? Who you been laying up with, girl? I never thought you'd turn out to be a tramp. Who you giving it up to, baby girl?"

Before she could put herself in check, her handprint was already embedded in Zach's face. Keisha looked terrified as she backed away, hoping that he wouldn't retaliate. She thanked God that her kids weren't there to witness this ugliness. They were outside with her downstairs neighbor, Sheree, and her three kids. Sheree had only lived in the complex a couple of months.

Zach just stood there in stunned disbelief. Reality had hit him as hard as Keisha had, and he didn't like this latest dose. His absence had had profoundly damaging effects on his family. The truth of it all had been kicking his butt ever since he was first released from prison.

Out of his rising anger and bitter disappointment, Zach backed Keisha into a corner. "Consider yourself lucky this time. If you ever raise your hand to me again, you will get hurt. I've changed, too, but you want to keep the blinders on. I'm trying hard, girl."

"I can do bad by myself! I don't need anyone to do bad with. But I know you're trying."

"You can't possibly know how hard, but you're not trying to see it either. I don't want to do this without you, but if I'm forced to I will rise to the challenge. Hear this if you don't hear nothing else. Those are my babies. I'm the only one they'll ever call Daddy. Keep the buster you're with away from my kids. You can drop Zach and Zanari off at my mother's house on your way out." Zach turned on his heels and walked out, slamming the door hard behind him.

Her very next thought was of Malcolm. If Zach knew she had a crush on Malcolm, he'd want to annihilate the both of them. If the kids ever mentioned to Zach the trip to Sea World, she was dead meat. Why hadn't she thought of that before? It would definitely be on between him and Malcolm if he ever found out. Zach had only seen Marlene and Jesse up at the prison, but he was well aware of how close Keisha had grown to them. He also knew that the Covingtons had a son, but he'd never be able to guess that he was the man Keisha was interested in.

During Keisha's idle times, thoughts of Malcolm kept her mind occupied off and on throughout the days and lonely evenings. Keisha felt a twinge in her heart as she thought of all the things

Malcolm had taught her and had helped her to see. He'd made her look inside herself and discover her inner beauty, something she hadn't known she possessed. He'd also made her realize she was worthy of nothing less than the very best. Malcolm always challenged her to be the best that she could be, to keep outdoing herself to reach the next level.

In Keisha's opinion, Malcolm was definitely the man. Was he the man for her? Was she falling in love with him, or were her feelings for him born out of gratitude? These were questions she had to find the answers to as soon as possible.

Michael smiled as he fastened the pearl necklace with the gold chain around Rosalinda's neck. He hadn't been able to resist purchasing the dainty gift set for her when he'd noticed it in the jewelry case at the jewelers where he'd taken his watch to have the battery replaced. He took the delicate, lever-back pearl earrings from the royal blue, velvet-lined box. "Can I have the pleasure of putting these on for you, too, Rosalinda? I'll be very careful."

Rosalinda reached up and gently brushed her knuckles across his right cheek. Her smile was warm and genuine. "No one has ever offered to put earrings in my ears. That's a really nice gesture. Thank you, Michael."

It pleased Rosalinda that Michael was still so thoughtful of her. He hadn't cooled off one bit toward her, constantly surprising her with sentimental gifts of candy, flowers, and sweet little greeting cards. The jewelry was his first expensive present to her. She had briefly considered not accepting the beautiful pearl necklace and earrings, but after thinking about it, she saw no harm in doing so. He'd said it was merely a token of his affection and that no strings were attached. She believed him wholeheartedly. There wasn't a day gone by that Michael hadn't tried to show her in some unique way of how much he truly cared for her.

Michael tenderly massaged each of her earlobes between his

thumb and forefinger before inserting the 14K gold-wired earrings into them. Rosalinda got goose bumps just before the warmth of his gentle touch soared right through her. The tender moments between them had begun to increase in frequency over the past few weeks. While never letting things get totally out of hand, Rosalinda and Michael were finding it increasingly hard to keep their physical desires at bay. Their hearts were quickly becoming entwined in a romantic liaison.

Finished with his delightful task, he stood back and gave her the once over. The white pearls and the gold chain were a striking contrast to the black, lacy pants set she wore. The top was cut low, allowing a full frontal view of the necklace. Michael had never seen Rosalinda wear her hair up. It was easy to admit to himself how sexy and sophisticated the upswept style made her look. Positioning his hands on both sides of her face, he kissed her tenderly on the mouth. "You're going to be the belle of the ball this evening, Senorita Morales. Are you ready to go?"

"Just about. I need to do a last minute checkup on my overall appearance. Do you think we could stop by a grocery store with a floral shop and get some roses for Miss Marlene?" Rosalinda asked Michael as she retreated down the short hallway. "Have any suggestion as to what we can pick up for Reverend Jesse? I know nothing about buying male gifts," she shouted.

"Yes to both questions. The roses are appropriate for them as a couple, but I have a great set of classy ballpoint pens we can give Jesse. I keep them in stock as gifts to special clients."

Carrying a lightweight sweater over her arm, Rosalinda popped back into the living room in Michael's guesthouse. "Ready to get this party started, Mr. Hernandez?"

"Ready as I can be, Senorita Morales. I love hanging out with you and your friends. Wait here. I'll bring the car right up to your front door. Royalty always has a chariot awaiting."

* * *

Marlene and Jesse were engaged in a lively conversation with Myrna and her husband, Raymond. The women were putting the finishing decorating touches on the extra table that had been set up in the family room, where the two men were comfortably seated on the sofa.

Despite feeling ill, Marlene had managed to look both chic and comfortable, dressed in an all-black Evan Picone designer label outfit. Decked out in the exact contrasting color, Myrna appeared smart and cool as a morning breeze in all white by Dior. Both women wore stylish pantsuits and mid-heeled pumps, the same color as their outfits. The husbands were debonair, dressed in dark slacks and dress shirts. Jesse's shirt was white, and Raymond's was a light beige.

The doorbell rang and Jesse got to his feet. "I'll get that, ladies. Excuse me, Ray. I won't be but a minute." Jesse strode out into the hallway and opened the door for the guest to gain entry. Jesse had to laugh, since it was Alexis. On time was a rarity for her; he'd never known her to be even a minute early at any of their events. "Alexis Du Boise, how nice to see you." Jesse embraced her briefly. "Welcome. Come on in. You're one of the first few to arrive."

"Shocked you, huh? Being on time has always been an issue for me, Reverend Jesse. While I'm in the process of making changes in my lifestyle and in me, I think being on time is a very important one for me to work on. Don't you?"

Jesse chuckled. "I can't argue with you on that," he said, leading the way into the family room. "Punctuality is important. By the way, where's your date?"

Looking a tad dejected, Alexis shrugged her slender shoulders. "We were never able to connect by phone. I've about given up on him, though I did leave on his answering service the address and phone number here at Marlene's suggestion. Hopefully, he'll get the message in time to join us. If not, the party will go on. I plan to show that I'm still alive this evening."

"Diva!" Marlene screeched upon seeing Alexis, running up to

greet her. The two women fell into a loving embrace. Marlene then stepped back. "Look at you. That's a mighty hot outfit you got on. Elegant, too. You sure love your red and it loves you. The color was made with you in mind. It's smashing." Marlene took Alexis by the hand and brought her farther into the room. "You remember my best friend, Myrna, and her husband, Raymond, don't you, Alexis?"

"Of course I do. Hello, Myrna and Raymond. Nice to see you again."

The other couple graciously extended their verbal greetings to Alexis, telling her it was good to see her, too. While Myrna hadn't gotten to know Alexis as well as Marlene and the others had, Marlene kept her informed. Myrna didn't believe it was fair that one woman should have it all. Alexis's natural beauty was just as astounding to Myrna as it was to Marlene. Myrna hoped she wouldn't have to bump her husband to keep him from staring at the widow Du Boise.

Alexis laughed heartily. "Keisha and Rosalinda are going to pass out when they find out I got here before they did. I was just telling Reverend Jesse that one of the ways I'm going to work on my image is by being on time."

The doorbell chimed again, causing an instant hush to come over the room. Marlene's cheeky response to Alexis's "on time" statement had been thwarted.

"Speaking of Keisha and Rosalinda, that might be one or both of them now. I think Michael and Rosalinda planned to pick up Keisha if I'm not mistaken. I'll get the door this time, Jesse. Alexis, do you want to come with me so I can the see the shock on the girls' faces, if it's them?" Marlene asked as she moved toward the hallway.

"That'll be fun." Alexis looked back at Myrna. "Want to come with us?"

Myrna shook her head in the negative, but thanked Alexis for inviting her along. "Girl, now that I've managed to lower myself down on this sofa, I'd better stay here. I might not be able to get back up right away."

Alexis beamed. "Okay. We'll be right back."

Alexis caught up to Marlene and looped her arm through hers. "You look mighty hot yourself, all draped in sexy black. How much weight *have* you lost already?"

"Nearly fifty pounds, but I tend to slow down on the diet. I haven't been feeling well lately. Jesse thinks the condition of my health might have to do with the weight loss."

Alexis looked concerned. "Please be careful. We can't have anything bad happening to you. How would we make it without you around to keep us in check?"

Marlene cracked up. "Don't worry about something like that happening. It's not that bad. Besides, Keisha won't have a problem taking up where I leave off. She's a bossy little cuss, but I love her to life."

"Who you telling? She loves to boss me around more than anyone else in the group."

Marlene quickly opened the door to the newcomers.

The subject of their last conversation was standing there with her hands on her hips, along with Rosalinda and Michael. "It's about time. Didn't you hear the doorbell? We only rang it ten times or more," Keisha rudely inquired. Then she spotted Alexis. "No way you beat us here. You must be ill." Keisha felt Alexis's forehead. "You're not sick, so what is it?"

Rosalinda giggled, squeezing Michael's hand. "I know what it is, guys. Alexis's new man is responsible for getting her here on time. That's the only explanation I can think of. You sure don't look sick in that red hot number," Rosalinda commented, kissing Alexis's cheek.

Smiling at Keisha and Rosalinda, Marlene and Alexis exchanged knowing glances. Then the four animated women embraced each other as if they hadn't seen each other in months.

Just as Marlene was about to close the front door, her handsome Malcolm, fashionably dressed in dark, attractive attire, slipped inside. Todd and his girlfriend, Arlissa, popped into the hall right behind Malcolm only seconds later.

"Sorry for crashing your party, Auntie Marlene. I hope it's okay for us to stay."

Though Marlene hadn't thought to invite the younger couple, she was always glad to see her godson and his girlfriend. "I'm so sorry about such a huge oversight. This little party was thrown together without much thought. I just wasn't thinking. Of course you can stay. You're always welcome here. Your parents are in the family room."

Since they'd all arrived at the same time, Marlene began to wonder if Keisha had come with Malcolm instead of Rosalinda and Michael. She quickly decided not to ask, as she warmly embraced Michael and then the rest of the guest arrivals. Marlene was once again on tenterhooks regarding her son's relationship with the young woman she loved like a daughter. Zach's recent release from prison had brought back her anxiety over the situation. Marlene was very worried.

Though Marlene wasn't accustomed to throwing dinner parties to include the younger couples, now that Malcolm was much closer to his parents and wanted to be around them more, she'd just have to get with the program and make sure they were always included. There were numerous alternatives for him and Todd to get into out in the world, but they'd never be as safe as they were inside their parents' homes.

The party was well underway. As Marlene had expected, the party had gone into full swing within minutes of the arrival of the last guests. Everyone invited was present, and the food was now warming for later consumption. As soon as everything was ready to serve, Marlene and Jesse would lay out on the tables all the delicious goodies.

The hosting couple hadn't been able to help themselves when it came down to sampling. Earlier, right after Sister Sharpe and her two sons had delivered the food, Marlene and Jesse had tasted each delightful entrée. It was Marlene who'd insisted on leaving the baked goods untouched. If Jesse had gotten his way, he would've eaten at least one whole pie.

The women were now congregated in the kitchen, helping Marlene in any way they could. When the doorbell rang, approximately thirty-five minutes after the last guest had arrived, Marlene looked at Alexis. Marlene had noticed that Alexis had started looking a little sad shortly after she'd arrived. Everyone was coupled off, and Marlene suspected that Alexis felt like the fifth wheel. Marlene prayed that Alexis's male friend was at the door. All of her other invited guests were accounted for.

Marlene's heart went out to her beautiful, widowed friend as she approached Alexis. "Can you get that for me, Alexis? I'd appreciate it."

Alexis looked unsure of herself, puzzled by Marlene's request. "Are you sure you want me to go? I don't know all of your friends."

"Absolutely. Just introduce yourself. Hurry up before they decide to leave."

Alexis patted her hair in place and smoothed the nonexistent wrinkles in her stunning red dress as she walked down the hallway to the front door. Then she stopped dead in her tracks, looking totally bewildered. It had just dawned on her that Marlene probably thought Jarreau Thornton might be the late arrival. Alexis had to take a few deep breaths. If Jarreau was the person on the other side of the door, she had to come off cool and calm. Never in a million years would she want him to know how his absence over the past week had affected her.

Alexis's hand trembled as she slowly turned the brass doorknob. Her smile lit up the night the same moment she laid eyes on Mr.

Thornton, who looked too good for her to even try and describe. "Jarreau," she gushed, obviously elated by his presence, despite her valiant attempt to hide it. Alexis silently scolded herself for failing to remain cool.

Jarreau drank in her stunningly elegant appearance. "Alexis, all I seem to ever be able to say to you is 'wow'!" He drew her into his loving embrace. "I'm sorry for being so late, but I just got your message when my plane landed a few hours ago. I was out of town on a business emergency. I immediately rushed home from the air-port to shower and change clothes. I hope your friends won't be upset by my late arrival."

"Not in the least bit," Marlene responded, with Keisha and Rosalinda following right behind her. "Welcome. We're thrilled to have you as a guest in our home. Alexis, would you mind doing the introductions? As you both can see, we have some very curious and nosy guests."

Marlene laughed while slipping her arms around Keisha and Rosalinda, hugging them affectionately. "No malice intended, girls. Let's be sure to make a great first impression."

Alexis was beaming all over as she proudly introduced Jarreau to her dear friends. As he told them how happy he was to meet them, all of the women appeared to be hanging on to his every word. He had passed the group of women's first personality test with flying colors.

Jarreau was polite and charming, and the women couldn't wait for him to reveal the rest of his hopefully wonderful attributes. There was no doubt about his fantastic good looks, which should be the least important element when looking for a responsible, considerate man, just another one of Marlene's teachings. This was the first man Alexis had ever brought around her girlfriends. The other three women cared enough about Alexis to make sure that Jarreau was worthy of her, even if she did have a lot of work to do herself.

Marlene knew the real test was yet to come. The men. What

would all the men in the family room think of Mr. Thornton? In Marlene's opinion, a man was always a better judge of a man's character than a woman could ever hope to be; she couldn't wait to hear Jesse's assessment of Jarreau at evening's end. The happy couple loved to lie in bed and indulge in lively conversation consisting of note comparisons after one of their private social functions.

Arriving in the family room with an entourage of beautiful women surrounding him could've easily made Jarreau the envy of all the males present. But the well-seasoned male guests in Marlene and Jesse's family room were very secure with themselves; the younger guys could've cared less. It hardly took Jarreau any time at all to fit himself right in with the guests, both males and females.

Marlene liked Jarreau already.

Chapter Ten

Completely soaked with perspiration, Alexis sat straight up in the bed, her heart beating erratically. The look of terror was in her eyes. Upon flinging her legs out of bed and struggling to her feet, she felt weak and disoriented. After practically stumbling into her lavish master bathroom, she turned on the cold water. Leaning over the marble sink, she splashed the cold liquid onto her face with her hands, gasping from the reviving coldness.

Returning to the bedroom, Alexis made herself comfortable in the overstuffed chair so that she could try to figure out what had frightened her terribly and had caused her heart to beat so frenetically inside her chest. Laying her head back, she closed her eyes, hoping to recall the nightmare that had awakened her prematurely. It was only three A.M.

R.J.'s image instantly appeared before her. He was alive and well, looking handsome and debonair as ever. Alexis moaned as she reached out to touch him, grasping nothing but air. Alexis then saw herself running to him, but when she flung herself into his arms, she hit the ground, nearly knocking herself senseless. She moaned again, only louder, resulting from sheer disappointment. The reality of him not being there was almost too painful for her to bear.

"Hey, sweet Lexy, you're in harm's way. You could get hurt badly. I'm no longer able to protect you. Please hear what I'm saying to you. I need you to really listen to me."

The voice alarmed and soothed her at the same time, sounding just like that of her deceased husband. Then she heard derisive laughter. Startled, Alexis turned around and saw that Mathis West was standing right behind her. The evil look in his eyes shook her up even more.

Wearing a menacing grin, Mathis started toward Alexis. "Thought he could save you, huh? Face it Alexis, R.J. is dead. I'm all you've got now. Stop fighting the inevitable. You and I are destined. You love money and I have plenty. I can make you happy. R.J. can't. I'm alive. He's not. You've been entertaining a ghost, or perhaps just a figment of your imagination."

Alexis heard herself scream, but she couldn't open her eyes. The images before her were so real, yet she knew without a doubt that R.J. was dead, had been deceased for over two years.

"Lexy," said the voice sounding like R.J.'s, "stay away from West. He's not at all who he says he is. Danger awaits you. Beware, sweet Lexy, beware!"

The images began to fade away just as Alexis's eyes flew open. "Please take me with you. Don't leave me behind, R.J. Please come back. I need you. It can be so different for us now. We are both seeking God. Please R.J.," she sobbed brokenly, "don't leave me here all alone."

A few minutes later, terribly forlorn and emotionally shaken, Alexis made her way back to the bed, climbed in, and put a pillow over her face to muffle her anguished cries. Although she knew she'd just been a victim of a bad nightmare, coupled with a desperate desire to have her husband back, Alexis still wondered if she should take the warning seriously.

Alexis felt extremely fearful. It now seemed to her that she was no closer to getting over R.J.'s death than she'd been right after the tragedy had occurred. How could she miss R.J. so desperately and at the same time desire to have a romantic relationship with Jarreau?

"Jarreau," she whispered, tasting the sweetness of his name on her lips.

Last evening she'd seen yet another side of him, one that she'd completely forgotten. The memories of how much fun he used to be in their youth had resurfaced during the dinner party at Marlene and Jesse's. He had positively wowed her friends. Charm and effervescence had oozed from him. Jarreau had enjoyed himself tremendously and made sure that everyone else did, too.

Marlene had pulled out all the oldie tunes she and Jesse had loved to dance to from the past as well as the present. Once Jesse had removed the throw rugs, exposing the magnificent family room's hardwood floor, the couple had begun the dancing. The party really came alive then. They even lip-synched a couple of Marvin Gaye and Tammy Terrell duets for their guests.

Jarreau was a smooth dancer, surprising everyone with his ability to execute all the latest dance steps. The brother admitted to learning the modern-day steps from watching the videos on BET. That was a real eye-opening revelation. He'd even attempted to teach everyone the newest version of the electric slide. Before the night was over, he had ended up dancing with every female in the room, tireless in his quest to have a smashing good time. Jarreau had also made fast friends with all the guys. His genuineness had shown brightly, like a beacon in the night. Malcolm and Todd mentioned that he was even cool enough to hang out with them sometime.

Alexis thought that Rosalinda and Michael were the most charming couple on the planet. Michael was also a smooth dancer, very light on his feet. He'd guided Rosalinda with ease through an array of salsa steps and other popular Latino dances. The couple had intrigued everyone while they'd performed their own cute and lively version of the Macarena.

Malcolm and Todd got in on the act by performing a few of their latest positive rap and R&B songs, with an inspirational flair.

Keisha surprised all the party attendees when she sang a couple of songs using Malcolm's old Karaoke machine. It turned out that she had a voice of an angel. The girl could sing. Keisha's star-quality talent had shone brightly on the night. Keisha's beautiful voice had prompted Malcolm into asking her to sing background on one of their songs. He also talked about her going into the studio to record with him and Todd.

Marlene wasted no time in telling Keisha that she should join the church choir. Keisha had been delighted by both prospects.

Todd's girlfriend, Arlissa Johnson, had a nice voice, too, very sultry. She and Todd had also performed a duet. Myrna and Raymond had danced quite a bit, but they didn't give any special performance as the others had. As Malcolm was heard saying several times during the evening, the Covington party was off the hook.

Alexis then thought of all the time she'd spent alone with Jarreau after the party. He had followed her home in his car and had stayed until around one-thirty A.M. or so. The rest of their evening had been rather romantic, though not reaching the levels of passion that Alexis had had in mind for them. However, just being around Jarreau was a real treat for her. Alexis was thrilled that he'd made it to the party and that he'd finally met her friends.

As if he hadn't danced enough at the Covington's place, Jarreau indulged Alexis in several more dances, all of them to slow songs. Luther Vandross was his favorite vocalist. It had been a dreamy time for them dancing to the love balladeer's passionate tunes. Although they'd talked a lot, they hadn't gone into depth on any particular subject. Before Jarreau had taken his leave, he and Alexis had shared a cup of coffee while nibbling on Marietta's freshly baked cookies.

In Alexis's opinion, the goodnight kiss had been just like the entire evening: the bomb, off the hook, to steal a couple of lines from the youth. Now she was face to face with her past again.

R.J. had come to Alexis in what seemed like a very real image, warning her of impending danger, and showing her that perhaps she still wasn't ready to move on. But she had to get on with her life. R.J. was dead and he wasn't coming back. All she'd ever have of him was the memories of their past. No matter how many times he showed up in her nightmares and dreams, she'd never be able to touch him. Though not his choice, R.J. had moved on without her.

Coming to grips with her past was way easier than deciding her present and future.

Rosalinda was surprised to see Maria Lopez standing in front of her desk at the telemarketing company where she worked. Seeing Maria again, after all this time, wasn't a good feeling. Rosalinda immediately looked around to see if anyone else was with her. Maria, possessing dark eyes and jet-black, waist-length hair was the beautiful girlfriend of one of Ricardo's boys, Rocco Sanchez. Rosalinda was in no doubt that Ric had sent Maria to deliver to her a threatening message of some sort.

Rosalinda said a silent prayer as she got to her feet. "Hello, Maria," Rosalinda greeted politely, trying to hide the fear she felt way down deep inside. Rosalinda did not want Maria to know how nervous and scared she was.

"Hola, Rosalinda." Maria looked all around the room. "Is there a private place where we could talk? I desperately need your help."

Maria's statement was yet another surprise for Rosalinda, though she wasn't about to leave the building with Maria. Rosalinda couldn't trust anyone in Ric's posse, especially the women. Gangbanging-females were often just as treacherous as the guys, if not more so.

Rosalinda pointed to an empty, glass-enclosed office. "We can go in there, but I only have a few minutes to spare. Follow me."

Once the women were seated, Rosalinda gestured for Maria to speak her mind. Rosalinda had sat down at the only desk with a hidden security alarm button. It was right at her fingertips.

Maria looked Rosalinda right in the eyes. "I need your help, Rosa. I want to know exactly how you did it."

Rosalinda shrugged. "Did what?"

"Break away from Ric. Rocco has been impossible to deal with lately. His drug use has gotten out of control, and he's drinking way too much. Something terrible is weighing on his mind, probably a drive-by or something just as bad. He gets crazy every time something bad goes down with him and the boys. I want out. Now!"

Rosalinda studied Maria's eyes and her facial expression, trying to discern if she was being honest or trying to pull something over on her. Rosalinda and Maria had not been close friends when Rosalinda hung out with Ric and his friends, which was really the only time they ever saw each other. Ric had told Rosalinda that Maria had two years of college under her belt, one of the things that Rocco was attracted to. He had made a bet with the boys that he could get her to drop out of college and become his sidekick. He won the bet shortly after meeting her.

"To begin with, Maria, I was never in the gang. You are. That alone will make it extremely difficult for you to just walk away like I did, though I'm hardly out of danger. The gang has been your family. They were never mine. Ric was my only tie to gangs."

"That's so hard to believe. He must've really loved you to allow you to lead a separate lifestyle than the one he lived. That never happens. If so, it's sure rare."

Rosalinda smiled but deep sadness was present in her dark eyes. "It hasn't been as simple as all that, Maria. No way. Ricardo often begged me to join the gang. There had come a time when he'd tried to insist on it, but my will not to become a part of it was stronger."

Rosalinda had never had any time for gangs. Taking care of her mother and working two jobs hadn't afforded her much free time during the week. Staying out of the gang was the only thing she'd ever been really adamant about with Ric. For whatever reason, he had allowed their relationship to remain separate, but it still had taken the same ugly toll on her.

The pressure for Rosalinda to join up had stopped altogether, after she'd helped to get him out of jail twice. Her having two decent-paying jobs had made his releases possible. Rosalinda couldn't be in a gang and hold down two jobs. The gang lifestyle just wouldn't accommodate steady employment. Gangs made their living off the streets through all sorts of illegal activities. Rosalinda now believed that her finances were more important to Ric than her being in a gang. She had finally come to realize that all he ever saw her for was for bail money and to put money in his prison account.

"I doubt that it was love, Maria. Ricardo isn't just letting me walk away scot-free either. But you already know that, don't you?"

Maria held her hand up in a halting gesture. "No one has mentioned anything like that to me. I know Rocco and Ric are hanging out, but Rocco hasn't mentioned you and Ric. I haven't even seen Ric since he's been out. Wherever he's holed up, no one's saying."

Rosalinda didn't believe Maria. She had a reason for being there, but Rosalinda didn't believe she was there for the reason she'd already given. "What do you need from me, Maria?"

"Like I said before, I need your help. I want to get away from under Rocco's control, but I'm really scared. Besides, I don't have any money or a job."

"Didn't you apply for county assistance for you and Rocco's baby?"

"Si, but I was told that I'd have to name the father so they could go after him and order him to pay child support. I was denied benefits when I told them I didn't know who the father was. That has worked for other people, but it didn't work for me. Rocco would've killed me if I had given them his name."

Rocco's killing you anyway, Rosalinda mused. She saw fear in Maria's dark eyes, the kind of fear that she'd often felt with Ric. Maybe Maria wasn't lying and really did need help. But Rosalinda had to wonder if she could afford to take that high of a risk and help Maria. What if Maria was lying just to set her up? Rosalinda felt completely torn in two by her sincere desire to help Maria and her dire need to protect herself.

Rosalinda was glad that she'd finally seen the light, but felt that her life was in more danger now than before. Ric had been severely scorned. Every day that he was out on the streets was a day that she would have to live in fear for her life. Even if they caught him, she still had to worry about the orders he might give his posse to execute against her.

Maria began biting her nails. "If I had money, I'd just up and leave. My older brother, Arturo, lives in Newark, New Jersey. He'd let me come there if I asked."

"Can he help you with your airfare or bus transportation?"

"I don't know. I don't want to ask him. He has three kids and a wife to take care of. I'd only stay with him temporarily, until I can halfway stand on my own two feet. Rocco doesn't know my brother. I'm glad about that. My brother would never approve of what I'm doing."

"Why don't you get a part-time job and save up?"

Maria shrugged. "Rocco would never let me work."

"Why not? Perhaps you can convince him that having a job would also benefit him."

"Rosalinda, you know Rocco and his macho behind. He would see that as me screwing with his dignity. He'd never allow it."

Rosalinda shook her head. Sitting across from her was the woman she could've so easily become and in some instances had become. Because she'd insisted on not joining the gangs and had continued working, she was way ahead of Maria in the game of life. At twenty-four, Maria already looked tired and washed out. It was possible that she'd had enough of living such a volatile lifestyle, Rosalinda considered.

"Maybe I can help you, Maria. Check the ticket prices for both the airlines and the bus, or even the train."

Maria shook her head. "The bus or the train. I ain't flying nowhere. The skies haven't been too friendly lately."

Rosalinda nodded with understanding. "Suit yourself."

"Rosalinda, please don't let anyone know I came here to see you.

Not even your cousin, Little Jesus. If word were to get out that I wanted to leave Rocco, we both know what would happen to me next. Promise to keep this our secret?"

"I promise. Call me here tomorrow." She handed a business card to Maria, since Ricardo already knew where she worked; he also had the private phone number to her desk. "I may be leaving this job in a few weeks, so you might not be able to reach me here after that."

Michael had wanted Rosalinda to give notice right away, effective immediately, though he understood that a two-week notice would leave her in good standing with the company, especially should she want to come back and apply for a job at a later time.

"If you're serious, Maria, I'll try to help. If you're not, please don't bother to call me tomorrow. If I don't hear from you, I'll know you've changed your mind."

Seated in Jesse's private study at the church, Marlene had just finished reading to Jesse from the list of situations that had arisen in the church. There were many needs that had to be met. Marlene also had typed up a list of the members who were sick in the hospital, shut-ins at home, and residents of nursing facilities and rehab centers.

Marlene handed a letter to Jesse for him to read. She couldn't wait to hear his response, hoping for him to be as excited as she was. The female inmates at the prison she'd visited for research had heard about her support group for women and wanted her to come talk with them. Although they were inmates, and not ladies in waiting, they thought she was someone they'd like to talk to about their situations.

Marlene was elated by their request for her to visit with them in a group setting. To get to meet these women was a real blessing. It would help her and Jesse understand the difference between the two groups. Knowing that their men didn't support these female inmates in the same way that the ladies in waiting supported theirs, Marlene hoped to learn more about how these women had landed in prison. Since she was armed with the knowledge that a lot of women were behind bars because of a man, she could hardly wait to hear the firsthand accounts.

Jesse looked up from the letter. "This is amazing. I'm eager to find out the outcome of the meeting. You are going to meet with them, aren't you?"

"I can't think of anything that would keep me away. I have so many questions. Meeting the female inmates will really shed a lot of light on the difference in support from men to women. This should be one enlightening experience."

"I agree. I pray that your project will have the blessings of God. Please keep me updated. Getting back to our meeting agenda, what's on the schedule for today, Wildflower?"

Marlene picked up her calendar listings. "Today we've scheduled the food pick-up from the food bank at 9:30 A.M. Reverend Lee Conklin is down to meet with you at 11:30 A.M.-12:00 noon. Lunch with the deacons is 12:30-2:30 P.M., but several of them can't make it. You'll have three hours until your next scheduled appointment, a 5:30 P.M. counseling session for you and the soon-to-be newlyweds, Brandy Sands and Dwight Randolph. And you're to counsel Samuel and Yvonne Carter on their marital problems at 7:30 P.M. Things are starting to look up for the Carters, but they still have a ways to go. I'm glad they're trying to work their problems out."

Jesse smiled sweetly at his wife. "Thanks to you. It was brilliant of you to tell Yvonne to look for something to do to keep her mind occupied. I'm glad you approached me about hiring her. She's doing a great job. Yvonne is only here three days a week, but she says having a part-time job has done wonders for her 'inner-self.'"

Jesse chuckled. "'Inner-self.' That's one of your favorite words, Marlene. I've lost count of how many times I've heard you say that. The Lord was the only one who knew how much both she and I needed help. Samuel's not too happy about her getting a job, but I've been preaching to him about his negative mindset. Hopefully, we can keep them out of divorce court. We both know that prayer and counseling works, Marlene. God is always in control."

"Amen to that. Let's move on down the list so we can cover everything before I leave. I have a tight schedule today as well."

Jesse stroked his chin. "When are we going to get back to delivering the food baskets to those that can't make it here to pick them up? I haven't done that since I've been home."

"Delivering the food baskets," Marlene iterated, shuddering at the thought. "Every time I think of you making those deliveries, I think of you getting arrested while doing a wonderful community service. What an unpleasant memory."

Jesse blinked hard. "I'm sorry for conjuring up bad memories for you, Mar. Forgive me. But that's one of the duties I miss most."

"I know." Marlene looked disillusioned. "I admit to purposely moving that duty from your schedule. I didn't want to reproduce old memories for you either. That was one horrific day. I've been so afraid of you reliving that memory if you started delivering the baskets again. It would hurt you so much."

Jesse got up from his seat and walked around his desk. After pulling Marlene up from her seat, he took her in his arms and hugged her tightly. He then held her at arm's length. "You are too thoughtful and you think of everything. Thanks for wanting to protect me. But, Mar, it's been over two years now. I need you to know that I can handle anything with God by my side. I'd like to add the delivery route back to my schedule. It's one of my favorite things to do."

Jesse snapped his fingers. "I have an idea. Let's do it together for the next few months. That way, you'll get to see how much pleasure I get out of it. You can be there to comfort me, should the need arise. What do you think?"

Marlene beamed adoringly at her loving spouse. She then gave him a warm hug. This was the one man that she would go through the fire for and with. *Yes, Jesse is a very unique man*, she mused. He never failed to amaze her.

"Brilliant idea, husband! Food baskets go out every Friday now, as opposed to how we used to do it every other week. We might be able to start this together next Friday, but I have to check my own schedule first. I'll also have to tell Reverend Clay Robinson that we're relieving him of that duty. I'm sure he'll be okay with it. He's still a bit overworked. He could probably use the break. The youth activities keep him hopping."

"I'm sure." Jesse kissed his wife full on the mouth. "Mmm, delicious. But we'd better get back to work before we get into serious trouble. Another kiss like that will have me slipping you out of here early." Smiling broadly, Jesse winked at his wife as he sat back down.

Laughing, Marlene reseated herself. "Don't get started with me, you old, charming saint. You know it doesn't take much for you to get me going. We still haven't made up for all the time we've lost."

Jesse threw his head back in laughter. "Girl, we'll never make that up. Besides, things are much, much better anyway. With Malcolm out of the house, we're free to express ourselves loudly." He couldn't help chuckling. "Don't you think so?"

Marlene giggled, covering her mouth so that those working in the outer offices wouldn't hear her. "I've never had any complaints in that department. But I have noticed that you're a little more amorous, way more often." She giggled again, blowing him several kisses.

Jesse felt proud as a peacock. He stuck his chest out even farther, eyeing his wife in a flirtatious manner. "Since I have a late evening counseling session scheduled, perhaps you should take a little nap before I get home." He wiggled his eyebrows suggestively. "Would you mind waiting up for me?"

"You got it, love."

"No, I haven't, not yet. But I'm definitely looking forward to getting it later."

While scolding him with her eyes, Marlene couldn't help blushing. "As you suggested a few moments back, Reverend Jesse Covington, we'd better get back to work. We've gotten way off track with this here burning-desires conversation."

Jesse gave her another flirting wink. "It's going to be hard to do, Wildflower."

For the next forty-five minutes, Marlene discussed with Jesse his scheduled duties for a two-week period. She then updated him on the happenings in the church, those things that she was privy to. The immediate emergency needs of several of the church members were laid out and discussed in great depth. While Marlene counseled many of the female church members and nonmembers, her job as personal advisor to her husband was the one she found the most joy in.

The meeting came to an abrupt end when Marlene noticed the time. She had promised to take Sister Wylie to the hair salon for her late-afternoon appointment.

Marlene gathered up her personal belongings and set them on the edge of the desk. She then walked around to Jesse's chair and gave him a sweet good-bye kiss. "I'll see you tonight. Do you have anything particular in mind for dinner this evening, Jesse? If I don't have on hand what you might want, I can stop by the store on my way home."

"Anything you fix for dinner is fine with me. It's the dessert I'm most interested in."

Alexis smiled brilliantly as Jarreau introduced her to his staff as his special assistant. The skeptical glances passing from one employee to another weren't lost on either Alexis or Jarreau. Alexis could clearly see the envy in a couple of the females' eyes. That Jarreau was having a love affair with his so-called assistant was probably the general consensus of those present, Alexis mused thoughtfully. She and Jarreau might be having a mild affair, Alexis thought, but her being in his suite of offices was all about business, and she planned to keep it that way.

No matter what they did outside the building, Alexis vowed to keep their relationship strictly platonic within the corporate structure.

Jarreau put his arm loosely around Alexis's shoulder, but only for a brief moment. "Alexis Du Boise will be helping us out with our major fundraising efforts. She has a lot of influential friends, the kind with bottomless purses and wallets. She's going to be a real asset."

Jarreau laughed to ease the tension. No one followed suit but Alexis. She immediately felt silly for doing so. It was obvious that she had her work cut out for her. These people weren't going to readily accept her as one of them. She was the enemy for now. It didn't take a genius to figure out that she'd have to earn their trust. One at a time, she mused, knowing she wasn't going to win over everyone all at once. Prayer and patience would see her through.

Tomika, a cute sister with short hair and long eyelashes laughed heartily. "I'm sure she has already become an *ass*et to you." Tomika's emphasis on the first syllable spoke volumes.

Carlotta, a beautiful young woman who appeared to be of mixed heritage, black and Mexican, snorted at Tomika's churlish remark. "Pay her no mind, Ms. Du Boise. Tomika always has a boulderlike chip on her shoulder." Carlotta double winked at Alexis. "If I can be of any assistance to you as you settle in, please don't hesitate to call on me. I was once a new employee, too. It's nice to have you join the staff. Welcome aboard!"

Alexis took Carlotta's hand and squeezed it gently. "Thank you. Your generous remarks have helped a lot. Please feel free to call me Alexis. I'm not into formalities."

Carlotta smiled at Alexis. "Okay, Alexis it is. Most everyone calls me Carly. I'd like it if you'd call me by the same. Please excuse me. Mr. T., take care. I'll talk to you later."

Alexis laughed, her twinkling eyes fixed on Jarreau. "Mr. T.! I like that one. All we need to do now is get you a bunch of gold chains and a few gaudy earrings."

Everyone laughed at Alexis's comment, including Tomika.

Jarreau feigned a punch at Alexis. "Okay, funny girl, let's get on with the tour."

Jarreau led Alexis down a long corridor where her private office was located. After using a key to open the door, Jarreau allowed Alexis to precede him. Her loud gasp made him smile. She was pleased at her new digs and that meant a lot to him.

Alexis's eyes swept the spacious, smartly furnished office. The modern wood furnishings were stained in subtle shades of gray and black, complemented by red and white accents. The huge picture window offered a perfect view of the bustling streets below and the beautiful park directly across the street.

Alexis jumped up and down like a school kid, clapping her hands and moaning with delight. After making her way over to the desk, she leaned over and smelled the fresh aroma coming from a huge red cellophane-wrapped wicker basket.

Turning back to face Jarreau, Alexis emitted her brightest smile. "You remembered after all these years. Unbelievable."

"So I did. The Alexis I once knew never ate candy or a bunch of gooey sweets. Although she loved an occasional pastry or two, her favorite thing to snack on was fresh fruit and unshelled nuts. You have a basket full of fruits and nuts for your eating pleasure. You might have to share some of the fruit so it won't perish. I, for one, won't mind helping you eat it. The basket is my way of saying welcome. I'm so happy to have you here."

Alexis thought of kissing him, passionately, but remembered her own cardinal rule: no improprieties in the office. "Thank you, Jarreau, for the beautiful gift basket. I'm glad to be here. I'm looking forward to working with you and your staff."

"You're welcome, Alexis. If you need anything, just ask. Someone will always be willing to help you out. I know there was a bit of tension out there earlier, but most of the staff members are great folk and real easy to get along with. Tomika is young and a bit unpolished, but she's a good kid. You'll make friends with everyone in no time at all."

"Thanks for the vote of confidence."

"No problem. I'll check on you in a while. Okay?"

"Sure thing. But if you have a few minutes more, I'd like to run something by you."

Jarreau pulled up a chair as Alexis settled behind her new desk. Unable to resist the temptation, Alexis twirled herself around in the swivel chair. She laughed and laughed, revealing how happy she was.

Jarreau looked amused. Alexis was like a little girl all over again. He knew that she was excited about her new job, thrilled that she might be instrumental in truly making a difference in the lives of others. It elated him to see her so excited. "I'm interested in hearing your thoughts. What's on your mind, Alexis?"

"Getting our first fundraiser underway. I have a few reliable people that I can call on to help me pull this together. While I have several wealthy folks that would see the importance of our mission, my few black friends, all of whom you've met, will go crazy at the opportunity to participate in a venture of this magnitude. I'd like to pull together a fall event. Did you see all the talent that was at Marlene and Jesse's house the night of the party?"

"Sure I did, but what does that have to do with fundraising?"

"Talent shows are a great way of raising funds, Jarreau. Can you trust me to pull it all together? Once I come up with a written proposal, I'll turn it over to you. I have the perfect person to help me write it. Marlene Covington, everyone's personal wonder woman."

Alexis's excitement was certainly contagious. Jarreau felt exhilarated by all her energy. "Jumping in with both feet first is what I love to see my employees do. You have my complete trust, Alexis. Just keep me in the loop."

"As you wish. You won't be sorry, Jarreau. I can promise that much."

He grinned. "I don't think I will be. I feel your energy. Dinner tonight?"

Alexis smiled beautifully. "If you promise me we can further discuss my ideas for the fundraiser before we get into our personal interests."

"You're on. My place. I'll print out the directions for you from Map Quest. See you around seven-thirty if my plans are okay with you."

"Seven-thirty, Jarreau. Your place."

Once Jarreau cleared the doorway, Alexis twirled around in the chair a few more times, laughing with pleasure. She felt energized. For someone who hadn't had a job since she was a teenager, Alexis Du Boise had landed an important one. She actually felt needed.

Her first fundraising venture would be off the hook, the social event of the year. She had to laugh at her choice of words. Ever since she'd heard Malcolm Covington repeatedly utter the slang phrase at his parents' party, she'd been using it readily. She had plenty of seed money to get the ball rolling, her personal donation to the foundation, of course. Alexis turned the chair around to face the window. Smiling, she looked over at the beautiful view of the park.

Seated in Keisha's living room, Malcolm looked from Keisha to Tammy, wondering how Zach had managed to get not only one, but two beautiful women completely under his control. He'd had a hard time believing that Tammy had allowed Zach to come live with her, after he'd heard the news from Keisha a few weeks back. Malcolm thought Tammy was very attractive, and he loved her heartwarming smile.

Much to Malcolm's surprise, Tammy had showed up within minutes of his arrival. He'd overheard her saying that she'd come there to make sure that Keisha was okay with her living arrangements with Zach, and to reassure her that it was strictly platonic.

Malcolm had stopped by to visit with Keisha and see how she was doing. This was the first time he'd been inside her apartment since Zach was released. He was trying to avoid any sort of altercation with Keisha's man, especially since she hadn't declared her relationship with Zach as history. Keisha was still on the fence about him, though she wasn't about to admit it.

Malcolm had had such a wonderful time with Keisha at his parents' party. Although she had arrived with Rosalinda and Michael, he'd driven her home in his car, where they'd spent over an hour just sitting and talking about the night's lively events. Malcolm was so astonished by Keisha's amazing singing voice and couldn't wait to record something with her. He thought they'd make a dynamic duo. Their incredible singing voices were a great blend.

Listening to Tammy talk to Keisha about her expansion plans for the two shops she owned gave him an indication of how intelligent Tammy was. He found her enthusiasm refreshing. This was a woman that knew what she wanted out of life; it was obvious that she knew exactly how to get it. The only thing that didn't add up for him was how she'd gotten all hung up on a guy in prison. That it had occurred through the U.S. mail was the most astonishing.

Keisha was also smart, too smart to be with a guy like Zachary Martin.

How in the world had these lovely, energetic sisters ended up with a man like Zach? Malcolm didn't want to be judgmental. He had no right to be. He used to be a taker and a user, too. If he could change his own life around, so could Zach. Mr. Martin had two very good reasons to change, his son and daughter. Zach felt compelled to pray for the brother, just as many people had prayed for him when he was a product of the world.

Malcolm then wondered if Zach had gotten a job yet. If not, he gave thought to trying to help him get on at one of the other county parks. Malcolm figured that his thinking might be a little crazy and that others might also see it that way. But Malcolm knew what it was like to be down and out, even if his own dilemma had been the direct result of making bad choices.

Malcolm realized that Zach couldn't even begin to take care of his kids without a gig. Had the County of Los Angeles not taken a chance on him, Malcolm didn't know where he'd be today, since his employment history had been one big blemish. He'd never held what one would call a steady job, which was hardly a consideration for gainful employment with a large, prestigious government agency like the County of Los Angeles.

Malcolm couldn't keep at bay the thought of him possibly getting to meet Zach one day. He really wanted to see just what the man was all about. Everything he'd heard about Zach had come from Keisha and Marlene. Since Keisha probably wouldn't agree to introduce them to each other, Malcolm knew he had to find a way to make it happen without her. He had to satisfy his curiosity about Zach once and for all. Even with those optimistic types of thoughts, Malcolm had serious reservations about how a meeting between them would play out.

Malcolm eyed Tammy with mild interest. "At your age, how'd you manage to become owner of one beauty salon, let alone two?"

Tammy smiled sweetly at Malcolm, wondering if he and Keisha had something deep going on, since Keisha definitely seemed interested in him on a personal level. Tammy thought he was drop-dead gorgeous. If Keisha wasn't romantically involved with him, though Tammy recalled her saying something about an attraction to him a good while back, Tammy would certainly like to get to know him better. She hadn't been in his company all that long, but he seemed like a pretty decent guy. She had also noticed how attentive and caring he was to Keisha, which could mean that he had a personal interest in her even if the feeling wasn't mutual.

"The first salon was willed to me by my grandmother. I then took some of the liquid assets that she left me and invested it in the second shop. No computerized system can ever take the place of a beautician. There will always be a need for those in my profession. However, I wish there were more blacks that owned beauty supply stores and nail shops. The Asians have a corner on those two markets in particular. They study us in depth, learning our likes, and then cater to them. Hair is in, lots of it. Braids, weaves, wigs, sister-locks, and so on."

Malcolm was keenly interested in investments. He was saving money so that he could invest it in something worthwhile. He didn't want to break his back working for the rest of his life. He loved his job with the youth; the county had a good retirement program, but he was also interested in becoming an entrepreneur. "So, Tammy, do you think there's good money in the beauty supply business?"

"Excellent money!"

"How much money do you think a person would need to invest in a store?"

"I don't know, but I can find out for you. Are you interested in owning a supply store?"

"You sure have me thinking about it."

"If you're serious, perhaps we could invest in one together. Would you have time to help run it? It won't run itself."

"Sure, after working my regular job. I work an occasional Saturday, mainly when we have a field trip scheduled for the kids. I'd have to stick with my full-time gig for a while. Are you serious about the possibility of going into business with me, girl?"

Keisha suddenly felt left out. She almost envied how Malcolm and Tammy had struck up a conversation so easily with each other. It surprised her that Malcolm was interested in owning his own business. Keisha was impressed with both Tammy and Malcolm. They had goals, something she was still learning how to set. Meeting them was something else.

Keisha cleared her throat, gaining the attention of her guests. "What about a third partner? This girl would also like to get in on a piece of the action. I'd also like to know how much money would be needed for the initial investment." Keisha didn't have two nickels saved up, but she had just joined the credit union savings plan. The first automatic deduction from her paycheck was to occur on her next payday. She had opted to start out with fifty dollars a month, at twenty-five dollars every two weeks.

It was now Malcolm who was surprised. "Are you serious, Keisha?"

Keisha looked Malcolm right in the eye, thrusting out her chin in defiance. "Just as serious as you are. I guess you don't see me like that. I'm not as stupid as I've been acting most of my adult life. Is it okay for this girl to finally have goals, too?"

Malcolm slid the back of his hand down Keisha's face in a loving gesture, wishing he'd shown a little more sensitivity toward her. "I've always been able to see you for what you are. Getting you to see your real self has been the problem. You're not stupid, far from it. We all make mistakes, Keisha. Both you and I are in the process of rectifying ours. Going into business with you two would be a blast. So, Tammy, do you really think this deal could happen?"

Tammy's eyes were bright with enthusiasm. "It's certainly something worth exploring. Maybe we should get together and discuss it in depth. Have any free time this week?"

Malcolm grinned. "You name the time and place; I'm there."

Keisha saw something almost magical happening between Malcolm and Tammy, but she wasn't exactly sure what it meant. Were they flirting with each other or was it just her imagination running wild? Had she been totally wrong in reading Malcolm's intentions toward her? Had she miscalculated his feelings for her? Since she hadn't been asked to attend the meeting, she felt a tad slighted and left out. She'd been denying any real feelings for Malcolm because she wasn't sure she could ever be over Zach. If that was the case, then why was she experiencing the unpleasant feelings brought on by burning jealousy?

The doorbell rang and Keisha looked toward the entry. She didn't know who was at the door, but their timing couldn't be any worse. For whatever reason, she felt like she didn't want to leave Tammy and Malcolm alone for a second, didn't want to miss a word spoken. The next ring of the bell had her reluctantly excusing herself. Slowly, she walked to the door, looking back at her guests all the while. A quick look through the peephole caused her heart to drop.

It was Zach.

Chapter Eleven

While praying for strength, Keisha opened the door to Zach. How to introduce Malcolm to her kids' father was pressing heavily on her mind. Zach was going to make his own assumptions about her and Malcolm no matter the truth. As sure as she was living and breathing, he was eventually going to accuse her of sleeping with Malcolm.

Zach smiled broadly as he handed Keisha several clothing store bags. "These are for the kids." When he tried to kiss her cheek, she pushed him away, hurting his feelings in the process.

"What is all this, Zach?"

Zach had a proud look on his face. "Open the bags and see."

Keisha, showing lots of attitude, made a dramatic showing of opening the bags and pulling out the contents. The clothes were darling, but how he'd managed to pay for them had her upset. The more she thought about it, the angrier she got. Grabbing him by the arm, she practically dragged him into her living room, where Tammy and Malcolm were seated. Keisha also had the bags of new clothes in tow.

Keisha looked from Zach to Tammy as she threw the bags down

on the table. "Which one of you thinks I'm dumber than dirt? Or do both of you share in that sentiment?"

Tammy looked shocked. "What are you talking about?"

Keisha posted her right hand on her hip. "Look, Sister Cookie, I really don't know what's going on with you, but I know Mr. Zach put you up to this vulgar scam. I know you want to help him out, but you can't support his kids for him. If anyone buys the kids' clothes, it should be him or me, and no one else. . . ."

"Just wait a minute, Keisha. . . ."

Keisha sucked her teeth hard, shaking her finger from side to side. "No, you wait! I've befriended you, Tammy, despite the fact that you were once involved with my man. But if you continue disrespecting me, I'll kick your behind to the curb just like I did your partner in crime. You all don't need to keep playing me. If Zach hasn't told you how I am, I will. I can get downright crazy when it comes to my kids. My boundaries are now clear. Don't step over the line again. Okay?" Keisha's hands swept over the clothes. "These cute little pieces of lint fluffs go back to where they came from. Hope you kept the receipts. Are you feeling me yet?"

Malcolm had a hard time believing what was going down. Keisha was acting like she'd lost her mind, all over new clothes for her kids. What did it matter who bought them? He saw nothing but good intentions in the act. Malcolm didn't like the way Keisha was handling things. However, he was glad that Zach was too busy watching Keisha's wild performance to focus on who he was and why he was in Keisha's apartment. He wasn't interested in a confrontation.

Tammy had a slight smirk on her face as she crossed her legs. "Are you finished, Keisha? If so, may I speak?"

"Have at it. But I'm warning you, don't try to con me. I'm barely revved up."

Tammy's laugh was sarcastic. "For starters, I had nothing to do with the purchase of these clothes. If you'd given me a chance to speak before you flew into a tantrum, you could've spared us all the grief and saved yourself some energy." Tammy turned to Zach. "I think it's time for you to enter Keisha's boxing arena. Don't you?"

Zach shot Keisha a hard look. "I don't have to explain a thing to you, but I will. I bought the clothes. Tammy had nothing to do with it. The clothes were bought with the money I made from working odd jobs for the last two weeks. I saved the money so I could do this for my babies. It was also my way of showing you I was trying to be responsible. So much for that! It would've been easier getting money the old way, but I decided to try a new avenue, just like you've been constantly nagging me about." Zach turned around and started for the door.

Keisha felt horrible for confronting Zach in front of her guests. She should've asked him about the clothes before assuming how he'd come by them. For someone who thought Zach would come into her house with assumptions about her and Malcolm, she'd done exactly what she'd expected of him. He never even got to meet Malcolm, let alone make assumptions.

"Wait, Zach! Don't leave yet."

Keisha got to the door just in time to have it slammed in her face. Tears filled her eyes. She had flubbed that one really good. Zach had tried to prove himself to her, but all she'd given him was a lot of attitude and sarcasm. How was she going to right that wrong? Zach was as stubborn as she was, which often made apologies between them darn near ineffective.

Looking glum, Keisha came back into the living room and dropped down on the sofa. "I blew that one big time."

Malcolm clapped his hands, his usual way of taunting Keisha. "Premier performance, Keisha. Too bad you weren't acting on a stage somewhere. You might've gotten an award."

"Don't start, Malcolm!"

"That's still your response to everything, isn't it? Do you know what you just did to that man's self-esteem?" Malcolm asked

Keisha. "If you don't know, I'll tell you. You just trampled all over it. You showed him no mercy, Keisha. What you did was foul."

Tammy reached over and rubbed Keisha's shoulders. "I have to agree with Malcolm. That wasn't what Zach needed from you. He's really trying. I hope you plan to apologize."

Keisha nodded. "For all the good it'll do me. Zach's head and heart are as hard as mine at times. We are both members of the mule family. I know I was wrong to put him down like that. I'll call him later, at your place. I owe you an apology, too. I'm sorry, Tammy. I should've asked questions before I jumped all over both of you. I hope you can forgive me."

"Without question," Tammy responded, giving Keisha a warm hug.

Keisha reached for Malcolm's hand. "I'm sorry you had to see that. It wasn't pretty."

"You're right about that," Malcolm seconded. "It was downright ugly. Had the kids been here, would you have performed like that in front of them? I sure hope not."

Keisha shook her head. "I wouldn't have. It might've been hard for me to hold my tongue, but I would've done it. My kids are not going to suffer another day through Zach's and my volatile relationship. I made that promise to myself, and I'm going to keep it." Keisha turned to Tammy once again. "Where has Zach been working?"

"He's been all over the place looking for work. He told me he had mowed about six different lawns for this realty management company. He did such a good job that they're going to let him continue to do it every two weeks. He also worked on a dump truck a couple of days."

Keisha's eyes widened with disbelief. "Hard labor and Zach are total strangers! He must really be trying to do things right. But he did take a course in landscaping while in prison. Maybe it will pay off for him. I hope so. I'd like to see him have some successes in his life."

Malcolm saw that Keisha's heart was softening rather quickly toward Zach. He wasn't sure how he felt about it. He liked Keisha enough, but there were a lot of things to still consider before getting into an exclusive relationship with her. Her kids had become a major concern for him, especially after his mother had lectured him about being careful with their fragile little hearts.

For right now, Malcolm decided it would be best to just focus on the music project he had in mind for them. That would give him enough time with her to see how things developed between them. He wasn't going to push for anything more than friendship at the moment. Both he and Keisha had a lot of very real issues to work through.

Malcolm got to his feet. "I'm hungry. What about you guys joining me? I'm buying."

"If you're thinking of McDonalds or Burger King, I'll pass," Keisha joked, laughing.

Malcolm pulled her up from the sofa and brought her in close to him. "Girl, I'm talking about some real food, steak and potatoes. Sizzler's Steak House is what I had in mind."

Keisha hugged him tightly. "Now that's what I'm talking about! I'm in. What about you, Tammy?" Keisha asked, looking over Malcolm's broad shoulder.

Despite the sudden envy she felt for Keisha having both Zach and Malcolm wrapped around her little finger, Tammy grinned. "I can go for the salad bar. Is it okay if I use the bathroom before we head out?" Keisha merely nodded her approval.

Once Tammy cleared the room, Malcolm lifted Keisha's chin with his two fingers. "I think a face-to-face visit with Zach will go over better than a phone call. You owe him that much."

Seated across from his ex-girlfriend, Cicely Kirkland, in the prison waiting room, impeccably dressed, Eric looked shell-shocked by the bomb Cicely had just dropped on him. It felt as though all the flying shrapnel and other dangerous debris from the bomb had struck the dead center of his heart. Since it was hard for him to make direct eye contact with her, because of deep shame and embarrassment, Eric kept his eyes averted.

The only time Eric had felt so sick inside was when he first discovered Cicely's out-of-control drug use. Learning now that Cicely had begun using drugs because of something he'd done to hurt her had him trembling within. His stomach was tied up in concrete knots. He'd never felt such shame as he did after hearing what Cicely had had to say.

That Cicely had known about his covert dalliance, though very brief, with his ex-fiancée, Traci Patterson, while he and Cicely had been still living under the same roof had come as a major blow to him. The shockwaves were still reverberating throughout his body.

Eric took a brief spin back in the past, hoping to buy himself enough time to think up the right words to say to Cicely. His love for her was never more apparent to him than it was right now. He felt it deeply. Her pain and suffering had also instantly become his cross to bear. The unbearable guilt weighing down on his heart almost made it hard for him to breathe.

Eric immediately recalled the late evening that Traci Patterson had called him to come over to her house due to the recent breakup of her latest relationship. She had been crying over the phone and had sounded so distraught. Since he and Traci had remained good friends after the split, he'd seen no harm in coming to her rescue, even though Cicely had been living with him.

In his attempts to console Traci on that fateful evening, one thing had led to another. Their covert affair had been going on for over a month, when Eric began to realize they just couldn't go back to where they'd once been. Traci was not what he wanted. He had totally lost those loving feelings, but the great sex had had him experiencing all sorts of wonderful things.

It was only after he'd committed the egregious wrongdoing that he'd come to understand what Cicely truly meant to him. He had immediately ended the affair with Traci to resume his once happy life with Cicely. Shortly after returning all his attention and affection back to Cicely, his world began to crash down around his ears. Cicely had suddenly turned into a stranger.

Eric finally made direct eye contact with Cicely. The tears streaming down her face cut him to the quick. "I just don't know what to say, Cicely."

Cicely blinked hard, fighting off her anger. "I guess not. I wouldn't know what to say, either, if I'd come off as self-righteous as you have. You hurt me, Eric, deeper than you can ever imagine. I never dreamed you'd be the one to destroy me in this way. I was wrong to trust you. Too bad I didn't know that back then."

Eric filled his cheeks with air and slowly blew it out. "Why didn't you say anything, Cicely? Why didn't you come to me with what you knew?"

"For what? So you could just stand up in my face and deny it? Lie to me without any compunction whatsoever? The bold-faced lies would've hurt even more. One of the things that hurt the most is that we'd been living nothing but one big lie. Everything about us was a nasty falsehood. I just didn't know when it had become that way, so I had to assume it was like that from the get-go. You disrespected me in the worst way possible, Eric Eldridge. And you did it with such ease. For such a self-righteous police officer, you acted out the part of a smooth criminal with veteran perfection. One problem. You weren't as smooth as you thought."

Eric knew that Cicely had made points that he couldn't even begin to argue with. Besides, he didn't want to mount a defense. His main objective now was to find out if they could get past the past and start their relationship all over again. They were having a baby. Although on his last visit she had hinted that the child wasn't his, his heart told him differently. "Can you explain how the drug use ties in with everything else?"

"Are you sure you want to know, Eric?"

"I did ask."

Cicely had been the type of person who harshly judged people on drugs. She had not an ounce of sympathy for their pitiful kind. She'd had no clue how easily addiction could occur. It couldn't happen to her. She'd never be that weak. Drug users were nothing but losers. Cicely Kirkland had been a winner all her life. Drugs and alcohol would never take her down and eventually shove her in the city sewer. She'd never become a statistic of near overdoses or death.

How quickly her tune had changed. One snort of cocaine had had Cicely singing away the blues and dancing to sweeter music. While lost in her white-powdered dreams, nothing could touch her. She was safe from all hurt, harm, and danger. However, when she'd awaken from her peaceful sleep, her soft whispers had turned into the loudest screams. The fear that had come with withdrawal pains had had her constantly looking for her next score, by any means necessary. Getting hold of that next fix had eventually become her main objective in life.

"One evening, when I'd gone out with my friends, after I learned you were still seeing Traci, I was offered a hit of cocaine. I was in so much emotional agony that night, so I snorted it without giving it any thought. Then I later smoked a joint. Both drugs took away my pain. It kept me from thinking of you, of us. I just didn't realize that it was only a temporary fix."

Cicely stared ahead blankly. Lost in the nightmare she'd created for herself, she no longer saw Eric seated across from her. No one was in the visiting room but her. Visions of her wandering the streets late at night filled her head. Cold and hungry, sweating profusely, and screaming out from the pain in her body were easy but excruciating recollections. The tears barreling down her cheeks were the only indication of what she might be going through.

Cicely finally looked up at Eric again, hating the fathomless pain she saw in his eyes. It suddenly dawned on her that Eric wasn't the cause of her addiction, just the source of her pain. He didn't shove those drugs up her nose or into her mouth. She only had herself to blame for that. This wasn't the end he would've wanted for her no matter how he felt about her.

Yes, he'd hurt her deeply, but she could no longer hold him responsible for what had occurred to her. The responsibility for the train wreck she'd made of her life laid solely with her. Clean and sober was starting to feel nice. Talking about her pain to Eric had helped a lot. What about her unborn baby? Was she about to deliver into the world yet another crack baby? For the first time ever, her hand went over her stomach, massaging it in a protective manner.

Cicely wiped her eyes and nose on the sleeve of her shirt. "When the pain returned, I had already learned how to purchase my relief on the streets. Then, when my pain just wouldn't go away, I kept getting deeper into the drug scene. I kept on using until I was hopelessly addicted. The first time I hit the crack pipe, the unbelievable high took me to a place I'd never been before. I didn't want to return from there. Reality was too darn harsh. One day, much to my surprise, I learned that I no longer had a reality. It eventually became easier for me to be weak than to remain strong. Petty crimes and prison lockdowns followed as my addiction continued to balloon out of control. End of Cicely Kirkland's pathetic story."

Eric gulped hard. "I wish you could've come to me and talked this out before things got so freaking bad for you."

"The same way you could've come to me and told me that you were back to rendezvousing with Traci again, Eric?"

Having no comeback, he merely nodded. "I see your point clearly. I'm not going to sit here and insult you with a bunch of empty ways to say I'm sorry. But know this, I'm here for you. I'm not going to leave you alone or without support."

"Because you care or out of your freaking guilt?"

"Out of love, Cicely. That hasn't changed. I take responsibility for hurting you, but you have to be the one to own the drug use. I didn't introduce you to that kind of lifestyle. You might want to take a close look at the people who did. Still, the choice was always yours."

"If only I could believe in you again, Eric. I can't."

Cicely couldn't help remembering how romantic Eric had been during most of their relationship. Then one day he'd begun to slip up badly. The difference in him had come as a result of having Traci back in his life. It was difficult to be all things to all people. Making love to two women, within the same time frame, had to have been taxing to his physical endurance. Especially since he was the type of man who put everything he had into pleasing his woman.

Cicely believed that Traci had gotten more of him during that time period than she had, since it seemed to her that he'd lost all interest in being at home with her. Him leading two lives had taken a horrific toll on both Eric and Cicely. Then it finally killed the relationship.

"I understand why that might be hard for you." Eric swallowed the uncomfortable obstruction in his throat. Crow didn't digest easily. "I know this is painful for you, but how did you find out about Traci and me?"

"My best friend, the juicy gossiper. Destiny saw your car in front of Traci's house late one night. When she told me about it, I told her there was no way, that she had to be mistaken. Destiny will go to any lengths to prove herself right, so she got into the habit of following you around. Then she brought me along for the ride a couple of times. With what I saw with my own eyes, I could no longer deny the truth. In the parking lot of Dante's Italian Restaurant, before you got into the car, you two were all over each other. That's when I actually witnessed my own man cheating on me right out in public with his ex-fiancée. End of another deplorable story."

Eric wasn't the least bit surprised. Destiny had always had it in for him, but not because of anything he'd ever done to her. He could never tell Cicely that Destiny's deeds were pure acts of revenge for him thwarting her own sexual advances toward him; she just wouldn't believe him. That didn't excuse his infidelities, not one iota. But Destiny was not whom she claimed to be to Cicely.

Best friends didn't go after each other's man. He'd never told Cicely about Destiny because he didn't want to see her hurt. Wrong choice, he now realized, though he'd hurt her far more than Destiny. But he wouldn't be a bit surprised if Destiny had introduced Cicely to drugs.

Destiny's recent visits to his home were starting to make sense now. As he thought of all the things she'd been saying to him, her motives became clearer. She had promised to help him with the baby if he won custody through the courts, even offering to change her work schedule to accommodate his in order to take care of the child. Her becoming a live-in had also come up.

It was now obvious to Eric that Destiny had had ulterior motives when she'd first told him about Cicely carrying his baby. It also looked as if she not only wanted to steal the man Cicely had once loved, but that she was now going after Cicely's child. It seemed to him that Destiny Powell planned to become an immovable force in his life one way or the other.

With all the wrongdoing he was guilty of, how would he ever be able to convince Cicely of the truth about her best friend? Cicely had just said she couldn't believe in him again. He instantly thought of what Reverend Jesse might advise him. "Patience," and "Wait on the Lord" were the phrases that came to mind. *Yes*, he thought. He would have to continue practicing patience.

Eric briefly covered Cicely's hand with his own. "How are you feeling today?"

She shrugged. "I'm coping."

"Is there anything I can do for you?"

Haven't you already done enough? Cicely successfully resisted the urge to use the stinging retort resting on the very tip of her tongue. Eric looked guilty enough. Never had she desired to hurt him, but that was before his indiscretions. Her main purpose in life had become to hurt him as badly as he'd hurt her. The storms of destruction that she'd wanted to rain down on him had somehow turned on her. She had managed to make herself the victim of all her vicious hate and anger. Eric was free. She was in captivity. Her plans had simply backfired.

Finding herself wanting to reach out to Eric came as a big surprise to Cicely. As hard as it was for her, she managed to curb her desire to touch his hand, to feel his satin skin beneath her fingers, to remember the times when it was so good between them. Those soothing hands had once belonged to her. She would be hard put to forget all the pleasures they'd brought her.

Everything about Eric was unforgettable, including the pain she'd suffered at his hands. Eric was guilty of breaking her heart into a million and one pieces. But she was the only one guilty of destroying her life in order to try and make him pay for what he'd done to her.

The issues on whom to blame for her life's struggles were now crystal clear.

That she still loved him wasn't at all a mystery to Cicely. Now that her belly was swollen with his seed, her love for him could never die. To detest him would be like hating her baby; her unborn child was a part of him. Of all the unsavory things Cicely had done for drugs, she'd never allowed anyone to enter her body. There were numerous other ways to effect sexual pleasures in exchange for drugs, all of which she'd done to get her own needs met. That she hadn't been raped was a miracle. That God had kept his angels encamped about her was the only explanation she could offer. Cicely came from a church home and was now attending services on the inside.

Cicely shook her head from side to side, as if she were shaking off a nightmare. "I'm ready to go back to my cell. I'm feeling really sick."

He looked alarmed. "Is it the baby?"

"Just plain old heartsick." Without uttering another word, Cicely got up and walked off.

Helplessly, Eric looked on, wondering if they'd ever be able to make it back to where they'd once been. Knowing he'd caused Cicely so much pain had him determined to try even harder. She was worth it. Their unborn child needed both parents. He vowed to keep them together as a family. Guilt was felt in spades; the deciding factor for him was his love for her.

Jesse folded his hands and put them atop his desk. Much to his surprise, seated across from him in the pastor's study was Easton Chapelle. Reverend Jesse had no clue as to why he was there, but he was sure about to find out. No appointment had been made by him to see Jesse; Easton had just shown up. "Nice to see you again, young man, though I am a bit surprised. How are you doing on this fine afternoon?"

Easton shrugged. "Don't know."

Jesse raised an eyebrow. "Okay. So why don't you tell me what I can do for you?"

Easton shrugged again. "I don't know that either."

Chuckling, Jesse raised both eyebrows. "If you don't know why you're here, how do you expect me to know?"

"Like I said, I don't know. I was just driving by here and the next thing I knew I was sitting in the church parking lot. I thought maybe you could tell me why I was compelled to come in here. You're the one with the direct pipeline to the man upstairs. Does God work like that? Did He send me in here?" Easton fidgeted in his seat like he was on speed. Sweat was popping out on his forehead in tiny beads. His eyes had the look of sheer fear in them.

Jesse was so puzzled by Easton's odd behavior that he had to take a minute to silently pray over the situation. Something was going on inside with this young man, but Jesse didn't know what. Perhaps the Holy Spirit was working on Easton. Otherwise, why would he just show up at the church out of the blue? Jesse had to wonder. Jesse didn't leave out the possibility that he was there as an advocate for evil. Satan and his followers were always at work. Unlike some of the Christians he knew, Satan's crew never took a day off from witnessing for their master.

Jesse moved from behind his desk and sat down in the chair next to Easton's. "Would you like me to pray for you or with you, son?"

Easton shot Jesse a hate-filled look. "I'm not your son. Don't ever call me that again."

"As you wish." Jesse closely studied Easton for several seconds before proceeding. "I really don't know why you're here, which makes it virtually impossible for me to know what to do for you. Until you can give me some idea of what you might need, my hands are tied."

Easton repeatedly pounded his fist against his thigh. "What I need is a decent set of parents for my child. I don't have what it takes to raise no frigging kid. After listening to that black guy talking about how he wanted custody of his kid to raise it on his own got me to thinking real hard about my son, Kyle. He's such a funny little guy. Trusting, too. But I think he knows I don't like him being around. He looks so sad at times. I don't have much of a heart, but I do feel something awful inside my chest when my kid looks at me like that. It's not fair for either one of us to be thrown together like this. What kind of God gives a child to a man like me?"

Jesse felt relieved, felt that they were finally getting somewhere. Easton had come to see him because he needed help. He was desperate now for some answers. While Jesse also believed that the Holy Spirit was at work within Easton, he also felt that Easton wanted to be helped.

Unwittingly, Eric Eldridge had sparked something deep inside of Easton, making him think about his own kid and what life might be like for him. Interestingly enough, Eric was to arrive within the next few minutes for his scheduled appointment. Jesse couldn't help entertaining the idea of continuing the session with both men present. Since Easton had mentioned Eric, though not by name, Jesse believed that Easton just might go for it.

"God may very well have given you a child, but when He does that, He sees it as a blessing for you, not as a curse. Your child was conceived because you willingly participated in the act of intercourse, which is how babies are made. So let's not go blaming God for what we humans tend to do in the heat of the moment, without ever thinking of the consequences. God has blessed you with a precious child; that's an irrefutable fact. Whether you're ready to take on that responsibility or not is the core issue. You can't send the child back, so we have to find a way to solve your dilemma, one that's beneficial to all concerned. Are you willing to let me help you find a workable solution?"

Admiration shone brightly in Easton's eyes as he looked up at Jesse. He couldn't believe that this big guy wanted to help him out, especially after all the insults he'd flung at him at some time or other. Easton's views on blacks as a whole hadn't changed much, but he was already changing his mind about Reverend Jesse. He saw that as a good start. He had just come to realize that he didn't like the way he felt, didn't like the way hating made him feel on the inside. His point of view had been instilled in him at a very young age, which would make it hard for him to overcome his hatred in a short span of time. That he wanted to change was the key.

"Any help you can give me I'll accept. Kyle deserves better than what I have to offer. I know that now. His mother is not much better than me in the area of responsibility. I have to convince her to let me see that Kyle gets the best life possible. If giving him up is what we have to do to achieve that, I'll convince her to sign papers expunging both our rights as parents."

Jesse frowned. "I want you to know up front that I'm not going to encourage you in that way of thinking. There are alternatives for your situation if only you're willing to learn what they are. I'll have to stand by any decision you make for your kid, but I don't have to like it. If I see that giving up your parental rights is the best thing for Kyle, you'll have my blessing. But I have to know without a doubt that he's better off with someone other than his natural parents. You can change your circumstances, Easton. With lots of guidance from God and His advocates, we can turn this situation completely around. Now that my hand has been shown, are you still willing?"

Easton only nodded his approval. He was too full to speak. He didn't know this God Reverend Jesse spoke so freely about, wasn't sure that he wanted to know Him either, but he had to admit to his burning curiosity.

Jesse rubbed his hands together in eager anticipation of helping Easton to work out his numerous problems, not just those that pertained to his child. Easton needed an entire spiritual makeover. Coupled with God, Jesse was one of the greatest makeup artists around.

Jesse clapped his hands one time. "In recalling you mentioning the brother who spoke about gaining custody of his unborn child, I have a suggestion." Jesse looked down at his watch. "Any time now my assistant is going to buzz me on the intercom to let me know my next appointment is here. Eric, the man you've mentioned, should be here any second. If he agrees to it, will you stay and sit in on our session? I may have to see him alone for a few minutes, so you'd have to wait in the outer office. What do you say to my suggestion, Easton?"

Easton looked uncomfortable. "I don't know about that, man. We sort of went head-to-head at the meeting. I'm not sure that can happen. I personally don't think he'll go along with it."

"If I recall correctly, Eric said he was there for his kid and himself. I don't see that as head-to-head. He could've gotten into a serious battle of wills and wits with you, but he didn't. This session can happen. Shall I give it the old college try?"

Easton still wasn't sure meeting with Eric would work. He was also fearful, but he wasn't sure of what. He'd been rude to the guy, no doubt. But as Reverend Jesse stated, it could've been much worse. Easton was having a really hard time believing any black man could help him, or would want to help him. This scenario was starting to come off like a badly rated feature film of some sort. *Black Guys Rescue White Guy from Self.* What a hard sell that would be to his group of socially deprived friends. Easton feared retaliation from his white supremacists friends, more than he feared anything else in the world, if they were to find out that he'd been hanging out with a bunch of black folks. He shuddered at the very thought, yet he remained seated.

Easton had to admit to himself that he started out thinking he could use the people he'd been referred to for his own purposes, but things didn't seem to be going in that direction. The fact that he no longer desired or even thought he could use them was the eye-opener for him. He had also learned that all blacks weren't as dumb and ignorant as he'd originally thought. He'd heard some intelligent stuff going on in that first meeting. It had shocked him to hear some of the big fancy words used, words that he hadn't heard before and didn't even know the meaning of.

Regardless of what he thought of blacks, he didn't know of any other way to go at the moment. Besides, a lot of headway had already occurred. If they seemed willing to help, he should be willing to accept it, but only within the spirit from which it came.

"Go for it, Reverend Jesse."

Just as Jesse had suggested, the intercom buzzed. Eric's arrival was then announced. Jesse came up with a last-minute idea. Instead of Easton waiting in the outer offices, he would go out and talk to Eric. He didn't want to give the young man an easy out. Easton would have to come past him before he could leave the building if he attempted to do so.

Jesse wasn't sure if he could convince Eric to sit in with him and Easton, but he figured he'd have an easier time convincing Eric than he'd had with anything to do with Easton. Prayer worked. As he left the study, Jesse was already deeply into prayer.

* * *

220

Jesse was thrilled at how well his counseling session was going with Eric and Easton. Eric had readily agreed to the meeting with Easton, making Jesse a happy camper. For the most part, Jesse was letting the two young men chop it up. He had an occasion to jump in every now and then, but only when he thought guidance was needed. They seemed to be handling everything quite well on their own. And Easton hadn't made one reference to differences in race, creed, or religion, which also made Jesse happy.

Eric leaned forward in his seat. "I can understand your fears about raising your son alone, 'cause I have them too. But I'm having a hard time with you entertaining the possibility of permanently giving up your parental rights. There are other ways."

Easton shrugged, which seemed to be a habit. "Reverend Jesse said the same thing. This little kid freaks me out at times. He seems so needy. Kyle always wants something that I don't know how to give. He likes to hug and kiss, which is downright awkward for me. Although she never gave it to me, I know my mother gave him a lot of affection. He always followed her around the house, looking up at her in adoration. How do I give him what he needs?"

"How long have you had sole custody of your son?" Eric queried.

"A little over a month."

Laughing, Eric slapped his hand down on his knee. "That's one of the problems right there, man. You haven't had enough time to adjust to this new situation. How often did you interact with Kyle when your mom was alive?"

"Next to never. I rarely stayed longer than an hour or so when I visited. Even when I was there, I was on the phone taking care of business. But I did catch myself closely watching how he interacted with my mother. I remember wishing she could've hugged and kissed me the way she did Kyle. In thinking about it, I may be jealous of my own kid. He definitely got more from her than I ever did. I often wondered if my father would've changed like my mother did. Kyle seemed to be the one to bring about the best in her. He may've been the only light in her life."

"Perhaps he was," Jesse remarked. "Grown folks make serious mistakes all the time with their kids. But children don't understand that because they're not equipped yet. Like you said earlier, Kyle is so trusting. Think about it. As newborns, they have to trust their parents for everything. They eat and drink what their parents give them and also have to wait on Mom or Dad to change their soiled diapers and give them a bath. They're helpless. That's often why the faith of a child is likened to the trust and belief in Christ. Children have no choice but to trust. When that trust is violated, trouble will eventually arrive. If everyone took on the faith and trust of God's little children, His Son's work would've been done."

Eric nodded. "I agree wholeheartedly with that. While we didn't do church things in our home, I got a lot of love. I remember when my aunt used to beat her kids something fierce. It was awful. My mother told me back then, that when a parent's anger is unleashed against his or her child, it's rarely about the child. She said it has more to do with what's going on in the parents' life and how they feel about themselves, and nothing to do with their offspring. I believe that. I've seen enough cases of horrific child abuse to cause me a lifetime of grief."

Eric wiped a tear from his eye. "What could a child possibly do to cause an adult to put them in a sink of boiling hot water or to lock them up in a closet and not feed them for days?"

"What? Are you a social worker or something?" Easton asked Eric.

Eric thought about the question for a moment, knowing he'd never reveal the nature of his job. "Not exactly, but something close to that. I work with society and all its forms of troubles, so I am privy to a lot of horrific situations."

Easton wanted to know more about Eric's profession, but he sensed Eric's reluctance to go any further into his job description. He decided instantly to respect Eric's right to privacy.

Jesse opened the Bible. "The Bible teaches us that Christ receives and blesses little children. This is written in Luke 18:15-17: 'And they brought unto Him also infants, that He would touch them: but when his disciples saw it, they rebuked them. But Jesus called unto them and said, Suffer the little children to come unto me, and forbid them not: for such is the kingdom of God. Verily I say unto you, Whosoever shall not receive the kingdom of God as a little child shall not enter therein.' You can read for yourself Matthew 19:13-15 and Mark 10:13-16. Both books refer back to the scriptures I just read."

Easton didn't like the way things were starting to go. He'd gotten antsy the minute Jesse opened the Bible. This wasn't something he'd bargained for. Jesse was well aware of it, too, but that hadn't stopped him from reading about what he thought Easton should hear.

Easton looked down at his watch. "Dang, I've been here over two hours now. It's time to move on. But I want to ask a couple of questions. How do I learn how to relate to my son? How do I try to meet his needs and my own?"

"Learning to relate to your son should be a piece of cake," Jesse advised. "In fact, Kyle will teach you how to relate to him if you let him. When he wants to be picked up and hugged by you, do it without hesitation. You'll know what he wants because his little arms will be so far outstretched you can't possibly miss the loving gesture. If he's hungry or thirsty, he'll find a way to let you know, and sometimes in no uncertain terms. Kyle will communicate to you his every need and want if you just listen and watch for the obvious signs. But you have to be there with him for any of it to happen, Easton. You have to be closely involved in his life."

"Reverend Jesse's right," Eric replied. "I'm going to add a little to what he's said. Your time is the most precious gift you can ever bestow upon little Kyle. Spend some quality time with your son, man. Get to really know him. Don't stay cooped up in the house with him. Take him out to the park or somewhere else fun. Just put in the time, man. The rewards are endless."

"Sounds like you already have kids besides the unborn one. Am I right?" Easton asked Eric, wringing his hands together from sheer nervousness. The subject matter had him freaked.

"I don't have any yet, but I am affiliated with many youth organizations. I volunteer my time to a lot of the children's activities. I'm speaking from experience, telling you just what I know. Trust me. Kids need quality time with their parents more than they need anything else."

"I'll keep all that you've said in mind, guys." Easton scratched his head. "There's also this matter of immunizations and other issues concerning keeping Kyle healthy. I have no clue what he needs there either. I'm just not there. Completely clueless."

Jesse was happy to hear that Easton was a concerned parent, despite all the silly hoopla he'd been trying to feed everyone. "Look around your house and in your mother's things for his shot record. If you can't find one, he may have to take them all over again. I'm sure your mother kept well-baby records. Look hard for anything pertaining to medical records and such. Then you need to start taking him in for regular medical and dental checkups. I'm a veteran dad," Jesse boasted, "even though Marlene took care of all the things we've just discussed. Let me know what you find out. I can refer you to a friend of mine at one of the local free clinics. She can tell you just what you need to do to make sure Kyle stays healthy."

"Thanks for all the great advice. I just hope I end up using it. This is still scary for me."

"You will," Jesse reassured him. "You will."

Easton got to his feet and the other two men followed suit. Easton knew Jesse wasn't going to let him get out of his office without prayer, so he just bowed his head and clasped his hands together. At that same moment Jesse began to pray.

Chapter Twelve

Rosalinda felt as if the telephone receiver was frozen in her hand. Chills ran up and down her spine as she sat at her desk listening to the frantic cries coming from Maria Lopez. From what Rosalinda could make out between Maria's screams and moans was that Rocco had done her in pretty good, that he'd left her badly beaten in a motel in downtown Los Angeles.

Rosalinda tightened her grip on the phone. Her sweaty palms had caused it to slide. "Maria, please try to hold on. You have to listen to me. You have to tell me exactly where you are so that I can get you some help. I can call 911 and give them your location."

"No, Rosa, no police. You have to come alone. If I get the police involved, Rocco will kill me for sure. I just need you to get me on a bus heading out of town."

Frustrated to no end, Rosalinda cursed in Spanish. "You're not thinking clearly. You need medical attention right away. After you get it, we can then think of getting you out of town. Now stop wasting time and give me the name and street address of the motel."

"I can't do that. I'm going to hang up and call someone else. . . ."

"No, don't do that, Maria. Please. Just tell me where you are. I'll come. I promise."

"No police?"

"No police, Maria."

Rosalinda's hand shook as she wrote down the information. Fear streaked through her at an alarming rate. Her heart beat much faster than normal. This was a crazy thing she was about to do, but if Maria died because she refused to help her, she couldn't live with that. The guilt would destroy her. Her life with Michael was just beginning; she didn't want to see it come to an abrupt end. Michael would know what to do. He'd be her backup. She'd call him as soon as she got settled into the car. Michael would see her through this just as he'd seen her through everything else. Michael Hernandez loved her.

Rosalinda prayed in Spanish to God for His assistance all the way down in the elevator. Upon reaching the parking garage, she got into her outdated hoopty-style ride and started the engine, praying that it wouldn't stall out on her. Seconds later she was pulling the car into traffic, hoping she could get into downtown before the rush hour began.

All sorts of things went through Rosalinda's head as she crept through street traffic, making her way to the freeway, where hopefully she could move a lot faster. Although Maria had given her the motel room number, Rosalinda wondered how she'd get inside if Maria were incapacitated. Surely the room door would be locked. The remedy then came to her with ease. The motel office would have a key, but they might not let her in. Rosalinda felt sure that someone from management would go in if they knew someone was hurt. Liability could become a major issue for the owners if their people refused to respond to an emergency situation.

Happy to have resolved that problem, Rosalinda reached over for her purse and removed her cell phone. She then dialed the two-digit code she'd set up for Michael. Her heart fell when the automated answering response system came on. He was probably still in court and had turned his cell off. She left a message and then called the office. Before she could give all the information to the administrative assistant, her cell went dead.

Rosalinda felt like kicking herself. She'd forgotten to charge her battery, once again. Since she rarely used her cell phone, she often forgot to recharge it. She then plugged her phone into the automobile charger and called back to complete her message for Michael.

Twenty minutes later, Rosalinda sped into the motel parking lot. The absence of cars was a very strange sight in L.A., but it was daytime. The setting reminded her of the sleazy motel she'd first met Michael in. She couldn't help laughing at that fiasco. The laughter eased the tension. However, what had unfolded afterward on that fateful night had turned out in her favor. Michael's test had shown her that she was no back-alley Suzy Q.

Rosalinda had proved herself to be an honorable woman, one with a conscience.

Rosalinda looked at the motel room number she'd scribbled down on a piece of paper. Her eyes then scanned the numbers on the doors. She spotted the room. It was on the second floor. The absence of an elevator was obvious. Rosalinda then located the set of stairs that led up to the room. She quickly got out of her car and walked to the steps, taking them two at a time, all the while praying that Maria was okay.

Upon reaching the target room, she knocked. The door came open, causing Rosalinda to step back in haste. She could see that the room was dark. "Maria," she called out. "Maria, are you in there? It's Rosa." She then heard a low, painful moan coming from within the room.

Rosalinda inched toward the door, although she felt that things weren't right. Something was telling her she was in danger. As her internal warning signals got stronger, she began to slowly back away from the door until she reached the steps. If still in her childhood, she would've slid all the way down the steps on her behind. Instead, she removed her shoes and hauled tail. Rosalinda was totally out of breath by the time she reached the bottom step.

Just as she reached her car door, relieved that she'd forgotten to lock it due to her state of mind, she saw Ricardo appear in the motel doorway. Quicker than lightning had ever hit, she was inside her vehicle. She couldn't hear his shouts and ranting, but his taunting fists, waving in rage, let her know his exact mindset. Ricardo had convinced Maria to get involved in his dirty work.

Maria had helped him set her up, the very thing Rosalinda had feared from the beginning.

Rosalinda's cell phone rang and she nearly jumped out of her skin. Upon seeing Michael's name and number on the tiny screen, she nearly came unglued from relief as she hit the talk button. "Michael! Oh, God," she cried into the phone, "Michael, I nearly got myself killed. I just barely escaped another dangerous encounter with Ric."

Michael stiffened at the mention of Ric's name, wishing he'd gone through with his plans to take out this menace to society. He quickly prayed for forgiveness, knowing he was dead wrong. Still, Ricardo had to be stopped, one way or the other. "Where are you now, Rosalinda?"

Michael sounded overly anxious to her ears, but she understood why. "Downtown. I'm leaving the area as we speak. Are you in the office or still at the courthouse?"

"I was just leaving the office to come over to the motel. I received both of your messages. Do you want me to come get you?"

"I'm close enough to the office. I'll come there. Please wait for me. I plan to leave my car there and ride home with you. I'm terribly shaken."

"I'll be waiting at the entrance of the building. In the meantime, I'll call the police and let them know what's happened and where. Be careful, my love."

* * *

Michael was so perturbed with Rosalinda for going to the motel alone and nearly falling into Ricardo's well-set trap. However, he didn't have the heart to chastise her. She still looked so vulnerable and shook up. Rosalinda was still young and naïve. Her desire to help and try to save someone else's life could've ended up with her losing her own. He didn't doubt for a second that Ricardo was capable of killing her. Ric had already gone to great lengths to get at her. Michael vowed to do everything in his power to keep that from ever occurring. God would do the rest.

Dressed in comfortable, nonrevealing nightwear, Rosalinda was stretched out on the sofa, her head resting on a pillow that rested on Michael's lap. Sweetly scented candles burned throughout the room, providing a romantic-but-relaxing ambience.

A hot bath and a vigorous but gentle neck rub and back massage from Michael had helped to calm Rosalinda down. By the time she'd reached the office building where he'd waited for her, she was an emotional basket case. Once her car was parked in his reserved spot in the multi-story garage facility, Michael had immediately driven her to the guesthouse, where he wasted no time in tending to her every need.

That Maria Lopez had set Rosalinda up didn't come as a big surprise to Michael. He could've told Rosalinda exactly what she was getting herself into had she shared with him Maria's trumped-up story. Unlike Rosalinda, Maria was a true gang member. He didn't like that Rosalinda still kept secrets from him, but he couldn't hold that against her. She *had* called him and left messages, which told him where she was going; that had to count for something. She wasn't a baby, so coddling her wasn't the answer either.

Michael no longer thought it was an issue of trust, since she'd told him many times how much she trusted him. That Maria had sworn Rosalinda to secrecy because of feigned fears was probably the real reason Rosalinda had taken matters into her own hands.

Rosalinda was a woman of her word, and Maria had more than likely known that.

In due time Michael felt that Rosalinda would come to share everything with him, in the same way he desired to share his entire life with her. Michael was in love with Rosalinda; there was no doubt in his mind about that. Getting her to love him back was now his main goal in life.

Michael looked down at Rosalinda. "Hungry?"

She smiled up at him. "A little. I don't think I can handle anything too heavy, though."

"Is your stomach still queasy?"

"Somewhat. Fear can wreak havoc on your insides. The quivers are still there. If only . . ."

Michael smoothed her hair with a flattened palm. "Shush, Rosalinda," he said in the gentlest tone possible. "You don't have to go back there. That episode is history. It's over. You're safe. Let's move on to greener pastures. What about some soup? I can run up to the house and get a can or two."

Rosalinda reached up and caressed Michael's lips with the pads of her fingers. "Thank you for being my hero." She then kissed two of her fingers and pressed them onto his mouth. "Going up to the house won't be necessary. I keep canned soup in the pantry. I'll fix it myself."

As she tried to get up, he gently brought her head back down. "Your hero is always on duty, Senorita Morales. I'll fix the soup while you continue to enjoy being a couch potato." He lifted her head as he got to his feet and then gently placed it back on the pillow. "What about some soft, mood music? Enrique Iglesias or Marc Anthony?"

"Both choices are soothing. I'll let my hero make the selection."

Michael's heart grew full. "That's the spirit."

Rosalinda's dancing eyes followed Michael until he disappeared around the corner. She then thought of how every single day in his presence was a new and exciting experience. He had introduced her to paradise. But there were times when she thought everything with them was too right, too nice, and possibly too easy. Were relationships ever really like that?

Michael offered very little resistance or opposition to anything she did or said. Was he afraid to speak his mind for fear of alienating himself from her? He seemed to want to please her without any thought to her pleasing him. Michael was so unselfish.

Though they weren't in a committed relationship, it felt like it. They had become each other's constant companion. Michael had given so much. All he'd ever gotten in return from her were a couple of passionate kisses and a bunch of constant thanks. Rosalinda thought it was time that she should give more, to show him how she really felt about him. Michael was so deserving of a lifetime of love and happiness. But was she the one to give it to him? She hoped so.

Her thoughts flew away as her hero came back into the room carrying a portable oak television tray. Before going back to retrieve the soup and eating utensils, he set up the wooden tray in front of the sofa where Rosalinda lay.

"Up you go." He reached for her hand, helping her to sit up. "The soup is really hot. I prepared it on the gas stovetop rather than in the microwave oven. Be careful so that you don't get your mouth burned."

Just as the soft Latin music waltzed into the room, Michael smiled softly. He then sat down next to Rosalinda. The wooden tray stationed between them kept him from making physical contact with her. But it didn't stop him from keeping his eyes hotly stayed on her.

Rosalinda had to wait for her soup to cool off. It really *was* boiling hot, just as Michael had warned her. She could barely wait to eat since her stomach had begun to growl.

Once Rosalinda had consumed her light meal, Michael immediately cleared away the tray and its contents. He then resumed his original seat, once again placing the pillow on his lap, encouraging Rosalinda to lie back down. Rosalinda offered no resistance to his gentle urgings.

As Michael looked down on his dark-haired beauty, he couldn't help smiling. He could see that her eyes were starting to droop shut. She looked as if she could fall asleep without a moment's notice. He thought he should go on up to the house so that she could get some rest, but his heart was telling him to stay. The night was still fairly young.

As though Rosalinda had read his thoughts, she sat up until her head was level with his chest and her bottom rested on the pillow. "I'm glad you're here, Michael," she whispered softly. "I feel safe, as if nothing can ever hurt me again. What would you say if I asked you to spend the night with me so we could make love until the wee hours of the morning?"

Michael couldn't have looked more shocked. His first reaction was to ask her to repeat herself, but he'd heard her loud and clear. That Rosalinda wanted him to make love to her filled him to the brim, even his eyes. He kissed the tip of her nose and then briefly traced her lips with his own. The sweetness of her mouth excited him. The heat of this passionate moment was rising up to engulf him, and his heart beat faster than normal. He fought hard to remain in control.

She kissed his ear. "Aren't you going to answer me?"

Michael groaned, fighting hard his desires. "The next time you make love to a man you'll be the missus. As much as it pains me, I'm going to help you honor that spoken vow. Let me know when you're ready to become the missus. Then we can resume this conversation."

Rosalinda stared deeply into his eyes. "Are you ready for me to be ready, Michael?"

"I think you already know. Until we both come to that end, your vow is safe with me."

The room was relatively quiet. All eyes were on Marlene as she sat in one of the numerous chairs forming a slightly broken circle inside the recreation room at the women's prison. Anticipation was high regarding what she had to say. She had first introduced herself to the one-hundred-plus female inmates and several women staff members who'd made the decision to be in attendance; many had chosen not to attend. Prayer followed.

Marlene then told the women a little about herself and how she'd coped with her situation when her preacher husband was a California inmate, though falsely accused. She also told them how she'd met three other women from totally different walks of life, women just like her, with the same set of circumstances. She then spoke of how they'd become great friends and how they continued to minister to each other to this very day.

Marlene picked up the plastic cup of water at her feet and took a sip. The use of glass products was forbidden. "I can't tell you how pleased I was to receive your invitation to come and speak before you. As some of you may know, my assistants and I have been running a support group for women waiting on men to get out of prison. Our group was what eventually encouraged my husband to start a group for men waiting on women to return home."

Loud laughter and hissing broke out among the attendees.

Marlene realized that the negative responses had more to do with the lack of support from men than anything to do with anything else. She'd heard enough about the nonsupport of men to understand why the women had responded the way they did. "I have somewhat of an idea regarding your negative feelings on the issue of men supporting their women behind bars. That's why I'm here, the reason I accepted your invitation. You asked for a group session and I was only too happy to oblige. This is your meeting. No formalities. Feel free to speak right from your seats. No one has to stand unless they want to. Many of your counselors are present to help things flow smoothly. This part of the session is now open to those who want to speak."

For several seconds the room was deathly silent. It didn't look as if anyone cared to be the first speaker. Just as a slender hand raised, sighs of relief could be heard throughout the room. All eyes turned toward the owner of the hand.

"Do we need to give our name, since a lot of us know each other?"

"It's up to each individual," Marlene responded.

"Okay, what the heck. I'm Melissa. Many of us are here to air out our feelings about how we were left high and dry by the men we loved and trusted. I did something really stupid to end up in here. I did quite a few small package deliveries for my boyfriend. I knew what was in them, but I did it anyway. You never think you're going to get caught. I got busted with the goods. I got time. He got off scot-free. But the real source of my anger is that he hasn't bothered to visit me, not even once. He has cut me off completely. He had his phone number changed after accepting a couple of collect calls from me. That really hurts."

"How long have you been in here, Melissa?" Marlene asked.

"I've been here a year and a half, with a year left to do. I'm afraid that I might go after him when I get out of here. I always have the same recurring dream of killing him. If anyone has some answers, I'd like to hear them. I'm still so freaking angry about my situation."

"Cut your losses and move on," a fellow inmate advised. "Killing him will only get you more time. Possibly life. It's just not worth it. The system will send you somewhere much worse than here. You don't want to do maximum-security. Medium-max is bad enough."

One of the counselors raised her hand. "Melissa, I'm surprised to hear you say that. In all of our sessions together, you've never once mentioned your dreams. A constant thought of killing another human being is serious business. I can arrange a referral for you to see one of the staff psychiatrists. You don't want to end up in prison for the rest of your natural life. If you go after your ex-boyfriend with the intent to kill, that could very well happen. You're so close to being released. We'll talk after the meeting. I promise to get you help."

Melissa nodded as she wiped the tears from her eyes. "Thank you."

The room was once again silent. It appeared that everyone was feeling Melissa's pain. Her story wasn't too different from other stories. Men had used these women, had abused them, and had eventually abandoned them. Marlene had been told by one of the counselors that desertion by their men was one of the most talked-about subjects among the female inmates.

Although it hadn't been mentioned as a requirement for speaking, another inmate raised her hand. It seemed to Marlene everyone was following Melissa's lead, the first to raise a hand.

"My story is similar to Melissa's but somewhat different. Like a dummy, I stored stolen goods in my apartment for my boyfriend and was later charged with receiving stolen property, which was later changed to grand theft. Like Melissa, I'm sitting in here rotting away and he's out on the street, probably doing the same thing. Men like my ex go on to find the next victim once they get stupid women like me imprisoned. I want to say something to Melissa."

She turned slightly in order to face Melissa. "He is not worth you giving up any more of your life for. Don't get into more trouble over him. Accept the help being offered so that you'll be mentally prepared when you're released. I'll be here for you if you ever need to talk."

The women that had spoken so far sounded very well educated in Marlene's opinion. They seemed to have lived a fairly decent life while on the outside. Each of these women thought their men loved them, just as they had loved in return. This wretched scenario brought a whole new meaning to the phrase, "What's love got to do with it?" It looked as though love had very little to do with what these young women had subjected themselves to.

Marlene saw the eager desire to participate when three hands went up at the same time. It seemed that everyone was starting to loosen up a bit. Sometimes all it took was one or two people to open up and get the ball rolling. Whether they knew or it not, these women really needed each other. They could find strength in one another, just as the women in the LIW support group had found. Marlene hoped this meeting would begin to forge a strong, unbreakable bond among the women who probably were desperate to belong to something meaningful. Fond and warm thoughts of Keisha, Rosalinda, and Alexis rested deep inside Marlene's heart.

"My dad is the only person to visit me," said the timid little voice of a woman who looked as if she were barely twenty years old. "He only brings my daughter to see me on special occasions, like my birthday or major holidays. He doesn't want her to be in this environment too often. I have a great father. Dad was so disappointed in me the first time I got arrested for solicitation. Although it kept on happening, he never abandoned me."

The young woman speaking seemed so familiar to Marlene, but she couldn't place her. Her tiny little voice sounded familiar, too. Marlene paid even closer attention to this speaker.

"My guy said I'd only have to do it one time to help him out of a financial jam. He said he needed the money desperately. One time turned to two, three, and then four. It continued until I became a full-fledged prostitute, working nightly the dangerous streets of L.A. Unlike some of the others, my guy did get me out of the county facility the first couple of times. But he started ignoring me when I kept getting busted. The last time I was sent way up here. That's when he left me to fend for myself. I also have visions of offing him. But I won't. I have my daughter to think of. By the way, Mrs. Covington, you know me. I went to high school with Malcolm. My name is Kamara Bauer. Please tell your son I said hello."

It took Marlene several seconds to find her voice. Sitting before her was a preacher's kid, Pastor Jeremy Bauer's daughter. Marlene was stunned out of her mind. Sweet Kamara had been in her own youth ministry at one time. How many times had she heard that little voice on the phone asking to speak to Malcolm? Far too many to count! What in the world had gone wrong? Kamara still looked like a little girl, but the freshness of her former innocence was definitely missing. Marlene prayed that Kamara would find her way back to God, just as Malcolm had.

"I'll certainly do that, Kamara. I'd also like to talk with you later. God bless you, child."

As time moved on, more and more women got the courage to speak. There was such a powerful need for release among them. Tears were shed. Lamentations were in abundance. Anger and other erupting emotions were loudly voiced. Not everyone in the room was there because of something they'd done for a man, but the numbers of those who were was astounding.

It was so sad for Marlene to see so many brokenhearted women, those of whom had been duped, all in the name of love. Her heart went out to each and every one of them. It appeared to her as if they needed a support group, too. She saw how it could do a lot of good. If a meeting of this kind could keep these women from physically executing their anger once they got out, it would all be worth it. Marlene instantly consulted with God on behalf of the women present.

Just as Marlene was about to adjourn the meeting, a woman with gray hair stood. She bit down on her lower lip, looking extremely nervous. "My crime was more stupid than most. The D.A. called it a crime of unbridled passion. I was so sick and tired of my husband cheating on me that I started to go insane. The last straw was when I came home from work early and found him in bed with another woman, my first cousin." She lowered her head. "Our fathers are brothers. We grew up together. Can you believe that? My own cousin! I do remember going off on him with my fists, but I can't remember shooting him. Obviously I did, or so they say. Thank God he wasn't killed. I did a lot of time in a maximum-security prison before I was sent here to finish my last few months out. Ladies, you don't ever want to go that route. It's hard, really hard."

"What did you do to your cousin?" a very attractive-looking sister asked.

"Apparently nothing. She wasn't harmed. Just him. To this day I still don't remember shooting him. I've often wondered if my cousin shot him. I don't remember going for the gun or firing it. It was kept in the nightstand drawer, so it was easily accessible. My hands were also negative for gunpowder residue. How can I draw only blanks on something so seriously unforgettable? I must've really been out of it not to remember such startling events."

"Why would your cousin shoot him?" someone asked.

"She tried to tell me that he was raping her when I first walked in. The boy had a condom on and there were a couple of unmentionable adult toys in the bed. I don't recall seeing any of that. I just remember it from the facts revealed in court." Looking forlorn and desperate, the older lady sat back down. Marlene could see her hands trembling from where she was seated.

There was no movement for a short time. Heads were hung low and eyes were filled with tears. Marlene thought she would take this quiet time as an opportunity to offer up prayer. Before she could begin, a middle-aged Caucasian woman got to her feet.

"I'm Nancy. Many of you know my story, since you've nicknamed me the butcher." A short-lived spurt of laughter came from the audience. "I was also transferred here to do my remaining time. I cut him to keep from being killed. Self-defense, but I was still convicted. My husband stomped me for breakfast, lunch, and dinner. His favorite pastime was beating on me. The difference between this time and all the others is that I was pregnant. I guess I felt that I had to protect my child. I carved him up like a Thanksgiving turkey, but not nearly as neatly. He lived, too evil to die. My mother told me that God wasn't through with him yet. He's living in serious pain. His scars will never allow him to forget. Regrets? Yes, that I'd let it go that far."

Nancy wiped a tear from the corner of her eye. "According to the prosecutor, I did nothing less than a hack job. Like the last speaker, I don't recall a lot of what happened. But I think I've simply blocked it out. Pleading temporary insanity got me a lighter sentence, though we'd hoped with his history of violence against me that I'd get no jail time. More police reports than you can ever imagine had been filed. They'd take him away, time after time; I'd always let him come back. My deepest regret is that I wasted more than half of my life on a man who had no respect whatsoever for me. A lot of us women call this love. Love it's not."✗

For the next hour, gut-wrenching story after story was told, all with a similar ring. Betrayed by the men they loved. Deserted by them in their darkest hours. Paying for his crime. Set up and then victimized by the one person they thought they could trust their life with.

Marlene's head was reeling by the time the last female inmate finished speaking. With the assistance of their counselors, some of them would get help. Many of them had never sought help; many would continue to keep the bitter secrets involving the betrayal of their men.

Marlene stood up to address the ladies. "We have heard some incredible stories here today, unbelievable ones, yet so very true. As women, we need to look closely at our circumstances. Then we need to look deeply into self and ask the difficult questions, the ones that are very hard to answer. Everyone here today should ask this question: What role did I play in allowing my situation to occur? We then need to explore the word *responsibility* in depth."

Marlene looked around the room, making direct eye contact with as many of the women as she could. There were so many sad faces in this room, so many broken hearts. Out of all the things she'd heard, she hadn't heard anyone take responsibility for their actions. It had all been about taking someone else's inventory, not their own. That was about to change if she had her way. This was another group that she vowed to assist in finding their way before their release.

"Ladies, we have to come to the conclusion that we're solely responsible for what goes on in our lives, that we're the masters of our own destiny. Just as I've told the members of my LIW group, no one can do any more to you than you allow. We give people permission how to treat us. Usually, we're treated like we treat our-selves. If we think we're nothing but a doormat, we can't expect a person not to step on us, since that's what doormats are for. If we treat ourselves with love and kindness, we more than likely won't accept anything less from another. Stroke yourself on a daily basis. Hear this if you hear nothing else I say today. *Self is the enemy we need to fear most. No victory will ever be as sweet as the victory won over self.*"

Marlene reached down for the cup of water and then drained it.

"At some point in our lives, each and every one of us has given up our power to another human being. We simply can't do that. We have to start making wiser choices for ourselves. No one but us should make the choice on how we should conduct our lives.

"I'm not going to stand up here and put the men down either. This is not about them. It's about us. Dare to be selfish by thinking of only yourself for a change. It's okay to be selfish in certain cir-cumstances. Give yourself permission to concentrate on nobody but you. I'm now going to leave you to think about all that was said here today. If you'll have me, I promise to come back. I won't aban-don you. My husband and I are in the business of rescuing souls. With the help of God's mighty unchanging hands, we can help you rescue you. Thank you. You've been very gracious in sharing. May God bless each and every one of you!"

Prayer ensued. Once it was over, the applause was thunderous. There was not a dry eye in the house, including Marlene's. Several of the women rushed up to give Marlene a warm hug.

The ride home for Marlene was tremendously emotional. The state of the entire world had her totally upset, yet she knew that prophesy had to be totally fulfilled before Jesus could come back for His people. Just the thought of rising up to meet Him in the sky brought tears to her eyes. His return was a day she was definitely looking forward to. Though there was much work still to be done on earth, tomorrow wouldn't be soon enough for Him to come back.

Tears rolled down Marlene's cheeks as she began reciting scripture.

"For the Lord himself shall descend from heaven with a shout, with the voice of the archangel, and with the trump of God: and the dead in Christ shall rise first. Then we which are alive and remain shall be caught up together with them in the clouds, to meet the Lord in the air: and so we shall ever be with the Lord. Wherefore comfort one another with these words. 1 Thessalonians 4:16-18. Amen!" Marlene shouted, feeling the Holy Spirit at work within her.

Marlene couldn't help but think of the manner of Christ's Second Coming as stated in the Bible, 1 Thessalonians 5:1-6: "But of the times and seasons, brethren, ye have no need that I write unto you. For yourselves know perfectly that the day of the Lord so cometh as a thief in the night. For when they shall say, 'Peace and safety,' then sudden destruction cometh upon them, as travail upon a woman with a child; and they shall not escape. But ye, brethren, are not in darkness, that that day should overtake you as a thief. Ye all are the children of light, and the children of the day: we are not of the night, nor of the darkness. Therefore let us not sleep, as do others; but let us watch and be sober."

Marlene was too emotionally full to continue speaking aloud. In her heart and in her mind she continued to recite the last few versus of 1 Thessalonians 5:7-11.

"God, thank you for bringing me into the presence of your precious children who are incarcerated. I have been so blessed by them and this dark, yet enlightening, experience. Father, please help Jesse and me to help them find their way back home to you. I know you await each of them with open arms. I know that it is your desire not to lose a one of the sheep of your flock. Please bless these women and men in a very special way. Keep them in your tender care. Amen."

Her thoughts then turned to the brief talk she'd had with Kamara

Bauer. She couldn't wait to tell Malcolm about the little girl he was once so fond of. Kamara had told Marlene she could share her woeful story with her son. She even said she'd love to see Malcolm again.

Marlene prayed that Malcolm would find it in his heart to visit Kamara. She wouldn't ask it of him, but she hoped he would see the need. Marlene thought Malcolm could minister to Kamara better than either she or Jesse. Malcolm would know how to speak Kamara's language. They were both from the same bad streets, the unsavory location of their own choosing.

This was yet another serious situation for her to pray over. God would deliver to her all the answers she sought. He hadn't failed her yet. "Seek and ye shall find."

Chapter Thirteen

As Alexis ran about the kitchen looking busy doing next to nothing, Marietta was up to her elbows in preparing the simple but hearty meal that her employer had requested. Alexis had told Marietta that Mathis West was a steak and potato man, so that's what the menu consisted of, complemented by fresh asparagus and a tossed salad. A light and fluffy angel-food cake served with fresh strawberries and homemade whipped topping was the chosen dessert, another of Alexis's favorites. The delicious scent of brewing hazelnut coffee filled the air.

Alexis wore a lightweight robe over her casual gray-and-pink sportswear to keep from getting any spillage on her while she attempted to make the whipped cream. She had purposely dressed down for the evening, though she intended to be solicitously charming. All she wanted Mathis to be hungry for was the food. No designer jeans or other brand-name labels graced her stunning figure, yet she still looked the part of a fashion model. Not a hair was out of place and her makeup was flawless, as always.

Alexis had not taken R.J.'s warning from her dreams lightly. She had a hidden agenda where Mathis was concerned. He could possibly help her fulfill one of her important missions. He apparently had a lot of wealthy friends, too, or so he'd boasted enough times. She hoped to convince him to speak with his friends on behalf of Jarreau's nonprofit organization. How to do it without revealing Jarreau's involvement was a bit sticky for her. Alexis was eager to make a success of her new job. Fundraising was the perfect job for money-people like her. Alexis was confident that she'd learn how to raise lots of cold cash as easily as she'd learned how to spend it. She had a nose for money, just one of the many benefits of having lived with R.J.

The doorbell rang, prompting Alexis to take off the robe, which she planned to hang in the hall closet on her way to the door. She wasn't through making the whipped cream, but she set it aside knowing Marietta would finish it up. It had to be Mathis and she didn't want to leave him waiting a minute longer than necessary. Everything had to be perfect. No screw-ups on her part. Mathis wouldn't suspect a thing. At least, not until the moment was upon him. Even then, she hoped he wouldn't be able to resist her pretentious charm.

The thought that she might be playing with fire did very little to quell her enthusiasm.

Seated at the superbly decorated table, the blessing already said by the hostess, Alexis smiled at Mathis, gesturing for him to dig in. One of the oldest clichés in the book was that the way to a man's heart was through his stomach. She wasn't interested in his heart. His wallet was what had her full attention. The old feminine wiles had a way of working every time when it came down to slipping the mean green from within the folds of worn leather.

Alexis was now sure about her newest purpose in life, since she had to wonder if she was getting into this fundraising thing just to impress Jarreau and to be near him. It was now clear to her that her mission was one of mercy, an undertaking sent to her through divine intervention. God was speaking to her heart; she was finally listening.

Mathis eyed Alexis flirtatiously, making her feel as if he thought she was part of the menu. "I was so surprised to get a call from you inviting me to dinner. I was also pleased." He grinned devilishly. "You don't have any tricks up your sleeve for me, do you, since your invitation came right out of the blue? Sometimes you're too complex for words, Alexis."

While trying to keep from looking guilty, Alexis's heart thumped wildly inside her chest. Talk about hitting the nail right on the head! Was her intent that obvious? It was at that very moment that Alexis decided to table her mission and let the chips fall where they may. God probably wasn't too happy with how she'd planned to use her feminine charms in persuading Mathis to open up his wallet for charity, anyway.

Despite her last thought, Alexis batted her eyes flirtatiously. She just couldn't seem to help herself. She was simply a huge flirt and loved to be in the company of men, those who held her in obvious adoration. "You know something, Mathis, I have to confess. You're not too far off the mark. I asked you here this evening because I desperately need your help for a very worthy cause, one that you could be very proud of. Your spirit of generosity is allowing me to come to you with this proposition," she flattered knowingly, gently covering his hand with hers for an added measure of persuasion. The contact only lasted briefly. Alexis did have limitations, not to mention scruples.

He appeared very interested in what Alexis had to say. The physical contact had also excited him. She saw that from the look in his eyes. She had no doubt that Mathis was a wolf in sheep's clothing. Among so many other things, Mathis and R.J. certainly had that in common.

"You have my undivided attention. Let me hear what's on your mind, Alexis."

Before Alexis could begin to lay out her proposal for Mathis, Marietta stepped into the room with the intent of telling Alexis she was leaving for the evening. Looking quite fearful, Marietta stopped dead in her tracks. Her skin suddenly appeared pale. She also seemed to have a problem voicing her reason for interrupting her employer's meal. Alexis could tell that Marietta's breathing was labored, too.

Alexis jumped to her feet, deep concern written all over her face. "Are you okay, Marietta? What's wrong? You look ill."

Marietta placed her hand over her heart. "I think I'm okay now, just a dizzy spell of some sort. I guess I'd better go lie down. No movie date for me tonight."

"I'll help you to your quarters, Marietta. Here, let me take your hand. Put your arm around my waist," Alexis prompted. "Do you think we should call 911?"

"No, no, nothing that serious, Missy. Don't need any loud sirens to stir up the night."

Alexis turned back to Mathis. "I'll be right back. I need to get her all tucked in. Go ahead and eat. I don't want your meal to get cold."

Mathis got to his feet. He guessed that Marietta was the housekeeper, since no formal introductions had been made. "Can I help in any way?"

Alexis gave him a reassuring smile. "It's all under control now. Marietta and I are used to taking care of each other. Thanks for your concern. Come on, Marietta, off to bed we go."

It would've only taken Alexis and Marietta a few minutes to make it from the main house to the outside guesthouse, but Alexis headed straight for one of the inside guest rooms. In spite of Marietta's objections, Alexis insisted that she stay in the main house for the rest of the night.

Once Marietta was dressed in one of Alexis's oversized T-shirts, Alexis helped her into the big, fancy, white, linen-dressed bed, beautifully accented by an ornate gold brass headboard. Completely fashioned in southern comfort décor, with white lacquer furnishings, the entire bedroom was luxurious. Marietta also had first-class digs in her fair-sized guesthouse quarters, but this grand bedroom was also nothing short of elegant. She felt like she was in paradise.

With Marietta all settled down in the bed comfortably, Alexis bent over and kissed her forehead. "The phone is right here. Use the second line to call me on the main line if you need anything. I promise to come running."

Alexis thought it was stupid of her to be so close to tears. But Marietta was the closest person to her in all of California, though she in no way discounted the closeness she now had with Marlene, Keisha, and Rosalinda. This was much different. Marietta had been like a mother to her. If something were to happen to Marietta, Alexis knew she'd be totally lost. Although she was now in constant contact with her parents and all of her siblings, all of whom planned to visit her again in the near future, Marietta had been there for her to lean on when she thought she had absolutely no one else.

As Alexis moved away from the bed, Marietta gripped her hand tightly. Alexis smoothed Marietta's hair back with her fingers. "What is it? Are you afraid to be alone, dear heart?"

Marietta shook her head in the negative, patting the side of the bed. Alexis wasted no time in honoring Marietta's gesture for her to be seated.

Marietta plumped the pillow behind her and sat higher up in the bed. "I haven't been feeling well the last couple of days, Missy, but I didn't want to mention it, at least not until after I see my doctor at the end of the week. But it was the sight of your guest that kind of pushed me over the edge. . . ."

Alexis looked perplexed. "Do you know Mathis, Marietta? What do you mean by that?"

Marietta shook her head. "I don't know him, but I've seen him coming and going on the premises numerous times while R.J. was alive. He always entered from the back end of the property. Never saw him up in the main house."

Alexis was downright shocked. It appeared that she wasn't the only one with a hidden agenda. What was Mathis playing at? What was he after? Something was terribly amiss. The short hairs stood up on the back of her neck. She then shuddered with fear, thinking of the day she'd come home after the funeral to find that the safety of her home had been compromised.

"From what you've been telling me about Mathis West, Missy, I know you didn't know him when R.J. was alive. He was definitely an acquaintance of some sort of your husband's. I'm certain of that. I've seen them together on the property, but I never knew his name. That man has purposely sought you out, for whatever his reason. You need to be extremely careful. Please beware of him, sweet child."

Alexis couldn't believe her ears. "Beware of him." The same words R.J. had said to her during the strange nightmare. If Mathis knew R.J., and she certainly believed Marietta, then Mathis had indeed duped her. But why? She, too, had a hidden agenda, but nothing as sinister as his seemed. She'd definitely be wary of him, but she needed to keep him around to find out exactly what he was up to. A person had to keep a close eye on possible enemies.

Alexis couldn't help wondering if Mathis West was one of R.J.'s partners in crime. Stupid to wonder, she mused. They only had the same kind of defects of character. R.J. had deceived her, too, for most of their married life. Whoever Mathis was, she was going to find out all she could about him. She had lots of friends in high places, too.

It suddenly dawned on her how Mathis had come to know where she lived the night he'd shown up at her home uninvited, without any warning. He'd been there before. Numerous times, according to Marietta. Another light bulb moment instantly flashed inside Alexis's head, making her dizzy with disbelief. She shook her head as if she could dispel all thought.

Had Mathis West been the one to remove the gaming equipment from the secret room?

Trembling inside, Alexis leaned over and brought Marietta into her embrace. "Please don't worry about me one bit, Marietta. I'm going to handle this matter very carefully. He'll soon be on his way, never to return as an invited guest, though I still plan to see what he's up to. I'll come back and check on you as soon as I show Mr. West the door. He'll have to understand that your illness has discontinued our evening. Tsk, Tsk!" Grinning devilishly, Alexis winked her right eye at Marietta.

Marietta winked back, catching Alexis's drift. "That's my girl! Since all these rooms are wired with emergency buzzers, don't hesitate to sound one off if you get into difficulty. I can call 911 from in here. He probably thinks you've taken me to my own quarters and that he has you all to himself. Be safe now. Just remember that I'm your backup."

"I will. See you shortly." Alexis blew Marietta a kiss as she left the room.

All sorts of things went through Alexis's head as she made her way back up to the front of the home. She didn't feel the least bit safe in her own residence, but she hadn't wanted to alarm Marietta. Alexis thought of getting the gun she kept in her nightstand drawer, but she dismissed that notion rather quickly. Statistics showed that people more often got killed with their own weapon than that belonging to the perpetrator. She didn't want to become a statistic. She had way too much to live for. Jarreau Thornton instantly came to mind.

Her internal alarms screeched when she saw that Mathis wasn't where she'd left him. His dinner plate was practically empty, with only a few crumbs scattered about. Where was he? Things were starting to feel eerie and very scary. She looked all around the room, eyes wide with trepidation. Alexis left the dining room, tiptoeing gingerly, because of the marble tile. Her shoes would undoubtedly cause a clicking noise upon direct contact. Then it dawned on her to remove them altogether. No alerting noises would come from stocking feet.

As she reached the hallway, she stood stock still, listening for any sounds of movement. Her eyes darted from side to side, trying to pick up the slightest shadow. Nearly creeping, she made her way to R.J.'s completely renovated study, playing on a hunch.

Then she spotted Mathis, just as she came upon the entry. His back was to her, and she was glad for that. God had granted much grace. That meant Mathis hadn't heard her coming nor could he see her. She then saw his hands roving all over the walls, as though he were trying to locate something hidden from view. Another startling light-bulb moment! He was trying to locate the secret wall.

The secret wall no longer existed. Renovations had removed it altogether, opening it up into one big room. The room looked totally different now that both rooms were combined. To make sure he didn't see her, Alexis backed away slowly. She walked all the way to the other end of the hall before she turned back and began calling his name. She had to get this man out of her house. "Mathis, where are you? Have you gotten lost in this big old place?" she asked jokingly, hoping to keep him unaware of her being on to him.

Mathis then appeared, as if he'd come out of nowhere, startling Alexis silly.

She quickly composed herself, swallowing her fear like it was a cool glass of water, instead of the burning acid that had risen in her throat. "There you are! I'm sorry that I had to leave you like that. It hasn't been all that long, but I'm sure it seems so to you."

Alexis knew that she had to give an Oscar-winning performance to outwit this shrewd cookie. If her life was in jeopardy, she was going to fight for it to the finish. Mathis was the one who was in the fight for his life if he thought she was just going to fall over and die.

As he reached out for her, she went into his embrace, feeling like she wanted to throw up. He held her away from him. "This house is much too big. I was looking for the bathroom and finally found one. It was when I came out that I got completely turned around. I've been wandering around here for several minutes now. It *is* easy to get lost in this much space."

I just bet you were, you clever dog. "I can attest to that. I used to get lost myself." Frowning, Alexis stuck her lip out in a pouting gesture. "I'm afraid I have bad news. I really must call our evening to an end. My housekeeper is feeling super lousy. I promised to come back and sit with her until she's feeling more comfortable."

Mathis eyed her suspiciously. "Why would you need to baby-sit a grown woman?"

"I don't see it as baby-sitting. Besides, she's much more than that to me than you realize. Marietta is my second Mom. I didn't expect you to be insensitive about this. I'm surprised."

Fearful of getting on her bad side yet again, he shook his head. "No, no, I understand. I'm just so disappointed. We can't seem to have a full date these days. I'll go now. What if I come by and check on you two girls sometime tomorrow? It won't be a problem for me."

"That's very nice of you, but so unnecessary. Marietta and I are used to fending for each other. We'll be fine. If I find that she's feeling better by tomorrow, I'll call you and perhaps we can set something up for over the weekend." Alexis had no intention of calling Mathis until she had him thoroughly checked out. His clever behind was about to go under the microscope. Lying to Mathis was a must for now. If he suspected her of being suspicious of him, she didn't want to think of what other nastiness could occur. He looked harmless, but he could be very dangerous.

A particular FBI agent came to mind, the one who'd been in charge of investigating R.J.

Miles Danvers was just another weak-in-the-flesh man who'd shown more than a casual interest in Alexis. He'd even had the nerve to hint to her that he had a real thing for brown sugar. All the while he'd flirted openly with her, Danvers had done his level best to put her husband behind bars. He had only succeeded in imprisoning R.J. Alexis would never even think of stooping so low as to sleep with the slimy likes of Miles Danvers, FBI agent extraordinaire.

Alexis couldn't get Mathis to the door fast enough, and she couldn't wait to close and lock it behind him. The alarm would be set instantly. Peace would be hard to achieve, at any rate.

At the door, Mathis took both of Alexis's hands in his, making her want to scream at him to get out and never come back. The agony had been prolonged enough. "Since I didn't get the after dinner dessert you promised earlier, what about a sweet kiss to send this big guy on his way. I'm sure it will be much sweeter than the cake."

Alexis nearly gagged, but she closed her eyes and offered him her mouth, anyway. As he tried to deepen the kiss, she pulled back from him. "Not ready for anything deeper than a light kiss or two. I hope you understand. Thanks for coming to dinner, Mathis. Good night."

An impatient sigh escaped his lips. "I understand. Good night, Alexis."

The moment the door closed behind Mathis, Alexis wasted no time in securing the house. She then took off running to the bedroom where a more-than-likely fearful Marietta awaited her. "Thank you, God," she prayed aloud. "Thank you for bringing me through yet another battle."

Keisha's heart ached as Zach tried to close Tammy's front door in her face, making her feel as awful as she'd felt a few nights back, when he'd slammed her own door in her face. At the risk of hurting herself, Keisha had forced her shoulder inside the door. "Zach, we need to talk. I came here to apologize to you. Please let me tell you what I came here to say."

Zach opened the door wide. He glared at her. "This has to be a first. Keisha apologizing! What, you done gone and found religion or something?"

Keisha pushed herself the rest of the way inside. "Cut the sarcasm long enough to hear me out, Zach. You know exactly why I thought what I did. I know your track record."

252

"There you go, all back in the past. Say what you got to say so you can go. I'm not getting into all that with you. You're always spoiling for a fight."

"So we just gonna stand out here in the hall? You're not inviting me in?"

"It ain't my place to be inviting no one in."

"Negro, please. I've been to Tammy's house a time or two before; she's been to mine numerous times." Without waiting for a response, Keisha started down the hallway and entered Tammy's newly all-leather furnished den, complemented by smoked-glass accents. Tammy had told Keisha that she'd recently done some redecorating and had purchased some new furniture. This was Keisha's first time seeing it. She found the room to be toasty warm and inviting.

Keisha plopped down on the sofa, looking back at the doorway. Zach was nowhere to be seen. His behavior was starting to get on her last nerve, just as her attitude had probably gotten on his over the new clothes. It wouldn't surprise her if he just left her sitting in there until she got tired of his game and stormed out. She and Zach were equally as stubborn. Bad combination.

Guilt over her uncharitable thoughts about him hit her full force when Zach finally entered the room, carrying a glass of soda and a bowl of chips. The boy had learned how to be hospitable. Would wonders never cease? Mr. Man was actually serving her refreshments.

He set the ice-filled glass of Coke on a coaster and set the chip bowl on one of the table's lace doilies. "Thought you might be thirsty and maybe a little hungry." He walked across the room and dropped down in the navy-blue, leather recliner.

Keisha thought Zach looked right at home. He seemed very comfortable in Tammy's private space. It was obvious that he was no stranger to her home, nor to her household belongings. For whatever reason, that bothered her.

Keisha took a sip of Coke while muddling over what to say,

though she'd already gone over her speech in her head a dozen times or more within the last few days. She set the glass down and picked up one of the sofa pillows, placing it in her lap. It was unusual for her to need a security blanket around Zach, but she did. "I guess I should just say I'm sorry for the way I acted with you a few nights back."

His eyebrows shot up. "You guess? Sounds like you're not sure if you're sorry or not."

Frustrated with herself, Keisha shook her head. "That didn't come out right. Zachary Martin, I'm sorry for my behavior toward you over the new clothes. It was unfair and unkind. I jumped to all the wrong conclusions. Can you forgive me?"

"You haven't convinced me that you mean what you're saying. For someone who's sorry, there was a lot of sister-girl attitude in your words and your body language. What, you feeling guilty 'bout something?"

Keisha threw up her hands in protestation. "What are you talking about now? The subject has definitely changed. We're no longer talking about my apology, are we?"

"You're not stupid. You know exactly what I'm getting at. Ol' boy was sitting all comfy in your apartment like he's been up in there a few times or more. What's up with that?"

"Like you're sitting all comfy here in Tammy's place? I guess I can ask you the same thing. What's up with that?"

Zach ignored her petulance. "Who is he? Better yet, who is he to you?"

"Please! Malcolm is Reverend Jesse and Mizz Marlene's son."

"Yeah, and what's that got to do with the price of milk? The second part of my question is still not answered. Who is he to you?"

"He's nothing to me." *Oh, God,* Keisha mused, upset that she'd gone there. Malcolm had become a dear friend, a confidant, and she'd just written him off as nothing. That would've hurt him so bad to hear her say that. Old ways died hard, but she quickly decided not to take another step backward. She no longer had to lie to anyone for any reason. "Malcolm's a good friend. He's been very supportive of the kids and me. He's in my life to stay. Deal with it!"

Zach leaped out of the chair and practically ran across the room, scaring Keisha to death in the process. Her eyes were wide with unknowing as he dropped down beside her and grabbed hold of her shoulders. "Keisha, tell me you're not sleeping with ol' boy. I couldn't take that. I know I've screwed up, but you got to at least give me a chance to try and get my family back. This brother needs a little more time and trust from you. You have to believe me when I say I'm trying, baby girl. It ain't easy out here in the real world. Employers have no sympathy for ex-cons. Most of them look at me as if I'm dirt once they find out I've done time."

The tears in Zach's eyes nearly stunned Keisha out of her gourd. That he might be feeling vulnerable, too, hadn't dawned on her in recent months. She could even feel the slight trembling of his body, as his thigh was resting close to hers. Taking him into her embrace was out of the question. He'd want more than she was ready for. Yet she felt deep compassion for him. Zach once again had the look of defeat upon his face. She'd have to find a way to encourage him, to be more positive with him, or he would end back up on the streets wheeling and dealing. Her kids deserved to have Daddy in their lives whether he was a part of hers or not.

She dared to take his hand, hoping he wouldn't read anything more into just a warm gesture. "I'm not sleeping with anyone, Zach. Sex is not even on my list of priorities these days. The kids are. They need you just as much as me. Don't give up on yourself. If you give up on you, you give up on them. Don't you think they'd like to have you around to tuck them into bed at night for a change?"

"I've been doing that since I been home. I see how much they love it. But I just feel so crazy at times and out of control. Prison has become a way of life for me, Keisha. It's all I've known most of my adulthood. I made the mistake of getting used to my circumstances."

"I know that. But keep reminding yourself that you're now free to take them to the park, the movies, and share in all the special holidays with them. I can't remember the last time you were free on Thanksgiving or Christmas. Your children live for Christmas from year to year, Zach. You haven't been home once to celebrate in their childish joy. We all have spent every Christmas of the children's short lives behind bars. That's the memory they'll have to live with for the rest of their lives if you go back inside. Try to create some sweet, new memories for them."

Hoping she was really getting through to Zach, Keisha wiped away a falling tear from his face. "Live for them until you can learn to live for yourself. Do whatever works to help you get through each miserable day. You haven't been out that long, yet you've managed to get some work. The world is cruel; such is life. Do you want to know what has helped me to keep my sanity through all these trials and tribulations? Through all this pain and suffering?"

His pain was soul-deep and he had no clue how to ease the awful aching. Keisha had been his addictive pain reliever for as far back as he could remember. In her absence he'd been forced into the agony of withdrawal, the worst kind of pain imaginable for an addict. His eyes connected with hers through the blur of his tears. Though he didn't make a verbal response to her question, his eyes told her that he desperately wanted to know her secret.

Keisha gently squeezed Zach's fingers. "Prayer, Zach. Lots of prayer. Prayer is the key."

"How do I learn to do that?"

Keisha's eyes filled to the brim as she recalled asking Marlene the same question. Marlene's response had changed her life. Keisha closed her eyes. "And it came to pass, that, as He was praying in a certain place, when He ceased, one of His disciples said unto him, Lord, teach us to pray." Luke 11:1 was the first scripture Keisha had learned to recite by heart.

Zach looked totally uncomfortable. Though he didn't recognize that it was his spirit aching for relief, Zach knew that he needed the weight of his burdens to be lightened. "I don't know anything about this. But I'm willing to try something new if it'll keep me from finding myself back up at the big house. How should I pray, Keisha?"

"I will pray with the Spirit, and I will pray with the understanding also." The book of 1 Corinthians 14:15. "Just like you're talking to an old friend, Zach. That's how I was told to do it. Tell Him what you need, and ask Him to guide your path toward that fulfillment. There's work that you'll also have to do, Zach. I've come to understand that we have to do our part. Then, when we see that we can't go any further on our own, we can then turn it over to God."

"Example."

"Okay. You can pray for a job. But a knock isn't going to come on the door. And when you say, 'Who is it?' 'job' is not the response you'll hear from the other side. You have to actively search for work, just as you've obviously been doing. I misjudged your intent and your accomplishments over the clothes for the kids. Thank you for making such a huge effort. Very sorry for the way I handled it."

He nodded. "I think you mean it." His expression grew pensive. "Is there still a chance for us, baby girl?"

Shrugging his question off would've been Keisha's normal response, but at this very moment she didn't want to offend or discourage him. He'd already had enough of both in his life. Zach needed to see some positives, which would hopefully keep the negatives at bay.

"You've had so many chances, Zach, that I really can't say for sure. At least not right now. Let's wait and see. I won't rule out the possibility altogether. All I want you to do is take care of Zach's needs for now. That's what I had to do to get strong. What about coming over for dinner tonight? I'll fix a couple of your favorites. I know the kids would love that."

He'd heard her, found it hard to believe, but he wasn't going to ask her to repeat it just in case he'd gotten it wrong. "What time?"

Keisha laughed heartily. "I see that you've forgotten the magic dinner hour. Six o'clock."

"What can I bring?"

Keisha was impressed with his comeback; so unselfish of him. "Ice cream and you."

"It's on. See you at six. If you're ready to go, I'll walk you to the door."

Jesse was so proud of Malcolm. His deep pride showed on his face. Malcolm had invited his parents over for dinner, but had asked his dad to come by early for a spirit-filled man-to-man. Jesse could hardly believe his son was all grown up now. Time was fleet.

Marlene would be along later, after she and Myrna finished working on the plans for Sister Wylie's surprise event. Malcolm had originally thought of asking Marlene to bring Keisha along, back when he'd first come up with the idea of cooking for his parents. That was before Zach had shown up at her apartment over a week ago. Malcolm didn't feel good about separating Keisha from her kids to do things with him, but it had to be that way. Marlene had etched their welfare upon his heart. He was determined not to hurt little Zach and Zanari.

This was the first time Jesse had been in his son's apartment since the new furniture delivery. The place looked good and well-maintained. The décor was very masculine, done in colors of burgundy and gray. Malcolm's numerous sports trophies, all of them won in high school, made really nice accents. Jesse loved all the family pictures Malcolm had placed on the mantelpiece. His was a loving family, a whole family of Covingtons. Jesse wasn't in any hurry for Malcolm to give him grandkids, but he hoped to eventually have two or three to spoil.

Jesse sniffed the air as he entered the small-but-efficient kitchen. "You got me waiting out there in the living room when it smells like all the goodies are in here. That aroma sure is familiar. Smells like something right out of yours and my mom's kitchens."

Looking a bit sheepish, Malcolm laughed. "It is. I called Mom this morning, and she gave me the recipe to Grandma Covington's spaghetti sauce. You remember how I used to sop up the leftover sauce with the last pieces of garlic bread? Grandma let me do it without a fuss, but Mom never did like that habit of mine." Malcolm made a waving gesture, pointing at the table. "Dad, go on over there and pull up a chair. We can talk in here. I'll join you in a sec."

Jesse made himself comfortable at the table. "Thank you, son. Back to you and the sauce. I don't think your mom minded. She just didn't want you to take those bad habits out of the house. Just think of someone in a restaurant making the mess you used to make. It was always about teaching you proper etiquette. Grandma Covington let you get away with far more than I ever did. That's grandmas for you. God love their sweet souls."

Jesse's eyes misted at the thought of his dear mother. As a mother-in-law, she was the exception to the rule. She loved Wildflower. He'd never heard the two women he loved dearly have so much as a cross word over anything. Mother Covington loved to cook and Marlene loved learning how to cook just like her. Two women working harmoniously in the same kitchen was indeed a miracle. Marlene didn't too much like having anyone else in hers, yet she'd been known to share her space a time or two when necessary.

"Dad, you look like you're having a flashback over there. Good or bad?"

"Wonderful, son. Any thoughts of your mom and mine are sweet treasures. So, what did you have on your mind when you asked me to come earlier than your mom?"

Malcolm lowered the flame under the sauce before taking a seat at the table. "Women, Dad! How did you know Mom was the one?"

Jesse cracked up at the perplexed expression on Malcolm's face. "I can't explain it, son. I just knew she was it for me."

"Ah, Dad, come on now. There had to be some telltale signs."

Chuckling, Jesse stroked his chin. "Well, my heart did beat a little faster than normal when she got on the bus that night. The seat next to me was the only empty one, so I quickly moved over to the window seat and let her have the aisle. She smelled sweeter than a field full of jasmine. I kept leaning in just to get another whiff of her delicious scent. That knock 'em dead smile of hers had my insides quaking. It came brightly when she thanked me for moving over, turning my knees to water." Jesse put his forefinger in the air. "But you know what, son? Despite all the captivating outward appearances, I'm in no doubt that the instant connection I made with her spirit was what let me know she was the one."

Malcolm frowned heavily. "How do you connect with someone's spirit?"

Jesse shrugged. "You'll know when it happens. And your life will never be the same again. Why are you asking all these engaging questions? Think you've found the one?"

Malcolm threw his head back in laughter. "Hardly! Women are too dang complex for me. I'm not sure I'm up to the task, Dad. Women are like a puzzle, hard to fit all the pieces together."

"What experience or experiences are you basing that on?"

"This thing with Keisha, for one. Listen to this. Zach brings over the kids some new clothes. She goes ballistic on him for that. It's crazy. Her complaints are the same whether he does something good or bad. The brother didn't stand a chance with her. She also accused Tammy of conspiring with Zach to buy the clothes. Keisha was out of control and dead wrong."

"You were there?"

Malcolm snapped his head to the side. "Yeah, I was there. Figure that one out. Zach was so mad at her that he stormed out of the place without us ever meeting. I'm sure he knows who I am by now. Keisha was supposed to go see him and apologize. She was sure he'd get around to asking about me. I can tell you this much. I'm glad our meeting didn't happen."

Jesse pursed his lips. "Why's that?"

" 'Cause the brother was boiling mad. The circumstances just weren't good."

"Then I'm also glad. I didn't know you were interested in meeting Zach, period."

"I wasn't in the beginning. Then I got to thinking about my relationship with Keisha. If she and I remain close friends, and I hope that we do, it'll probably be better for me to meet him. I don't want to hang out with her behind his back. That's not cool. It's just asking for trouble."

"Only friends?"

"Only friends?" Malcolm reiterated. "The question of the millennium! That's what I really want to talk to you about, Dad. I need your advice. Mom will be here in a bit so I'd better move this right along. She's okay with you keeping what I say in confidence. I asked her first. She understands about the men thing."

Jesse raised an eyebrow. "This sounds serious."

"It is, Dad. But crazy, too."

Grinning, Jesse crossed his legs. "I can hardly wait. You know how I love to use real life situations to get my point across to my congregation. Maybe I'll receive some good, racy material for my next sermon."

"Okay, Dad, stop clowning me."

Jesse chuckled. "It's all good. I'm ready to hear what you got going on. No more clowning. I promise."

"Thanks, Dad."

Malcolm went on to explain to his father his real dilemma as best as he could. He knew Jesse would give it to him straight, just what he needed. Malcolm had a few decisions to make.

* * *

Marlene looked at her only child with deep admiration, so proud of who he'd become. She'd always loved her son; now she really liked him as a person. He had also earned her deep respect. His growth was as astonishing as that of Keisha and Rosalinda.

Alexis had grown, too, but she wasn't yet as fully secure with herself as were the others. Marlene felt confident that Alexis would eventually come into her own. Alexis had her own agenda and time schedule, never dancing to anyone's tune but her own. Alexis Du Boise was a highly polished gemstone with a few rough edges to buff and shine. In Marlene's opinion, Jarreau Thornton was just the kind of buffer Alexis needed to help her smooth her life out.

"You really worked that Covington sauce, son. Grandma Marie would be so proud of you. Mr. Malcolm has turned out to be a great chef. What do you think, Reverend Jesse?"

Jesse shrugged. "He learned from his mom and grandma, two of the best cooks I know of. Your mother was right; the sauce was kicking. You did a good job, son. Thanks for having us over. This was one of the nicest evenings we've had since the party at our place."

"No problem. I hope we can do this more often, Mom and Dad. It's not every day a son gets to entertain his parents in his own place. One that he's paying for on his own."

Marlene got to her feet. "You can say that again. Is it okay if we move into the living room, Malcolm? I have something I want to share with you."

"Sure. Does anyone want coffee and dessert to take along?"

"I'd like to come back and have it here in the kitchen. In fact, I can talk to you in here as well as in the other room. Is it okay if I do the serving?" Marlene asked Malcolm.

"No, Mom. Just sit back and let me cater to you and Dad for a change. Okay?"

"You won't get any arguments here," Marlene remarked. "Cater to me, child!"

Once the coffee and chocolate-fudge mousse cake were served,

Marlene told Malcolm about Kamara Bauer being in prison and why she'd been sent there. Malcolm was as stunned as Marlene had been when she'd first realized that she knew one of the female prison inmates. Much to Marlene's delight, Malcolm volunteered to go visit Kamara the first opportunity he got. She was pleased that he'd made the decision to visit Kamara without any prompting from her.

Chapter Fourteen

Marlene and Jesse's idea for a coed support session had caught the interest of many. The large number in attendance inside the recreation area at the women's prison consisted of the LIW group, the UTW group, and the female inmates Marlene had spoken to a few weeks back. Several of the counselors were instrumental in getting approval from the warden to hold the special session at the prison. Seeing the good in it, the warden had approved, and was also in attendance.

Special passes to enter the prison gates and the session had to be obtained by Marlene and Jesse. The passes were then passed out to each of the members in their respective groups, and valid IDs were to be presented at the prison. Nothing like this had ever been done by this prison, so a lot of red tape had to be cut through. No one could gain entry without a pass and ID check. The prison also had a team of guards on alert should anything out of the ordinary occur.

Everyone was seated and ready to go, when another male entered, the same guy who always seated himself in the back of the sanctuary during the UTW sessions. Frank Armstrong had read about Jesse's idea for the support group in a newsletter on his job. Then he'd later heard several of his coworkers talking and laughing about the group in the company break room. Frank was employed as an administrator at a large company that manufactured automobile tires. The general consensus among his coworkers was that no one in his right mind was going to attend a support group. But they didn't have to deal with what Frank was dealing with.

Glad that he'd managed to attend, Jesse nodded in Frank's direction, hoping he'd soon reveal his reasons for coming to the meetings. Jesse was sure the young man was carrying a heavy burden of some sort. Frank look like a deeply troubled man, another man who didn't know how to go about finding relief for what bothered him. Jesse had just what he needed, but Frank had to first ask for it. Being a patient man, Jesse would wait on Frank for as long as it took.

Frank once again took a seat in the back of the room. He had been the last person Jesse had processed for the coed meeting. To request his special pass, Frank had shown up in Jesse's office only a couple of days before the session, which had meant more red tape for Jesse to tackle because of such short notice. Frank's visit had been their first face-to-face encounter.

The meeting came into session with Jesse reading a few passages from the Bible, followed by a humbling prayer, which he hoped would set the mood. Reverend Jesse Covington was in partnership with God on everything he took on. Jesse would no more think of leaving God out of any of his messages than he could forget to breathe, because God had chosen him as the messenger. A messenger of God delivered the Master's message, nothing more, nothing less.

Marlene had a few powerful words to say as well. In the interest of time, she immediately opened the floor and reseated herself next to Jesse. The seats had been set in rows this time. Because of so many chairs to be arranged, the circle formation hadn't been possible.

"Since it appears that no one else is going to volunteer to go first, I'm going to get things started," said a young black woman. "I want to begin by thanking Reverend and Mrs. Covington for making all this possible."

Applause followed her statement.

"My name is Stella, and, yes, I wish I could get my groove back. But that's not going to happen for a very long time. I've always heard older women say that 'men will be men,' as if that makes their despicable behavior okay. Dogs will be dogs, too, 'cause they don't know how to be anything else. Men do, yet they don't. My man used me until he used me up. My fault? You better believe it. No one forced me to drive the getaway car for him. While he was robbing liquor stores, I waited outside with the car engine running." Stella took a deep breath.

"All he had to do was tell me he loved me and that this was the last time I'd have to prove my love to him. He proved his to me when we finally got busted; he turned state's evidence against me, getting less time than I did. The mastermind behind the robberies got less time than his accomplice. What a wonderful justice system we have here in America, the home of the brave and the land of the free! My question to any of you guys who want to answer it is this: Why do men disrespect us women so much? Why do we have to work so hard for love?"

A burly, black guy wearing a red-checkered shirt jumped to his feet. He rubbed his hands together, as though he were eager to speak. "Willie G., here. I'm just the one to answer that for you, my sister. If any man disrespects you, it's because you women disrespect yourselves. Women always seem to be looking to some man for affirmation. Save yourselves from the dogs of the world instead of thinking some no good man's got your back. You allow the crap to go on for years and years before you decide you're sick and tired of it. Most of you just want to hear yourselves talk, because you know you're not going to do a darn thing about him. You're better off shutting up and putting up with it if you're not going to end it. I'm out."

Willie G. sat down only to get right back up. "I guess I left you wondering how I know these things. I'm here because my sister is spending life behind bars because she stayed too long, got beat down one time too many. She ended up killing him before he eventually killed her."

Stella had no comeback. Willie G. was right on the money. Women often disrespected themselves in the name of love. She knew about that from firsthand experience.

A young, black female inmate got to her feet and looked over at Willie G. "What did you mean when you said we'd be better off shutting up and putting up with it?"

Another brother raised his hand to speak but didn't get up. "It's like this. It means that you say something, but rarely do you do anything about it. Women fling around ultimatums all the time, but you don't arise to the occasion. Men walk over you because you lie down at their feet and let them step on you. You work harder at love 'cause you're loving the wrong man."

"If that's the case, what does that say about you as a man?" a member of the LIW group asked. "What respectable man hangs around a dishonorable woman?"

"Look here, lady, I'm not going to get into a war of words with you. My sister is also locked up behind some stupid bull-corn. What kind of woman sells herself to keep her man in crack? A woman who has no respect for herself and no kind of direction in her life is the kind of woman that a no good man completely dogs out. She wasn't raised to be nobody's trick. My Momma and Daddy would die if they were alive. I thank God that they're not here to see how she turned out. And you all need to stop putting us men all in the same category of some of these lowlifes you all deal with. In my opinion, a man who mistreats a woman isn't a real man. It's only his genitals that makes him so. You seem to work hard at picking the wrong kind of men."

Eric Eldridge was the next person to stand up. He looked around the room for several seconds. There were a lot of different age groups represented here, but the younger ones were much larger in numbers. Some of the female inmates still looked like scared little teenagers. He would be willing to bet that many of them were just barely in their early twenties.

"Men versus women is nearly always the name of the game. It shouldn't be that way. I'll tell you why in a second. I'm a member of the UTW support group run by Reverend Jesse. My pregnant girl-friend is behind bars. Drugs. I only learned a few weeks back that she started using drugs for something I did. . . ."

"What else is new?" a white, female inmate interrupted.

Eric gave the sarcastic speaker a slight smile. "I can understand why you'd say that. But I do believe it cuts both ways. Contrary to popular belief, women aren't exempt from causing men pain. At any rate, I was dumbfounded to find out that my lady started using drugs because of me. She found out that I was cheating on her with my ex-fiancée. While I won't take blame for her involvement with drugs, I do take full responsibility for her pain and suffering. . . ."

"A little late for that, isn't it, since she's already locked up behind your sorry behind?" the same female inmate asked.

"My woman is locked up for committing felonies, not because of a broken heart; she used and sold illegal drugs. In looking back, I can now see how communication problems played a part in this madness. She didn't come to me with what she knew about me, and I didn't ask her why she'd changed so much until it was too late. I ended the affair with my ex after I realized how much my current woman meant to me. I went back to my girlfriend and never gave the brief fling a second thought, never felt a moment of guilt. It was over for me. But a nightmare including white-powder dreams had just begun for my girlfriend."

Easton looked on in deep admiration of Eric. His respect for Eric had grown by leaps and bounds. He and Eric had forged a spe-cial friendship in just a few short weeks. Easton never dreamed he'd ever call any man of color 'friend.' But that was exactly how he thought of Eric, as his friend. Eric had helped him work through so many issues. Easton felt the same about Jesse.

Eric paused for a second to reflect. His statements had had a profound effect on even him. "I want to say a few more things, then I'm clearing the floor. This is directed to both the men and women. It's true that we men show disrespect to our women, but it is also true in the reverse. My advice to all of us is to respect and love each other. More importantly, love and respect for self is the most important in the codes of morality. Respect is crucial to the survival of any relationship.

"Whether we're aware of it or not, men and women teach their sons and daughters by example. Women, teach your sons to respect themselves, you, and other females. But please don't disrespect and put their fathers down in front of them. Men, take time with your sons and teach them self-respect and how to respect you and the women in their lives. If they see you disrespecting their mothers, they will do one of two things: take on the behavior, or challenge you to a fistfight because they don't like the disrespect. That's a given."

A huge grin spread across Eric's face. "I'm pleased to announce that my girlfriend and I have decided to work things out no matter how difficult it gets. We're hoping to get married before the baby arrives, which will hopefully occur in a regular hospital. Regardless of the birthplace, our child will be in my custody until she's released. We're doing this because we love each other, not just because of our baby. Thank you."

Eric was highly aware of the fact that marrying a woman behind bars might adversely affect his career. Because of what Reverend Jesse had taught him about patience, and also waiting on God for the answers, he was no longer worried. God would take care of his every need.

Jesse was thrilled by Eric's news. *Hope does float*, he mused. *But prayers are always answered from way above the clouds. Thank you, Jesus*, Jesse silently prayed.

Marlene noticed that the room was deathly still ever since Eric had taken his seat. His comments appeared to have everyone deep in thought. He had made some heavy statements, none that could be challenged, either. This meeting was turning out better than Jesse and Marlene had dared to hope for. The participants were opening up their thoughts and letting them pour out like falling rain. A thorough cleansing of the mind and the spirit were good things indeed.

Keisha, as a representative of LIW, thought it was time for her to show her growth as a former "lady in waiting." She stood up and introduced herself. She then went straight into her own nightmare of a story, not leaving out anything of importance. "I'm sure many of you have heard before what I'm about to say, but I'm going to spell it out anyway, just in case someone hasn't heard it. We attract to us exactly what we are. If we're insecure, we'll attract an insecure mate. Confidence will draw to us a confident partner. Low self-esteem has to be present in both parties for it to survive. The only person who's going to put up with someone suffering from low self-esteem is that person's mirror image." Kiesha looked around at all the people who reminded her of herself, especially those who'd already spoken.

"I suffered terribly with esteem issues. I've made a lot of positive changes in myself and I now know how to set firm boundaries. I've also learned how to enforce them. Anyone coming at me incorrect these days won't be hitting on anything but a brick wall. The changes in me will hopefully have a positive impact on my kids for years to come. I'm setting much better examples for them. Thank you for allowing me to share." Keisha smiled at Marlene as she took her seat.

Rosalinda quickly followed Keisha's lead, also stating that she was a member of LIW. "I agree wholeheartedly with what was just said. We need to look closely at all the relationships we've had, from the very first one to the very last, including our present ones. If each relationship has the exact same or similar problems as the others, we're simply repeating the same old patterns. We keep repeating the same mistakes because we haven't worked on or changed our own behaviors. It all goes back to attracting to us what we are.

"If we make the necessary changes in ourselves, the circumstances around us will change. Your mate will respect the change, continue to try and bring you down because of it, or move on to the next victim. I know. Been there, done that. Making positive changes in my life has brought about positive experiences. Thank you."

Rosalinda didn't go into what Ricardo had tried to do to her by using Maria to trap her. She'd wanted to keep things on as much of a positive note as she could. Rehashing the past had a way of rebounding negatively. It also kept alive the pain of the past.

Marlene couldn't have been any prouder than she was of Keisha and Rosalinda. These two young women were prime examples of what positive changes could bring about in a life of nothing but negative circumstances. They had finally learned to beat what had once seemed like insurmountable odds. By becoming the captains of their ships, Keisha and Rosalinda had learned to effectively steer each of their courses in life. Rough waters would always lay dead ahead, but they'd also been taught how to change directions and chart a new course when needed. Marlene had equipped them with a sturdy umbrella to protect them from life's often-stormy conditions.

Keisha and Rosalinda now knew how to come in out of the rain.

Easton stood when Jesse looked his way, though he didn't feel pressured by the mere glance. He leaped right into his story, which took him less than five minutes to tell. He then went into detail about his problem with bigotry, one of the worst of all his problems.

"You see, I never thought I'd have any men of color as friends. I was taught by my dad to hate all people of color, and then I hung around people with the same views. I can't eradicate a lifetime of bigoted brainwashing in just a few weeks. I admit to still having a long way to go."

Easton pointed at Jesse and then Eric. "These two men are the most down-to-earth people I've ever come across. They're real men. I kept seeking them out because of their show of strength, despite my feelings about their race. They had something I wanted, though I didn't know what it was. These two guys have helped me tremendously. Thanks to them I've decided not to give up my parental rights to my son. The chances of his mother and I getting back together are nil and none, as the Lakers' Chick Hearn used to say," Easton remarked, laughing. "But we have amicably agreed upon the custody issues. Our son will live with me. Once she's out of prison, we'll work out the issue regarding visitations. I won't keep his mother away from him unless she once again becomes a danger to him and herself. Reverend Jesse has helped me to locate a reputable day care center for Kyle. As for the issue of bigotry, I'm proud to call these two brothers friends. They have taught me the real meaning of colorblind. Thanks."

Jesse and Eric both silently applauded Easton. Jesse was surprised that none of the men had questioned him about his reasons for hating people of color, though grateful for the nonoccurrence. Being reared by a bigot was enough of a reason. Jesse was also glad that Easton's speech was very tactful. It didn't appear to him that anyone had been offended by his remarks.

Frank had often trembled at the UTW meetings while listening to the men tell their war stories about women. He'd been attending the session for several weeks now, yet hadn't spoken a single word about his grave situation. Besides a nod or a verbal greeting, he'd remained silent. He had started coming for the same reason everyone else had come: support.

Frank just hadn't built up enough courage to air his dirty laundry in public. He even feared what it might result in. Although there had been a few other cowards at the UTW meeting, he saw himself as the biggest coward of all.

Frank Armstrong's personal story would make all of the men seem like heroes.

His former lover's sad face flashed before his eyes. He instantly blinked back the tears, wishing he could shake Anita's pitiful image right out of the inside of his head. Frank hated that he'd become so emotional over the past few months. It wasn't so long ago that nothing bothered him. Ice water had filled his veins in place of warm blood. There hadn't been a warm or tender thing about him. He didn't know where this sudden conscience had come from, but it was kicking the mess out of his black behind.

Frank practically jumped up from his seat, as if he'd been poked by a cattle prod. He appeared to be in a daze as he looked around the room, focusing more on the female inmates than anyone else. After a few seconds, he gazed over at Jesse. As their eyes connected, Jesse gave Frank the thumbs up sign. "I'm so new at this, so please bear with me. I'm nervous, too."

Cheers and softly spoken comments of encouragement helped to spur Frank on.

"I had my girlfriend take my car to get it washed because I was running late for a rendezvous. Though the possibility always existed, I really didn't think the Feds would stop the car if I weren't in it. Having followed the car to the automated car wash I frequented, they'd surrounded it before she could get out. The bust went down hard. I was never implicated, though they knew I was the man in question. It was also my car. She was prosecuted to the full extent of the law. One of my buyers was a very twisted narc. He saw getting her as a way to make me suffer. If I continued selling drugs, he knew he'd eventually get me. He was mistaken about me suffering, until recently, when my conscience started to bother me something fierce."

Frank stopped a minute and took a couple of deep breaths. He'd gotten most of it out, but the hardest and the worst part was yet to come. Courage didn't come easy for cowards.

"The car apparently had been under surveillance for a long time. The real problem is this. I have a very high-paying administrative job, but my woman friend never knew about my second career. Though completely innocent of all charges, I left her holding the bag, thinking she'd get a lighter sentence, being a woman. She never knew a cache of street drugs was cleverly stored in the trunk.

This woman never told the Feds anything in her own defense. Without me even asking, she decided to take the fall. That's what's been keeping me awake at nights for the past several months. I'm not saying that I'm not glad that she did it. But why would she do that?"

"You should be asking yourself why you let her take the fall," one inmate said. "It's obvious that you don't have the same kind of love for her that she has for you."

Eric stood up. "Lady, that doesn't translate into love. What she did was plain stupid. It was not about love. She made herself a willing victim, which is known as martyrdom."

Eric turned to Frank. "Sir, what's stopping you from going forward now? This thing can still be reversed, but you'd have to go at it very aggressively. As far as the courts are concerned, a jury proved her guilty, and they'll feel that they have no further obligation in the matter. Perhaps we should talk after the meeting. I also suggest that you proceed with caution."

"I'd like to talk with you. Thanks. In all honesty, the fear of being locked up is what kept me silent," Frank responded. "As for the jury, there wasn't one. She did a plea bargain."

Loud gasps and instant murmurings could be heard all over the room.

One of the newer brothers from the UTW stood. "Men like you don't deserve to live. You're the lowest form of lowlife. You wear a white collar by day and a black hood by night. In my hood we call you Dr. Death. More people, many of them young kids, are dying because of your deadly poison. Your day will come. Count on it. Someone is probably lying in wait for you right this moment. Men like you thoroughly disgust me. You'll get yours sooner or later."

Fearing that things might get out of hand, Jesse went up to the front of the room. He then turned to face the audience. "Ladies and gentlemen, let us not allow our tempers to boil over. It took a lot of courage for this man to share his story with us. We're all here for the same reason. We have to learn to give support as well as receive it." Jesse put his hands behind his back.

"I don't deny that his actions are despicable, but we all can change. We've heard enough evidence of that today. His conscience is obviously bothering him. He came to our group to find relief. We also have to be ever mindful of God's laws. Forgiveness will come to everyone that seeks it. There is not a one of us in this room who doesn't need forgiveness for something or other in our past or present. We'll all fall short of the glory of God. It'll do all of us well to remember that when wearing our judgmental robes. Also, everyone needs to remember that what's said in this room stays here. That's an oath of membership. People have to feel free to speak their mind without the fear of judgment or other possible repercussions."

Jesse went right into prayer. The moment was ripe for it. He was sure that a lot of serious issues were on the minds of everyone in the room. There was no better time to ask God to intercede on their behalf. Jesse's recently written sermon for the upcoming Lord's Day was perfect for this group. He'd had a different lecture in mind for this session, but the Holy Spirit was moving him to deliver his church sermon now.

"People, I know you didn't come here to hear me preach a sermon today, but my heart is heavy with the things that I believe need to be said. With your permission, of course, I'd like to share a special sermon with you. My sermon is simply entitled *Unaccustomed to Waiting.*"

Jesse noticed the nodding heads from some of the members of the UTW group. He had promised them a tie-in as to why he'd chosen the UTW name for the group. Now it was time to fulfill the promise, though he hadn't intended for it to come today. "My sermon is very fitting for this occasion. Can I get an amen to show your approval?"

The approvals from the audience members came through loud and clear.

Jesse's huge smile revealed his deep pleasure at the positive responses. "If you had your Bibles here with you, I'd have you read three scripture texts this afternoon, somewhat unusual, but necessary for today's sermon. However, I'm going to read them to you."

Never leaving home without it, Jesse flipped quickly through his Bible.

"We'll start with Proverbs 20:22: 'Say not thou, I will recompense evil: but wait on the Lord, and he shall save thee.' I'll now move on to Psalms 46:1: 'God is our refuge and strength, a very present help in trouble.' Now for the last one, Psalms 46:10: 'Be still and know that I am God.'"

Jesse closed the Bible and looked out into the audience, his expression a solemn one.

"Be still and know that I am God," Jesse reiterated. "That can be very hard to do since we live in a time when often it's very difficult to remain still, and, if ever, not for very long. Ours is the age of 'instants.' No one wants to wait. Instant oatmeal, instant grits, microwave popcorn done in a minute. Hurry up, hurry up, hurry up! I want mine now. Can't wait! Amen!"

A few loudly voiced amens filtered through the room.

Jesse pulled out his handkerchief and mopped his brow, a force of habit. He wasn't sweating a bit. "But, instant gratification, this isn't something new. Impatience has been with us almost since the beginning of man and/or woman." Jesse chuckled. "I said man or woman, because there are many people that believe God is a woman. Speaking of woman, formed from the rib of a man, Eve wanted to know as much as God, although God had an appointed timeframe in which He would have taught both her and Adam all they needed to know. Couldn't wait, was offered a shortcut, so they bit into the forbidden fruit. Here we are today, still biting into that desire to have everything instantly. It takes time, part of God's plan. And even with our knowing, some things God will hold back.

"The secret things belong unto the Lord our God: but those things which are revealed belong unto us and to our children forever, that we may do all the words of this law." (Deuteronomy 29:29)

Jesse gave the audience a huge smile. "I wish I could rush this sermon, but I can't. However, I'll try not to get too longwinded. Is that okay?"

He received another loud round of shouting approvals.

Jesse opened his Bible again. "I have many important words to share with you from God's word. We're going to look at three recorded events in biblical history. These recordings rebound even down to today. Marlene, please write these texts down to copy later and give to the counselors to pass out. Once they're in your possession folks, you can peruse them at your leisure. Hopefully we'll get the chance to talk about them in depth at another session. I don't plan on this being my last time to stand before you. God willing. Amen.

"Let's get started. Genesis, chapters 16-18, tells the story of Abram and Sarai and God's plan for them. It tells how Sarai took matters into her own hands through her hand-maiden, no pun intended, that has the world in a state of turmoil even to this day. The Arabic nations are descendants of Ishmael and the Jews are the descendants of Isaac; both were children of Abraham. Sarai, viewing herself as 'dried-up' at age 76, decided to help God with His plan. Couldn't wait on the Lord any longer. By the way, God changed their names from Abram to Abraham and Sarai to Sarah with huge ramifications on future mankind. I liken it to Genesis 18:14 where it says, 'Is anything too hard for the Lord?' He's Alpha and Omega, the beginning and the end. There is nothing too hard or too difficult for Him, Amen! I have to tell it like it is. God is God and He can do all things!

"Some of you already know the story," Jesse continued. "Abraham was one hundred years old and Sarah was ninety when Isaac was born. It took a little time, but it was in God's time that the promise was fulfilled. Wait on the Lord! If you're not accustomed to waiting on Him, you should try it out. You'll never know what you're missing until you give God a try."

Jesse pointed at the plastic water pitcher stationed on a side table. "Mrs. Covington, please, if you don't mind." As the dutiful wife, Marlene poured a cup of water for her husband and then handed it to him, smiling broadly as she did so. Jesse thanked her and gulped it right down.

"Our second text deals with an impatient people. This story is recorded in Exodus 32. When the people saw that Moses delayed to come down out of the mountain, they approached Aaron and instructed him to make them some gods because Moses may not be coming back; thus, the golden calf and mass pandemonium. Have mercy, Lord, on your wayward, impatient people. We're very much included in that statement, too.

"The children in the wilderness didn't want to wait any longer for what they wanted. And, we, pardon my grammar, ain't no different from them. Amen! Give me what I want now, not tomorrow, but right now. Ironically, as the people were rebelling, God had already given Moses the law, had written it with His own hand: 'Thou shalt have no other gods before me.' For every action, there is a consequence. Jesus simply stated this. 'If you love me, keep my commandments. If my people, which are called by my name, shall humble themselves, and pray, and seek my face, and turn from their wicked ways, then will I hear from heaven, and will forgive their sin, and will heal their land.' (2 Chronicles 7:14) 'Wait on the Lord and He shall save thee.' (Proverbs 20:22)

"Folks, it's all good! Wait on the Lord, and in His time, He'll give us what we need. Moving right along into our third and final portion of scripture that deals with a man, chosen by God to lead His people, who got a little impatient. Saul couldn't wait any longer, and took matters into his own hands, changing the course of his life for eternity. This particular story is found in 1 Samuel, chapter 13. Especially pay attention to verses 6–14.

"Saul was the first king of Israel handpicked by God to lead the people. The O'Jays had a song popular a few years back, actually a few decades for you young folks. It was entitled 'You Got to Give the People What They Want.' Some of you don't know what I'm talking about, 'cause that was back in the seventies, the 'It's all right, have a good time Impressions,' the 'Do your thing Isaac Hayes' days. Amen!

"But even back in that day, it wasn't a new thing for God to give the people what they wanted. God is good and has always been good. He'll sometimes give you what you ask for just so you'll fully understand later that He knew what was best for you all along. The people wanted a king; God gave them a king. God gave specific instructions. The king was instructed to wait for Samuel's arrival and for Samuel to offer a sacrifice unto God on behalf of the people; the king couldn't wait, too impatient. He offered the sacrifice himself, and it cost him his kingdom and eternity. Saul was unaccustomed to waiting. Each of these biblical characters was unaccustomed to waiting. Be still and know that I am God."

Jesse closed his eyes. "Let us pray. Our Father and our God, Alpha and Omega. Grant us this day peace that surpasses even our own understanding. May we learn today to trust in Your plan for us, be patient and wait on You. May we study Your word and cherish the examples given on mankind's struggles since creation and how You have loved us, even when we seem to not love ourselves. May we walk today, holding on to Your unchanging, steadfast hand. In Jesus' name we pray. Amen."

Jesse opened his eyes and looked at the crowd. The falling tears dripping down many faces told him that his sermon had reached those who may've needed it so badly. Every message wasn't for everyone, but God had a certain message for everyone.

God always delivered His message to those who needed it the most.

Jesse raised his hand. "Let us please stand and recite the Serenity Prayer. If you don't know it, please listen to the words carefully so that you might carry them out with you.

"God, grant us the serenity to accept the things we cannot change, the courage to change the things we can, and the wisdom to know the difference. Amen. This meeting is adjourned."

Chapter Fifteen

Alexis and Marietta had everything ready for Alexis's friends by the time they'd arrived at her Bel Air home. Although Marietta had been asked by Alexis to join their group, feeling much better now, Marietta had to decline since she'd already made plans for the evening.

When Alexis didn't know what to do regarding her situation with Mathis West, she called on the very people who'd seen her through the worst days of her life. Not a single one of her friends had turned down the last-minute invitation to her home.

Marlene had been the first to arrive at Alexis's home. Keisha and Rosalinda had come together in Rosalinda's car. In spite of the fact that Rosalinda no longer lived in the apartment building next to Keisha's, the two longtime friends still managed to see each other quite often.

Marietta had filled the table with all sorts of delectable finger foods as soon as everyone had arrived. Alexis thought the impromptu get-together with her friends should be informal, relaxing, and fun-filled. Although her fears about Mathis ran deep, she thought the camaraderie, laughter, and light bantering among them would help to put her at ease.

Looking a tad impatient, Keisha chewed the food she had in her mouth. "What's your crisis this time, Mrs. Du Boise, drama queen of the new millennium?"

Seeing that Keisha was already getting wound up, everyone laughed.

"Why don't we wait until we're finished eating before I get into it, drama princess?"

"If we wait until then, Alexis, we'll all be too stuffed and ready for a nap. You'd better tell us what's up while we're still alert," Keisha responded cheekily.

Laughing, Alexis sucked her teeth at Keisha. "Miss Impatient, as always. Don't you ever stop dispensing the flip comments?"

"No! And you'd miss it too much. You know you live for my sarcasm." Keisha dramatically jerked her head about for a few seconds more, rolling her eyes at Alexis. "As a matter of fact, I've been watching my mouth a lot lately. Ever since I falsely accused Zach and Tammy of playing me. So there, Mrs. Du Boise. Eat your words and don't choke on them."

"It's about time you checked that mouth of yours," Alexis shot back, clapping her hands together. "At Keisha's impatient suggestion to get on with it, here's the real deal."

Alexis jumped right in and laid out for her friends in painstaking detail her strange encounter with Mathis, holding everyone's rapt attention. For the next twenty minutes or so, she told all the information she'd learned from Marietta, and then some, about the man in question.

So stunned by what Alexis had to say, Marlene's mouth had fallen wide open. "Sounds like you need the LAPD, not us."

Alexis shook her head. "I thought of that. But I'm not sure if I want to see another brother behind bars. Besides, he hasn't committed any specific crime to speak of. If I called the police, what do I say? I caught a friend of mine roving his hands over my walls, as though he were looking for something? They'd think I was nuts."

"But look at all the lies he's told you," Rosalinda chimed in.

Alexis shrugged. "Hearsay. All of it is just his word against mine."

"Go ahead, Attorney Du Boise!" Rosalinda laughed heartily; the others followed suit.

"Girl, all the days I had to sit still in that courtroom, I had no choice but to listen to the proceedings. That's how I picked up on the legal jargon. I'm glad I took something worthwhile away from that depressing courtroom. I wish it could've been R.J. instead." Alexis's sadness came and went in a fleeting moment. The melancholy mood was brief for the others as well.

"Alexis, this sounds serious, but what do you think we can do?" Marlene asked.

Alexis shrugged once again. "I don't know. Really, I don't, but I think I know exactly what he might be after."

"What?" the others asked simultaneously, making Alexis laugh.

"Remember the secret wall?" Alexis inquired. Everyone nodded. "After seeing Mathis running his hands over the wall, it was obvious to me that he was looking for something. The renovation of the secret room didn't reveal anything else mysterious that I know of, so I decided to check out other rooms in the house. Well, I found another secret panel just last night."

Her eyes bulging with keen interest, Keisha's mouth fell open. "Where'd you locate it?"

"Get a load of this. In the master bedroom that R.J. and I once shared. His walk-in closet is where I discovered the control panel. It's the first time I've been in there since all of his clothes were removed and donated to the various churches and charities. I can actually see the fuse box now. Instinct told me to open it. The button is inside the box, another shiny silver one just like the previous one. Clever behinds. Both R.J. and Mathis, partners in crime. Hit the button and a large panel of the closet opens."

Alexis leaned forward in her seat and rested her elbows on the table, heightening the near tangible anticipation. "You'll never guess in a million years what I found in there."

"What?" The same simultaneous responses from before had come.

Alexis cracked up. "Come on, divas, I'll show you. I have to warn you, though. If you have a weak heart, stay behind. Marietta is still in total shock."

Alexis got up from the table, and the others quickly followed, leaving behind the unfinished plates of goodies. Food hardly matched the excitement and high anticipation of viewing another of Alexis's secret rooms, causing them to wonder what else R.J. had hidden.

Since she had opened it up several times now, Alexis didn't waste a moment in revealing the contents behind the panel. As the wall panel opened slowly, wooden shelves began to come into view. What had everyone screaming and going absolutely bonkers were the contents of the dozens of shelves. None of the women could believe what each was actually witnessing.

Alexis laughed at all the shocked expressions. "I warned you! Is this not too much?"

"This is what Mathis West is after," Marlene said in complete awe. "We've never met the guy before, but I wish we had. He may not have gotten away with as much as he has. Alexis, you sure know how to pick them. This is an incredible moment for me."

Keisha waved her hands in the air. "Yeah, and we need to devise a plan to trap his clever butt, just like Tammy and I set up Zach. But it's going to take all of us, possibly including Reverend Jesse and Michael. We need some tough men for this job."

"I agree," Rosalinda weighed in. "Let's go back into the dining room and hash this over. We've got to pull together a really solid plan, since we have no evidence to take to the police."

The others agreed. As soon as Alexis closed the wall, they all made a beeline back to the dining room, each wondering how Alexis always managed to be surrounded by mega drama.

Marlene looked troubled as she reclaimed her seat at the dining room table. "Ladies, can I have your attention for a moment? I've got something that needs to be said before we go talking about putting any plans into action."

Everyone looked in Marlene's direction, nodding approval.

"I'm beginning to think that it's much too dangerous for us to take on a man like Mathis West. We don't know what lengths he'll go to, to get what he's after—and we all know what that is now. No disrespect intended to his memory, but we know R.J. was associated with Mathis in some way. That brings the illegal gambling casino to mind. I say that we talk to Jesse and Michael first. Then we should let them decide how this dangerous situation should be handled. We might be a tough group of sisters, but I don't think we want to take on this very clever man. There may very well be other people involved in this complex situation. If that's the case, what are we going to do then? Take Mathis and all of his henchmen on? I don't think so!"

Alexis nodded. "I think you're right, Marlene. If I had more evidence, I'd go ahead and turn it over to the police. For whatever reason, I don't want to see this man behind bars unless he has committed a serious crime. If he and R.J. were partners in the casino, illegal gambling and income tax evasion may be his only crimes, just as it was with R.J."

"Only!" Keisha huffed. "No matter how big or small, a crime is a crime."

Alexis slammed her fork down on the table. "Oh, Keisha, don't you start with your self-righteous rhetoric!" Alexis shouted. "I don't know about the others, but I'm not in the mood to hear it. Your boyfriend has been no lesser a criminal than my husband. In fact, his crimes have been worse than those R.J. was guilty of. You didn't want to see Zach behind bars any more than I wanted to see R.J. locked up. So save your indignation for someone who doesn't know anything about your private business, which is no less scandalous than mine."

Keisha was speechless at the knockout punch Alexis had just delivered right to her midsection. Alexis had certainly taken her down to the mat, and had also put her in her place; Keisha was now deciding if she wanted to stay there or risk starting another round. Alexis looked ready to take her on if she decided to make a comeback.

Keisha finally concluded that it was best for her to be quiet and not come out of her corner. Conceding to the opposition never came easily for Keisha; her decision to concede showed how much she'd grown over the past two years.

Alexis stared coldly at Keisha. "No comeback?"

Keisha was finding it increasingly hard not to throw down the gauntlet, but she knew it wouldn't solve a thing. Feelings and pride would just get hurt, including hers. "No comeback whatsoever, Mrs. Du Boise. Thank you for offering the opportunity, though."

"Good!" Alexis remarked triumphantly, wondering if Keisha had suddenly taken ill. She couldn't remember a single time that Keisha had backed down from anything. The girl was always primed and eager to do battle. In Alexis's opinion, Keisha's sarcastic tone alone had been a comeback in itself.

"Ladies," Marlene intervened, "can we now get back to our original discussion?"

"Yeah," Rosalinda chimed in. "Marlene and I aren't interested in seeing another catfight between you two. I agree with what Marlene said about this situation being dangerous. Let's turn it over to the guys. They'll know what to do. We don't want to run up a tree we can't climb down from without getting hurt."

Keisha raised her hand. Everyone looked at her like she was crazy, wondering why she was seeking permission to speak. It was certainly a first for her.

"Why are you suddenly raising your hand, especially when you've never had a problem just blurting out anything that comes to your silly mind?" Alexis asked Keisha.

Keisha curled her fingers in and then thrust her fingernails out like a set of claws, meowing and hissing like a cat. "You don't want me to scratch your pretty little face with these acrylic daggers, now do you? I love you but I'll hurt your evil behind." Knowing she was acting downright juvenile with Alexis, Keisha couldn't hold her laughter in. The others laughed, too.

Alexis got up from her seat. After walking over to Keisha, she leaned down and hugged her warmly. "Why do we always seem to provide such pure entertainment for these two? We make a fool of ourselves every time we get together. Why do you think that is?" Alexis asked.

" 'Cause we're like oil and water; we just don't mix. Both of us are just plain crazy. This little group would be boring as hell if you and I didn't liven things up. Mizz Marlene and Rosalinda would be sorely disappointed if we didn't unsheathe our claws at least once during our little get-togethers. Of course, they won't admit to it. They're too prim and proper for that."

Alexis cracked up. "Yeah, I guess you're right. We *are* entertaining. I'm glad we don't take things personal, at least, not for very long. Since we've all agreed that we should turn things over to the guys to handle, let's do something fun to while away the rest of the evening. What about listening to a bunch of oldies while we play Monopoly or UNO?"

"I'm all for that," Marlene said jovially. "Anything is better than watching you two."

"Me, too," Rosalinda seconded. Keisha saw no choice but to go along with the program.

Reverend Jesse and Michael arrived at Alexis's place within an hour of Marlene and Rosalinda phoning them to come there for an emergency meeting. Jesse and Michael listened intently to what Alexis, Marlene, and Rosalinda had told them about Mathis West, his lies and strange behaviors, and the secret panel found in R.J.'s walk-in closet. The secret room, the onetime gambling casino, was the stage setting for the unfolding of the latest episodic drama in the life of one Alexis Du Boise. Jesse also wondered if West had removed the gaming machines.

Jesse stroked his chin. "I believe this is something for the cops to handle. What do you think, Michael?"

Michael raised his eyebrows. "Not one shred of evidence to present to back up any allegation of criminal intent on West's part. Alexis, do you feel that your life is in danger?"

"I really don't think so, but what do I know? When I met Mathis at an upscale party one evening, I had no idea he had any connections to R.J. It has been proven time and time again that I'm lousy when it comes down to judging someone's character. The evening he showed up at my house uninvited was the first time I had any inkling that something could be amiss. Still, I dismissed it. I was more concerned with his control issues than anything else."

Jarreau Thornton had shown up at Alexis's place near the end of the story, so he really didn't have much of a clue as to what had gone down prior to his late arrival. A business meeting had held him up much longer than had been anticipated. However, he'd heard enough to know that Alexis hadn't mentioned a thing to him about Mathis West being a possible threat to her. That not-so-tiny bit of information caused him to cast Alexis a look of utter displeasure.

Keeping secrets was how Alexis had lived her entire adult life. It looked to Jarreau as if nothing had changed. The secret-keeper was still at it. It seemed to him that Alexis led two totally separate lives, with a split personality for each.

On one hand, she played her life out as the sophisticated rich woman who had the world at her fingertips, someone who was extremely intelligent, confident, and unconquerable. On the other hand, she definitely appeared confused as to who she was and seemed unsure about her position in life. There were times when she acted as if she were unable to make any decisions without having someone to constantly guide her through the entire process. Jarreau wanted to have a special place in her life, but her unpredictable behaviors had kept him on guard.

Jarreau made eye contact with Alexis. "From what little you've told me about Mathis West, and then hearing the tail end of this conversation, I get the impression you know next to nothing about this man. I was once your best friend, yet you failed to share any of this incredible story with me. You really have to learn to trust your true friends, Alexis. It seems to me that you've been placing your trust in the wrong people for far too long. You must learn to be more careful. The world doesn't give a darn about who you are and what possessions you might have."

Alexis looked regretful. "I'm sorry, Jarreau. I didn't want to worry you with this." *If you'd come around more often, I might've felt comfortable enough to do so.* Outside of their business dealings, Alexis was highly perturbed with his frequent absences in her life. She planned to tell him so later, once they were alone. That is, if he didn't leave before the others.

"That's exactly what true friends are for, Alexis. If that's what it takes to keep you safe, you can worry the hell out of me," Jarreau stated emphatically. "Friends care about each other."

Sweet, misguided Alexis, Jarreau mused, *once again caught up in a completely foreign world, a crazy world that will eventually chew you up and spit you out if you don't learn to practice extreme caution around those persons who are of the world.* From rags to riches was still Alexis's only claim to fame. Jarreau had a hard time believing that this little slip of a girl from New Orleans had ever been truly happy and comfortable in her Cinderella fairy-tale life.

R.J. Du Boise had popped into New Orleans in hopes of taking the city by storm with his flashy style of dress, dashing charm, and inexhaustible amounts of cash. He then quickly sold to a young, wide-eyed-with-wonder Alexis his ideology regarding all the fancy goods and services that money could buy. Jarreau was convinced that she'd never fully bought into her expensive new identity. It now appeared to him as if the lavish lifestyle had been all but forced on her.

R.J. and the shady characters that had once surrounded him had constantly put Alexis's very life in danger, yet she seemed so oblivious to the criminal element she now found herself right back in the midst of. Danger always existed around any type of illegal operation.

Michael wasted no time in coming up with a viable solution. After running a thorough criminal background check on Mathis, as an officer of the court, Michael alone would confront Mathis with the suspicions. In his experience with criminal minds like Mathis's, Michael believed wholeheartedly that Mathis was a smart enough conman, one who was deep enough into illegal dealings, not to want this situation to come to the attention of the local or federal authorities. According to Michael, often it was just the threat of exposure that was enough to send packing a man who had no desire to face life inside prison walls.

Although there was no evidence of any wrongdoing on his part, Mathis had no way of knowing whether a smoking gun existed in this instance or not. Michael was a great poker player, one who knew exactly how to bluff his way into a win. He knew all the many ways the con games were played. He could write an almanac on the inner workings of the criminal mind.

If Mathis West were in any way connected with R.J.'s gambling operation, Michael explained to the others that it would behoove him to lose himself as quickly as he'd appeared in Alexis's life. Mathis's interest in Alexis had been by sheer design, not by happenstance, as she once believed. Marietta Grainger could corroborate at least that much since she'd seen him in the company of R.J. on numerous occasions. Though R.J.'s criminal activities were hidden completely from view of his wife, the housekeeper had seen many a strange happening from her living quarters, which were located near the private back entry to the tunnel.

On the other side of the coin, Jesse agreed with Michael, but he also believed that once Mathis learned that the wall had been destroyed during renovation, that he'd have no reason to continue hanging around. Surely he'd think that what he was after had already been discovered and was no longer available to him. No one was sure if Mathis knew about the wall of unmarked money hidden behind the panel in the walk-in closet, but it seemed that his only interest was in the secret wall once housing the gambling casino. Jesse also thought that the house should be fully searched to find out what other hidden treasures it might hold.

Neither Jesse nor Michael wanted to know what Alexis planned to do with that mountain of cold cash. For sure, she couldn't bank it, not without arousing serious suspicion.

Alexis's guests, with the exception of Jarreau, all left shortly before ten P.M.

Since Jarreau was out in the kitchen retrieving a bottle of wine and a couple of glasses, Alexis rushed around the room lighting all the candles. Although she planned to have a serious heart-to-heart with Jarreau, she thought the candlelight would help dictate the mood. The last thing she wanted was for an argument to ensue between them. Alexis simply needed to know his intent toward her. If she had her way, there'd be no more beating around the bush regarding their personal relationship.

One way or the other, it was time for a resolution.

Jarreau came back into the room and set the tray laden with wine and glasses down on the coffee table. As he went about the business of opening the bottle of merlot and pouring the dark, aromatic liquid into the crystal wine stems, he noticed that the atmosphere had changed. It appeared to him that Alexis might have a few romantic notions inside her pretty little head.

Alexis moved from the chair and came over and sat alongside Jarreau on the sofa, her mission clear in her mind. Alexis began to put her personal feelings on the line, asking the difficult questions she needed the answers to from him. She also told him how she felt about him ducking in and out of her life whenever it suited him. He was attentive enough when he was with her, but then she wouldn't hear from him for days at a time.

His intense, frowning expression was somewhat of an indicator to Alexis that she had put him on the spot and that he didn't like the idea of her forcing the issues. Jarreau eyed her closely. "I don't know what to say about all this, Alexis. What is it that you want me to say?"

Alexis's frustration clearly showed on her face. She wasn't crazy about the noncommittal responses she'd just received from Jarreau. She needed some answers regarding his on-and-off-again presence in her life, but he seemed reluctant to come clean. Since it appeared that he was eventually going to disappear on her altogether, she quickly decided to put both of them out of their misery. It was obvious that he wasn't happy spending too much time with her. The candles she'd lit looked like a silly idea to her now. The right mood just wasn't happening. It was as if she didn't even exist for him.

Alexis moved closer to Jarreau. Daring to take his hand, she massaged the back of it.

"This situation is no good for us, Jarreau. It's not working between us the way I thought it might. I'm sorry, but I don't think we should see each other in this way again. However, I'd love to remain friends with you."

He eyed her with cold suspicion. "If that's what you want, Alexis, you got it. I think I've been waiting for this moment to occur since our first kiss. Thanks for being honest and up front. I no longer have to wonder where I stand with you."

Alexis looked puzzled. "What are you talking about?"

"You and your inability to commit and to make any serious decisions for yourself. I was right to guard my heart around you. But it still got broken despite my attempts to protect it from you. You've managed to destroy my heart all over again. Why should I be surprised? I've known this would happen all along. R.J still owns your heart, still controls your every move from the grave. One heart, one love has been your motto from the day you first laid eyes on him."

Jarreau got to his feet. "Good-bye, Alexis."

"Oh, hell no!" she shouted at the top of her lungs. "I'm not going out like this. You need to sit your fine, black tail back down and explain your chilling comments to me, because I don't know what you're really saying."

Looking totally bewildered, Jarreau decided to sit back down. The last thing he wanted to do was leave Alexis while she was so upset. Their friendship meant everything to him. "Alexis, it's real simple. I love you. But you're still in love with R.J. I only wish that you could return my feelings. It was the same way when we were in high school. I was in love and you saw us as nothing more than friends. As tough as it is to swallow, that's life."

Alexis couldn't believe her ears. Jarreau confessing his love for her had rocked her world. Was she dreaming or what? But she had to take issues with some of his statements. How could he think she didn't return his feelings? She'd only been sending every signal imaginable. Of course she still loved R.J., would always love him. He had been her entire life, but he was no longer there for her.

Alexis was desperate to move on with her life. Having Jarreau in her life would make moving on so much easier. Her feelings for him already ran pretty deep. There was no doubt that she could love him. Jarreau was the most lovable man she'd ever known.

"What makes you think I don't share in your feelings, Jarreau? Why do you feel that I've destroyed your heart?"

"How *can* you feel as I do? Putting your love for R.J. aside, you had at least one other man on the string, Mathis West. For all I know there may be other men waiting in the wings. Guys have always flocked around you like crazy, Lex. It bothered me to no end that you were seeing Mathis and me at the same time. Why you couldn't figure that out is a mystery to me."

Alexis felt somewhat ashamed. "Maybe so, but you don't know why I continued to see him." Her hackles began to rise.

"At first, I continued to see him out of loneliness. You were coming and going in and out of my life whenever the mood hit you.

Then you'd disappear on me for days at a time. Nor did you bother to call me during those times. Mathis was just a stand-in. I hate to admit that I was using someone like that. But from all indications, I was the one being used big time. If you really want to know the truth, I could barely stand the man, even before I knew what he was really after. It was you that I wanted all along. I didn't know any better when we were younger. I know better now. I know that you're a wonderful human being and I couldn't do any better for myself than you. How's that for truth?"

Upon seeing the tears in her eyes, Jarreau brought Alexis into his embrace. "Are you saying that I got it all wrong?" he whispered into her ear, wanting so desperately to keep her in his life.

"Emphatically so! As for R.J., you're right on the money about him. I'll always love him, Jarreau. He was my husband. What I feel for you is totally different from what I shared with R.J. I know you think you're taking a risk by involving yourself with me again, but I'm ready to move on, ready to love unconditionally again," she cried. "I need you to trust me to know my own heart, Jarreau. I'm scared of getting my heart broken, too. Can you give me a chance to show you how ready I really am to move forward with our personal relationship?"

He kissed her gently on the lips. "Your heart is safe with me. Chances of a lifetime and new beginnings are ours to claim. I'm a patient man. I love you, Lex."

Alexis kissed him back. "I know I can love you, too, Jarreau. My feelings for you run very deep. I longed for you in your absences. Forgive me for failing to convey those strong feelings to you. Thank you for giving me the opportunity to live and experience love again."

Alexis trembled all over as she comfortably positioned herself across the bed. While looking down at her wedding rings, she rolled them around on her finger. Time for completely letting go was now. These rings were a part of her past. A new lease on life was her future.

Alexis lifted R.J.'s picture from the nightstand and laid it on the bed, placing it out in front of her. Tears fell from her eyes as she studied his handsome face. "R.J., I'll always love you. You know that. It is now time for me to move on and let go of the past. Although there are times when I wish it was possible, you're not coming back to me." A rolling tear splashed from the corner of her eye.

"There was a time when I never failed to ask your permission for this or that, but today I'm telling you my plans. I'm finally letting go. I'd love to have a sign from you that it's okay, but it's happening regardless. I have a chance at happiness again.

"I know you and Jarreau didn't get along because of your intense rivalry over me, but you always admired him for bowing out so gracefully. You once told me that he handled the defeat like a real man, even better than you thought you would've done."

Alexis laughed at the memory of that day and time. R.J.'s ego had loomed larger than life in his triumph over Jarreau Thornton. No one could tell him that he wasn't the man.

"I never saw it the way you both did, because I wasn't into Jarreau that way back then, though you never really believed that. Things have a way of changing, when you least expect them to. I'd love for you to give Jarreau and me your blessing, my love. I don't know if forever is in the cards for us, but we are taking our relationship to another level. Happiness is right at my fingertips. I've granted myself the permission to love again. Rest in peace, my darling R.J."

The distinct scent of fresh flowers suddenly filled the air. Alexis felt frightened by the sweet aroma in the absence of blossoms. Then a calming effect came over her, instantly removing all her fears. Her love of fresh flowers allowed her to believe that the unexplainable perfumed scent had been R.J.'s way of giving her his blessing, his way of releasing her. Nothing else would make sense to her.

"Whatever it takes for me to get on with my life. Thank you, R.J."

Alexis removed her large diamond solitaire and then her gold diamond-studded wedding band, kissing each one. She then clutched the rings in her closed fist. Since she and R.J. had no children, she would save them for her first nephew to give to his bride-to-be. R.J. would like that. She was sure of it. Before slipping under the covers, Alexis got out of bed and knelt down.

It was now time for Alexis to have a personal conversation with God and to also pray for His blessings in abundance. God had never failed to keep any of His promises.

Chapter Sixteen

Keisha couldn't believe her eyes as she walked through her apartment. The first thing she noticed, despite the dimly lit room, was how clean and neat the place looked. Malcolm had obviously cleaned up for her. Then she spotted the romantically set table adorned with a fancy lace tablecloth, accented by a magnificent centerpiece of unlit candles. That blew her away.

As she remembered Malcolm's earlier phone call to her job, her heart nearly skipped a beat. He'd called to tell her she'd forgotten to give him Zanari's asthma medication when he'd picked the kids up early that morning as a favor to his mother. Marlene was taking them out with her for the day. His call had resulted in Keisha calling the manager to let him into her apartment. So that's how he'd managed to get all this done, she marveled, with help of the management.

Management wasn't that familiar with Malcolm, but her word was good enough to get him inside. His visits to the apartment were also more frequent as of late, but she noticed that he always came after the kids were in bed. Keisha and Malcolm's relationship hadn't progressed any further than a close friendship, lots of mutual encouragement, and positive vibes. They were a long way from romance and intimate contact, but she loved having him around.

Keisha fought a hard battle to keep her tears at bay, though deeply touched by all that Malcolm had done to create a romantic setting for her. That there was only one plate on the table caught her attention. Malcolm obviously wasn't planning to share this evening with her. She found it so odd, yet quite intriguing. It seemed as if he'd done this all for her.

Though romance was nonexistent for them at this point, she had to admit they'd grown a lot closer. Constant productive conversations were having a positive impact on each of them. Although he hadn't been around the kids in a good little while, Malcolm's initial tentativeness toward her kids was what pleased her the most.

Although Zach loved his children like crazy, he hadn't ever involved himself in their day-to-day care. Zach had shared much of his time with little Zach before jail; all of Zanari's experiences with her dad had been from behind bars. Their shyness and aloofness with Zach right after his release was probably what set him on his course for change.

Wondering if Malcolm had cooked, too, though no food odors were present, Keisha entered the sparkling clean kitchen. It appeared as if Malcolm had done a thorough cleaning job throughout the apartment. *No pot-and-pan food action in here*, she mused, after looking around for several seconds.

Just as Keisha passed the oven, a delicious food smell of some sort passed by her nose. Upon opening the oven, she saw the Kentucky Fried Chicken box. Opening the container revealed a full wing dinner, original recipe, her favorite KFC meal. Malcolm was gaining in popularity. This was too much for her to believe. That he knew so much about her likes was astounding. It also meant that he paid close attention to the things she'd tell him.

Smiling to herself, Keisha moved on toward the bathroom off her bedroom so she could wash up and change before eating her surprise meal, though she'd first have to nuke it for a couple of minutes in the microwave.

After flipping on the bathroom light, Keisha stopped dead in her tracks. The bulbs had obviously been changed in the lighting fixtures. The room now reflected a soft, yellowish glow. Laid out across the rim of the tub were a brand new fluffy white bath towel and a sponge ball. Malcolm had set on the counter a variety of colorful bath salts and rich-looking oils and lotions.

The sight of the aroma-therapy candle caused her tears to flow unchecked.

As she recalled telling Malcolm, eons ago, how she'd love to be able to afford candles and feminine products to spoil and pamper her anatomy with, her entire body shook with the force of her emotions. Malcolm had remembered that, too. That also amazed her.

Instead of just washing up as originally planned, Keisha immediately ran herself a hot bath, barely able to wait to use the scented oils and lotions. A quiet time for relaxing and reflection in a luxurious bath appealed to her tired senses. Her stress levels weren't nearly as high as they used to be. Still, there were times when the nervous tension got the best of her.

Keisha laughed like a silly schoolgirl as she poured the bath salts under the running water, watching the riot of bubbles explode atop the water. She then slowly drizzled in the lavender-scented aromatherapy oil, causing little rivulets to appear. Her giggles filled the air.

Without further ado, Keisha stripped out of her clothes and installed her body into the steaming water. As the oils and bubbles caressed her body like the gentle hand of a lover, her emotions were once again triggered. Keisha thought it was rather sad that she hadn't ever taken the time to pamper herself with something as simple as an inexpensive bubble bath.

Keisha had nearly two hours to pamper herself before Zach arrived with the kids. Marlene was dropping them off to him at Lucian's after their outing. Keisha had arranged for Zach to bring them home to her later, since she would still be at work when it was time for Marlene to drop the kids off.

Zach had gotten his driver's license back, another positive on his list for change.

Too much time spent at the prison had left Keisha very little time for herself. Putting too much of her hard-to-come-by money on Zach's books had barely left her enough money to take care of her kids properly. She and the kids had gone without for far too long. If Zach was finally coming to that realization, it was about time. If only Zach had set up the romantic setting for her.

The doorbell rang all too soon, interrupting Keisha's sentimental journey. It had to be Zach with her babies. Her body was still a little wet, but she didn't have time to finish drying off. Her kids were impatient. Zach would have fun by lifting them up to lean on the bell just to annoy her. He was an impatient one, too.

Keisha quickly slid into sweats and then ran for the door, knowing she looked less than presentable, since her sweats were wrinkled. There was a time when she wouldn't dare to let Zach see her looking anything but her very best, before bearing the sole responsibility for two kids came into play. Zach was lucky to get a smile and a pleasant hello these days.

Her heart did a double flip at the two little smiling faces looking up at her. Zanari had an angel painted on her face and little Zach had some sort of cartoon caricature on his. Both the kids had on new shoes. She wondered if they were gifts from Marlene. Keisha's heart grew full as she lifted her children, one at a time, giving them a big hug, telling them how much she'd missed them.

Zach and Zanari then ran off to their rooms to play and watch television. Keisha read to them for a half an hour each night after their baths and just before bedtime. No playing and television were allowed once the reading was over. It was lights out for her little charges.

Zach had been grinning from car to ear ever since he'd trooped in right behind the kids. All Keisha could do was stare at him, wondering what he was so happy-faced about.

Fearing that he'd messed up with her again, he sighed heavily. "Aren't you at least going to say something, Keisha?"

Keisha shot him a sassy look. "Hi! Is that enough for you?"

Zach's face showed his growing impatience. "I can't believe you. I thought you would like all the things I did just for you. I'm in a no-win situation. Nothing I do ever pleases you."

Completely dumbfounded, knowing she was probably looking stupid, Keisha nearly fainted at Zach's remarks. It was Zach, not Malcolm, who'd cleaned the entire place. But how had he gained entry to the apartment? With Zach staring her down, Keisha couldn't think clearly.

But she had to quickly think of something, if no more than a word or two to appease him. His good deeds couldn't go without reward regardless of her questions about how he'd gotten in.

Smiling broadly, Keisha pulled Zach to her by his hands and gave him a big hug. "Bend yourself back in shape, Mr. Man. I was just messing with you," she lied. "Awesome! Everything is fantastic, down to the KFC, though I didn't get a chance to eat it yet. Thank you for being so thoughtful and kind, Zach. Very special gestures coming from you to me." She laughed. "After seeing the place, the candles and all, I thought you might've tried your hand at cooking dinner for me, too."

Zach chuckled, relieved that she was genuinely pleased, though he didn't buy her lie about just messing with him. He also knew why she'd lied. "You know I can't cook. If Momma hadn't had a lot to do today, I guess I could've had her whip up a little something, something for you. I have good news and I was trying to put you in the mood to celebrate with me."

Lucian! The mention of Zach's mother caused Keisha to think that Zach had somehow gotten a hold of the spare key she'd given to Lucian when Zanari was ill. Keisha had simply forgotten to ask tor the key back. Keisha didn't like the implications. Either Zach had possibly stolen the key from his mother, or Lucian had just completely disregarded her feelings about her giving it to her son. Keisha decided it was best to deal with it later. Zach needed much praise from her right now. He'd catch holy hell later if he'd stolen the key from Lucian.

Keisha's curiosity was highly aroused regarding the good news. "Let's hear it, Zach."

He beamed, sticking his chest out with pride. "I got a full-time job, a legal one. Although I'm on a ninety-day probationary period, I'm going to do everything I can to stay on as a regular employee. Home Depot is taking a chance on me. They know about my felonies because I thought it was important to tell the truth. Are you excited for me, baby girl?"

"Beside myself with excitement. Proud, too. Join me while I eat my KFC? If you haven't eaten, I'll even share." Her face clouded. "Oh, my God, I haven't asked if my children have eaten. Have they?"

"Chuckie Cheese. Just before I brought them home. As much pizza as those two kids ate, I'd be surprised if they weren't already in the bed asleep. Keisha, your kids eat like you do. A lot! Is that dinner invitation still open?"

She rolled her eyes at him. "Like you haven't eaten dinner over here lately. Of course, but I have to warm my dinner in the oven. I lost track of time while soaking in those luscious bubbles you bought for me. Let me go slip out of these sweats. I'll be right back." She turned around to face Zach. The kids' new shoes, do you know anything about them?"

"Yeah, I do. I bought them. Any problem with it?"

"Nope. Just a need to know. I'm off and running."

"I'll have everything on the table when you get back. Why don't you change into something cute while you're at it?" Knowing he'd taken a big risk with that not-so-subtle remark, he waited for her comeback with bated breath.

Zach had made Keisha blush for the first time in a very long while. "I just might do that." She suddenly had the desire to kiss him to show her appreciation, but she immediately thought better of it. They hadn't shared any intimacy whatsoever since he'd been home.

Rushing any major sort of intimacy between them could turn out to be a mistake. The hug she gave him was just a hug; a kiss was a much more intimate act. Things felt kind of nice the way they were. The relatively slow pace that she'd set for herself reminded her of how it had been between them in the very beginning. Zach hadn't pressured her for sex back then. They had slowly let their relationship progress into something more intimate.

Keisha rushed into the bathroom, where she washed her face again and then applied fresh makeup. Putting on clean underwear came next, since she hadn't had time to put them on under her sweats because of the doorbell. She couldn't believe how bubbly she felt inside. After all the anger she'd displayed toward Zach in recent months, the euphoric feelings were a nice change.

In deciding what clothes to wear, she surprised herself by not wanting to wear anything provocative. Besides, Zach had said "cute." Cute was okay, so she opted for a cute, loose, black V-neck top and a pair of not-too-tight white jeans. This was as provocative as she was willing to get for now. The new choices she was making made her feel really good about herself.

This all seemed so darn crazy. She and Zach having a fast-food KFC dinner by candlelight felt strange, but rather exciting. Could troubled couples really recapture the magical glow that often came along in the beginning of a budding romance?

Well, the candlelight and romantic setting gave her a reason to be somewhat optimistic about the odds. Zach had really pulled out all the stops, really pouring it on thick. But would it last? There was only one way to find out. Did she dare run the risk?

An intimate dinner for two was quite a stretch for the former

Zach. The Zach he'd eventually become, not the one she'd first met and fallen instantly in love with.

Only for a minute did Keisha allow her mind to come to rest on sweet Malcolm.

The flowers on the table were beautiful. Zach must've placed them there while she was out of the room, Keisha mused, unable to keep herself from smiling all over. She couldn't help wondering why he hadn't brought them in when he first came in, but she had a pretty good idea. Rejection wasn't a good feeling. It wasn't so odd for Zach to think she'd reject him yet again.

Zach's eyes danced with appreciation as he checked out Keisha's outfit. Although he thought it was a little conservative for the old Keisha, he liked the new, wholesome look she was sporting. He also noticed that Keisha wasn't wearing as much makeup as she used to. He liked the fresh-face look, too. It was obvious to him that Keisha had changed in more ways than one. He had to admit to himself that he was intrigued with all the new changes.

Zach removed one of the roses from the cellophane paper and handed it to Keisha. "Red roses are supposed to be for lovers. I know you don't see me like that anymore, but I hope I can change it back to the way it used to be. I've missed you something terrible, baby girl."

Keisha felt all warm and fuzzy inside. Despite her desire to just fall into his arms and melt, she smiled softly instead. "Time, Zach. I don't know where time will lead us, and I refuse to promise a thing. But we have to take time to get to know each other all over again. I'm not the person you used to know. You're not the same person I fell in love with. I'm not nearly as gullible or vulnerable. Time and circumstances have changed us both. You may come to find out that you don't like the new me. But I do. That's about all I can say for now."

Zach took ahold of her hand. "You've said enough to let me know where things stand. I think you have a good idea about us getting to know each other again. I've changed, too, more than you know, Keisha. It's hard for me to believe how much I've missed out on by keeping myself in trouble. Prison is not a nice place. People often become much harder and tougher than from when they first went in. The horrendous living conditions often found in jails and prisons can make even those who are innocent become hard-core. I'm not going to make any excuses for myself. I've nearly blown most of my adult life away. Keisha, I want to change. Not just for you and the kids, but for me, too. Hang in there with me for a little while longer? I can make it."

The changes in Zach were hard for Keisha to believe, yet the evidence of such was irrefutable. He'd even lost the street lingo, at least around her and the kids. A big change had also occurred in his style of dress. Zach was finally starting to act like a man, finally starting to take on as much of the responsibility for his children as he was capable of right now.

Although she still feared that he'd go back to his old ways, she felt as if she had no choice but to hang in a bit longer and give him the benefit of the doubt. He certainly seemed sincere enough. He'd already made good on a lot of his promises. Things were definitely looking rosier these days. The kids absolutely loved having Zach around. They had bonded once again.

Keisha put the rose up to her nose and inhaled the sweet scent. "Let's take it one day at a time, Zach. That's all I can offer."

"That's more than I'd hoped for, baby girl. Ready to eat?"

Nodding, Keisha smiled broadly at Zach. "Let's do in this KFC."

Rosalinda looked at the clock and freaked out, seeing that she'd be late for her dinner engagement with Michael, wishing she had waited until the next day to come back and clean out her desk. Rosalinda had finally convinced herself to accept full-time employment at

Michael's prestigious law firm. The money offered was darn good and would help her to continue with her education. Accepting the offer was one of the best decisions she could ever make.

To save on time, Rosalinda emptied the entire contents of one drawer into an empty box to sort through later. It was almost dark outside, and she wasn't anxious to leave the building alone, though security personnel were also available as escorts.

A sudden shuffling noise caused her to turn around with a start. Her heart instantly leapt into her mouth. Ricardo looked more menacing than he had the last time she'd encountered him. Shards of deep fear shot completely through her.

His grin was taunting. "Hello, Rosa. How are you?"

The hard rolling *r* in the pronunciation of her name gave her a clear indication of his agitated state of mind. No doubt that she was in imminent danger. The harder he rolled the *r*, the angrier he was with her. He came toward her and she backed away.

"You should stay put. You have nowhere to run. You're finally caught in my snare. I'm sure you thought it was over when Maria failed at her mission. Her lies to you are now a reality. You should see her. She's a battered, bloody mess, all because of you. You didn't make things easy for her. I just asked how you were doing. Think I can get an answer?"

Rosalinda merely shrugged. Fear had temporarily robbed her of her voice. She swallowed hard, knowing she had to find a way to speak. If not, severe consequences would occur. "Okay," she said weakly, hearing the distinct sound of fear in her one-word response.

"Just okay? That's not what I heard. A little birdie told me you're living high on the hog. Behind security gates, I hear. Did you and your lover think gates could keep me from getting to you? Maybe so, but I knew you'd screw up sooner or later. You always were predictable."

Rosalinda saw no immediate escape route, since Ricardo had the entrance covered. If only she could manage to get into one of the private offices and lock the door. Each had an exit leading into the hallway. She could also take time to call 911 before fleeing to the elevator.

His laugh was acidic. "I knew I'd get to you sooner or later. Just had to be cautious and patient. I finally have you right where I want you, Rosa. No security. No Michael Hernandez."

Quicker than Rosalinda could blink an eye, Ricardo had her by the hair, one of the cruel ways he loved to cause her pain. He also knew that she was extremely tender-headed. Fighting her tears, Rosalinda winced as he locked up her hair in his hand, pulling it all the while. Then his mouth came down hard on hers, forcing his tongue past her clenched teeth.

The thought to bite Ricardo's tongue as hard as she could was only a fleeting one. Fearing dire retaliation had instantly nixed that thought. Rosalinda cringed inwardly, careful not to show outward disdain, wondering how she'd ever stomached his vulgar kisses before. The alcohol and marijuana breath had always been there, but never gagging her like it did now.

For a few moments, in hopes of calming herself down, Rosalinda allowed herself to think of Michael's sweet kisses, the sweetest she'd ever had. She looked up at the large office clock. It sounded as if it was ticking away right inside her head. The minutes were growing louder and louder. Michael was probably starting to worry about her by now. She was thirty minutes late for their dinner date. The worst part of all was that she hadn't told him she was stopping by the office to clear her desk. He had no way of knowing where she was.

Once again, her carelessness had gotten her into big trouble.

As Ricardo forced her back onto the desk, Rosalinda's heart felt as if it was bursting out of her chest. The pain was so unbearable she thought her back was breaking. Her screams rent the air as Ricardo's strong hands ripped her blouse completely open. As her buttons flew in every direction, all Rosalinda could think about was what he intended to do next.

Ricardo might take her against her will by brutal force, but not without a bloody fight.

Rosalinda's strength seemed to have grown tenfold as she pushed Ricardo off her with a force of power she never knew she possessed. She spotted the scissors at the top of the box in the same instant that she went for them.

Rosalinda showed Ricardo the scissors. "No, you're not doing this to me. Do you want to add aggravated assault and rape to your already extensive rap sheet? Though I'm sure that many of your crimes have been more serious than what I have firsthand knowledge of, especially those surrounding your gang life, you've only been arrested for the lesser ones. You should quit while you're ahead."

Ricardo gave her a menacing grin, causing her to shudder. "Rape? We've had sex too many times for anyone to believe that, Rosie. They'll just think you're a little loco," he said, coming toward her again.

Adrenaline pumping through her body at a high rate of speed, she lightly pressed the sharp points of the scissors into her stomach. "I'll kill myself before I let you violate me sexually. If you intend to rape me, you'll have to do it over my dead body. Do you hear me?" she screamed, tears streaming down her face. "You don't have my permission to assault me."

Ricardo laughed derisively. "No one will ever believe I raped you."

"On the other hand, no one will believe that you *didn't* stab me with these scissors. The police already know you've been trying to set me up for the kill. You may not get arrested for rape, but the charge of murder one just might become your reality. Is that what you want?"

Ricardo's eyes appeared glazed over as he stared blankly at Rosalinda. The scissors at her stomach had him freaked out, something he hadn't bargained for. He couldn't believe she'd stab herself to keep him from touching her, yet something was telling him she wasn't just bluffing. He loved Rosalinda. He didn't want to hurt her. But if he couldn't have her, no one else would either. She belonged to him. How had she come to hate him so much?

Murder, rape, aggravated assault, he mused, comparing them to the lesser charges he'd already served time for. The vulgar possibilities burned him up on the inside while traipsing through his brain at breakneck speed. Maybe he wasn't as ready to take things as far as he'd once thought. He had long since decided to mess her up so badly that no one would want her, including Hernandez. He had a different sort of end in mind for his former attorney. Just the thought of Michael touching Rosalinda in the intimate way in which he used to caress her drove Ricardo insane. That Rosalinda had traded him in for a sophisticated suit rankled him within.

But now, seeing the awful fear in her eyes had him sick to his stomach. How had Rosalinda ended up with the likes of him, the woman who couldn't stand to hurt a fly? He had to wonder why she wasn't as repelled by him before as she seemed to be now. He knew the answer. Denial came easier than facing the truth. Bad memories of the past hit him full force again.

Ricardo suddenly began to shake all over, as if he was possessed by a demon of some sort. His eyes appeared reddish, bloodshot. How had things gotten so far out of hand? A wave of horrific memories washed up in his mind, providing him with the answer to his question. His trembling increased as the bad memories of his late childhood continued to assail his mind.

"They won't believe you!" he shouted, his eyes wide with terror. "No one will believe I made you have sex. They didn't believe me. What makes you think they'll believe you?"

The tears streaking down Ricardo's face shook up Rosalinda something awful. She'd never seen him cry. He was always so hardcore, so tough acting. His mother's absence in his life had gotten him emotional at times, but she'd never known him to shed a single tear over it.

What Ricardo had said was slowly sinking into Rosalinda's befuddled mind. *They didn't believe me,* he'd said. *Believe him about what?* The weird look in his eyes frightened her as she looked over at him. Her thoughts became even more frantic at seeing the murderous expression on his face. *God help me,* she cried inwardly. *Help me get through this perilous situation. I can't do it without you, Lord.*

Ricardo moved forward until he was within inches of her face.

Scared senseless, her breathing was now coming in shallow gasps. Rosalinda quickly backed away from him, repositioning the scissors against her abdomen, gripping them tightly.

Ricardo stopped dead in his tracks before he also took a couple of steps back. "Would you really try to kill yourself to keep me from touching you?"

Rosalinda glared hard at him. "You don't want to find out. Neither do I. I don't want to live with the kind of emotional pain and scars caused by rape. I won't let you rape me, Ric."

"Stop using that word!" he yelled, putting his hands over his ears, as though he needed to shut out the sound of her voice. He then fell to the ground, trembling all over, moaning like he was in physical pain. "Stop saying that," he cried.

Rosalinda's heart nearly stopped ticking as she watched him writhing around on the floor in agony. Then her eyes darted all around the room, looking for an open office to make a quick escape to. Since Ricardo was still blocking the exit doorway, and she couldn't tell which office was unlocked, she'd have to wait him out and pray that he'd come to his senses.

Where was security? This had been going on for over nearly thirty minutes now and no one had come around to check the offices. It then dawned on her that no one knew she was there. It was customary for an employee to call in and alert security when working after regular hours. She had only come there to pick up her things. A security check might not occur any time soon.

Ricardo's sudden howling cries recaptured Rosalinda's attention.

Ricardo pounded into his left palm with his right fist. "He said no one would believe me if I told anyone about what he was doing to me. He told me everyone would think I was a demon possessed, that they would lock me away in a rubber room inside an insane asylum."

Alarm as well as concern for Ricardo arose sharply in Rosalinda's breast, causing her breathing to shallow even more. A feeling of discomfort had long ago settled inside her chest. She swallowed hard before attempting to converse with him. It seemed to her that he was crying out for help. "Who said that to you, Ric? Did something bad happen to you?"

As he looked up at her, his eyes appeared to roll to the back of his head. "You don't care about me, Rosie. You won't believe me, just like he said. You were the last person I thought would betray me. You're no different from the others. No one ever believed me."

Rosalinda's frustration with this situation continued to grow. She felt like screaming to ease the tension, but she knew that she had to remain in control of herself. "If you don't tell me what you're talking about, you'll never know if I believe you or not, Ric."

His tears flowed unchecked. "It doesn't matter. He's right. No one will ever believe me. He's dead now, so nothing can happen to him. Not ever."

"Ric, were you raped by someone?"

While getting to his feet, Ricardo put his hands over his ears again. "Don't use that word again, Rosa. I'm warning you!"

"Okay, Ric, I won't. Please talk to me. Please tell me what happened to you."

Ricardo stopped his maniacal pacing and sat down in the middle of the floor. "I was a ten-year-old altar boy. Imagine that! I trusted everyone and everything back then. It was the people I trusted the most that hurt me the worst. He was right. No one believed me, not even my own mother. My mother called me a liar. Said that my awful sins and dirty little secrets of the mind had to be kept quiet. I ended up confessing to the very person who hurt me, confessing to something that I now know wasn't mine to confess. He knew I was telling the truth about him, but he didn't say nothing."

"Who is *he*, Ricardo? Who's this person you're talking about?"

"You know who he is! Everyone knows who he is, but no one ever tells." Ricardo's tears continued to flow unchecked. "No one confronts him or talks about him without reverence. He's the man! He's the man everyone trusts, Rosa, yet he did bad things to me for over four years."

At the same moment Rosalinda's heart went out to Ricardo, she spotted Michael outside the door. Rosalinda waved Michael off, hoping she could convince Ricardo to surrender to the police so that he could get some serious help. It seemed to her that he needed some sort of psychiatric treatment or counseling. Rosalinda had always had a penchant for being the rescuer.

A lot of men, former altar boys, were presently going through the same trauma Ricardo was going through. She could only guess that Ricardo was talking about a priest or some other powerful church head. If so, he was only one of countless victims. This serious problem within the church had reached epidemic proportions, yet statute of limitations had already freed many of the perpetrators in the state of California.

It looked as if Ricardo had been acting out his unfathomable pain, committing lesser crimes and then violent ones because of the violence perpetrated against him as a ten-year-old innocent. Ricardo had paid hundreds of times over for someone else's act of violence. With the accused dead, Ricardo was right about nothing happening to the person who had violated him, at least not in a court of law. God was the highest authority, held a much higher court, to which everyone would answer for his or her sins. Ricardo was also wrong about one thing, that no one would believe him.

Rosalinda believed him, without a shadow of a doubt.

Knowing she had backup should Ricardo decide to turn on her, though she really didn't think he had any fight left in him, Rosalinda knelt down in front of Ricardo and took hold of his hand. "I don't know if it helps any or not, but I believe you, Ric. There comes a time when all of us need help. Do you want help for your pain?

You're not alone in this, Ric. There are many men who've been subjected to the same horrendous treatment by someone they trusted. . . ."

Before Rosalinda could finish her pleas for Ricardo to seek help, cops poured into the room. Her begging them not to handcuff or hurt Ricardo fell on deaf ears. "He needs help," she cried out, wishing Ricardo had talked to someone about his pain a long time ago. Apparently he had, she recalled. But his very own mother hadn't believed him. How sad was that?

Unable to watch the inhumane way in which the officers were handling Ricardo, Rosalinda rushed into Michael's arms and pressed her face against his chest. With her breathing labored, she found it hard to speak. Her heart hadn't dislodged itself from her throat yet.

Rosalinda remained deathly still until Ricardo was taken from the room. The last look he gave her nearly brought her to her knees. The deep regret she saw in his eyes could not be denied. In return, she gave him a reassuring smile, praying all the while that he'd get the help he so badly needed. Ricardo was still very young and there was always hope.

Michael felt her entire body trembling as he brought her even closer to him. "It's okay, Rosalinda. I'm here with you now." He kissed the top of her head. "It's finally all over."

With tears in her eyes, Rosalinda looked up at him. "For me, yes, but will it ever be over for Ricardo? I don't know how much you heard before I spotted you, but what he told me wasn't at all a pretty story. Ricardo was sexually assaulted when he was an altar boy, at only ten years old. He said it went on for an entire four years. His life of crime may be the direct cause of what happened to him back then. He needs psychiatric help, Michael. He'll never change if he's denied help to deal with the pain of his past. He still has a lifetime ahead of him. Can you try to intercede on his behalf? Please."

Michael had turned quite pale. Hearing Rosalinda tell Ricardo's story made his compassion rise. "Are you asking this of me because you're still in love with him, Rosalinda? Or do you have other reasons?"

Rosalinda shook her head. "Compassion, Michael, plain and simple. I had to feel something for Ricardo once, or I don't think I would've stayed with him as long as I did. But I know now that it wasn't love. I'm sure of it, since I hadn't learned to love me yet. But we've already discussed all that. I want help for him because I care about him as a human being. Will you try to get Ricardo some kind of help? He didn't deserve what happened to him."

"No child ever does," Michael commented.

With tears in her eyes, Rosalinda went into his embrace and looked up at him. "It's all over now. I'm here with you. We're both safe. By the way, how did you know where to find me?"

He laughed. "It wasn't easy. But since you'd finally accepted my offer to work at the office full-time, I gave this place a serious thought or two after I had exhausted all my other attempts to locate you. When I pulled into the parking garage, your car was there."

"But how did you know something was amiss?"

Michael shook his head. "I really didn't, not at first. When I talked to security to try and gain entry to the building, they told me that no one had called in to report they'd be working late hours. That caused me concern, so I convinced them to check it out since your car was there. Once we saw what was going on, security alerted the proper authorities while I kept a close eye on you and Ric. I'd only been there a couple of seconds when you saw me and waved me off."

"Thank God you thought of coming here!" Her body began to shake all over.

In a soothing manner Michael rubbed Rosalinda's arms. "You're alright now. Everything else is under control. Let's get your things together and get out of here. You never have to come back here again."

Relieved that it was finally over, Rosalinda put her trembling hand into Michael's. "I really don't have the stomach for dinner after all this drama. A hot bath seems more appropriate. Rain check on dinner, Michael?"

He kissed her forehead. "No problem. However, I think you should stay up at the main house with me until you're fully recovered from this latest episode of terror."

She smiled with devilment in her eyes. "In one of your guest-rooms?"

"Only for a short while. That is, if you're now ready to become the missus of my home?"

Tears filled her eyes, causing them to shine like a million brilliant stars. "Are you saying that you're ready for me to become the missus, Michael?"

Michael brought her back into his arms. "Nothing would make me happier than to have you as my missus. I love you, Rosalinda Morales. Will you marry me as soon as possible, say in the next week or two?"

Rosalinda kissed him passionately. "I love you, too, Michael Hernandez, with all my heart. Yes! I'll marry you. Tomorrow wouldn't be too soon."

He kissed her passionately. "Let's hurry home so we can make a toast to the official engagement of Rosalinda Morales and Michael Hernandez, the soon-to-be Mr. and Mrs. Michael Hernandez. We will shop for the ring tomorrow."

Michael looked upward to heaven. "Thank you, God, for answering my prayers. I pray that you will bless this holy union for all eternity." The happy couple's tears mingled as they sealed their promise of marriage with another staggering kiss.

Despite all she'd been through, Rosalinda couldn't wait to tell all her friends the wonderful news. Rosalinda Morales was marrying a beautiful man, an attorney no less. Would wonders never cease? Rosalinda knew her good fortune had nothing to do with wonders. God had been doing a powerful work in her life for as long as she could remember. He hadn't changed a bit. Rosalinda had been the one to change and to make the positive changes in her relationship with God. God had only been waiting for her to seek so that she could find Him.

Just as he'd answered Michael's prayers, God had also answered hers.

Chapter Seventeen

Alexis was both surprised and alarmed to find Mathis West standing at her door. Whether to let him in or not was a big concern for her. He had once again shown up without calling. His unexpected visit could mean that Michael had already spoken with him about their suspicions. Was he there for a confrontation? Since she'd opened up the door without thinking, the same mistake Rosalinda had made with Ricardo way back when, Mathis was already in her face.

Something in the back of Alexis's mind was telling her to face down this man once and for all. She couldn't continue to be fearful of him and allow his intimidation of her to continue. She was ready to let him know that she'd just entered into a committed relationship with Jarreau and that she wasn't free to see him anymore. Mathis had to understand that the friendship was over.

Drat, she mused, *that probably wouldn't work, anyway*. He was after the money, not her. And all the time she'd spent in his company, she'd believed him to be completely enamored with her sweet self. Alexis had to chuckle at that vain thought. At any rate, she had to get this over and done with. Mathis was already looking a little impatient.

Alexis was all forced smiles as she folded her arms across her chest. "I'm really surprised to see you, Mathis. I thought we had an understanding about calling before showing up. I can't imagine you forgetting how upset I was the last time."

He looked slightly abashed. "I only need a few minutes of your time. I can assure you I won't be showing up again unannounced. I can say what I need to say without coming in."

Alexis's curiosity was quickly aroused. That he didn't want to come inside was puzzling, but it also offered her a sense of relief. "Okay. What is it you want to say?"

He rubbed the back of his neck. "I have to go away, Alexis. I came to say good-bye."

Alexis turned the corners of her mouth down. "Away? Where?" As if she cared.

"That really doesn't matter. I'm a man who goes wherever his business takes him. I no longer have any business dealings in California."

"You're closing your architect firm?"

Alexis now knew that no such firm existed. Mathis had lied about that, too, yet he did possess an architectural engineering degree. In fact, he had been employed as an architect for several years, and had been very successful at it. Mathis's background check revealed that he was self-employed as a drifting high-stakes gambler. He went wherever the money led him, in hopes of finding the pot of gold at the end of the rainbow. He didn't always have lots and lots of money as he'd touted, but Michael had reported to Alexis that Mathis was far from broke. The mega kitty R.J. had left behind would've set up Mathis for life, had he been able to get his hands on it.

"Sometimes you have to move on to bigger and better things." Mathis laughed inwardly. He had purposely dodged her question. For the first time in his life, his lies actually bothered him. A man hated to lie to a woman he'd fallen hard for. Falling for Alexis had not been a part of the plan, but he couldn't imagine any man not falling for her, despite her unattractive rudeness.

Mathis also thought of the visit he'd had from Alexis's friend, Michael Hernandez, who had made him see that the windfall wasn't available to him. Mentioning offshore banking by Michael had Mathis not knowing what to think in that regard. Mathis had no idea of the walled-in bank in Alexis's walk-in closet. Michael had strongly suggested that Mathis should move on to greener pastures elsewhere. The real threat of prosecution had Mathis seeing eye-to-eye with the young defense attorney. Just the thought of doing prison time was enough to deter Mathis.

Michael had also presented to Mathis his entire criminal history, facts that were undeniable. When things got too hot in one place for high-stakes gamblers, they simply moved on to another one. Las Vegas and Atlantic City were two of Mathis's favorite haunts. Mathis had also considered Biloxi, Mississippi, for setting up a brand new operation.

Mathis couldn't believe that the wall had been destroyed without anyone finding the money. He couldn't help wondering if there were a few wealthy construction workers running wild around the city. He couldn't have imagined that R.J. would've moved the money to another location. R.J. had often promised to share some of the money with Mathis, even if he got a long sentence. But when he'd gotten a message from R.J., via one of his friends, asking him to remove the gambling equipment from the house, Mathis had eagerly done so. Like Jesse, Mathis never knew the name of the person he'd spoken to over the phone.

Mathis had gone to the house that day, only to learn that the code to the secret vault had been changed; the combination had died with R.J. Mathis had sold the equipment for a good sum of money, but it hadn't been nearly enough to retire him in the lifestyle he'd had in mind.

Eager for them to go their separate ways, Alexis broke into Mathis's musings by calling out his name. She then extended her hand to him. "Well, I guess this is good-bye. I hope you find that pot of gold at the end of the rainbow."

Interesting analogy, Mathis mused. "If it exists, I'll find it. Take care of yourself, Alexis. Sorry it couldn't have been different between us."

"Things always turn out just the way they're supposed to. Predetermined destinies. So long, Mathis. Godspeed!" Alexis was so giddy with relief that she extended to Mathis a warm hug. The fear of intimidation had been conquered. Mathis no longer frightened her in the least. By giving Mathis West just enough information to make him think he had even more than he did, Michael Hernandez had handled his business like a pro. Alexis also thanked God that Mathis wasn't the type of high roller who was in the game to win it at all costs, by any means necessary. "Blessings in abundance, Mathis."

"Thank you, Alexis. God bless!"

Alexis silently thanked God and then Michael as she closed the door on Mathis's retreating form. Mathis West was finally out of her life for good. Ridding herself of him had gone much smoother than she'd anticipated. She couldn't wait to call Michael and get the rest of the details regarding his meeting with Mathis. That it was finally all over was the main thing.

Alexis was free to live her life without fear; free to give, take, and share; free to express her feelings freely; free to love; free, period. No more unmanageable obstacles barred her way. The path was clear. Money would never be an issue. She might not be able to just take it out of the wall and bank it all at once, but nothing could stop her from doing a lot of good with it.

Jarreau's handsome image popped into her head, giving wings to her brightest smile. The Blacks In Crisis organization would receive the first of many sumptuous donations. Although she'd always seen the money as a surefire backup plan, Alexis had every intention of taking her fundraising duties seriously. Alexis had something to prove to herself, and to no one but herself.

* * *

Seated on the sofa in her living room, Keisha felt extremely nervous about what she had to say to Malcolm. He had just come over to see her and had made a quick run to the bathroom. He wasn't going to like the decision she'd finally come to about her future, but she simply couldn't deny the desires of her heart. She loved Zach, had always loved him. Her relationship with Malcolm was a great one, but a romantic liaison had yet to occur. Had their relationship taken a romantic turn, she might've been singing a different tune. Malcolm had it going on and she had been very attracted to him.

Just the thought of Malcolm getting hurt caused her to cringe. He'd been so good to her, good for her. Although he hadn't been personally involved with the kids, he'd had a very positive impact on them. They had liked him instantly. His reasoning for not involving himself too closely with the kids was a perfectly sound one. She had no problem with anyone who wanted to protect the hearts of her children. She'd begun to realize that it wouldn't work between them when he first began to exclude the kids from their outings; he hadn't given a reason for it then. Not knowing had hurt her at first.

Malcolm, dressed casually in khaki Dockers and a navy-blue, silk T-shirt, came back into the room and plopped down in the chair that faced where Keisha sat. He eyed her for several moments, curious about why she'd called him over. She had sounded anxious to him over the phone. He couldn't help wondering if she'd heard anything about him. If she had, he thought he should tell her himself before she got herself all worked up.

He licked his lips, feeling a bit nervous. "Keisha, I know you said you wanted to talk to me, but I have something to say to you before you say anything. Is that okay?"

Keisha smiled. "As long as you're not going to tell me you don't want to marry me before I tell you I just won the lottery," Keisha joked. Keisha was referring to a television commercial that everyone seemed to get a big kick out of. This was certainly a similar situation in her opinion. Her eyes suddenly pierced him like a perfectly aimed arrow. "I think what I have to say may be more important, Malcolm. Can yours wait?"

Malcolm rubbed the side of his temple with the palm of his hand. "No, it can't. Just sit still and listen for a change. Think you can do that?"

Rolling her eyes at him, she nodded. "Whatever!"

He moved over to the sofa and put his arm around her shoulders. He then turned sideways so that he faced her. "We've become so close, girl, closer than I ever dreamed. You've come to mean a lot to me. We have something very special."

Hoping he wasn't going to confess to loving her, or worse, ask her to marry him, Keisha gulped hard, her heart racing like crazy. Causing him pain wasn't something she could easily bear. They were both children of the night, caught up in unfortunate circumstances, brought together by need and the pain of the past.

Malcolm kissed the side of her face. "Although we've grown close, Keisha, I feel differently about you than you might think. I thought it was more than that in the beginning. I do love you, girl, but it's more of a brotherly love than a romantic type. I'm not in love. I wanted to be your rescuer, but I only realized that I might cause you more pain than Zach did. You see, Keisha, I love you like a sister. I'm not prepared to be a daddy, nor do I think I'm ready for a committed relationship. If I were prepared to settle down, I'd still be thinking through this entire matter. I don't want to hurt you or the kids. I had to come clean before somebody got hurt in this deal, including me."

With tears brimming in her eyes, Keisha began laughing uncontrollably. Malcolm thought she was hysterical, which made him feel awful. He tried to take her in his arms to comfort her, but she doubled up on the sofa, holding her stomach from her agony, or so it appeared as such to Malcolm. That made it impossible for him to hold her. Malcolm couldn't feel any worse than he did at the moment. He had hurt the one person he would've moved heaven and earth to see that she never had to suffer any hurt again.

Keisha suddenly threw herself in his arms, shocking him speechless. "Oh, Malcolm, you have no idea what I've been putting myself through ever since I called and asked you to come over here." Tears came to her eyes and she wiped them away. "You've turned everything in my world right side up again."

Malcolm nudged her shoulder. "What are you talking about?"

Taking his hand, Keisha looked deep into his eyes. "I love you in the same way you love me, like a sibling. It's Zach that owns my heart. I don't know why, especially after all the hell I've been through with him, but he's the man for me. With all the recent positive changes he's made in his life, I must confess that I've fallen even deeper in love with him. I was so scared to tell you." She kissed him and then hugged him, too. "I know you don't like Zach, but do you think you could try to get along with him for the sake of us all?"

Malcolm blew out a gusty breath of relief. "Girl, this is so darn crazy. You and I both are nuts." He laughed. "It looks as if we both put ourselves through a lot of unnecessary grief. I really didn't want to hurt you, but I couldn't let you think we could be more than we are right now. I do respect you, girl. A lot. I also love you, Keisha Reed. And I'm happy to share you with my parents. Still want me for a big brother?"

Keisha grinned. "Correction: little brother! Yeah, you're a keeper. Plus, I like having your sorry butt around. If nothing else, you're always good for a laugh or two."

While hugging each other, they both dissolved into laughter.

Malcolm grazed his finger down the side of Keisha's face. "As for your question about Zach, I'm feeling you, big sister. We've already had a man-to-man talk about you and the kids. We understand each other, so you don't have to worry about any drama between him and me."

Gasping in horror, Keisha looked shocked. "When did all this talk take place? Zach hasn't mentioned anything about meeting you to me."

"I met him at Tammy's place."

Keisha raised an eyebrow. "At Tammy's! What were you doing at her house?"

"Discussing a little hair biz. Tammy's cool."

Keisha had seen a twinkle of affection in Malcolm's eyes each time he'd said Tammy's name. "Oh, no! Say it isn't so! You got a thing for Tammy, don't you? Oh, my God, this is sick. Zach and me, and you and Tammy. Unbelievable!"

"It's more than believable to me. Tammy has a good head on her shoulders, and she has a great sense of humor. I'm very attracted to her. I had a talk with Dad about my attraction to her the night I had my parents over for dinner. Dad gave me a lot of good relationship-building pointers during our sincere man-to-man discussion. Dad's the one who urged me to come clean with you about my true feelings as soon as possible."

"Really now! This is some interesting stuff going on up in here. But we'll get back to you and Tammy in a minute." Keisha struck her temple with her forefinger. "So, tell me what you and Zach discussed in your little man-to-man with him. My curiosity won't let me wait."

"In confidence?"

"Straight up. Whatever we talk about stays right here, Malcolm. I promise."

"He was a little huffy with me at first, before he questioned me about my relationship with you. I told him the truth, that I was once interested you in a romantic sense, but that I later realized I loved you like a sister. He seemed happy to know that. We didn't get into anything too deep, but we had a decent conversation. I later told him about a few places to apply for a job, where his record might not hold him back. My friend at Home Depot promised to try and give him the benefit of the doubt. He's hired a couple of guys just home from prison. They worked out well for him."

Keisha was amazed by his comments. "So, you're the one who told him to go to Home Depot. That was really thoughtful of you."

"A man can't do anything without a job. Zach can't take care of his kids if he doesn't work. Rehabilitated prison parolees often get an unfair shake. No one wants to hire them because of their records; if they don't find work, it's back to the big house. Catch-22."

Keisha shook her head. "That's really sad, isn't it? I really don't believe Zach is going to be a repeat offender this time around. His head finally seems to be screwed on halfway straight. You see, Malcolm, Zach and I aren't too much different from each other. We've always fed off of each other's insecurities. I'm far more secure now. He's getting there." Keisha had a sudden light-bulb moment. "Did you also have something to do with Zach cleaning my apartment?"

Malcolm laughed. "I wondered when you were going to get around to that. He and I were only minutes into our conversation when my mother called me on my cell phone asking about Zanari's meds. So we could finish our talk, Zach rode along with me. It was then that he started talking about wanting to do something nice for you. He told the manager the same thing once we got there. Only because she knew him did she let him stay and do his thing. He promised to let her know when he was leaving your place. By the way, how did he do with his plan?"

"Fantastic! He really put it out there." Laughing, Keisha rubbed her forehead. "I thought you did it at first. Then, when Zach told me he was the one, I felt downright stupid. However, I recovered enough to give him his props. His thoughtfulness and endless attempts to please me has put our relationship on an upward spiral. I'm sure it's going to work for us this time."

Keisha playfully punched him. "Now we can get back to Tammy. You really like her, huh, little brother?"

"I feel a little something, something for her. She's a really nice girl. She's smart as a whip, too, really savvy in business. Can you be down with it if a personal relationship does develop between us, big sister?"

Keisha cracked up. "This is so crazy. You and Tammy! She's not

324

the woman I'd handpick for you, nor is Zach the man you'd pick for me, but Tammy is a super person. She's all heart. Just don't go playing with her mind and her emotions. She's fragile enough as it is. Come correct with her, little brother, and you'll have my blessing."

Keisha stuck her hand out to Malcolm. "Deal?"

"It's a deal, Keisha."

"What about ordering in a couple of pizzas? The kids are with Zach for the night."

"I think I'd like it better if we went out for pizza. Don't want to give Zach any reason to distrust me. Okay with you?"

"All right with me. But don't worry about Zach. I've made it clear to him that you and I have a special relationship and that I'm not giving that up for anything." Keisha smiled softly. "Would you like me to call Tammy and have her join us for pizza?"

Malcolm shrugged. "That works for me, but I'll be the one to make the call. Can't have my big sister arranging dates for me. That'll definitely blow my image, girl. Maybe you should call Zach, too. We can double-date." Malcolm cracked up. "How lame does that sound? My boys would clown me big time if they heard me say that. Anyway, I hope Tammy's home. I'd love to see her tonight. She's great company."

Keisha looked at him hard, paying close attention to his eyes. "Ooh, do I know that look! Tammy's got you whipped already— and she hasn't even given you any. Has she?"

"Keisha, don't go there. This is a different kind of feeling altogether. Nothing sexual. I like this feeling, in fact. It feels real good."

"I hear you, boy. I feel the same way about my new style of relationship with Zach. It definitely has a different feel to it. Maybe I *will* call Zach and see if he wants to meet us. If Lucian's home, she'll probably watch the kids for him." Keisha looked at the clock. "It's only five-thirty. We can be back before eight if she has plans to go out. Otherwise, Zach can just bring the kids along. We *are* a family." Keisha laughed. "Family. It finally has a nice ring to it."

"Let's put the wheels in motion, girl. I'm getting hungry! With or without Tammy and Zach, we're going to go eat." Malcolm pulled Keisha into his arms. "Thanks for understanding where I'm coming from." He kissed the tip of her nose. "By the way, you and the kids are very much a part of our family, too. Mom and Dad feel the same as I do."

Keisha hugged Malcolm with all her might. "The understanding has been mutual. Thanks. Though you're not mine, you're still the man, Malcolm Covington!"

While everyone Marlene had gotten involved in the surprise party had been assigned a duty of some sort, not a single soul had been assigned to keep an eye on Annie Wylie. No one had checked on Sister Wylie. Sister Wylie had written the note to Marlene, the one she held in her hand. Marlene had already read it at least twenty times over the past couple of days.

Sister Annie Wylie and Brother Paris Sheldon had run off to Las Vegas to get married. The couple had eloped to avoid all the prying eyes and the silly gossip. Marlene couldn't help laughing at how those two had decided to handle their wedding plans. Annie and Paris had simply done things their way, the only way that was more than likely right for them. *Bravo, for them*, she mused, smiling broadly. *Bravo!*

Much to both Marlene's dismay and delight, the birthday party for Sister Wiley wasn't going to happen. The couple had certainly thrown a monkey wrench into all the well-laid plans, since the happy seniors were already honeymooning in colorful Las Vegas, Nevada. It seemed to Marlene that all the hard work had been for not, until Marlene quickly decided the party should go on as planned.

Marlene looked all around the beautiful fairy-tale, ballroom setting. A surprise birthday party had turned into something that could've only existed inside Marlene's thrilling imagination and creative energies. Since there had been numerous other occasions for them to celebrate, Marlene had immediately gone to work on creating new plans for all the new guests of honor: Michael and Rosalinda's engagement; Keisha and Zach recommitting themselves to each other and the kids; Alexis and Jarreau entering into a committed relationship; the exploration of a new relationship for Malcolm and Tammy; Cicely and Eric's upcoming nuptials; Easton living up under the same roof with his son, Kyle; and Zach's very legitimate, two new jobs. Jesse and Marlene's continuing love story of "until death do us part" was celebration enough.

Ricardo Munoz had even written a letter to Reverend Jesse asking if he would please visit with him, a request that Jesse was only too happy to oblige. Miracles were happening everywhere. All one had to do was believe in the power of God.

While there were numerous other just causes to celebrate, the most important to Marlene and her friends was the gift of giving, the gift of friendship, and the priceless gift of love from one woman to the other.

Marlene's, Keisha's, Rosalinda's, and Alexis's arms flew wide open to greet each other.

Dear Readers:

I sincerely hope that you enjoyed reading **UNACCUSTOMED TO WAITING** from cover to cover. I'm very interested in hearing your comments and thoughts on this host of men, women, and children who prayed continuously to bring themselves out of the darkness and back into the light from above. These parents fought courageously alongside their kids to bring about victory at the end. I love hearing from my readers, and I do appreciate the time you take out of your busy schedules to respond.

Please enclose a self-addressed, stamped envelope with all your correspondence and mail to: Linda Hudson-Smith, 16516 El Camino Real # 174, Houston, TX 77062. Or you may e-mail your comments to *LHS4romance@yahoo.com*. Please also visit my Web site and sign my guestbook at *www.lindahudsonsmith.com*.

About the Author

Born in Canonsburg, Pennsylvania, and raised in the town of Washington, Linda Hudson-Smith has traveled the world as an enthusiastic witness to other cultures and lifestyles. Her husband's military career gave her the opportunity to live in Japan, Germany, and many cities across the United States. Linda's extensive travel experience helps her craft stories set in a variety of beautiful and romantic locations. It was after illness forced her to leave a marketing and public relations career that she turned to writing.

Romance in Color chose her as Rising Star for the month of January 2002. *Ice Under Fire*, her debut Arabesque novel, has received rave reviews. Voted as Best New Author by the Black Writer's Alliance, Linda received the prestigious 2000 Gold Pen Award. She has also won two *Shades of Romance Magazine* awards in the categories of Multicultural New Romance Author of the Year and Multicultural New Fiction Author of the Year 2001. Linda was also nominated as the Best New Romance Author at the 2001 Romance Slam Jam. Her novel covers have been featured in such major publications as *Publishers Weekly*, *USA Today*, and *Essence* magazine. Linda was recently named as Best New Christian Author by *Shades of Romance Magazine* for 2003.

Linda is a member of Romance Writers of America and the Black Writers Alliance. Though novel writing remains her first love, she is currently cultivating her screenwriting skills. She has also been contracted to pen several other novels for BET Books.

Dedicated to inspiring readers to overcome adversity against all odds, for the past three years Linda has served as the national spokesperson for the Lupus Foundation of America. In making lupus awareness one of her top priorities, she travels around the country delivering inspirational messages of hope. Her Lupus Awareness Campaign was a major part of her ten-day book tour to

Germany in February 2002, where she visited numerous U.S. military bases. She is also a supporter of the NAACP and the American Cancer Society. She enjoys poetry, entertaining, traveling, and attending sports events. The mother of two sons, Linda shares a residence with her husband, Rudy, in Texas.